"Would you like to have dinner?"

Randi studied him intently. "Thanks for the offer, but I don't think that's a good idea."

"Why? Aside from the case, that is," Cedric said as he closed the distance between them.

She instinctively took a step backward. He towered over her five-eight height by a good six inches. Aside from the case, she didn't have a legitimate reason, except for wanting to steer clear of men for a while. "Since there is a case, nothing else matters."

A small smile crept onto his face, and he folded his arms across his wide chest. "And if I promise we won't talk about the case? Are there any rules against it?"

"Not that I know of, but I—"

"Think of it as my way of apologizing for being such a hard-ass. One dinner won't get you into any trouble."

In her estimation, dinner would only be the beginning of trouble, because Randi knew he'd be charming—like now—and she didn't need or want *charming* in her life. Yet she heard herself say, "Okay, one dinner and no talk about the case."

He unleashed a full dimpled grin that made her breath stack up in her throat. The half smile she'd seen on the website photo didn't come close to capturing this sexy version, one a woman would sell her soul to touch, as Iyana had pointed out. But Randi wouldn't be selling her soul *or* touching. After tonight, there would be nothing between them except what pertained to the case.

Sheryl Lister is a multi-award-winning author and has enjoyed reading and writing for as long as she can remember. She is a former pediatric occupational therapist with over twenty years of experience and resides in California. Sheryl is a wife, mother of three daughters and a son-in-love, and grandmother to two special little boys. When she's not writing, Sheryl can be found on a date with her husband or in the kitchen creating appetizers. For more information, visit her website at www.sheryllister.com.

Books by Sheryl Lister

Harlequin Kimani Romance

It's Only You
Tender Kisses
Places in My Heart
Giving My All to You
A Touch of Love
Still Loving You
Sweet Love
Spark of Desire

Visit the Author Profile page
at Harlequin.com for more titles.

SHERYL LISTER
and
ELLE WRIGHT

Spark of Desire & All for You

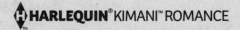
HARLEQUIN®KIMANI™ ROMANCE

ISBN-13: 978-1-335-45840-7

Spark of Desire & All for You

Copyright © 2019 by Harlequin Books S.A.

The publisher acknowledges the copyright holders of the individual works as follows:

Spark of Desire
Copyright © 2019 by Sheryl Lister

All for You
Copyright © 2019 by Leslie Wright

PLEASE RECYCLE · THIS PRODUCT IS RECYCLABLE ·

Recycling programs for this product may not exist in your area.

This edition published by arrangement with Harlequin Books S.A.

For questions and comments about the quality of this book, please contact us at CustomerService@Harlequin.com.

Printed in U.S.A.

H HARLEQUIN®
TM www.Harlequin.com

CONTENTS

For Maia

Acknowledgments

My Heavenly Father, thank you for my life
and for loving me better than I can love myself.

To my husband, Lance,
you continue to show me why you'll always be
my #1 hero! I couldn't do this without you.

To my children, family and friends, thanks for your
continued support. I appreciate and love you!

A very special thank-you to my daughter Maia for
her help and guidance. That forensic science degree
is already paying off. Love you!

They always say to find your tribe
and I've found mine. They know who they are.
I love y'all and can't imagine being on this journey
without you. Thank you for keeping me sane!

A very special thank-you to my agent, Sarah E. Younger.
I can't tell you how much I appreciate having you
in my corner.

SPARK OF DESIRE

Sheryl Lister

Dear Reader,

If you've kept up with this series, you know that Cedric has adamantly stated his preference for remaining single. Randi has her own reasons for shying away from relationships, but the problem is love doesn't always play by the rules. That old adage about sparks turning to flames is true in this case and it was a pleasure to watch them fall in love. What I also enjoyed about writing this story was having a heroine as a former firefighter and a current arson investigator. I hope you will, as well.

Can you believe there is just one more single Hunter? Jeremy's time is coming...and soon.

As always, I so appreciate all your love and support. Without you, I couldn't do this. I love hearing from you, so be sure to email and let me know your thoughts.

Much love,

Sheryl

Website: SherylLister.com

Email: sheryllister@gmail.com

Facebook: Facebook.com/SherylListerAuthor

Twitter: Twitter.com/1Slynne

Instagram: Instagram.com/SherylLister

Chapter 1

"Look at all of DeAnna and Nolan's grandbabies. All five of their children have married."

Cedric Hunter added more ice and drinks to the three coolers and tried to drown out the sound of his mother's voice. His aunt, uncle and most of the Gray family lived in Los Angeles but had come to Sacramento to celebrate their paternal grandmother's eightieth birthday. The weekend turned out to be a good one with the late March temperatures running slightly warmer than normal in the low seventies.

"And Lorenzo is smitten with Desiree. Even Alisha has remarried," she added in reference to his cousins, the adult children of his father's twin brother. She placed her hands on her hips. "If everybody else can find someone and settle down, why can't you and Jeremy?"

He groaned and closed the lid. He used to love family gatherings. "Mom, I'm not looking to settle down.

With Dad and Uncle Russell retiring last year, I've been spending more time on the business. It doesn't leave much time for socializing." His father and uncle had come into the office one morning almost a year ago and announced to Cedric and Lorenzo that they were retiring that very day, leaving Cedric and Lorenzo to run their family-owned construction company. It was true that he'd been spending lots of hours at the office, although he still made time to play. However, marriage wasn't on his radar. "Maybe you should be having this conversation with Jeremy. He's the romantic."

"You're the oldest, Cedric, and you're not getting any younger."

Cedric winced. "Wow, Mom. You act like I'm two years from being sent to a retirement home. I'm only thirty-six."

"Closer to thirty-seven," she muttered.

"Hey, Ced. Can you come help me move these tables?"

He glanced over at his brother. "Yeah. Be right there." Cedric kissed his mother's cheek. "If it's meant to happen it will." He said the words to placate her, but he had no intention of settling down. He didn't have a problem with the idea of commitment or marriage. He just didn't see those things for himself. He preferred a little variety in his life. Cedric crossed the yard to where his brother stood waiting.

"You looked like you needed a rescue," Jeremy said with a laugh, grabbing one of the tables.

Cedric shook his head. "Mom has been on me nonstop since Alisha got married last month." His younger cousin had been married previously, until her first husband left her, eight months pregnant with a two-year-old in tow.

But her new husband treated her like a queen. Cedric picked up another table and they carried it a short distance, setting it near another one that held wrapped gifts at one end and an elegantly decorated cake at the other.

"Well, you'd better get moving. Do you need any help finding a potential wife?"

He shot his brother a glare. "You know what you can do with that—"

Jeremy leaned toward Cedric. "You might want to watch your mouth. Mom is standing not too far behind you and you *know* she hears everything."

Cedric clamped his jaws shut, glanced over his shoulder and caught his mother's gaze. Growing up, he'd never understood how she could hear everything they said, whether she was in the room or not. "Lucky for you." Before he could say anything else, his cousin Lorenzo joined them.

"Need help?"

"Yeah." Cedric nodded toward the remaining table.

Lorenzo picked it up and brought it over. "Why are you moving these?"

"I think they're getting ready to do the cake and Mom wants all the tables close together," Jeremy answered. "Did Ced tell you Mom's on his case again about settling down?"

Lorenzo grinned and clapped Cedric on the shoulder. "Forty is right around the corner, so you might want to get busy."

Cedric shrugged off the hand. "Shut up. You're right there with me." He and Lorenzo had been born two months apart.

Jeremy burst out laughing. "That's what I said. It

would be a shame for him to be flashing an AARP card while taking his kid to day care."

Lorenzo joined in the laughter.

Cedric didn't. "I've already stated my position, so there's no need for me to repeat it."

"Yeah, I know. There isn't a woman alive that can make you change your bachelor status." Lorenzo gestured around the yard. "Take a look at all our cousins. They all said the same thing and were adamant about remaining single. Hell, I even said it." Lorenzo had been put off relationships for a long time after his ex-girlfriend had stolen money from him and hidden drugs in his home. "And look at me now—I wouldn't trade what I have with Desiree for anything."

"That's all well and good, but I simply like being single."

Jeremy smiled. "So do I, until I meet Mrs. Right, but I guarantee there's going to be a woman who'll make you change your mind." He pulled out his wallet. "A hundred dollars says you'll be ready to take that walk down the aisle by the end of the year. That's roughly nine months. Care to take the bet, big brother?"

Cedric snorted. "If you want to waste your money, fine."

"Two hundred says he'll be a goner by summer," Lorenzo said.

"Whatever." Cedric pivoted on his heel and stalked off.

"Everybody, it's time for cake," his mother called out.

The family gathered around the tables. Cedric's grandmother sat as regally as a queen at a table that had been decorated in her favorite colors, pink and green, to represent her Alpha Kappa Alpha sorority. After Cedric's mother gave the count, the family sang happy birthday, then boisterously broke into the Stevie Wonder version, complete with dancing. Cedric watched in amusement as his grandfather helped his wife to her feet and the two joined in. "Go, Grandma!" She didn't look a day over sixty and could still get her groove on. Once the noise died down, his mother and two aunts coordinated cutting and serving the cake and ice cream.

Cedric took his cake and sat at the table across from his cousin Morgan. She and her pro-football-player twin brother, Malcolm, were the youngest of their generation in the Gray clan. "How's the sports agenting world?"

Morgan adjusted her toddler son on her lap. "It's good. This one right here keeps me so busy, I'm not adding any more clients right now." She'd left her job as an attorney for their family's home safety company to pursue her dream.

"How many clients do you have now?" Cedric ate a bite of cake.

"Seven." She fed Omar Jr. a piece of cake and he grabbed the fork.

Cedric chuckled. "I guess you're not moving fast enough." Before he could say anything else, his cell buzzed. He fished it out of his pocket and frowned, not recognizing the number. "Let me answer this, Morgan." He connected. "Hello."

"Hello, is this Cedric Hunter?"

"May I ask who's calling?" Before the man on the line could answer, Cedric's phone chimed, alerting him that an alarm had gone off at the strip mall site.

"This is Detective Brian Warner from the Sacramento Police Department, and I'm calling to let you know there's been a fire at one of your construction sites."

Cedric's heart almost stopped. "Excuse me? What?" He jumped to his feet and scanned the yard for Lorenzo. He spotted him on the far side and waved him over, still listening to the detective. "Thank you. I'll be right there." *I don't need this right now.*

"What's wrong?"

"There's a fire at the strip mall site."

Lorenzo's eyes widened and he muttered a curse. "Let's go."

Cedric quickly explained to his father and his uncle what had happened.

Uncle Russell rose to his feet.

"We got it, Dad," Lorenzo said. "Let everybody know and we'll be back as soon as we can."

Cedric and Lorenzo got into Cedric's car and sped off. "We haven't even started the wiring," Cedric said. "Only the foundation and frame have been completed, so I can't understand how a fire got started." This would put them behind schedule, and there'd be the added cost of replacing materials, not to mention the hassle of dealing with the insurance company. They would also need to contact their client, but Cedric wanted to wait until he saw how much damage the building had sustained. He gripped the steering wheel tighter. The closer he got to the site, the more his gut began to churn. His cousin's tight jaw let Cedric know Lorenzo was feeling the same turmoil.

When they arrived at the construction site, Cedric could only stare. They had seen the smoke several blocks away and all he could think about was the amount of time and money they'd spent going down the drain. Police cars and fire engines surrounded the area and he had to park halfway down the block. The flames looked to be under control but almost a third of the building lay charred. It wasn't until he felt the tightness in his chest that he realized he'd been holding his breath.

"I can't believe this," Lorenzo muttered. "Who could've done this, and *why*?"

Cedric had no idea, but he knew it hadn't been an accident. "I wonder if some punk-ass kids were out here playing stupid games." Along with the acrid smell of smoke, he detected the unmistakable scent of gasoline. He and Lorenzo started toward the site but were stopped by a police officer.

"I'm going to need you to stay back."

"My name is Cedric Hunter and this is my cousin Lorenzo Hunter. This is our site. A Detective Warner called me."

The man nodded. "Wait right here and I'll get him."

Cedric scrubbed a hand down his face. "I don't even want to think about what Preston is going to say." Preston Davies was a millionaire real estate developer who owned several commercial buildings.

Lorenzo nodded in agreement. "He's not going to be happy. I just hope it doesn't take them too long to release the site. The quicker we can get this cleaned up, the better off we'll be."

Cedric glanced over at the half-burned building again and sighed. How had they gotten in? A metal fence surrounded the property.

"Mr. Hunter?"

Cedric and Lorenzo turned at the sound of a man's voice. "Yes," they both answered.

The man divided a glance between the two. "Which one of you is Cedric Hunter?"

"I am." Cedric stuck out his hand.

"I'm Detective Warner," the man said, shaking the proffered hand.

"Can you tell me what happened? Who did this?"

"We don't know. We've canvassed the neighborhood, but so far no one has seen anything. Have you had any problems on the site recently?"

"None."

"Any disgruntled employees?"

"No. You think someone working for us did this?"

"I'm just covering all the bases." The detective asked several more questions. "It looks like whoever did this cut through the fence over there." He pointed.

That answered the *how* question, but still not the *who*. "Any idea how long it'll be before we can start cleaning up after they put out the fire? This is going to set us back and I'd like to avoid further delay."

"You'll have to take that up with the fire investigator."

"Any way I can talk to him now?"

A slight smile tilted the corner of Detective Warner's mouth. "I'll see what I can find out from Randi."

"Thanks." The detective ducked under the yellow tape bordering the site and walked over to the opposite side of the building where he spoke with someone writing on a notepad. After a few minutes, he came back.

"Randi will be with you in a few minutes." He handed Cedric a card. "If you think of anything that might give us a lead, give me a call."

Cedric nodded and pocketed the card. He paced back and forth. "This is insane. Who would do this?" He didn't have a clue as to whom or *why* someone would torch the site. They'd been in business for nearly thirty years and this had never happened before. He stared as the firefighters went around with the hoses battling the blaze. Because the roof hadn't yet been constructed, the fire was fought from the ground.

"I wish I knew," Lorenzo said grimly. "I just hope it doesn't take long for the investigator to release the site. I'm thinking we might need to pull a few people off the other projects to help with the cleanup in order to make up time." As a civil engineer, Lorenzo oversaw the planning, budgeting and scheduling and made sure the sidewalks, parking lots and other roadways associated with each project were intact. Cedric, with his construction engineering degree, took care of site staffing, materials and making sure the buildings went up on time.

He mentally went down the list of current projects. "I'll have to see. I don't want to put any of the others behind schedule, either. I may end up hiring a few temporary workers." They continued to mull over options. After several minutes, Cedric glanced over his shoulder and, although his view was partially blocked, saw that the fire investigator still hadn't moved. "What is he doing?" he mumbled.

"Who?"

"The fire investigator." He checked his watch. It was almost five, nearly an hour after he'd received the call. "We've been waiting for almost fifteen minutes."

Lorenzo shrugged. "Looks like he's still making notes."

"Well, I wish he'd hurry up." Patience had never been one of Cedric's strong points.

"I'm sure he'll be over when he's done."

Cedric hoped so. He needed to know something… *anything.* After another forty minutes, Randi still hadn't so much as looked their way and Cedric felt his patience slipping. "I've had about enough of this. I'm going over there." He threw up his hands. "He knows we're waiting." He took a step and Lorenzo placed a staying hand on his arm.

"No you're not."

Cedric lifted a brow. "And who's going to stop me?"

Lorenzo blew out a long breath. "Look Ced, I know you're anxious. So am I. But I don't think charging over there demanding answers is going to win you any brownie points. You don't want to piss the investigator off and risk us not getting any answers."

"I know, I know." He closed his eyes, drew in a deep breath and let it out slowly. He opened them and gasped as the fire investigator approached.

"I'm Randi Nichols. I apologize for keeping you waiting, but I wanted to document as much of the scene as I could before it got dark."

Cedric couldn't utter a word.

Lorenzo cleared his throat. "Hello, Ms. Nichols. I'm Lorenzo Hunter."

Between her sultry voice, arresting green eyes and shapely body, every gorgeous inch of *her* had Cedric's attention. She wore jeans, a zipped-up black jacket, work boots and a baseball cap. He finally found his voice and extended his hand. "Cedric Hunter."

Randi reached out, then paused. "Sorry." She removed her latex gloves. "Let's try this again," she said with a little laugh, shaking his hand.

Lorenzo chuckled and said for Cedric's ears only, "Looks like I might be getting that two hundred dollars sooner than I thought."

Cedric disregarded his cousin's comment, but he couldn't ignore the instant attraction he felt toward the very sexy fire investigator.

* * *

Randi Nichols had sensed the site owner's eyes on her as she sketched the perimeter of the building. She wouldn't be able to get inside the building until it had been vented and the fire chief determined it was structurally safe. But the incident commander had assured her they would preserve the evidence as best they could. She'd interviewed the first officer on the scene and would interview and do a walkthrough with the first-in firefighter once they'd extinguished the fire. She made her way over to where the two owners stood and introduced herself. A slight smile curved her lips at their reactions. She got the same shocked stare from men nearly every time. Randi just hoped they wouldn't behave like some others she encountered who seemed to think the only thing a woman could do on the job was get coffee. She studied the two of them. Both were good-looking and stood a few inches over six feet. They looked enough alike to be brothers. Cedric had slightly more muscle on his chiseled frame than Lorenzo. And his interest in her seemed to go beyond surprise. His dark brown eyes bore into hers and for a fleeting moment something inside her reacted. Randi quickly shook off the crazy feeling.

"We've been waiting for over an hour," Cedric said.

She chalked up the impatience in his voice to his worksite being burned and tried to keep her voice calm and even. "I know and I appreciate you waiting. There isn't much I can tell you until the investigation is concluded, but I will need to set up a time to talk with you."

"Do you have any idea how long it'll take before we can get back to work? I smell gasoline, so I know it wasn't an accident."

"I don't know. And you could be correct." Even

though she could almost guarantee the fire was the result of arson she refrained from saying so. She'd always been cautioned not to make assumptions without all the evidence. "I understand how frustrated you must be and we'll do everything we can to get you back on your site as soon as possible."

"No, I don't think you have any idea how frustrated I am right now." Cedric sighed heavily and ran a hand over his head. "I don't have time for this."

Randi conceded him that point. No one ever had time for a fire that disrupted workflow and destroyed lives. "Is there a time we can meet on Monday?"

"Yes." He handed her a business card. "I'll be at another site in the morning but should be back around three."

His hand brushed against hers during the exchange, and she was surprised by the softness. She'd noticed it when they shook hands, too. With him being in construction, she'd have expected them to be roughened by calluses. "Will four o'clock work?"

"Fine," he responded tersely.

"Thanks for your time," Lorenzo said and frowned at Cedric.

"You're welcome. I'll see you on Monday at four." She handed him one of her cards. "If you need to reschedule, just give me a call."

Cedric nodded, his eyes locked on hers. "Thanks." He pivoted on his heel and strode off.

Randi watched him as he and Lorenzo took up a position several feet away, near the area where the firefighters worked. Fortunately, no other structures had been damaged and no lives lost. Turning her attention back to where it needed to be, Randi made her rounds and interviewed the few people who had been standing around. No one had seen anyone near the building. More than once as she went about her tasks, she caught Cedric staring her way. It took another three hours before the firefighters had the fire completely out.

"Hey, Randi."

She spun around at the sound of Detective Brian Warner's voice. "Hey. Anybody see anything?"

"Not one person." Brian shook his head. "You know as well as I do, people are real hesitant to give up information these days."

"Tell me about it," she murmured.

"You heard about the task force?" When she nodded, he said, "The mayor wants to nip this in the bud before it gets out of control. Not sure how he heard about this one or the fact that it's suspected arson, but..." He shrugged.

Randi lifted a brow. "He thinks they're connected?"

"I've no idea, but apparently he's good friends with the construction company owner from the first fire and if there's a connection, he said he wants to be on top of it." That fire had been two weeks ago and they still had no leads.

"Always politics. I wish he'd get more involved when it comes to our budgets."

Brian laughed. "Tell me about it. The first meeting is tomorrow at eight."

There goes my Sunday. "Hopefully, it won't last too long."

"Hopefully. See you later."

After he left, Randi went to find the fire chief. She spotted him talking to Cedric and Lorenzo and decided to wait until they finished their conversation. She didn't want another round with Mr. Personality. She wasn't fond of Cedric's attitude, but she couldn't deny his good looks. She also sensed his attraction to her beneath the gruff exterior and briefly wondered what his smile would be like. She immediately dismissed the thought. *I need to be focused on finding an arsonist, not worrying about the man's smile.* She'd always been able to hold her own in any situation and had worked to prove herself in a male-dominated profession, but something about the way Cedric stared at her had her off balance or *something.* As much as she hated to admit it, she felt a tug of attraction toward him.

Chapter 2

Instead of sleeping in on Sunday morning like she had planned, Randi found herself seated in a conference room with people from the local police and fire departments, two ATF agents and Detective Warner. The fire chief headed the meeting, which started promptly at eight.

"Let's get started." Chief Milton Anderson had been Randi's captain when she started as a twenty-three-year-old recruit almost a decade ago. Unlike some of the men in her unit, he'd never treated her differently because of her gender and she had the utmost respect for him. "The mayor is chomping at the bit to catch whoever is setting these fires."

"Has the first one been connected to this one?" an officer called out from the back.

"Not yet, but there were some similarities. The only thing we know for sure is that both fires were at construction sites and deliberately set. We'll know more once all the evidence has been processed. Randi, you're all set to go."

"Thanks, Chief." A small part of her had hoped the construction site hadn't been released. She'd worked late six days straight and was exhausted. But Randi knew the drill and fires didn't care whether you were rested or not. She texted her team the information and asked them to meet her at the site at ten. She took a sip of the coffee she had picked up on her way in and hoped the jolt of caffeine would kick in soon.

The chief continued with his briefing, then gave everyone their tasks. An hour later, the meeting ended. "We'll meet again on Tuesday at eight."

As they all filed out, one of the ATF agents stopped Randi.

"You have a minute?"

"Sure."

"I'll walk you out."

Randi studied him a long moment, curious as to why they couldn't talk there, but nodded. She had worked with Jason Marks on a few cases and considered him one of the good guys. They didn't speak until they'd exited the building and were halfway across the parking lot. "What's up? Do you have some other information on the case we're not privy to?" she asked with a smile. The feds were notorious for taking over local cases.

Jason chuckled. "No. We're just here to assist if needed. The mayor called the governor, who's a good friend of my boss…"

She laughed. "I get it."

He glanced around, then spoke quietly. "I know you're looking to apply to the agency and I wanted to give you a heads-up that there's going to be a position opening at the end of the summer."

She stopped walking. "I didn't see anything posted on the website."

"It hasn't been advertised yet. You're good people, Randi, and we could use someone with your expertise and professionalism on our team."

Inside, she bubbled with excitement but kept her voice calm. "I appreciate the endorsement and the heads-up. I'll be watching for the announcement."

He nodded. "See you later. Let me know if you need help with anything on the case."

"Thanks." They parted ways and she continued to her car. Randi got in, started the engine and pulled out of the lot. She smiled, thinking she might just be able to reach her goal sooner than planned *and* without having to move away. She did a little fist pump. When applying, all applicants had to sign a mobility statement, acknowledging they could be relocated at any time. As she drove, she thought about what she needed to do to prepare. The ATF required each person to take and pass special agent and assessment exams, and a physical-task test comprising sit-ups, push-ups and a mile-and-a-half run.

Randi was in good shape—she'd had to be as a fire-fighter—and continued to work out regularly. However, due to the many hours she had worked recently, she hadn't been to the gym in nearly two weeks. She would have to find time because she wanted to do everything in her power to get that job.

She arrived at the site first and parked at the edge of the property. While waiting for her colleagues, she answered a few emails and confirmed dinner with her sister for later in the evening.

When her team arrived, the five of them went about the arduous task of collecting evidence. One of Randi's forensic science professors had mentioned wearing two pairs of gloves to make it easier when having to document samples and Randi had continued the practice to this day. The gloves kept them from cross-contaminating the evidence and while processing a scene, it wasn't uncommon for her to go through more than a dozen pairs. She continued the task, placing pieces of wood, soil samples and other findings into separate containers, sealing them and labeling each one.

Starting from the least damaged area and progressing to the most heavily affected, Randi searched for the point of origin, paying close attention to burn patterns along the partially completed walls. Fire tended to burn upward and outward, but she didn't find any of those patterns, further strengthening the theory that the fire had been deliberately set. They found three points of origin with erratic burn patterns. Whoever had set the fire had intended to burn the entire building. That, along with the lingering smell of gasoline, left no doubt in her mind that this was arson. She made sure to carefully document the scene, writing her observations and descriptions, sketching and marking each area, and photographing and taking videos of everything.

The sun had begun to set when the team started packing up. All the evidence would be transported to the lab by one of her team members. "Be extra careful maintaining the chain of custody. The mayor is involved and he'll want every detail." And she didn't want any problems when it came time to prosecute.

"Will do," Jada said, placing the various containers into the back of the van. The young woman had joined the team less than a year ago and often shadowed Randi or the other senior member, Marlon Wilson. "I'll leave a copy on your desk."

"Thanks. Before you leave, I'm going to do another walkthrough to make sure we didn't miss anything."

"I'll come with you," Marlon said. "I'll take the back."

He started toward the rear of the building and Randi went in the opposite direction. Near one of the points of origin, a partially covered, blackened piece of wood caught her attention. She added a second pair of gloves and squatted down. She could see something written in gray paint on one side. "Hey, Marlon, can you come get a shot of this?" There shouldn't be paint, since the building hadn't been completed.

Marlon came to where Randi knelt, and complied. After she moved the top piece of wood, he took another picture. "This means it's personal."

She studied the written words. "Yeah, it does." Cedric's dark, penetrating stare filtered through her mind. She wasn't looking forward to telling him. They collected two other pieces of evidence, made plans to meet in the morning and went their separate ways.

Before driving off, Randi called her sister to let her know she'd be there in an hour. It took her half an hour to get to her Natomas condo from Elk Grove. Once there, she showered quickly and changed into jeans, a long-sleeved T-shirt and tennis shoes. Her stomach growled, reminding her that she hadn't eaten since breakfast. At the site, Randi had stopped long enough only to down a protein shake. She grabbed three crackers and a slice of cheese to hold her until she made it to Iyana's place and went out to her car. Luckily, her sister lived only fifteen minutes away.

"Hey, Randi," Iyana said when she opened the door. They shared a quick embrace before Iyana stepped back to let Randi enter.

"Hey." Randi sniffed. "Please tell me that's my favorite food I smell."

"Come see for yourself."

Randi followed her to the kitchen. She smiled when she saw the enchiladas, Mexican rice, black beans, chips, salsa and guacamole. She immediately scooped some of the guacamole onto a chip and popped it into her mouth. Her eyes slid closed and she moaned. "You make the best guac *ever*. Ooh, and sangria."

Iyana laughed. "You always say that. I decided to try a tropical sangria this time... Moscato and rum."

"Say no more. Just pour me a glass."

"I guess that trip to Puerto Vallarta three years ago is still paying off. Well, in one way, at least," she said wryly.

Randi gave her sister a sympathetic look. "I still want to rip his heart out."

"You and me both." What was supposed to be a romantic getaway with her fiancé had turned into a disaster when Iyana caught him cheating with a woman he had invited to the resort. She'd sworn off dating since then. Iyana waved a hand. "Let's not ruin a perfectly good meal." She picked up two plates and handed one to Randi.

"You don't have to tell me twice." They shared a smile and filled their plates. She continued to observe her sister. Although Iyana was her usual upbeat self, Randi could still see remnants of pain. At thirty-two, Randi was one year older and had always looked out for Iyana. She hated to see her hurting.

"Are you investigating that construction site fire?" Iyana asked as the two settled in the family room. She turned on a rerun of *The Color Purple*. "The news reports imply it was arson."

"Yep. That's why I was late." Between mouthfuls, Randi filled her sister in on the basics without getting too detailed. "I'm meeting with the owners tomorrow."

"That won't be fun. I know I would be pissed off if somebody torched all my hard work. All that money gone down the drain."

"No, it won't." Once again, thoughts of her first encounter with Cedric surfaced, from his curt manner to the intense way he had stared at her. She really wanted to know what he'd been thinking. Or maybe she didn't. Randi glanced up to find Iyana viewing her curiously. "What?"

Iyana angled her head and narrowed her gaze. "There's something about the way you said that."

"I don't know what you mean. I just agreed with you that the conversation won't be fun."

"Have you met the owners yet?"

"Briefly yesterday. Why?"

A smile spread across Iyana's lips. She forked up some rice, chewed, then asked, "What does this owner look like?"

Randi shrugged. "He's a nice-looking guy, maybe mid-thirties." In reality, Cedric was *fine* with a capital F. And though he wore the owner's hat now, his muscular body let her know he had done more than sit behind a desk. She could imagine how many women had stopped to watch him while he worked on some building. Not many men could make her stop in her tracks, but Cedric Hunter had not only done that, he'd also invaded her thoughts. She jumped when she felt something hit her cheek. Randi glared at her sister. "Why are you throwing chips at me?"

"Because I called your name three times and you're so busy thinking about that owner, you can't hear me."

"What?" She waved her off. "I'm not thinking about Cedric." She muttered a curse. That was all the ammunition Iyana needed.

Iyana's grin widened. "Thanks for providing confirmation. Obviously, the brother is more than good-looking to have you all drifting off into space."

Randi didn't respond.

"Cedric, huh?"

"I told you I met him yesterday, along with the co-owner, Lorenzo Hunter."

Iyana set her plate on the coffee table, wiped her hands on a napkin and picked up her phone.

Randi bit into a chip. "What are you doing?"

"Looking him up. What else would I be doing? The news said the company's name was…" She made a show of thinking, then snapped her fingers. "Hunter Construction." Her fingers moved rapidly over the keyboard and a moment later, her eyes widened. "*Have mercy!* Is he the one with the locs or the one with that sinfully sexy smile? I mean, both of them would make a sister sell her soul for a touch. All this chocolatey goodness and those killer dimples, mmm-mmm. I guess the construction business does a body good."

Randi shook her head and chuckled. "You do have a way with words." She leaned over to see the photo. Just as she had suspected, the smile transformed Cedric's already handsome face.

"Hey, just because I've spent the last two months

painting muscles and whatnot on bodies doesn't mean I don't recognize the real thing when I see it." Iyana worked as a movie makeup artist. "And you didn't answer my question."

"The latter one."

"I see why you were all in la-la land. He's sure to melt all that iciness you've built up since—"

"Don't even say his name, and you're one to talk." Randi had spent the better part of a year trying to forget the fiasco of her so-called relationship. She refused to be with any man who couldn't accept her and her job…*as is*. If that meant being labeled an ice princess, as Iyana sometimes called her, Randi would wear the name gladly. At least her heart would be intact. Sure, she wanted to find the *one*, but she was done settling. "In any case," she said, refocusing on her food, "the only thing I'll be discussing with the Hunters is the fire."

Still looking at her phone, Iyana said, "Whatever. All I know is this brother looks like he could thaw a blizzard." They burst out laughing.

Randi lifted her glass in a mock toast. "I'll concede you that point." She sipped the sangria. "This is really good. What else is in it?"

"Pineapple and orange juices, and the fruit."

"You'll have to give me the recipe."

"I'll write it down before you leave. Back to those fine men. Are they brothers?"

Randi had wondered the same thing, since the two favored each other, but as she'd told her sister, their only conversation would be a professional one and that question didn't fall within that scope. "I have no idea. Now, can we just eat and watch the movie? You're making me miss my favorite parts." She'd see Cedric tomorrow, and that would be soon enough.

Cedric and Lorenzo spent the balance of the weekend trying to move resources around and putting together ads for temporary workers, then they hit the ground running Monday morning. Cedric had spoken to Preston and, as he suspected, the man was not happy. He couldn't blame Preston because he felt the same way. Before heading out to one of his other sites, he met Preston at what was left of the strip mall frame.

Preston shook his head and let out a deep sigh. "The police have any leads?"

"Not yet. I'm meeting with the fire investigator this afternoon, so hopefully I'll know more then." Mentioning the fire investigator made Cedric think of his reaction to Randi. He hadn't expected a woman, and he definitely hadn't expected the jolt of sexual attraction that hit him. Preston's voice pulled him out of his thoughts.

"This is going to set us back weeks and I already have the tenants lined up. How long will it take to clean up and restart?" The planned South Sacramento mall would house business and medical offices, a restaurant and coffee shop.

Cedric glanced around the property. "At least three to four weeks, minimum. I'll have to order more lumber and I won't know how much is needed until I get inside."

"Thank goodness for insurance," Preston muttered.

"Agreed." Cedric hoped they didn't have to haggle with the insurance company and wait forever for them to cut a check. He peeked at his watch. "I need to get across town to another site. I'll let you know what the investigator says."

"Thanks, Cedric." Preston stuck out his hand.

"We'll try to keep as close to the original schedule as possible."

Preston chuckled. "You always do. That's why I like working with you." He had used Hunter Construction for two other commercial buildings previously.

"And we appreciate your business. I'll be in touch." Cedric and Preston went to their respective cars and Cedric drove out toward Rocklin to check the progress of the manufacturing warehouse. His cell rang five minutes into the drive. He connected the Bluetooth. "Hello."

"Hey. You and Preston still at the site?" Lorenzo asked.

"We just left."

"The insurance company called back and we have to wait until we get the fire report before they can do anything. I sent some photos already."

Cedric merged onto the freeway. "I figured as much."

"Speaking of the fire report, I hope your attitude is better when you meet with Ms. Nichols today."

"What are you talking about?"

"You know exactly what I mean. You almost took the woman's head off."

"I did not."

Lorenzo let out a snort. "Yeah, you did."

"Well, she had us standing there forever and I couldn't get her to admit it was arson, even though you could smell the gasoline fifty feet away. She's the one being difficult."

"Maybe, but your problem goes deeper than that."

He frowned. "Meaning?"

"You're attracted to her, plain and simple. Not that she's going to give you the time of day now."

"The only thing I need her time for is to let me know when I can get back onto that worksite," he lied. His cousin knew him well and that momentary pause when she introduced herself had been a dead giveaway.

Lorenzo's laughter came through the line. "Is that what you're telling yourself? I can't *wait* to see how this plays out."

"There's nothing to play out."

"Whatever. See you when you get back to the office."

Cedric disconnected. If he were being honest with himself, part of him wanted to see her to find out if the vibe he felt flowing between them had been his imagination. Randi had been the epitome of professional during their interaction, but he sensed something, saw it in her eyes for a split second. He turned up the music and refocused on the road. He'd deal with Ms. Nichols later.

Forty minutes later, Cedric pulled into the worksite. He donned a hard hat, climbed out of the truck and sought out the foreman.

"Hey, Cedric."

He spun around at the sound of his name being called. The foreman, William Coleman, waved from the other side of the site and Cedric started in his direction.

Will met Cedric halfway. "I heard about the fire. If you need me to help with the cleanup, let me know. I can work a few hours in the evening and on the weekend." Will had worked for the company for as long as Cedric could remember. When Cedric and Lorenzo had taken over the company and needed to fill their old supervisory positions, they'd offered the construction supervisor job to Will, but he declined, citing he'd rather be outdoors than cooped up in an office every day.

"I appreciate that, Will. Is everything running smoothly here?"

"Yes. No hiccups. We should be finished by summer, right on schedule."

Cedric and Will pored over the blueprints for several minutes, discussing next steps, then did a walkthrough of the site. More than a few of the workers expressed their willingness to help get the burned-out worksite up and running again. Cedric truly appreciated his employees and considered them family. If it turned out that he did need to pull some of them in to assist, each would get a bonus in their checks.

He said his goodbyes and headed back to the office, but not before stopping at the Sandwich Spot in Roseville to get his favorite, the Throw Down—marinated chicken, barbecue and teriyaki sauces, mozzarella cheese, lettuce and tomatoes, all on a soft roll. He splurged and ordered a side of fries, too. Between the late hours he'd worked over the past couple of weeks, all the food he had consumed at his grandmother's birthday party and today's sandwich, Cedric would need to spend extra hours in the gym to work it all off. He had been only three times in the last fourteen days. Thinking about the gym reminded him that he needed to schedule a time for his cousin Khalil to come back up and see the progress of the fitness center he'd contracted them to build. Khalil owned two Maximum Burn gyms in LA, and was expanding to the northern side of the state. The gym would be ready by the end of summer.

Cedric arrived at his office later than he anticipated

and had only fifteen minutes to eat before his meeting with the fire inspector.

"Hey. You went to the Sandwich Spot and didn't tell me?" Lorenzo said, entering the office. "You know that's wrong."

Cedric unwrapped half of the sandwich and took a hefty bite without answering. It tasted so good he groaned.

Lorenzo reached over and snagged a few fries.

Cedric sighed and pushed the other half of the sandwich across the desk. "Don't say I've never given you anything."

Lorenzo laughed, but quickly snatched it up. "Aw, thanks, cuz."

They ate in silence for a few minutes before Cedric wondered aloud, "Do you think she'll confirm the arson? I've racked my brain all weekend and can't come up with one reason why someone would deliberately set fire to the building."

Lorenzo shrugged. "I hope she'll have something to tell us. I've wondered the same thing. I also thought about whether it had something to do with Preston and not us."

Cedric popped a fry into his mouth and chewed slowly. "I hadn't considered that. Maybe someone who wanted that piece of land?"

"Or something," Lorenzo said, reaching for another fry.

"Why are you stealing my food? Didn't you have lunch?"

"No. I had to meet with Joanne this morning, check on the community center building and deal with the insurance company."

Cedric shook his head and moved the bag of fries closer to himself. "You already have half my sandwich, so you're not getting any more of my fries." He checked the time. "We have about five minutes."

Lorenzo ate the last bite of the sandwich and stood. "I'm going to get some water. I'll be right back."

Cedric rolled the chair back, reached into the mini refrigerator he kept in the office and retrieved two bottles of water. "Here."

"Thanks."

He finished the last few fries and drained the water bottle, then disposed of the empty packaging before popping a mint. His intercom buzzed. "Yes, Loretta."

"Your four o'clock is here."

"Thanks. I'll be right out." He was up, around the desk and halfway across the office before he caught himself and slowed his steps. He told himself he was eager to see Randi only to find out what information she had on the fire. But that went right out the window the moment their eyes connected. "Ms. Nichols."

"Mr. Hunter."

Cedric felt the same underlying attraction he'd experienced on Saturday. "Right this way." He stepped aside to let her enter his office. Today, she wore the same work boots and another pair of jeans that hugged her curvy bottom. He followed the sway of her hips, then waved her into one of the chairs across from his desk. "Please have a seat."

"Thanks. Detective Warner had planned to be here, but got called away."

Lorenzo offered a greeting and took the chair next to her.

"So it was arson, right?" Cedric asked.

Randi nodded. "Yes. The fire was set in three different places—at both ends and behind the structure. Evidently, someone wanted the entire building to go down."

He leaned back in his chair. The fact that it hadn't
burnt to the ground meant the fire department arrived
quickly, and he couldn't be more grateful. Having a third
of the building burned was bad enough, but if they'd had
to start from scratch after eight months of hard work…
Cedric didn't even want to think about it. "But why?"

Randi shifted in her chair. "I'd hoped one of you could
shed some light on the situation. Have you had any problems lately?"

"Nothing lately, no," Lorenzo said.

Cedric sighed. "I can't think of one reason why someone would do this. Our employees are like family and,
for the most part, get along well on the job."

Randi divided a glance between Cedric and Lorenzo.
"No disgruntled employees, no one you've fired recently
who might be holding a grudge?"

"I haven't fired anyone. Zo, you fired that tech last
year." He tapped his finger on the desk, trying to remember a name.

"Joey Abrams?"

"That's him."

"Do you think he would do something like this?"
Randi asked.

Lorenzo shook his head. "No. He was far too lazy.
I couldn't even count on him to spend fifteen minutes
going over the contractor's work order, let alone walk
the entire site. Besides, last I heard he'd changed fields
completely."

She wrote something on her notepad. "I'll have Detective Warner check him out anyway. Can you think of anyone else?"

Cedric and Lorenzo both said no. Then Cedric asked, "Is there something you're not telling us, Ms. Nichols?"

Randi handed them a photo.

Cedric's heart nearly stopped. "Where did you find this?"

"Near one of the points of origin. So, again, are you sure there isn't anyone who comes to mind who might have a grudge of some sort?"

He shook his head slowly, still trying to make sense of the photo. On one of the two-by-fours, he could make out the first three letters of his name. The only visible letters before that were *ay*. And the only word that came to mind with those letters was *pay*. Someone wanted him to pay for something. But he had no idea what. Or why.

"I thought that fire would destroy all the evidence," Lorenzo said.

"Not necessarily. It distorts it, but we look deeper than the norm. This is a crucial piece of evidence. I'm sure whoever set the fire didn't expect this to survive, but fire is unpredictable." She asked several more questions that mirrored the detective's. "I'll need to rule out everyone who's worked at the site, and that includes fingerprints and background information. I'll need the same from both of you."

"You think I'd burn down my own site?" Cedric asked incredulously. He tossed the photo across the desk. "What about this?"

"I'm not saying that at all. This is just standard procedure."

She held his gaze without flinching, piquing his interest even more, despite his anger. He rose from his seat.

"I'll have my assistant pull together the information. Is there anything else you need?"

"Not at the moment."

Lorenzo's assistant, Tanya, knocked softly on the door and poked her head inside. "I'm so sorry to interrupt. Lorenzo, your wife is on the line and she says it's important."

"Thanks." Lorenzo hopped up. "Ced, I need to take this. You can handle the rest without me?"

Not taking his eyes off Randi, Cedric said, "Yeah, I can handle it."

Chapter 3

Randi shifted in her chair. She'd been fine while Lorenzo sat in the office, but now with just her and Cedric, she sensed the same undercurrents she had the day they met. He stared at her in awkward silence, making her change positions again. "I hope everything's okay." She wanted to ask if he was married as well, but curbed the urge. She didn't care. Or at least that was what she told herself.

"So do I. Will my employees have to go to the police station to get fingerprinted? This will be uncomfortable enough without them being subjected to a visit to the precinct."

His voice held a slight edge and she understood how this might affect his workers. "I'll talk to Detective Warner and see what can be arranged." Randi stood. "If you think of anything, let me or Detective Warner know."

Cedric slowly came to his feet and nodded.

Today he wore a pair of well-worn jeans that clung to his strong thighs, and a long-sleeved T-shirt with the company logo across the front that outlined the muscles of his arms and chest. She could see small spots of dirt and speculated on whether he'd been working on one of his other sites. Her sister's comment about construction doing a body good came back to her. "Thanks for your time." She headed for the door.

"Hang on a second and I'll get the information you wanted from my assistant."

She paused at the door. "You can just send it to me or the detective. My information is on the card I gave you and I can give you Detective Warner's if you don't have it."

"No need to do that when you're already here. It'll only take a couple of minutes."

He came around the desk and strode across the room with a walk so sexy she wanted to ask him to do it again. *Get it together, girl.*

"I'll be right back."

Randi moved aside to let him open the door at the same time he moved, and their bodies collided. She jumped back and nearly tripped over his foot. Cedric's strong arm came up and steadied her. "Sorry," she mumbled.

"My apologies," Cedric said at the same time. He stood there a moment longer, then opened the door and exited.

She blew out a long breath. *This is ridiculous. I do not get all worked up over a man.* To make sure the same thing didn't happen again, she walked over to the window and glanced out at the traffic. She checked her watch. It was after five and she wanted to get to the gym.

Her workout clothes had been in her car for the past two weeks. She would check emails and review the evidence from the comfort of her condo later on.

"Here you go."

Randi spun around at the sound of Cedric's voice. "Thank you." She scanned the sheet he handed her. It contained the names of every worker, along with their addresses, phone numbers and years at the company.

"Is this what you need?"

"Yes. I'll pass this on to the detective. I'll be in touch." She started for the door, keenly aware that he was watching.

"Do you have to go back to your office?"

She turned back. "No. I can work just as well from home tonight."

"Would you like to have dinner?"

Randi studied him intently. "Thanks for the offer, but I don't think that's a good idea."

"Why? Aside from the case, that is," Cedric said as he closed the distance between them.

She instinctively took a step backward. He towered over her five-eight height by a good six inches. Aside from the case, she didn't have a legitimate reason, except for wanting to steer clear of men for a while. "Since there is a case, nothing else matters."

A small smile crept onto his face, and he folded his arms across his wide chest. "And if I promise we won't talk about the case? Are there any rules against it?"

"Not that I know of, but I—"

"Think of it as my way of apologizing for being such a hard-ass. One dinner won't get you into any trouble."

In her estimation, dinner would be only the beginning of trouble, because Randi knew he'd be charming—like now—and she didn't need or want *charming* in her life. Yet, she heard herself say, "Okay, one dinner and no talk about the case."

He unleashed a full-dimpled grin that made her breath stack up in her throat. The half smile she'd seen on the website photo didn't come close to capturing this sexy version, one a woman would sell her soul to touch, as Iyana had pointed out. But Randi wouldn't be selling her soul *or* touching. After tonight, there would be nothing between them except what pertained to the case.

"Deal. Any particular food preferences?"

Randi opened her mouth to say Mexican, but changed her mind since she'd just eaten some yesterday. Another reason she needed to hit the gym. "No."

Cedric went to his desk and picked up his phone. "There are several restaurants around the area. I'm sure we can find one to fit both our tastes." He typed for a moment, then came back to where she stood. "See if there's anything that catches your attention."

She leaned over to see the phone as he scrolled slowly through the choices. Some she hadn't heard of, and others she recognized but had never visited. "Have you ever been to Yard House?"

"Yes. The food's pretty good. You?"

"Not yet."

"Check out the menu and see if it's something you'd like to try. They have everything from burgers and pizza to steak and seafood."

She scanned it briefly. "That sounds fine. Is it far from here?"

"Ten, fifteen minutes. It's across the street from the Roseville Galleria Mall. We should take the streets instead of the freeway since most people are just getting off work. I'm going to add us to the call-ahead list to cut down on the wait time." He did that and pocketed the phone.

She'd been to the mall but didn't recall seeing the restaurant. "I'll follow you."

"Okay. Let me go talk to Lorenzo for a minute, then we can go."

Randi smiled. "Sounds good." She followed him out and stood in the waiting area until he returned.

He came back a short while later and grabbed his jacket from his office. "See you in the morning, Loretta."

"Bye, boss. I'm right behind you."

"I'll lock the door on my way out." He faced Randi. "Ready?"

"Yes." She walked out to the parking lot in front and pressed the remote lock on her Acura. She startled when Cedric came up behind her, reached around and opened her door. She hadn't even heard him approach. "Thanks," she mumbled and got in. He closed the door and sauntered a few spaces over to a dark gray Mercedes. Randi started the engine and pulled out behind him. All during the drive, she wondered if she'd made a mistake in accepting Cedric's offer. She hadn't been on a date since breaking up with her ex a year ago, choosing to focus on her career instead. When they arrived, they had to circle a few times to find parking. A spot opened up near the entrance and Cedric motioned for her to take it. A few minutes later, he joined her at the front of the restaurant and escorted her inside. She stood off to the side while he spoke with the hostess.

"They said it should be about ten minutes." He held up the little pager. "With this crowd, I'm glad I called ahead. I forgot it was happy hour, too."

"Me, too." The upscale bar and grill had a large crowd of people waiting inside and out. Randi surveyed the area and saw several NBA and NCAA basketball games on in the bar. March Madness was in full swing.

After a few minutes, Cedric leaned close to her ear. "Do you want something from the bar?"

His heat surrounded her and it took her a moment to answer. "No, thanks. I'll just wait until we're seated. But if you want to get something, we can go over."

He shook his head. "I'm good."

After a couple of minutes, Randi asked, "Is Lorenzo's wife okay?"

"Yes, she's good. Thanks for asking. Are you married?"

"No. You?"

"No... And I'm not seeing anyone." He spoke that last sentence staring directly into her eyes. Her pulse skipped.

"Are you and Lorenzo brothers?"

He chuckled softly, recognizing her attempt to change the subject. "We're cousins. And he's more than happy to let everyone know he's a couple of months older."

Randi laughed. "Hey, as the oldest, I'm with that. My sister probably won't agree."

"I do have a younger brother who occasionally forgets his place," he said with a smile. The pager buzzed. "That's us." Cedric handed it to the woman behind the counter and a young man led them to a booth.

"Your server will be with you shortly," he said and handed them menus.

"Thanks." She opened her menu and perused the pages. The first thing that caught her eye was the variety of street tacos, but since she had already told herself she wouldn't indulge two days in a row, she turned the page and kept looking. "What's good here?"

Cedric looked up from his menu. "Depends on what you like. The burgers are pretty good, the rib eye and shrimp combo isn't bad, and if you like spicy foods, you might want to try the jambalaya."

Randi went back to perusing the selections. "I think I'm going to have the jambalaya."

He set the menu down. "I'm going to have the same."

The server came to take their drink order. She chose a mixed drink called Paradise Found and Cedric selected beer. Since they had made a decision on their meals, they gave that order, as well.

"Would you like an appetizer?" Cedric asked.

"No, thank you."

He handed the menus to the server and waited until the woman left. "You can't discuss the case, but am I allowed to ask how you got into this career?"

She smiled. "You're allowed. When I was nine, my best friend's house burned down. They never found a cause—or if they did, we weren't told—and it bothered me. I wanted to know why, so I decided to get degrees in fire science and criminal justice. I worked as a firefighter for almost six years and when a position opened up in the fire investigative unit, I applied and got the job."

"I'm impressed. Not many women would venture into such a dangerous field."

Randi eyed him. Was he another man who didn't think women belonged in a male-dominated arena? "Are you saying women *shouldn't* be firefighters?"

Cedric lifted his hands in mock surrender. "I'm not saying that at all. I think it's cool. They say women don't work in construction either, but we have five women in our company who can wield a hammer better than a lot of men. I'm all for women choosing whatever career makes them happy."

"Oh. Glad to hear it."

He laughed softly. "Better now?"

"Much," she said, joining in his laughter. "You're not so bad, after all."

"Thanks. I want to apologize for my less than stellar behavior."

"I totally understand that you're frustrated."

"It's still not an excuse in my book and I'm sorry."

"Apology accepted." The sincerity in his voice and in his eyes touched her in a way she didn't expect. Not good.

The server returned with their drinks. Cedric lifted his beer. "To good conversation." Randi touched her glass to his, then took a sip. He studied her over his drink. He had no idea why he had impulsively asked her to dinner, but sitting across from her now, he could admit attraction played a part. Curiosity played another. As he'd told her, not many women entered her field, and his admiration for her went up several notches after hearing her story.

"I'll turn your question back to you. Why construction?"

"I grew up around it. My father and uncle started Hunter Construction when I was seven and I wanted to be like them. Dad bought me a little tool belt and let me follow him around on a few sites." He smiled at the memory. "I started with the company as a teen, working from the bottom up. I love being able to take a drawing and bring it to life."

"That's really cool. When did you take over as owner?"

"Last year the two of them called Lorenzo and me into a meeting and said they were retiring, effective immediately. Then they left to take our mothers on a cruise. We always knew they'd planned to leave the company to us, but I have to say I expected the transition to be far different."

Randi's eyes widened and her mouth fell open. "Just like that?"

"Just like that. My expression probably looked like the one you're wearing now," he added with a shake of his head. "Our heads were spinning."

"It couldn't have been easy taking over without warning."

"No, it wasn't, especially since we both headed up divisions in the company. It took us several months to find replacements for our positions, and until then, we did both." Cedric recalled the drama that happened right after the takeover. They'd been in danger of losing the business. Now there was the fire. If he didn't know better, he'd think someone had it in for him. He glanced up when he felt a touch on his hand.

"Are you okay?" Randi asked with concern. "You seemed a million miles away for a minute."

It took him a second to answer because the warmth of her soft hand on his elicited a strange feeling inside him. He gave it a gentle squeeze, and didn't let go. "I'm good." The server returned with their food and Randi quickly pulled away, as if she'd realized what she had done. Their eyes held for a lengthy moment before she looked away.

"This looks good. I'm going to have to do an extra workout this week with everything I've been eating."

Cedric smiled. "I hear you." They ate in silence for a few moments, then he said, "You mentioned working out. I imagine you had to be in good shape as a firefighter with all the gear you wore."

Randi nodded. "It was pretty grueling having to climb massive ladders, carrying heavy equipment to or from the scene, lifting people, but I wouldn't trade the experience for anything."

"Sounds like you miss it. Was it hard being a woman in that environment?"

She shrugged. "Sometimes. There were a couple of guys who acted like I was inferior and incompetent, but thankfully, that wasn't the general sentiment." She leaned forward. "The craziest thing a guy said to me was that his wife wouldn't like the situation—meaning me bunking in the station with all the guys."

"Are you serious?"

"Very. I looked him dead in his eye and told him, 'You'd better find another job, then, because I'm here to stay.'"

Cedric burst out laughing. "I would've loved to see the look on his face. I bet he didn't come at you that way again."

"You'd win that bet," she replied, using her fork for emphasis.

The conversation tapered off and as they continued to eat, Cedric found himself wanting to know everything about the fascinating woman sitting across from him. When they finished, he leaned back in his chair and studied her again. He couldn't remember the last time he'd met a woman with as much spunk as she seemed to have. The server brought a dessert menu. "Would you like to have dessert?"

Randi patted her stomach. "No, thank you. I can't eat another bite." She handed the young woman her plate. "Can you box up mine to go?"

"Sure. I'll leave the check and be right back." She picked up Cedric's plate and left.

"You didn't even finish your food."

She laughed. "But I wanted to. I'm trying to get back to my healthier eating habits. I've fallen off the wagon over the past few weeks and my body is letting me know."

Cedric's gaze roamed over her. "I don't know what your body is telling you, but I don't see one thing that's *off the wagon.*"

"Um... I think it's time to go." She opened her purse and reached for the bill.

He frowned and snatched it up. "What are you doing?"

"I'm paying my part, what does it look like?" She stared at him as if he should know.

"Please put your money away, Randi." He withdrew his credit card and placed it in the folder, making sure to keep it on his side of the table.

"You don't need to pay for mine. I mean, this isn't a...a date or anything."

"No? Then what would you call it?" he asked, amused.

"I don't know." Randi waved a hand. "It was just dinner."

He smiled inwardly at her flustered state. "A dinner *date.*" The server returned with her food in a bag and took the bill.

Randi skewered Cedric with a glare.

He chuckled. "Why are you upset about a man wanting to take you out to dinner?"

"I'm not upset. I appreciate the gesture, but it's not necessary since this is a one-time thing."

She had mentioned that they would have only one dinner back at the office and he hadn't argued. However, he knew there would be more. The attraction between them would eventually reach a boiling point and they'd have to deal with it. Cedric signed the bill, pocketed his card and slid out of the booth. He extended his hand to Randi. "Am I allowed to help you up, even though you don't consider this a date?"

Randi slapped her hand in his palm. "Ha-ha, funny."

He assisted her but didn't let go of her hand as he escorted her out of the restaurant and to her car.

She opened the door and faced him. "Thanks for dinner, Cedric."

"You're welcome. I enjoyed it."

"So did I."

His gaze dropped to her lips. The way she smiled tempted him to find out if they were as soft as they appeared. "I'll be right behind you. And before you say anything, I'm only following you home because it's what I do. You can thank my father and uncles for my good manners."

She shook her head. "That's fine."

Cedric closed her door behind her and walked the short distance to his car. A smile curved his lips. While it was true that his father and uncles had drilled into his, Jeremy's and all their male cousins' heads the proper way to treat a woman, Cedric had a little something else in mind. Kissing her.

Chapter 4

Randi glanced in her rearview mirror and saw Cedric behind her. She must have been out of her mind to agree to let him follow her home. Okay, so she thought it was cool he wanted to be all chivalrous, but they weren't dating, so he needed to save that for some other woman. Their dinner conversation played in her mind. His father and uncle had to have had the utmost trust in Cedric and Lorenzo to turn the company over to them without warning and at such a young age. She frowned. He'd said he had worked there for twenty years, so that meant he had to be older than she originally thought. She'd put him around her age, but realized he had to be a few years older.

She rehearsed in her mind what she would say once they reached her place. A quick thank-you for dinner and for making sure she got home safely, then send him on his way. Easy. Randi pulled up to her complex, punched in the gate code and drove around the side to her condo. Cedric parked in one of the few uncovered spots nearby and got out of his car.

"Nice area," he said as they walked to her unit.

"Thanks." She stuck the key in, unlocked the door and faced him. "Thank you for dinner and for making sure I got home safely."

"You're welcome." He moved closer and brushed a kiss across her lips.

Whatever else she had planned to say went right out of her head. Instead, she asked, "Would you like to come in for a minute?"

He gestured for her to go in first, then closed the door behind him and rested against it. He must have sensed her hesitation because he said, "Second thoughts?"

"No. What about you?"

Cedric laughed softly. "I never have second thoughts about spending time with a beautiful woman."

The brother was smooth. "Um, would you like something to drink?"

"No, thank you." He wrapped an arm around her waist. "What I want, with your permission, of course, is to kiss you."

Randi's gaze dropped to his sexy lips. She shouldn't even be contemplating saying yes, but his smile and those dimples were doing her in. And what happened to her little send-him-on-his-way speech? He leaned down, leaving a mere inch between their mouths. "Yes." Before she could get the word out good, his lips came down on hers. His tongue tangled around her own and she lost all track of time and place. He reversed their positions and her back hit the door. She moaned at the feeling of his hard body pressed against hers. Randi ran her hands up his strong arms and over his muscular chest.

"Not one part of your body has fallen off the wagon," he murmured as his hands traveled from her thighs and hips to her breasts, caressing each part before moving to the next.

His touch set off a blaze and she arched closer. She wanted to feel more of him…all of him. Her hands slid beneath his shirt to touch his bare skin and she felt the muscles of his abs contract.

Cedric let out a low groan and stilled her hands. "Doing that is going to get you into trouble."

She stared up at him. "I can handle any amount of trouble you can dish out."

He lifted a brow. "You sure about that?"

"Positive." Common sense said she should stop this right now, but she'd left all her good sense behind the moment she invited him inside her home.

A smile tilted the corner of his mouth. "Then let's see how much trouble we can get into."

Once again, he captured her mouth in a scorching kiss, this one more intense than the previous one. He brought his hands up to frame her face, angled his head and deepened the kiss. Randi felt every inch of him, especially the solid bulge of his erection pressing against her belly.

Cedric lifted her to the fit of his body and trailed kisses along her jaw and neck. "Can you handle this?"

The only thing she could manage was a soft moan. He reclaimed her mouth and gently sucked on her tongue while slowly gyrating his lower body to the same rhythm. A flurry of sensations whipped through her and she sensed herself on the brink of an orgasm already. She wrapped her legs around him and he gripped her hips, moving her in time with him. Her body trembled and she came in a rush of pleasure. She tried to tell herself it was because it had been a while since she'd been with a man, but Randi knew that had nothing to do with it. The man knew his way around a woman's body and they were still fully clothed.

He eased her to her feet and slowly, methodically divested her of her clothing. He continued to use his hands and mouth to tease and heighten her desire.

When it came time for his clothes, Randi moved his hands away. "It's my turn."

Cedric spread his hands in surrender. "By all means."

She treated him to the same unhurried pace, gliding her hands beneath his shirt once again to touch him. Using her hands and mouth, she caressed and kissed her way up his body. She removed his shirt and tossed it aside and couldn't take her eyes off his smooth chest and rock-hard abs.

"Problems?" he asked with amusement.

"None at all. Just admiring the scenery." Her hand went to his belt.

"Hold on a minute." He squatted down to remove his work boots and socks, then straightened. "I'm all yours."

She wanted to tell him that he didn't belong to her and she didn't belong to him, but for tonight, she'd just roll with it. She resumed the task of undoing his pants and pushing them down and off. His erection strained against the navy boxer briefs and Randi ran her hands over his length before hooking her thumbs in the waistband and removing them. Her gaze roamed over his nakedness. The man didn't have one ounce of fat anywhere. Cedric retrieved a condom from his wallet and slid it into place. "My bedroom is down—"

Cedric slowly shook his head. He grasped her buttocks and lifted her in his arms. They shuddered as their bare bodies collided. "Right now, right here."

Randi closed her eyes and clung to him, her legs wrapped tightly around his waist and her arms clasped around his neck. He locked his mouth on hers and eased his shaft inside her until he was embedded deep within. He didn't move for several seconds and she opened her eyes. As if that was what he was waiting for, he began moving, plunging deep and retreating in a slow, erotic cadence that sent heat spiraling through her. She moaned. He kept up the pace, each stroke going deeper and deeper. She didn't realize they had moved until her back hit the cool wood door. Cedric planted his feet and increased his movements. He dipped his head and latched onto an erect nipple. The contact sent a jolt straight to her core and she cried out. He sucked and licked until her body trembled, then lavished the same sweet torture on the other one. "Cedric," she whispered on a ragged moan.

"What, baby?" He transferred his kisses to her exposed throat. "I'm going to work your body in every way and give you everything you want," he said in an intense rush. His words heated her even more.

"Don't stop."

"I won't stop until you ask me to, until you tell me you've had enough."

He kissed his way back to her mouth and moved in and out, mimicking the movements of his lower body. Pressure built and flared out to every part of her body and she erupted again with a force that snatched her breath. She screamed out his name.

Cedric drove into her faster and moments later, he went rigid, threw his head back and exploded. He let out a low groan. "Damn, girl." He rested his head against hers, their breathing ragged. "Soon as I catch my breath, round two. This time in a bed."

Randi chuckled softly even as her body tingled in anticipation. He gripped her tighter around the waist, holding her in place. As her breathing slowed, she felt him growing hard inside her again. Her head popped up.

"I'm going to stay inside you until you're completely satisfied."

No problems there. He'd already satisfied her, but her body was ready for more.

Cedric woke to Randi's hot tongue skating across his chest. He sucked in a sharp breath.

"Wake up, sleepyhead. Time for round three."

He hardened immediately. "We're going to have to be a little creative, since I only had two condoms."

Randi held up a condom. A slow grin spread across her lips. "Then it's a good thing I have one, huh?"

"A very good thing." He gritted his teeth as she rolled it over his engorged length, teasing and tormenting him. He muttered a curse.

"Problems?"

"Yeah, just one."

Her brow lifted. "And that would be?"

"I'm not inside you."

She smiled. "I think I can help you with that." She lifted one long, toned leg, straddled his body and lowered herself inch by inch onto his erection, swirling her hips in a figure eight.

Cedric groaned.

"I think I want to take a little ride."

"I'm game," he said with a grin. She braced her hands on his chest and slowly moved up and down. His hands made a path up her smooth honey-colored skin and settled on her breasts. The soft light from the nightstand lamp afforded him the opportunity to see the play of passion on her face. He massaged the full mounds, then leaned up to capture a pebbled nipple between his teeth and tugged gently, drawing a sharp cry from her.

"Cedric!"

The sound of her husky voice calling his name and the subtle color change in her eyes sent his desire into overdrive. He grabbed her hips and guided her to move faster. Her hands dug into his shoulders and each time she came down, Cedric thrust up to meet and match her strokes, going deeper each time. Her inner muscles clenched him tight and he could feel himself teetering on the brink of his control, but he wasn't ready for it to end. His body trembled slightly and he closed his eyes as the sensations intensified. "I can't get enough of you." He pulled her into a passionate kiss.

Abruptly, she broke off the kiss and let out another scream as she climaxed all around him.

He tightened his hold on her hips and growled hoarsely as an explosive orgasm ripped through him. She collapsed on top of him and he wrapped his arms around her. Breathing harshly, he kissed the top of her hair. He'd known from the moment they met it would be like this between them. Now he had to convince her.

At length, Randi slid off his body and lay on her back.

Cedric rolled his head in her direction and studied her pensive expression. "Regrets?"

She didn't answer immediately. Finally, she said, "As much as I should have them, no, I don't."

He leaned up on his elbow. "I hear a *but*."

She blew out a long breath. "We can't do this again, Cedric."

"Why not?"

She met his eyes. "You do remember I'm investigating the arson at your site."

"And you do remember that I promised not to ask you any questions about the case." He stroked a finger down her cheek. "Baby, I won't do anything to jeopardize the case or your job. I just want to spend time with you and explore whatever we've got going on."

"I don't know. I'm not really looking for some kind of permanent relationship."

"Neither am I." He gathered her in his embrace. "And you said yourself there aren't any rules against us seeing each other."

"But I can imagine the looks I'd get from my colleagues if they see us together."

"So, if I act like there's nothing going on between us in public until the case is over, would that make it easier on you?"

Randi sat up and observed him. "You'd do that?"

"Of course. If it means I can have you to myself in private, I'll ignore you all day."

She burst out laughing and flopped back down on the pillow.

Cedric chuckled. "What? You said you didn't want your coworkers eyeing you. I'm just trying to help a sistah out."

"More like trying to help yourself out," she mumbled, still laughing softly.

"That, too." He nuzzled her neck and idly stroked her thigh. "So, what do you say?"

"I can't think while you're doing that."

"So that would be a *yes*?"

She lifted her head and kissed him. "That would be a *yes*, Mr. Hunter." She laid her head on his chest and draped an arm over his midsection.

They lay quietly for a while. He wanted nothing more than to make love to her again, but he had to be in San Francisco early in the morning. And he never stayed the night at a woman's home or she at his. He didn't want to give the impression that the relationship was anything more than physical. He and Randi were on the same page and that suited him just fine. "I need to get going. I've got an early morning in Frisco."

"What time do you need to be on the road?"

"Six."

Randi looked over at the nightstand clock, then back at Cedric. "You're going to be exhausted. It's after midnight and you have to drive home. I hope you don't live far."

"I live in Rocklin."

Her head came up sharply. "That's not close. We were already on your side of town for dinner and you followed me all the way over here. You could've been home by now."

Cedric pulled her on top of him. "True, but if I hadn't followed you home, I would've missed out on this incredible night with you."

"Mmm-hmm, I bet you say that to all the women."

"I don't have *all* the women. I'm very selective." Even more so in the last year. In his younger days, he might have had a different woman every other month. Now his liaisons lasted a bit longer and were fewer and further in between, but he still had no desire for anything permanent. He chalked it up to getting older and minimizing the drama in his life. "And I don't ever cheat."

"I'm glad you cleared that up because I don't share, even if it's for a short time."

"Then we're in agreement." He slanted his mouth over hers in a hungry kiss. He'd meant it to be only a short one, but the erotic way her tongue tangled with his had him contemplating one more round. It took all his control to end the kiss. "I've got to go."

"I know," she said with a sigh. "I have an early meeting, too."

"Where's your bathroom?"

She pointed to the other side of the room. "Right through there."

Cedric went to do a quick cleanup. He'd shower once he got home. When he came out of the bathroom, Randi was leaning against the bedroom door wearing a robe. She followed him out to the front and watched him dress. "I'll call you tomorrow."

"The number on the card is to my office. Let me give you my cell."

He dug his phone out of his pocket and input the number she recited. He hit the call button and let it ring a couple of times. "Now you don't have to worry about getting my number." He gave her a quick kiss, being careful not to touch her, then stepped out into the brisk night.

"Drive safely."

"I will. Good night."

"Night." She gave him a little wave and closed the door as he loped down the walk.

It took Cedric half an hour to get home and he headed

straight for his bedroom. As he emptied his pockets, he noticed the light flashing on his cell. He read the text from Lorenzo, sent a quick reply and went to shower. Afterward, instead of going to bed like he should have, he found himself standing outside on the balcony off his bedroom. The brisk air blew across his bare chest as he stared up at the clear black sky. The temperature had dropped, taking the night into the forties. He stood there, ignoring the chill and thinking about Randi. Though he hadn't been surprised they'd ended up in bed, he just didn't think it would be so soon. Tonight, he'd told her he'd go along with the pretense of nothing going on between them in public, something he'd never done with a woman, and he didn't understand it. He'd never gone through these kinds of lengths to be with someone. Why her? And why now? *Looks like I might be getting that $200 sooner than I thought.* Lorenzo's words rang in Cedric's ears and he promptly dismissed them. It wasn't the first time he'd been attracted to a beautiful woman and it certainly wouldn't be the last. Neither of them was looking for anything long-term, so he'd enjoy the ride until it ended. And like always, it would end.

Chapter 5

Randi sat in the back of the conference room Tuesday morning drinking her second cup of coffee. It had taken a good two hours for her body to come down off the high she'd been on with Cedric. Even now, the remnants of last night's encounter played havoc with her mind. On some level, she had known sex with him would be incredible and parts of her were eager for a repeat. She'd told herself one and done, but it had taken only a kiss and a suggestion to make her fold and agree to continue seeing him. Pushing the seductive memories aside, she refocused her attention on Detective Warner's voice. A few of the test results had come back and confirmed what they already knew: the cause of the fire was arson.

"We're still waiting on the results from the paint used to write the message found at the Hunter Construction site. For now, I want that information to stay in this room. The less the arsonist knows, the better chance we'll have of catching this guy or guys. My guess is that whoever set the fire wrote that message for their own personal satisfaction and never intended for it to survive. Randi, you met with Cedric and Lorenzo Hunter yesterday, right?"

The mention of Cedric's name sent her mind back to the two of them naked against her door. "Ah, yes. Neither of them could think of anyone who would have set the fire, no disgruntled employees. I have a list of all the employees who've worked on the site. We found fingerprints in the unburned areas and I'm sure most of them will belong to the crew."

"If we're lucky, maybe one will belong to the arsonist. Let's talk after we're done here."

Randi nodded. Once the meeting ended, she went over her notes while waiting for Brian to finish a call he'd received from the police chief.

Brian headed her way. "Sorry about that. The chief wanted an update."

She stood. "I wish we had more to tell him."

"I really hope we can catch a break with that partial message."

"That still doesn't help us find the arsonist from the first fire. Have you found something connecting the two?" She hadn't been the lead on that case but had a message in to get a copy of the report.

"Not yet."

She handed him a sheet of paper. "Here's the list of employees."

He scanned it. "With this many, it might be easier to go out to the site to get the prints, rather than try to find a way to get them all in here."

"Maybe. The Hunters weren't too keen on having their employees dragged into a police station."

"Have you released the scene yet?"

"No. I wanted to wait until I got all of the lab results back, just in case they need additional samples. I should have everything back by tomorrow at the latest."

"Okay. I'll call Cedric and see if I can go to their office to do the fingerprints. Will you be available to go?"

"I should be able to. Let me know the time."

"I'll call right now." He removed a business card from a folder and made the call.

Randi almost blurted that Cedric wasn't in the office but clamped her jaws shut. She wondered how much sleep he'd gotten and whether his energy levels were as low as hers at this moment.

Brian moved the phone away from his mouth and whispered to Randi, "They're both out of the office, but the assistant is calling Cedric." A few minutes later, he hung up. "They can have everyone at the office tomorrow at one. Will that work with your schedule?"

She checked her calendar, saw the time slot was empty and added it. "Yes." The thought of seeing Cedric so soon after their night filled her with mixed emotions. Instead of the terse, impatient man she'd thought him to be, he had turned out to be charming, fun and incredible in bed—an impossible combination for any woman to resist. Randi would be the first to admit that the lines between physical and emotional could easily become blurred, and though she'd agreed they could continue to date, parts of her wondered if she was setting herself up for another heartbreak.

The next afternoon, Randi and Detective Warner arrived at the Hunter Construction office building as scheduled. As they neared the entrance, she said, "You know I really don't need to be here for the fingerprinting."

Brian held the door open for her. "Hey, we're partners and you need to be in the loop."

The small two-story building sat on the corner of an industrial complex. Inside, the receptionist directed them to Cedric's assistant down the hall.

The woman smiled at their approach. "Good afternoon, Ms. Nichols."

"Hello, Ms. Franklin. This is Detective Warner."

They exchanged greetings.

Ms. Franklin stood. "Cedric asked that I show you into the conference room. It's on the second floor." She led them to the elevator and up to the meeting area. "I'll let Cedric and Lorenzo know you're here."

"Thank you," Detective Warner said.

Randi watched as Brian set up his equipment. Her phone buzzed and she dug it out of her pocket. Jada had sent a text with the news she was waiting for. "The other lab results are in," Randi told Brian. She'd go over them when she got back to the office.

"Good. Let me know if there's anything about that paint."

"It would be nice to catch a break." She started to put the phone back and it buzzed again. She read the message from her sister: Just finished the makeup on a fine brother. Made me think of those construction workers. Married? Single? Looking for a bae for a night? Update?

Randi shook her head at her sister's antics, but couldn't suppress a smile. She typed back: You are a crazy nut! The one with the locs is married. The other is single. Don't know about the other question. Not the

entire truth, but she didn't plan to kiss and tell…at least
not yet.

"Sorry to keep you waiting."

Randi turned at the sound of Cedric's voice. His dark
gaze made a lazy path down her body and back up. A
soft pulsing began between her thighs. The slow grin
that curved his lips made her speculate on whether he
knew the effect he was having. Shaking off the vibe, she
extended her hand. "Mr. Hunter, thanks for your time."

Cedric clasped her hand, giving it a gentle squeeze,
then circling his thumb in her palm before letting go.
"No problem." He turned to Brian. "Detective Warner."

The two men shook hands. "Mr. Hunter."

"How do you want to handle things? Just about everyone is here and I can send them up whenever you're
ready."

"That's fine. I apologize for the inconvenience."

"No problem. I just want you to catch whoever did
this." He turned to Randi. "Has anything come back on
the testing that will help identify the arsonist?"

"I don't know yet. I'll be going over the results when
I get back to the office and will let you know if anything stands out. I'm hoping we can release the site by
the end of the week."

His eyes never left hers. "Great. My client is anxious
for us to get back to work."

Randi had asked him to be professional when they met
again and he was doing a good job. Outside of that little
stunt with the handshake and the banked heat reflected in
his eyes, one would think they hadn't spent several hours
indulging in the most passionate night she'd ever had.

Voices made her look away. Several men and two
women streamed into the room, followed by Lorenzo.

She stood off to the side while the detective gave instructions.

Brian handed her the employee list. "Randi, would you mind checking each person off the list as they're fingerprintcd?"

"Sure."

Cedric walked over. "I'll go first." He leaned close. "Having a little problem with that agreement?" he asked as he passed.

She didn't answer.

He made sure to cross her path after finishing and said for her ears only, "You're not the only one because all I want to do is strip you naked and make you scream my name again."

Randi's gaze flew to his and her pulse skipped. She tried to keep her voice neutral. "You're all done, Mr. Hunter." She called the next person on the list and hoped Cedric would leave the room. She'd never played these kinds of sensual games and it was all she could do to pretend to be unmoved by the subtle touches and the heat of his body near hers. A few minutes later, he came back to where she stood and she braced herself. Cedric leaned over her shoulder pretending to look at the list.

"Are you guys close to being done?"

"There are still seven more to go." She took a step to create some distance between them and he moved right with her.

"Come by my office and I can help us both," he whispered. He raised his voice. "Sounds good. If you have a moment, can you stop by my office before you leave?"

"I rode with Detective Warner, so—"

"We're almost done here, Randi. I can finish up," Brian said. "I'll wait for you."

"Oh, okay." She glanced over at Cedric's amused expression. If she said no, undoubtedly there would be questions. She did a quick survey of the room to see if anyone else was paying attention. The employees stood around talking and laughing. Lorenzo seemed to be the only person looking their way. The smile on his face told her he knew exactly what was going on.

"It won't take long," Cedric said.

Randi handed the list back to Brian. "Be right back."

Cedric gestured to the door. "After you."

She waited until they were in the elevator before speaking. "What are you doing? You're supposed to be acting professional."

"Oh, I was being very professional. If I wasn't, I would have kissed you the minute I stepped into the room." Cedric closed the distance between them and murmured against her lips, "Like I'm going to kiss you as soon as I get you in my office."

Luckily, the elevator chimed and stopped her from doing something crazy like grabbing *him* and planting her lips on his, not caring about who saw. She followed him to his office and before the door closed good, the kisses started. Randi couldn't tell who was more eager. Her hands roamed over his chest and up to frame his face, holding him in place as she devoured his mouth. She lost herself more and more with each stroke of his tongue. He pulled her closer and she reached between them to cup the solid ridge of his erection.

Cedric broke off the kiss sharply and jumped back. "Don't do that."

A sly smile tilted the corner of her mouth. "No? Why not?"

"Because."

Randi pressed her body against his and he groaned. "You'll need a better answer than that, Mr. Hunter." She leaned up and kissed him again. "You started this, remember?"

"I do, and I plan to finish it...later."

"Promises, promises."

He held her around her waist and chuckled. "Didn't expect you to be this playful."

She shrugged. "There are a lot of things you won't expect when it comes to me."

He lifted a brow. "Is that a challenge?"

She backed out of his arms. "Time will tell. I have to go."

"I'll call you later."

"Okay." She stood there a moment longer, warring with herself and wanting nothing more than to continue.

Cedric folded his arms. "You should probably go before I break my promise to remain professional. Otherwise, everybody in this building is going to know what's going on between us."

Randi read the heated warning in his eyes and walked out of the office while she still could. She nodded to his assistant on her way to the elevator. Once there, she hit the up button, leaned against the wall and released a deep sigh. This was moving too fast. *Way* too fast.

Cedric didn't get the all clear for the construction site until late Friday afternoon and he spent Saturday and part of Sunday checking out the damage and trying to get an estimate of how much material he needed to order. Monday morning, his crew was on-site at six to get started with the cleanup. He made sure the foreman and more experienced construction engineers su-

pervised the careful removal of debris. Because of the
many projects the company had going, Cedric couldn't
pull anyone from the other sites, so they'd hired seven
temporary workers to assist with the cleanup, another
expense they hadn't planned for.

He continued his walk around the building, stopping
to make notes on his iPad. He heard a car, looked over
and saw Lorenzo drive up. "Hey," he said at his cousin's
approach. "What time did you get in last night?"

Lorenzo surveyed the damage with a grim stare. "Hey.
Almost two in the morning. They couldn't fix the issues
with the door, so they put us on another plane, which
didn't leave for another three hours."

"How did things go in Chicago?" Lorenzo had left
right after the fingerprinting to accompany Desiree to
visit her mother. Her mother's Alzheimer's disease had
progressed to a level where she could no longer live alone
safely and they had begun evaluating different housing
options.

He shook his head. "Man, her sisters are still at it. Between Patrice complaining about the cost and Melanie
complaining about one thing or another at *every* facility we went to, I wanted to pack up my mother-in-law
and bring her back here. The one good thing is that Desiree's brother stepped in and told them they could stay
home or shut up."

Cedric laughed. "At least she had one person on her
side for a change."

"Tell me about it."

"I know this has to be hard on her. How is she handling it?"

Lorenzo sighed. "She puts up a good front, but I know
she's worried, especially since we can't be there all the

time. She broke down once and it felt like my heart was being ripped from my chest because I couldn't do anything to help."

"You love her, Zo, and that's what she needs."

"Since when did you start doling out relationship advice, Mr. I'm-Staying-Single-Forever?"

"Just because I'm not married doesn't mean I don't know what it takes to be in a relationship." He went back to his iPad. He knew from observing his parents, aunts and uncles, and grandparents over the years the importance of communication, compromise and just being there.

"Speaking of relationships, what's going on between you and the arson investigator?"

He feigned innocence. "I don't know what you mean."

Lorenzo stared at him in disbelief. "So you're going to act like you don't know what I'm talking about? I watched the two of you in that conference room. I thought you were going to kiss the woman right in front of the whole crew."

Cedric focused on his task and ignored Lorenzo. He *had* been a heartbeat away from doing just that and more. He'd wanted to run his hands over every inch of her golden skin. "Do you plan to stand here all day or work?"

"That bad, huh? Well if it's any consolation, she wants you as much as you want her." Cedric still didn't say anything. Lorenzo studied him a long moment. "You never said how your dinner went."

"It went fine," Cedric said and squatted down to inspect an area.

"Must've been better than fine since you didn't reply to my text until two in the morning. Sounds like you got caught up in the moment," he added with a chuckle.

Cedric whipped his head around and stared at Lorenzo's retreating back. He knew his cousin had added that last bit to remind Cedric that he had said the same thing when Lorenzo and Desiree missed dinner reservations early in their relationship for the same reason. Damn.

He finished his inspection, locked the iPad in his car, then donned a pair of gloves and jumped in to help with the cleanup.

Everyone stopped for lunch midday and Cedric found himself scanning the faces of each worker, wondering if one of them had set the fire. He dismissed the notion. As he'd said before, Hunter Construction was a family-oriented company. He trusted these people.

His thoughts went back to Randi. They had talked briefly twice since that incident in his office, but due to their work schedules, they hadn't been able to find time to see each other. The memory of her long legs wrapped around his waist surfaced in his mind and Cedric felt himself getting aroused. She'd matched his drive and energy, and he had to admit it was one of the best nights of sex he'd had in a long time. He placed his sandwich on the wrapper and wiped his hands on a napkin. Impulsively, he pulled out his phone and dialed her office. He wanted to hear her voice.

"This is Randi."

"Hey, Randi. It's Cedric."

There was a brief pause on the line. "Um, hey. What are you doing calling me at the office?" she whispered.

Cedric chuckled. "Relax, baby. This is official business."

"Oh."

"I was calling about the fire report. The insurance company wanted an estimated time frame."

"I should have it done in a couple of days. There were a few results I needed clarification on. As soon as I get that information, I can finish it. I'm surprised they didn't come out to do their own inspection."

"They're sending someone out tomorrow."

"Well, you shouldn't have any problems with regards to it being labeled arson. Both the police report and mine will corroborate that."

"Thanks. I appreciate that."

"How's the cleanup going?"

Cedric scanned the building. "It's going to take two weeks minimum to get everything cleaned up and hauled away. The damage ended up being more extensive because of the water, so it'll put us behind by at least a month."

"I'm really sorry, Cedric."

"I know. There is one good thing that's come out of this, though."

"What's that?"

"Meeting you. Oh, wait, I'm not supposed to be mentioning that, right?"

"Right," Randi said with a laugh. "Professional."

"Then I should probably get off this line."

"Yes, you should. I'll let you know when I have the report ready."

"Thanks. Talk to you later."

"Bye, Cedric."

He waited five minutes, then dialed her cell.

"Cedric, I thought we agreed—"

"This isn't your office phone, it's your personal one."

"True, but… I thought you said you were going to talk to me later."

"It is later."

She burst out laughing. "I can't with you."

"Actually, you can…as many times as you want. You did it exceptionally well the other night, I might add."

"You know what I mean."

"Yeah, I do, but this is what I mean. The next time I see you, I'm going to take my time removing your clothes, then I'm going to kiss my way up your beautiful body. I'll start at your ankles and work my way up those gorgeous long legs, your thighs. Mmm, I might have to stay there for a while, especially once they're spread wide so I can—"

"Cedric!" she whispered sharply.

"What? I'm not on your work phone. You don't want me to kiss you or touch you?"

"I didn't say that. I need to call you back."

Cedric heard the beep indicating the call had ended and smiled. He picked up his sandwich and continued eating. A few minutes later, his cell rang. He saw Randi's name on the display and answered.

"Okay, Mr. Hunter, two can play this game," Randi said before he could open his mouth. "I'll let you kiss your way up my body only if I can do the same. There's a lot of territory to explore between those strong thighs of yours and I don't plan to miss one *centimeter*. And yes, I love the way you touch and kiss me and I'm going to show you how much the next time we're together. Now I have to go."

He bowed his head and tried to get a grip on the fire rushing through his veins at her words. "You can't just leave me hanging like this. I'm liable to show up at your house to collect."

"I'm leaving you the same way you're leaving me."

"And how's that?"

"I think you already know the answer to that question. Bye." And she was gone.

Cedric sat there wondering how he'd lost control of the conversation. She'd turned the seduction tables on him in a way that had his entire body primed and ready. He picked up the bottle of cold water next to him and gulped down the contents without stopping. It didn't help. Nothing would except more of her.

Chapter 6

Randi let the bathroom wall take her weight and closed her eyes. She didn't know what had possessed her to call Cedric and play his game. She glanced down at her hands. They were still shaking, and her heart still thumped as if she'd been running the 400 in track practice. Every molecule in her body wanted to drive out to that construction site and get him to do everything he'd said and more. She heard someone open the bathroom door and jerked away from the wall. She nodded a greeting to the woman who'd walked in and went over to the sink to wash her hands. Randi wet a paper towel and blotted the moisture from her forehead and neck. *Get it together, girl. You have work to do.* She took a quick glimpse into the mirror, discarded the paper towel and dried her hands on another one, before heading back to her desk.

She tried to focus her attention on her computer but

kept being distracted by the thoughts of that phone call and the sound of Cedric's voice in her head giving her a play-by-play of what she knew would be another amazing night. She needed to slow this relationship—or whatever they were doing—down. It would be too easy to get caught up, and she'd done that enough to last a lifetime. Besides, Cedric had been very clear about not looking for anything serious, and so had she. But keeping her emotions separate from everything else had never been easy, despite her best efforts. Randi figured this thing with Cedric would most likely burn out within a month or two, and she could handle that.

For the balance of the afternoon, she worked on compiling the data from the lab into her report. Once she finished, in addition to providing a copy to Cedric and the insurance company, she would need to disseminate the information to the various state and federal databases, as well. The information helped to identify fire trends and develop procedures.

At the end of the day, Randi had made good headway on the report but was no closer to finding the arsonist. She stretched to relieve the kinks in her neck and back, then picked up the phone to call Brian.

"Detective Warner."

"Brian, it's Randi. I've got some information on the paint."

"What did you find out?"

"It's a high-end oil-based composition. Each manufacturer has their own ingredient formula that contains different proportions of pigment and binders. Hopefully, the lab can narrow it down for us. I'll email you the information."

"Thanks. But anyone could've purchased the paint and we have no idea when."

"True." It would be like searching for a needle in a haystack, but it was all they had at the moment. "I'll let you know if I find anything else."

"And I'll do the same. Hang on a minute, Randi." She heard muffled voices, then Brian came back. "I've got another call. Talk to you soon."

She hung up, sent the information to him, then shut down her computer. Since she was leaving at a reasonable time, she decided to go to the gym. With traffic, it took her over half an hour to reach her destination.

Randi changed, locked up her bag and went out to the treadmill for a fifteen-minute run to warm up. Afterward, she did her weights and core exercises. By the time she finished, she was hot and sweaty, but working out felt good. Thankfully, she lived only five minutes away. Once home, she parked in her spot and trudged to her unit. Her stomach growled. She dropped her bag on a chair in the kitchen, placed her phone on the counter and went to the freezer to take out some shrimp for an avocado shrimp salad. Randi set it in a bowl of water to thaw while she took a shower.

She picked up the bag and started down the hallway to her bedroom. The sound of the doorbell stopped her. Randi groaned, set the bag down and walked back to the door. She glanced through the peephole and gasped softly. *What is Cedric doing here?* Great. Sighing, she opened the door.

Cedric eyed her from head to toe and a slow grin curved his lips. "Hello, beautiful."

Randi reached up and tried to smooth her hair back. She knew she looked a hot mess and, after the intense workout, smelled worse. "Hey." She backed up and let him in. "I hope you don't make a practice of just popping up unannounced."

His smile widened. "Actually, it wasn't unannounced."

Her brows knitted in confusion. Then it dawned on her…their conversation from earlier in the day. "You didn't say you were coming over. You said you were *liable* to show up."

He waved a hand. "Same thing. I see why you're in such good shape. Hard workout?"

"It's not the same thing, and yes, I did an intense workout. I was just about to shower."

"Don't let me stop you." He rubbed his hands together and wiggled his eyebrows. "I'll even wash your back for you."

A vision of his hands sliding down her wet back sent heat straight to her core. "Ah, I don't think that's a good idea," Randi said with a nervous laugh.

He closed the distance between them and wrapped an arm around her waist. Unlike her, he smelled freshly showered. "I don't think you want to get this close."

"I'm not afraid of a little sweat, are you?"

"Cedric, I really need to clean up." She squirmed and tried to back out of his arms.

"I know." He nibbled her bottom lip and placed lingering kisses along her jaw. "But you owe me at least a kiss first for all that talk earlier."

Her mouth dropped and she leaned back. "*Me?* I'm not the one who started it."

"No, but you did a hell of a job finishing it," he murmured, still teasing her with butterfly kisses on the corner of her mouth.

She still couldn't believe she'd said all those things

Spark of Desire

to him. He settled his mouth on hers and slid his tongue inside her parted lips. The kiss went from slow and gentle to hot and demanding in a nanosecond. She came up on tiptoe and met him stroke for stroke. Sensing things were about to get out of control, she eased out of Cedric's embrace, took his hand and led him to the living room. "Can I get you anything?"

Cedric's brow lifted.

"Not that."

He chuckled. "Nah, I'm good."

"Okay. I'll be out in a minute." Randi hurried down the hall to her bedroom. In the bathroom, she took a quick shower, instead of the leisurely bath she'd planned. Though she told herself it was too soon to sleep with Cedric again, she felt a little disappointed that he hadn't joined her. She put on a pair of comfortable sweats, a long-sleeved T-shirt and socks. As she walked out, she glanced in the mirror and saw her hair sticking up everywhere. She redid her ponytail and went back to the living room. Cedric was leaning forward, typing on his phone. "I'm back."

He typed a second longer, then stuck the phone in his pocket. "What are your plans for the night?"

"Nothing much. Just dinner and going over a couple things from work. I'm making a shrimp and avocado salad if you want to join me. Or is that not something guys eat?" she added with a grin.

He stood. "I eat salad sometimes, but I can't say it's ever been the whole meal."

She hooked her arm in his and guided him to the kitchen. "There's a first time for everything. Besides, there's enough stuff in it to make you full." She directed him to a stool at the small breakfast bar. "Have a seat." He scanned the area.

"I like your place. How many bedrooms do you have?" Instead of sitting, he leaned against the bar.

"Two." Randi started to tell him that he'd been there before, but remembered that the last time he came over, she hadn't given him a tour of anything except her bedroom. She liked the open layout of her place and how each room flowed into the next. She'd added splashes of blue to break up the standard eggshell-painted rooms and a variety of plants to liven up her living room.

"I like the flow of the rooms," he said, echoing her thoughts.

"I guess as a builder, you'd notice these kinds of things. What's your place like?"

Cedric came to her side of the bar. "It's a little bigger. How about I invite you over and you can see for yourself?"

She should have expected him to say something like that. She opened the bag of shrimp, placed them on some paper towels and patted them dry.

"Well?"

Randi glanced over at him, then back to the shrimp, which she dumped into a bowl. "Well what?"

"My place."

She went to the refrigerator for the salad mix, cilantro and two ears of corn she'd cooked on the grill over the weekend. "Still waiting on the invite."

He shook his head, stood behind her and wrapped his arms around her. "Will you come to my place? I promise to be on my best behavior."

That's what I'm afraid of. "Yes."

"Check your weekend schedule and let me know if you're available." He released her. "What can I do to help?"

She studied him. "You cook?"

He placed a hand over his heart as if offended. "Of course I cook. I've been living on my own for almost two decades. How else am I going to eat?"

Smiling, she shrugged. "Hey, for all I know, you could be doing takeout every night."

"That's just wrong." Cedric moved to the sink and washed his hands. "Just tell me what you want me to do."

"You can slice and dice the veggies and cut the corn off the cob," she said, pushing the vegetables toward him. Randi got a salad bowl from the cabinet and handed it to him.

"That's it? I thought you wanted me to do some cooking."

"Oh, I think I'll wait to see your *real* cooking skills when I come to your place." She paused. "Dinner comes with the visit, right?"

He sighed in mock exasperation. "Keep talking and all you'll get is some cheap fast food."

Randi laughed. They worked in silence for a few minutes. She seasoned and sautéed the shrimp.

"Do you always do such an intense workout?" Cedric asked as he arranged all the vegetables in the bowl atop the lettuce.

"Not always, but I want to apply for a position at the ATF and have to pass a fitness exam." She hadn't meant to blurt out that information. She waited for the usual response she had gotten from men when she shared her ambitions.

"The ATF?"

"Yes." When he didn't respond immediately, she turned from the stove.

"I think that's pretty cool."

She stared at him, searching for some hint that he

might be just saying it to placate her. She found only sincerity.

"Randi, I told you before I think it's great that you follow your dreams, regardless of whether society considers them appropriate for a woman. My cousin Morgan pursued a career in sports management and she's been pretty successful. Do what makes you happy."

"Thanks." She stirred the food.

"You know that's the second time you've almost bitten off my head when it comes to your job. Was your family against your choice or something?"

Randi turned off the burner and poured the shrimp onto a plate. "No, they were very supportive." She and Cedric hadn't known each other very long and she hesitated telling him the real reason. However, their relaxed camaraderie made it seem as if they'd been friends for much longer. "Just about every guy I've dated had a problem with my job. In their minds, it was too dangerous. I even had one tell me he didn't think I should work out so much because he didn't want to date a woman who could bench press more than he could."

Cedric threw his head back and laughed. "You're kidding me, right?"

"No."

Still chuckling, he kissed her temple. "Some men are idiots."

"Yeah, and that idiot found himself blocked and deleted one minute after that phone conversation." She added the shrimp to the salad bowl. She noticed that instead of just dumping everything into the bowl haphazardly, Cedric had grouped the avocado, corn, tomatoes and cucumbers separately as if he were presenting a meal on some cooking show. "Now I just need to make the dressing. It's a honey-lime vinaigrette."

"Sounds good." He stood off to the side and watched her add the ingredients to the blender. "No measurements?"

"Nope." It was her favorite dressing and she had memorized her own tweaked version of the recipe. She blended it for a few seconds, then removed the lid. She got a spoon from the drawer, scooped up a small amount and handed it to Cedric. "Taste."

He nodded. "This is good. I like the balance the honey gives it. I was expecting it to be really tart."

Randi figured since she had a guest she should serve the dressing in that fancy cruet her mother had given her. If she could find it. She searched in the cabinets, moving from one to the next.

"What are you looking for?"

"The salad dressing bottle my mother gave me."

"You don't need to mess up another container. Just pour it out of the blender." He carried the blender and salad bowl to the kitchen table, then came back for the plates she had placed on the counter.

That earned him a brownie point. She threw in another when he took the food to the table. "I have some iced mango tea, but I have to warn you, it's not too sweet."

"That's fine. I probably need to cut down on my sugar intake anyway."

Smiling, she poured two glasses and joined him at the table. He seated her, then took the chair opposite. "Well, time for the taste test," she said.

"You get yours first, baby."

The way the endearment flowed from his lips made her pulse skip. And with his gentlemanly ways, she could see a stack of brownie points coming by the end of the night. Throw in the way he made love and she might as well hand over the whole pan. How was she going to keep from falling for this man?

Cedric forked up a portion of the salad. After chewing and swallowing, he said, "Okay, I might be able to handle this as a meal."

She smiled. "You can always add additional shrimp or even chicken to make it more filling."

He sipped the tea. "Now this tea, on the other hand.. I think you need to get your definition of *not too sweet* straight. This qualifies as not sweet at all. I need a little sugar in here." He frowned and she laughed. "I'm serious. Where's the sugar?" He'd tasted sour foods with more sugar than this tea. Where was the sweetness from the mango?

Randi shook her head and rose from the table. She brought back the sugar canister and a spoon. "That tells me you really do need to cut back on your sugar intake. I'm sure you know that maintaining all those nice muscles you have is going to take more than just hitting the weights. Eating right is important, too."

He groaned. "Please don't tell me you're one of those health nuts."

"How can you say that when you saw me eat almost all of that jambalaya the other night? And my sister and I stuffed ourselves on my favorite, Mexican food, the day before. I'm not a health nut, but I do try to eat relatively clean about seventy-five percent of the time. I fall off the wagon every now and again."

"I try to do the same, but it isn't always easy when I get stuck in the office or out at a site." Lately, his eating habits had been less than stellar, but if he could have

this salad or something similar once or twice a week—
he would definitely need to add more meat—it would
get him back on track. He lifted a forkful of food. "So
thanks for helping a brother out."

She toasted him with her own fork. "I do what I can."
They continued to eat. "Earlier you said you'd been living on your own for almost twenty years. Exactly how
old are you?"

Cedric added a couple of teaspoons of sugar to his tea
and stirred. "Thirty-six. My mother would say closer to
thirty-seven," he added with a wry chuckle. "How old
are you?"

"Thirty-two." Randi angled her head. "I would've put
you closer to my age, rather than closer to forty."

He lifted a brow. "Are you calling me old?"

"No," she said with a little laugh. "An old man
wouldn't have been able to do all the things we did last
week." She tossed him a wink and went back to her food.

"You've got that right." He didn't need any reminders
of that night or the phone call today. His body had been in
a state of arousal since she opened her door to him. If he
were being honest, he'd admit that she had sparked something inside him that he couldn't seem to shake. Nothing
else would explain why he'd left his house and driven
across town to see her. They finished the meal in silence.

"Did the sugar help your tea?" she asked as she stood
and took her plate and glass to the sink.

He picked up the glass and downed the remaining
liquid. "Yep." He scooted the chair back and pulled her
down onto his lap when she passed him on the way back.
"But it didn't help this craving I have for your kisses."
Not giving her a chance to answer, he slanted his mouth
over hers in a deep, scorching kiss. As always, she gave

as much as she took and in the blink of an eye, she shifted until she sat straddling his lap and whipped off his shirt. His head fell back as the warmth of her tongue skated across his chest.

"I told you I was going to show you how much I like the way you touch me."

Groaning, he sat up and removed her shirt. She didn't have on a bra and he wasted no time taking a hardened nipple into his mouth. Somewhere in the back of his mind, Cedric thought he heard a phone buzzing, but he ignored it. The sound came back again.

Randi let out a sigh of frustration. "I should probably see who that is. I'm on call." She slid off his lap, crossed the floor and picked up her phone. "This is Randi."

Still breathing harshly, he scrubbed a hand down his face. He stared at her standing there with her beautiful breasts bared and her lips thoroughly kissed and hoped whoever it was on the line would make it quick.

"Text me the address," he heard her say. A minute later she hung up. She came back to where he sat and gave him a look of regret. "I have to go."

"Another fire?"

She nodded.

He wanted to ask about it but remembered his promise. He got to his feet.

"Rain check?"

Cedric smiled. "You'd better believe it, and preferably on a night when you're not on call."

Randi stroked a hand over his hardened length. "Problems?"

"*Big* problems."

Her mouth gaped and she swatted him on the arm. "I

can't believe you." She grabbed her shirt off the floor and pulled it on.

"What?" he asked, reaching for his shirt and putting it on. "You asked and I answered."

"Don't act all innocent, Cedric Hunter." She rolled her eyes.

"I have no idea what you're talking about." He picked up his plate and glass and took them to the sink.

She quickly covered the bowl of salad with some plastic wrap, poured the remaining dressing into a container and placed them in the refrigerator.

"I'll hang out in the living room while you change and walk you out."

"Okay."

While waiting, he tried to will his body back to calm, but he had a hard time because he kept hearing her bold words in his head. He drew in several deep breaths and let them out slowly. It still didn't help.

"I'm ready."

Cedric spun around at the sound of Randi's voice. Once again, she had on jeans and her boots. "Is it far?" he asked as she locked the door behind them. They walked the short distance to her car.

"Not too far."

He brushed a kiss over her mouth. "Be careful."

"I will." She got in the car, started it and backed out.

He walked over to his own car parked a short distance away. *It's going to be a long night.*

Chapter 7

Tuesday evening, Randi dragged herself home and straight to the bathroom. She had gotten less than four hours of sleep the previous night and had spent all day at another burned construction site collecting evidence. That made three within the last month—all arson—and they still didn't have any leads. A few of the officers speculated on whether some joyriding teens were cruising around torching sites for the fun of it, but her gut told her it had to be something else, particularly since they all followed the same pattern. To make matters worse, it had started raining late in the afternoon and she looked like a drowned rat. Tonight, she planned to take a long bath, if she could stay awake long enough. She also had to do her hair. More and more she was beginning to think going natural, as her sister had suggested, might have some merit. But for now, she was in for a night of washing, blow-drying and flat-ironing. She stepped into the shower to rinse away the grime and wash her hair, then ran a tub of hot water to relax in.

Randi sank into the warm water scented with her stress-relief blend of bubble bath and sighed pleasurably. She leaned back against the towel she'd rolled up and closed her eyes. The heat seeped through her chilled bones and she felt the tension release. She didn't realize she was drifting off until the sound of her phone ringing startled her awake. Randi jerked upright, dried her hands on a towel and retrieved the cell from the edge of the sink where she had placed it. She noticed a missed message from Cedric; she would look at it when she finished her call.

"Hey, sis," she said.

"Hey, Randi. I was just checking on you. I saw there was another fire last night and I know you're on the case."

Randi frowned. "How did you know?"

"It was on the local news and I caught a glimpse of you at the site."

"Oh." She had been so focused on her task that she hadn't even noticed the news crews.

"I know you're tired, and if you haven't eaten, I'll bring over some chicken tortilla soup."

"That sounds so good. Thanks, sis. I'm in the bath right now, then I have to do my hair."

"I figured as much. I'll see you in about half an hour."

"Okay." She ended the call and placed the phone back in its spot. She washed up quickly, dressed and dried her hair. She'd wait until later to flatiron it.

Randi finished just as her doorbell rang, and she went to let her sister in. The two women embraced.

Iyana entered and handed Randi a bag. "I'm glad it

stopped raining. Hopefully, it'll hold until I get back home."

Randi lifted the bag and sniffed. "This smells so good. You really need to share some of these recipes." She started toward the kitchen with Iyana following. Once there, she got a bowl, filled it with some of the soup and stuck it in the microwave for a minute.

Iyana shrugged out of her jacket, hung it on the back of a chair and sat. "I know you can't say much about the case, but do you think these fires are connected?"

"I don't know right now. The only thing I can tell you is that they were all arson." The one last night bugged her because on her way to the scene, she had passed two other construction sites within two miles of the torched one. Why hadn't those been set on fire, as well? Surely, if she'd passed them, the arsonist would have, too. That alone made her question the randomness. No, those companies had been targeted for some reason. Cedric had been targeted. But why? Randi removed the bowl from the microwave, added cheese and tortilla strips and came to the table.

"I don't understand people," Iyana said. "Why would somebody do something so asinine? Someone could be killed, not to mention all the money and time it's costing. Speaking of money, have you talked to Mr. Hottie recently?"

She'd gone way past just talking to him. Twenty-four hours ago, she had been straddling him, half-naked, right here at this table. "Yesterday." She ate a spoonful of soup.

"Well?"

Randi glanced up. "Well what?"

Her sister sighed impatiently. "You said he's not married, unlike that fine brother of his?"

"No, he's not. And he and Lorenzo are cousins, not brothers."

"Sounds like you two talked about more than just the fire. I think he has potential. You should let him know you're available, too."

She and her sister had always been each other's confidantes. "He already knows," she said, not looking up from the bowl. Iyana sat silently for a full minute and Randi could feel her penetrating stare.

"Go ahead and spill it."

She set the soup aside and sighed. "I went to follow up with them last week. A detective was supposed to meet me there but got called away at the last minute. After I finished asking my questions, Lorenzo left to take a phone call from his wife."

Iyana smiled. "Leaving you and Cedric alone."

Randi nodded. "We wrapped up the meeting and I was getting ready to leave, and he asked me out to dinner."

Iyana rubbed her hands together. "That's what I'm talking about! Obviously, you didn't turn him down."

"Obviously," Randi said, trying to hide her own smile. "Anyway, he was a complete gentleman—opened my car door, wouldn't let me pay." She paused. "He followed me home to make sure I was safe. His words."

"Aw, that's so cute. I didn't think men still did that. Apparently, I've been hanging around the wrong ones."

"You and me, both."

"Is he a good kisser?"

"Who said I kissed him?"

Iyana snorted. "Girl, please. Granted, the brother followed you home for safety reasons, but I guarantee you that wasn't the only thing on his mind. He was looking for a little sugar." She laughed.

Smiling, Randi shook her head. "You sound like Grandma." That had always been their grandmother's moniker for kissing. Iyana's expression said she was waiting for an answer. "Yes, he's a good kisser." Better than good.

"Ain't nothing like a man who knows how to make you wet from a kiss. And if you lie and say he didn't, I'm taking my soup back." She reached for the bowl.

Randi chuckled and quickly moved the bowl away. "Why are you being so nosy? I told you he kissed me. It was no big deal." She lowered her head and pretended to focus on the soup, hoping her sister couldn't tell it wasn't the whole truth. She could.

"Because you're holding out on me. You're being awfully defensive and you are lying. *Lying.* Wait." Her eyes widened. "Did you two *sleep* together?" When Randi didn't answer, Iyana brought her hands to her mouth and squealed. "You did. Big sister is getting her groove back." A sly grin curved her mouth and she leaned forward. "Did he make your toes curl?"

"Hell, that and everything else," Randi confessed. They both screamed like teenagers and fell out laughing. When they finally calmed themselves, Randi said, "I agreed to a short affair with him, with the understanding that we wouldn't talk about the case. I'm not sure it was a good idea, though."

"You just said he was all that and a gentleman. I don't see the problem...unless you're afraid physical is going to turn emotional."

"Bingo. You know how hard it is for me to keep those emotions separate after a while. I'm also concerned that I might be transgressing some work rule." As she'd told Cedric, she had never come across a policy forbidding it, but she always played by the book and this made her feel somewhat antsy. "I'm sure it'll burn out before it goes that far, so it should be fine. He's not looking for anything serious, either." Randi figured if she reminded herself often enough to keep it light, it would save her some heartache down the line.

"Friends with benefits."

"Something like that." The conversation tapered off and she finished her soup. "Do you have a long day tomorrow?"

Iyana checked her watch. "Yep. I have to be on set at five in the morning. It'll take me a couple of hours to make my client look twenty years older. The team has already done some of the facial prosthetics, so I'm hoping things will go smoothly. Then, next Monday, we'll be going down to LA to shoot some scenes. I should be back by Wednesday."

"Let's do dinner Thursday or Friday."

"Works for me. I haven't eaten steak in a while, so…"

"Yeah, okay. I can take a hint," Randi said with a laugh.

Iyana stood and put on her jacket. "It's a darn shame that I'm thirty-one and going to bed by ten. *Alone.*"

"You're not the only one. I have a meeting in the morning and then it's back out to the site. I hope it doesn't rain again." Randi didn't relish the thought of slogging in the mud to collect samples, and she wanted to preserve as much evidence as she could. She had been searching for another message left by the arsonist, but so far had come up empty. "Thanks again for the soup," she said as they walked to the door.

"You're welcome. I hope you catch a break in the case soon."

"Me, too."

Iyana opened the door and jumped back with a gasp.

"Girl, what is wrong with—?" Randi's eyes went wide. "Cedric. What are you doing here?" Seeing him reminded her that she had never checked the message he had left.

Cedric smiled. "Hello, to you, too." He slowly dropped the hand that had been poised to ring the bell.

"Um, hey," Randi said. Iyana elbowed her. "Oh, Cedric, this is my sister, Iyana. Iyana, Cedric Hunter."

"Cedric, it's *very* nice to meet you."

"Same here." He divided a glance between them. "Are you two leaving?"

"Oh, no," Iyana said, opening the door wider. "Come on in, Randi's in for the night. I was just leaving. You kids enjoy yourself." She walked out the door and mouthed behind Cedric's back, "He is fine, fine, fine!" Then pretended to swoon.

Randi bit her lip to keep from laughing. "See you later. Text me when you get home."

"I will. I'm sure I'll be seeing you again, Cedric." Iyana waved and sashayed off.

She shook her head at her sister. Instead of doing makeup, she should be on the stage. She closed the door and faced Cedric. "I wasn't expecting to see you tonight."

He stroked a finger down her cheek. "I had a late meeting in the area and I wanted to make sure you were okay. I know you had a long night and day with the fire."

The sweet gesture, coupled with his sincere concern had her heart racing. "I'm okay. Exhausted, but okay. But it goes with the territory, so..." She shrugged.

"I saw the news. Do you think it's connected?"

"I don't know."

"And if you did you wouldn't tell me."

Randi opened her mouth to reply and he cut her off with a searing kiss. He moved closer and she felt every inch of his hard body against hers, sending heat flowing all through her. She wanted nothing more than to take him to her bedroom for a repeat of their first night. However, that didn't line up with keeping things light.

Cedric eased back a fraction. "If you're off on Saturday, we can do dinner at my place." He touched his mouth to hers again. "Get some rest, baby."

She reached up and caressed his face. "I will. And I'll let you know about Saturday. Thanks for checking on me. You look tired, too." She could see the lines etched in his forehead and guessed the stress of having to clean up and restart the building project was already taking a toll on him.

"Long day and it'll be even longer tomorrow."

"Then I'm not the only one who needs to rest." She came up on tiptoes and pressed a soft kiss on his lips.

"Good night." He opened the door and paused with his hand on the doorknob. "Oh, and tell your sister thanks."

Her brows knitted in confusion. "For what?"

"She thinks I'm fine," he said, amused.

"Oh, my goodness. You heard that?"

Cedric winked. "Yep."

He laughed and strolled down the walk, leaving Randi with her mouth hanging open. She closed the door and shook her head. "This man." Not falling for Cedric would take a Herculean effort.

Cedric added more charred wood to the dumpster. They had been working twelve hours a day since Monday, and four days later it seemed as if they hadn't made any headway. He seriously considered coming out tomorrow, but he'd been trying to adhere to his father's advice about keeping balance and not working on the weekends. Besides, his cousin was coming up to check on the fitness center progress and planned to spend the night, so it would be useless to start in the afternoon.

"Man, I haven't worked this hard in over a year," Lorenzo said, tossing in another bundle.

"I hear you." Since taking over the company, they'd spent most of their time in the office, instead of working hands-on at a site. And if they came out to a site, it typically ended up being no more than a few hours, never an entire day or week. "Did you send the fire and police reports to the insurance company?"

"Yeah. I forwarded them right after you sent them to me. Hopefully, it won't take long to cut the check. The adjuster said two to three weeks. We're okay financially right now, but if we take on those two potential projects, it might stretch us a bit."

Cedric grabbed another load and threw it in. "When are we scheduled to meet with them again?"

"Not for a couple of weeks."

"Good. Hopefully, all this won't scare them off. That's the last thing we need." If developers believed their buildings might go up in flames, they'd start taking their business elsewhere, and that would spell disaster for Hunter Construction. Cedric's phone buzzed. He took off his gloves and pulled the cell out of his pocket. He read the message from his cousin and smiled. "That was Khalil. Their plane gets in at two." He checked his watch. That gave Cedric and Lorenzo three hours.

"Lexia and KJ are still coming with him?"

"Yep." He pocketed the phone and pulled his gloves

back on. "I told them they could stay at my place tonight, rather than going to a hotel. I figure we can do dinner around seven. Jeremy said he'd get there a little early to get the meat started on the grill." He'd also invited Lorenzo and Desiree, Lorenzo's sister, Alisha, and her husband and two children. They had always made a practice of getting together when one or more of the cousins visited.

"You should invite Randi," Lorenzo said as he gathered up another load for disposal.

Cedric glared. "I don't recall you bringing Desiree to a family gathering two weeks after you started dating her." He'd only ever brought one woman home—his senior prom date—and only because his mother insisted so she could take pictures.

"I don't recall you being sympathetic. In fact, you were the one who told my mother about her."

He laughed. "All I said was tell Desiree hello." Lorenzo had been eager to leave a family dinner so he and Desiree could go on a weekender.

Lorenzo paused with a stack of debris. "You know what they say about payback. Your time is coming and I'm going to have a front-row seat. I'm putting my money on Randi."

"If you want to waste your money, fine. Two or three months from now, Randi and I both will have moved on."

"Uh-huh. If that's what you believe. You forget I've known you your entire life. You have never reacted to a woman the way you did with her."

Cedric shrugged. "She's a beautiful woman." He blew off the comment, but Lorenzo was right. No other woman had *ever* rendered him speechless. And no other woman had invaded his dreams. He chalked it up to strong sexual attraction.

They worked for another two hours, then he and Lorenzo left to pick up Khalil and Lexia from the airport. Lorenzo drove his car, so he could drop Lexia and KJ off at Cedric's house. Afterward, he would meet them later at the house.

When they arrived, Khalil surveyed the two-story building. "You outdid yourself, cuz. This turned out better than I'd hoped."

"Thanks. You said you wanted it to be similar to your original one. I'll start installing the flooring next week." After Cedric and Lorenzo had visited Khalil's LA fitness center to get a sense of the layout and discuss what Khalil wanted, Khalil had given them free rein to come up with the design. "Let's go inside." Using the blueprint, Cedric pointed out where everything would go on both floors. Having two stories would allow ample space for Khalil to incorporate his accessible equipment for those with various disabilities.

"Are you still on schedule for it to be finished in June?"

"Yes. If everything goes as planned, we might be done the last week of May."

Khalil spun around. A wide grin covered his face. "Now that's what I'm talking about." They did a fist bump. "Maybe we can turn it into the next family reunion." He glanced around the room again. "Malcolm should've come up to see it." He took out his phone and snapped several pictures before they headed back to the car.

On the drive, Cedric asked, "Did he decide whether he's going to retire this year?" Malcolm played professional football as a running back and had mentioned hanging up his cleats. He planned to join Khalil in the fitness business.

"He hasn't made an announcement yet, but I think he's done. He said he's tired of seeing the twins' milestones by video. He missed their first steps and barely made it home for their first Christmas."

"Yeah, that would make me consider retiring."

"Speaking of families, when are you going to get started?"

"I'm just going to be the cool uncle."

Khalil folded his arms. "You're still singing that tune? I guarantee there's going to be a woman who'll make you change it."

A vision of Randi floated through Cedric's mind and he promptly dismissed it. "I keep telling y'all there isn't one woman who can make me change my *song*. I like being single."

"Said every one of us. And *all* of us are married. Hell, I yelled the loudest about staying single and you know my story. Trust me, you want the *one* who can give you everything you think you'd be missing. There's nothing like it."

"So you keep saying," Cedric muttered and turned up the music.

Khalil chuckled but didn't say anything else.

When they arrived at the house and entered, the almost two-year-old Khalil Jr. ran over to his father. *"Daddy!"*

Khalil scooped up the toddler. "Hey, little man."

"Hey, KJ," Cedric said.

"Hi, Unca Ced."

Cedric smiled. Technically, KJ was Cedric's first cousin, once removed. However, to make things less confusing, the cousins had all decided that the kids would call the adults uncle or aunt.

Pretty soon, the house was full of food, conversation and laughter. After dinner, they settled the kids in the family room with a movie and snacks, while the adults sat in the kitchen.

"Now that little ears are out of hearing, Ced, what's going on with those fires at construction sites?" Alisha asked. "Lorenzo said they think it's personal."

Khalil shifted on his stool to face Cedric. "You didn't say anything about that."

"They found a partially burned piece of wood with a few visible letters. It was just 'Ced' and two letters before it—*A-Y*."

"Someone wants you to pay for something," Lexia said.

Jabari, who had been standing between the family room and kitchen, came over to the table. "Do you need me to look into it?" The former military officer now co-owned a tech company and served as its chief security information officer. He had a background in cybersecurity.

"Nah, not right now. I'll wait to see what Randi turns up." Too late, Cedric realized he'd used her first name.

"Randy?" Alisha asked, reaching for a strawberry from the fruit tray in the center of the table. "Who's he?"

"*She*," Lorenzo corrected, "is the fire or arson investigator. And the woman who's going to make me two hundred dollars richer. I've never seen a woman make Ced speechless, but she did."

Jeremy burst out laughing. "Wait, what?" He whipped his head around. "Ced, you're dating the investigator? Zo, why didn't you tell me?"

"I just did." He smiled and lifted his beer bottle in a mock toast to Cedric. "Checkmate."

Cedric opened his mouth to tell Lorenzo just what he could do with his checkmate, but remembered the children. "It's nothing."

"Oh, it must be something if she had my big brother tongue-tied."

Cedric waved him off. "Jeremy, it's just physical attraction. Y'all act like it's never happened before, and I don't know why." He gestured around the room. "None of you would be married if you hadn't been attracted to your women."

Jabari draped an arm around Alisha's shoulder. "Bingo."

He met the amused gazes of everyone around the table and realized he had played right into their hands. He lifted his beer bottle and took a swig. "Again, it's nothing." At least that's what he kept telling himself.

Chapter 8

"I don't know why you drove all the way over here to pick me up, Cedric," Randi said as she followed him out to his car early Saturday evening. "It would've been easier to just give me your address and let me drive over. It doesn't make sense for you to make two round trips. That's just a waste of gas."

Cedric held the car door open. "Are you done?"

She didn't comment. They had argued about it earlier when he called and shared his plans. Well, she had argued. He'd flat out refused.

"It doesn't matter whether you live here or across the street from me, I'd still pick you up and bring you home. Those are the rules." He placed a kiss on her temple. "Now stop fussing and get in the car."

She dropped down in the seat and couldn't decide if she was mad or flattered. He closed the door and got in on the other side. "Whose rules?"

He started the car and pulled away before answering. "My family's. My father and uncles drilled into my head, and my brother's and cousins' heads, that there are certain rules where a woman is concerned. Always open doors, stand when she comes into the room and—" he slanted her a quick glance "—*always* pick her up and drop her off at her door."

She couldn't remember the last time she'd had a man do all of those things. She'd certainly never had a man stand when she entered a room…until now. All those times Cedric had stood, she'd attributed it to him stretching his legs or to the kiss that sometimes followed. It hadn't dawned on her that it had to do with his upbringing. It made her curious about all the other men in his family, particularly his father. But that's as far as it would go because she would most likely never meet them. "Impressive," she said.

"Not really. It's just the way we are."

"Okay. I guess I can't complain. It is kind of nice."

"You've never had a man do all those things?" Cedric asked with surprise.

"Maybe an opened door here and there, and they picked me up most of the time, but the whole standing thing, nah." Randi could see how a man might do those things if he was serious about a woman, but not one he was having a fling with.

He lifted her hand and brought it to his lips. "Now you know."

They fell silent and she watched the passing scenery.

"Are you on call tonight?" he asked.

"No, we're on a rotating schedule. But I will be starting Tuesday." She saw his smile in the fading light. "Why?"

"Just want to make sure we'll be able to enjoy the evening without interruption."

"Oh." The tone of his voice made her pulse race. She didn't even pretend to not know what he meant and she didn't want any interruptions this time, either. Her desire had been simmering below the surface ever since that interlude in her kitchen. Randi made herself comfortable in the seat, settling in for the ride. At length, she asked, "How long have you lived in your place? Is it a condo? House?"

"It's a house and I've lived there three years. When my cousins come up from LA, they can crash there, rather than a hotel, especially when they're only staying overnight."

Randi turned in her seat toward him. "Sounds like you all are pretty close."

"We are. We used to spend summers together—either there or here. Looking back, I don't know how my parents and aunts and uncles put up with all the noise."

She laughed. "How many of you are there?"

"Nine."

"At one time?"

"Yep," Cedric said with a chuckle. "Two boys in my family, two in Lorenzo's—he has a sister—and there are five LA cousins, two girls and three boys."

She sat back and shook her head. "My parents moved to the LA area five years ago when my dad's company transferred there, and they decided to downsize. The two-bedroom house barely holds eight of us during the holidays and it gets a little loud. I can't even imagine that level of noise. We always stayed a week with my grandparents in the summer and I thought it was rowdy with my sister, me and my three cousins, but *nine*. They probably would've put us out after a day."

"Oh, they did threaten to a few times, especially when we got into fights." They laughed. "But we always had a lot of fun."

They continued conversing and laughing until Cedric parked in the driveway of a stately two-story home. "This is nice," she said.

"Thanks." He got out and came around to her side.

Standing outside the car, Randi surveyed the neatly manicured lawn and house.

Cedric smiled. "Come on." He escorted her up the curved walkway to the double doors. He opened one side and gestured her in.

She stood in the entryway and stared. Gleaming wood floors, an elegantly curved staircase leading to the second level and high ceilings greeted her. Each room flowed into the other, and the open layout made the space seem even grander. She followed him past the living room and dining room to a large kitchen boasting stainless steel appliances, two islands with bar stools and an eat-in table for six. A comfortable-looking family room sat on the other side with a stone fireplace and black leather furniture. A large television had been mounted on the opposite wall.

"Well?"

"It's fabulous. I guess when you said you wanted something bigger, you meant it."

Cedric laughed softly.

"I can fit two of my condos in here." She'd thought her sixteen-hundred-square-foot, two-bedroom home was spacious, but she could run laps in his house.

"Have a seat. Can I get you something to drink? I have wine, tea, lemonade."

Randi sat on the sofa. "Wine, please."

"Red or white?"

"White." He went over to a wine cooler and retrieved a bottle. She scooted back and her hand hit a small object. She froze. *A pacifier?* It had never occurred to her that he might have a child. He had never mentioned one. She scanned the room and noticed a few board books and a small box of toys. She ran a hand over her forehead. Had he been married to the mother? Did he still have a relationship with her? More important, she asked herself, did she want to be involved with someone who had children? Granted, with his confession in the car about how his father had raised him, she couldn't imagine he'd be negligent in taking care of any children he might have fathered. But still. Cedric's voice broke into her thoughts.

"Here you go."

She accepted the glass and took a long drink. "Thank you."

"Is something wrong?" Cedric lowered himself next to her.

"I'm not sure." She held up the pacifier. "Why didn't you tell me you had children?"

He took the pacifier and placed it on an end table. "Because I don't. That belongs to KJ, my cousin Khalil's son. They came up yesterday so Khalil could see the progress on the fitness center we're building for him. The books and toys are here because Lorenzo's sister has two children and they spend some time here. I keep a few things so Alisha doesn't have to pack up so much when they visit."

"Oh."

"If I did have children, would that be a problem?"

She thought for a moment. A few of her divorced friends often cited the struggle of finding a man who was willing to date a woman with "baggage," as they called it. It would be unfair to do the same thing. "No. No, it wouldn't. You're building a fitness center?" she asked, changing the subject.

Cedric smiled knowingly and sipped his wine. "Yes. This is the third one. There are two in LA."

"Did you build those, too?"

"No, but we modeled ours after the original site. If you want, I'll show it to you when you have time."

"I'd like that." Even with the strip mall being half burned, Randi could tell he had great building skills.

He stood. "I'm going to start dinner."

She followed suit. "Do you need any help?"

"Nope. But you can keep me company."

"And make sure you're not trying to pass off some takeout as your own," she said with a sly grin.

"Whatever, woman." But he was smiling.

Randi made herself comfortable on a bar stool across from where he worked. "So, what are we having?"

"I decided to splurge a little. We're having crab-stuffed shrimp over white rice with a basil cream sauce, sautéed asparagus and some of my mother's homemade French bread."

"Mmm, sounds fabulous, especially the bread. That's probably one of my most favorite things to eat. A nice warm loaf with butter... But I've been trying to cut back."

"And hers is the best. She makes me a loaf and all I have to do is pop it in the oven. One of these days, I'm going to go over and have her teach me how to do it. But for now…" He held up the loaf. "This is it. Besides, since you're already questioning my cooking skills, I wouldn't want to ruin the meal." He set the temperatures on his double oven.

She rolled her eyes. "I never said you couldn't cook."

Cedric cut her a look. "Uh-huh." He went to the refrigerator and removed several items, then set them on the counter.

Randi sipped her wine and observed as he expertly added ingredients to a bowl of crab and mixed it gently. He seemed to be quite comfortable in the kitchen. The last guy who had "cooked" for her had ordered from one of those online meal services, heated it up and presented it on a plate. It turned out to be overcooked because he couldn't even follow the heating instructions. She'd found out only because she'd gone to throw something away in the kitchen and saw the empty containers. However, as Cedric stuffed the crab mixture into the jumbo sized shrimp and wrapped them in bacon, she knew she was in for a treat. She slid off the stool and wandered over to the sliding doors on the other side of the kitchen. "This is nice," Randi said of his sunroom. It was walled in on three sides and the fourth side opened to a large backyard. Two semicircular sectionals surrounded a sunken fire pit. "This looks like a cool place to relax. What do you do when it gets cold?"

"Thanks. Push that button on the wall."

She pushed the button and a wall of tinted windows rolled down like a garage door, effectively enclosing the space but still allowing for the view. "This is fabulous!"

A few minutes later, Cedric washed his hands and came to stand next to her. He opened the sliding glass door and motioned her through.

The area extended past the kitchen and had another entry from the family room. It housed a couple of loungers with a small bistro table between them, a gas fireplace and a dining set for six. "Can we eat out here?"

"We can eat anywhere you want." He kissed her softly.

Randi turned to face him and kissed him again. She could see herself getting addicted to the way his mouth moved over hers. It left her breathless every time. *Remember, keep it light, girl.*

Placing butterfly kisses along her jaw, he whispered, "If you don't want burned food, we'd better stop. We can save this for dessert."

"Oh, we're having dessert, too?"

"Absolutely. Something sweet and then a little something wicked."

She had no clue what the sweet dessert might be, but the look in his eyes left no doubt in her mind about the wicked part. And she couldn't wait…for either.

"You can relax out here if you want." He turned on the fireplace. "If you get cold, there are blankets in that chest over there."

She glanced in the direction he'd indicated. She couldn't help but wonder how many other women he had invited to his home, how many he'd cooked for. Not that it should matter. As long as he didn't entertain anyone while they were together, whom he saw before and after her wasn't any of her business. "I think I will. Let me know if you need my help."

Laughing, Cedric shook his head. "When I'm done, you're going to want me to cook for you forever." He went still, as if realizing what he'd said. Their gazes held for a long moment. "I'll call you when dinner's ready," he said softly. Before leaving, he turned on some music. "Is this okay?"

The smooth R&B sounds flowed through hidden speakers. "Perfect." Randi waited for him to disappear into the kitchen before collapsing in one of the loungers. She blew out a long breath. She could feel her emotions creeping into the mix and she had to find a way to keep them out. Her heart and her sanity depended on it.

Cedric braced his hands on the counter and muttered a curse. *What am I doing talking about forever?* That word had never been part of his vocabulary when it came to relationships. Hell, he didn't even do long-term commitments. His liaisons never went beyond two or three months. After that, women began to think he wanted something more than what he was offering—mutually satisfying physical pleasure. The end. As it stood, he had already broken his rule about bringing a woman to his home. He'd done it only once, not long after he moved in. Halfway through the evening, the woman had started making insinuations about the relationship, and he clearly stated they were not up for discussion. After that, the only women who'd visited were family. As for preparing a meal, he'd never done more than throwing a steak on the grill or picking up takeout when it came to cooking for a woman. He didn't need to be sending out any other crazy signals that might be interpreted as permanency.

He checked the bread in the top oven and the shrimp in the bottom. They would be done in another five minutes, so he started on the basil cream sauce. He'd done some prepping earlier and had chopped the onion and garlic and made the pesto and roux. While the sauce reduced, he sautéed the asparagus. A minute later, he removed the bread and shrimp from the oven and placed them on the stove. Once everything finished cooking, Cedric fixed their plates. Instead of just dumping the rice on the plate, he used a small bowl to mold it, arranged the shrimp around the mound and drizzled the sauce on top. He added the asparagus and surveyed his work, satisfied that the presentation looked good.

Cedric didn't know why he was going through all this trouble for a dinner. As he carried their plates out to the sunroom, he began to think he should finish the meal and skip dessert. He was getting in too deep. "Dinner's ready." He placed their filled plates on the table.

Randi came over. "Oh, my goodness. Look at you with all this nice presentation. I feel bad now that all I served you was a salad. Next time, I'll have to go all out."

He smiled. "I hope it tastes as good as it looks." He didn't stop to analyze why her praise made a funny feeling swirl in his chest. "I'll be back with utensils, bread and butter, and the wine."

"I'll help you so you don't have to make two trips." She followed him inside.

They gathered everything and went back out. He waited for her to take the first taste of the shrimp with the rice and sauce. She moaned and the sound sent a jolt of desire straight to his groin. Cedric took a huge gulp of his wine.

"This is really, *really* good, Cedric. This sauce is to die for." She moaned again.

"If you want to finish your dinner, I'm going to need you to keep the vocal responses to a minimum. Keep it up and I'll be the only one eating tonight." Her stunned expression made him smile.

"Well, since you went to all this trouble and I don't want all your hard work to go to waste, I'll just—" Randi mimicked zipping her lips and smiled. She took another bite, leaned back in the chair and pretended to swoon.

He was enjoying her playful nature and it drew him even more. He picked up his fork and dug in. Halfway through the meal, Randi's phone buzzed.

Randi went over to the small table to retrieve it. "Sorry." She answered and listened for a minute or so. "Thanks for letting me know. I was hoping to find something more."

Cedric tried not to eavesdrop, but it proved to be impossible with her standing only a couple of feet away. When she ended the call, he wanted to ask her whether it had to do with the fire at his site, but held back.

She reclaimed her chair and continued to eat. "Is there any more of the sauce?"

He sensed some tension rising. "Yeah. I'll get it." He pushed away from the table and went inside. He filled a small bowl, brought it back and handed it to her.

"Thanks." She added more to her food and set the bowl on the table. "I know you're wondering about the call. I wish we had a solid lead, but we don't."

He studied her. He could see she was conflicted about saying anything. Technically, she hadn't, and he didn't want to put that kind of pressure on her. He grasped her hand. "I appreciate you telling me. Yes, I was curious, and I won't lie, there are times I want to ask a million questions. Like I told you before, I respect you and your job and I'd never do anything to jeopardize it." He didn't want their evening to be ruined.

Relief flooded her face. "Thank you," she whispered.

"Now, as you mentioned earlier, I did go through a lot

of trouble to prepare this meal, so no messing it up with this conversation. We need to go back to before the call."

A smile blossomed on her face. "Deal." Randi slid her finger through the sauce, sucked it off and moaned. She tossed him a bold wink. "You said to go back to how it was before the call."

Cedric couldn't stop the laughter that burst out of him. "You're a lot less serious than you seem on the job. Are you always like this?"

"Not always."

"What's different?"

"Must be the company I'm keeping." She shrugged. "You're fun to be with."

"I enjoy being with you, too." Neither looked away and the temperature rose between them. *So much for skipping dessert.* They finished the rest of the meal in companionable silence while the music played in the background. He clasped his hands together on the table. "Can I get you anything else?"

"Not right now. I'm stuffed. What's for dessert?"

"Make-your-own sundae."

"Ooh, that sounds good. Give me about twenty minutes to digest this food and I'll be ready."

He stood and extended his hand. "We can relax out here, unless you want to go inside and watch TV or something." He helped her up.

"No. Out here is good."

He sat in one of the loungers and pulled her down onto his lap. As she made herself comfortable, her bottom moved suggestively over his groin. Cedric's body reacted with lightning speed and he sucked in a sharp breath. His plan had been to just hold her, but before he could stop himself, his hands began a sensual tour over her curves as he rained kisses across her jaw and the exposed column of her neck.

Randi moaned softly. "I thought we were going to have dessert."

"Later," he murmured. "Right now there's something else I'd like to have." He stood with her in his arms, then carried her upstairs to his bedroom and placed her on his bed. He slowly, erotically removed her clothes and whispered all the ways he planned to make love to her.

"Cedric," she called on a strangled moan.

"What, baby? Don't you remember our phone call?" He slid down her body. "I told you I would start at your ankles." He placed a lingering kiss on each one, then alternately kissed and licked his way up one leg, then the other to her knees. "I'm beginning to think this is a far better dessert, sweetheart." He continued his quest upward and nudged her thighs farther apart. She was already wet and his desire climbed higher. Cedric slid two fingers inside her and she cried out, arching her body to his touch. She writhed beneath him, her gasps filling the room. His kisses found their way to her belly and farther to her breasts. He kept up the twin assaults until she came with a loud cry. He stood, removed his clothes and donned a condom. "Ready for more?"

"Oh, yeah." She sat up as he joined her on the bed. "As I recall, there were a few things I promised to do to you, too." She kissed him until he lay flat on his back and proceeded to kiss and lick her way down his body.

The feeling of her hot tongue making its way over his belly had him harder than he could ever remember being. By the time she got to his thighs, he couldn't take it anymore. He flipped her on her back and drove into her with one hard thrust. Her inner muscles clamped down on him. She was so tight, so wet. His eyes slid closed and his body trembled. Cedric gripped her hips and set a hard, pounding rhythm that shook the bed. Randi wrapped her legs around his waist and met his every stroke. Her nails dug into his back and her thighs gripped him tighter. He lifted her legs higher and plunged deeper and deeper, bringing her to a hard, shuddering climax that made her scream his name. She was still catching her breath when he shifted positions, turned her over and entered her from behind. He held her closer and thrust deeply. Groaning with pleasure, he moved faster and faster until his orgasm roared through him with such force, it shook his entire body and tore a hoarse shout from his throat. Before he could recover, he came again in a rush of pleasure that made bright lights flash behind his eyes. His head hung limply and his breaths came in short gasps.

As their trembling tapered off, Cedric withdrew, rolled to his back and gathered her in his arms. She gazed up at him with a smile, and emotions unlike anything he'd ever felt surged through him. *What in the entire hell...?* He tried to dismiss the feeling but it wouldn't go away. His heart started pounding in fear. Now what was he going to do?

Chapter 9

Randi spent the first part of the week with Detective Warner, re-interviewing some of the witnesses from the last two fires in hopes that one or more of them had remembered something. However, they came up empty. Now, on Thursday morning, the two of them hit the road again, this time to track down information on the paint used at Cedric's site. "How is it that not one person saw anything, especially at Hunter Construction? That fire was set in broad daylight," Randi said.

"I wonder. It's getting harder and harder to conduct investigations these days with no one wanting to get involved unless there's reward money dangling in front of them. Whatever happened to doing the right thing?" Brian asked. "Where's the first paint store located?"

She glanced down at the printout and recited the address. The lab had narrowed down the paint ingredients to two companies in the area. Randi had thought they'd caught a break when fingerprints at the latest site came back as belonging to someone who had been fired three weeks ago. But the man had no connection to the other construction companies. He had also relocated out of state and had an airtight alibi. That had been the phone call she'd gotten at Cedric's house on Saturday night.

A soft pulsing between her thighs began as the memories rushed through her mind. After making love that first time, they'd gone into his bathroom to shower. She had teasingly told him the stall looked big enough for a party. She would never forget Cedric's response: *I've never had a party in my shower before, but there's no time like the present.* They used every inch of the enclosure—the walls, the bench, the floor—and found that yes, it was absolutely big enough. After a short nap, he took her on another sensual ride before they fell asleep in each other's arms. They never did get dessert, but as he had pointed out, they'd shared a much better sweet treat. By the time it had ended, she knew she was falling for him. Randi didn't know what to do with the feelings because she was certain he didn't feel the same. He'd made the rules clear and she had agreed. *This is exactly why I should've walked away after the first night.* She was so deep in thought she didn't realize they had made it to the store until the car stopped.

Brian parked in front of the small paint store located in West Sacramento and they went inside. He introduced himself and Randi to the young woman behind the register. "Is the owner available?"

"Um, sure. Wait right here and I'll get him."

A moment later, she returned with a middle-aged man of average height with sparse blond hair and a belly that looked to have seen one too many beers.

"I'm John Atwell. How can I help you folks?"

"Paint that may have come from your store was found at a fire scene a couple of weeks ago," Brian said. "We'd like to know if you have any recent purchases on file." He provided the color and dates.

"Let me check." The store owner went to a computer and searched the records. "Sorry, but I haven't sold that particular shade of gray in over three months."

"Can you give us the name anyway?" Randi asked. The person could have purchased the paint earlier and not used it until the night of the fire.

The man wrote down the name and address on a piece of paper and handed it to the detective.

"Thanks for your time."

"You're welcome."

Randi and Brian exited and drove twenty miles in the opposite direction to the second store. The paint color hadn't been sold in two years, so they thanked the owner and left.

In the car, Brian asked, "Do you have to rush back to the office? I want to check out Mr.—" He glanced down at the paper. "Mr. Upshaw."

"No."

"Good. Then we can grab some lunch before heading back."

With any luck, Mr. Upshaw would turn out to be their arsonist. But her hopes were dashed the moment the man opened his door. With his walker and portable oxygen tank, he couldn't make it twenty feet, let alone set a fire and get away quickly. He told them he had purchased the paint for his granddaughter's high school space project. Randi and Brian thanked him for his time and got back on the road.

They ended up at Chevys Fresh Mex out on Garden

Highway, which didn't hurt Randi's feelings at all. Of course, the food couldn't hold a candle to Iyana's, but it would do in a pinch. Because it was almost two, the lunch crowd had come and gone and they didn't have to wait for a table. She chose the lunch mix with tortilla soup and a chicken quesadilla, and Brian opted for steak fajitas.

Over the meal, she and Brian discussed their next steps. "I was really hoping this lead would pan out," he said. "The mayor is all over the chief, and the chief is breathing down my neck for some information to give him."

"I understand their frustration, because I feel the same. But we can't just wave a magic wand and make a suspect appear." Randi dipped a chip into the salsa and popped it into her mouth.

He chuckled. "That would be nice. Maybe I can borrow my daughter's Harry Potter wand that we bought when we took our vacation to Universal Studios. She swears the thing is real."

Randi shrugged. "Hey, I'm for anything that'll help." They shared a smile. "Anything else come back on the fingerprints?"

"Nothing from Hunter Construction. I'm still waiting on a couple more from the Premium Dynamics fire." Silence rose between them for a few minutes. "I saw you talking with Special Agent Marks a couple of weeks ago after the meeting. Does he have any leads?"

"No. He said he's taking a backseat, unless we need him. Why?"

Brian focused his gaze on her. "Just wondering. You know as well as I do that sometimes the Feds tend to take over, whether it's justified or not. And with the mayor being involved, I wanted to be sure the rest of us aren't being left out of the loop."

Randi didn't know whether to laugh or be angry. She'd worked with Brian several times and this was the first time she could remember him questioning her loyalty. "I'm trying to decide if I'm offended or not."

"Sorry, Randi. I don't mean to offend you. You're one of the few people I trust. It's just that I noticed the way he hustled you out of the building and into the parking lot to talk, and I guess I jumped to conclusions. I'm trying to put the pieces together and I feel like I'm missing something. I apologize."

"Apology accepted." She debated telling him the real reason she and Jason had been talking, and decided to keep it to herself for now. She didn't want anyone to get wind of her seeking employment with the ATF. She finished her food and wiped her hands. "I need to get back to the office. There are a few more lab reports to review so I can get the fire report out on Premium Dynamics. The insurance company isn't very patient."

"Yeah, I know. Same with the police report." When Randi made a move to pay, Brian said, "I got it."

He made the drive back to her downtown office in ten minutes. She got out and told him, "I'll let you know if anything turns up."

"Thanks. And Randi?"

"Yes."

"I'm really sorry. I like working with you and I don't want it to be uncomfortable."

She smiled. "We're good, Brian."

He nodded. "See you later."

Randi couldn't be mad at him. He was one of the good guys and had always treated her with respect. She'd give him a pass this time. Inside, she went over the lab results on some of the samples and didn't see anything that would put them anywhere closer to finding the arsonist. She tapped her finger on the desk. "There has to be something," she mumbled. This guy couldn't be *that* good, or were they looking at a professional, someone possibly hired to carry out the job? Somehow, she didn't see that. Everything in her felt it was personal. But why? Automatically, her thoughts shifted to Cedric. She had forgotten to text him about dinner. She picked up her cell and called him. "Hey, Cedric," she said when he picked up.

"Hey."

"Just checking to see if we're still on for tonight."

There was a pause on the line. "Actually, I'm going to have to cancel. We're pretty behind at the site and I'll be working overtime for a while to get back on track."

Randi stared at the phone for a lengthy moment. *"Oo-kay."* She waited for him to offer an alternative, but he remained silent. "So, are we rescheduling or what?"

"I'll let you know."

"Oh."

"I'm coming," she heard him say. Then he came back on the line. "I have to go. I'll talk to you later."

"Don't worry about it." She pushed the end button, tossed the phone on her desk and released a deep breath. "I guess that's that." She turned back to her computer. At least it had ended before she invested too much of her time. And her heart.

Cedric sat in his office Friday evening staring out the window. He should have been going over the specs for the next project, but he hadn't been able to stop thinking about Randi since their short conversation yesterday. The emotions she evoked in him scared the hell out of him and he needed some time to think. He'd thought having a little distance would help, but less than an hour after talking to her, he had wanted to call her back. He got up and paced the office. He could still hear her husky voice in his ear and feel her kiss on his body.

"Hey. How late are you planning to be here?"

He stopped and turned at the sound of Lorenzo's voice. "Probably another couple of hours. You headed home?" Since getting married, Lorenzo had made a practice of leaving the office no later than six thirty, unless they had an emergency.

"Yeah. I figured you'd be leaving, too. You and Randi aren't going out?"

"No." Cedric went and dropped back down in his office chair.

Lorenzo came over, propped a hip on the desk and folded his arms. "Did she end things already?"

"Not exactly."

"Hmm, then that means you did."

"Not exactly."

Lorenzo shook his head. "What *exactly* does that mean?"

"We were supposed to have dinner last night and I canceled. She wanted to know if we were going to reschedule and I told her I'd let her know."

"And she said?"

"She said don't worry about it." Those four words had been eating at him all day. He'd never had a problem ending a liaison or moving on. This time, his head said he should be constructing a temporary ramp, but his heart seemed to want a bridge.

Lorenzo started laughing. He whipped out his phone and typed. "This is great. I can't believe it."

Cedric frowned. "What's great and who are you texting?"

"Seeing you being brought to your knees. And I'm texting Jeremy to tell him to get my money ready. You might as well get yours ready, too." He laughed harder.

"I don't owe you anything, because nothing has happened."

Lorenzo wiped tears of mirth from his eyes and sobered. "Look, Ced, I know you always said that you'd never settle down with one woman. By the way you're acting, you realize Randi might be challenging that position, and it's probably scaring the crap out of you. I get it. I was there, too, remember? But you don't have any demons to fight like I did, no trust issues or anything. Wait, you don't, do you?"

"No," Cedric grumbled. He buried his head in his hands. "This wasn't supposed to happen. Just sex, no, no…other stuff."

"If it helps any, falling in love isn't a bad thing with the right person. And Randi may very well be that person for you."

"Can't it just go away?"

"I'm afraid not, cuz," Lorenzo said, clapping Cedric on the shoulder. "And the fact that you've already slept with her this early in the game—more than once, I'd say, given how miserable you look—will make it that much harder to let her go."

"She's already given us the report and if I have any questions about the case, I can call the detective, so technically, I don't need to see her." Even as Cedric said the words, the thought of not talking to her or kissing her didn't sit well.

"True, you don't need to see her. Problem is you *want* to. Want some advice?"

"Not particularly, but I'm sure that's not going to stop you."

Lorenzo's phone buzzed. He checked the display and chuckled. "That was Jeremy. He said he can't believe you're caving so fast."

"I'm not caving," Cedric said through clenched teeth. *Reason number twenty why I stay away from emotions.* He didn't have time for all these distractions. He jumped up from his chair. "I'm going home." He couldn't concentrate and would only be wasting his time trying to read the document.

"My advice is to decide what you want. If it's Randi, don't let anything stop you from going after her."

Cedric had no idea what he wanted or *if* he wanted it.

"By the way, you said something when I was falling for Desiree and fighting it. It was the time Brandon, Khalil and Malcolm showed up."

Cedric remembered that day. It happened not long after his and Lorenzo's fathers had retired. The cousins had come up to offer assistance. With Brandon being the oldest and heading up his own family's company, he had a wealth of experience to share.

"I tried to tell you all that things with Desiree and me were casual and you said, 'You do remember that this is how it started with the cousins and look how they ended up.' It's your turn, Ced." Lorenzo straightened from the desk. "And now I'm going home to cook dinner for my beautiful wife. She's had a lot on her plate these past few weeks and deserves a little pampering."

"Tell her I said hello." After Lorenzo left, Cedric packed up and followed suit.

He spent a restless night trying to figure out his next move with Randi. The way he saw it, he had two options: bite the bullet and call her or let it go. By Saturday afternoon, he had decided on the former. He picked up the phone to call, then set it down again. What would he say to her? The short fling he had proposed no longer seemed appealing and he, who said he would *never* pursue anything outside of a physical relationship, wanted more. Cedric ran a hand over his head in exasperation. What if she didn't? She had readily agreed to his terms because she hadn't wanted anything permanent, either. *This isn't hard*, he told himself.

He remembered his cousins all sharing what they went through to get their women—the missteps and uncertainties. The one common denominator: it was worth the risk. He picked up the phone again and it rang in his hand. He smiled.

"Hey, Mom."

"Hey, baby. I'm cooking dinner tonight for you and your brother. We haven't talked since your grandmother's party and I wanted to see how things were going. You both have been working extremely hard."

"It's been a long couple of weeks for sure, and I know Jeremy has been putting in lots of hours to get his company off the ground." The robotics engineer had struck out on his own two years ago after making a name for himself in the area of prosthetics. "What time?"

"Around six. Oh, I should've asked if you'd be busy or out on a date first."

Cedric smiled. His mother never failed to slide in a comment about his love life. He wondered how she would have reacted if he'd said he did have a prospective woman in his life. "Six is fine. I'll be there. Do you need me to bring anything?"

"No, honey. I'll see you in a little while."

He disconnected and checked the time. He had a good three hours to mow his lawn, do a short workout and shower before going over to his parents' house. He left the balcony off his bedroom, laced up his sneakers and got started.

He made it to his parents' home a few minutes after six and used his key to enter. He and his brother both had keys, but used them only when his mom and dad were expecting them. He found his mother in the kitchen, standing over the stove. "Hey, Mom." He bent and placed a kiss on her smooth brown cheek.

"Hi."

"You need help with anything?"

"Nope. Your dad and Jeremy are in the family room. We'll be ready to eat in a few minutes."

"Okay." Cedric found them watching a basketball game. "Hey, Dad. What's up, little brother?"

"Seeing as how I'm a good three inches taller than you, who's the *little* brother?" Jeremy said, unfolding his tall body from the love seat to tower over Cedric like he always did.

"The four-year difference in our birth certificates says you are."

Their father chuckled. "You two have been having this argument since you were teenagers. How's the cleanup going, Cedric?"

Cedric dropped down into a recliner. "It'll probably take another week, at least, to finish hauling away all the debris. I've already started ordering more lumber, but I want to wait until everything is gone to get a true measure. We've gotten the reports from the fire inspector and police and turned them over to the insurance company. They said we should receive a check in a couple of weeks."

"Good."

He waited for his father to say more, but he didn't. They'd had a long talk when Cedric first took over the company. His dad always offered to help when some crisis or situation arose, even as he allowed Cedric and Lorenzo to make the final decision. It was one more reason he loved and respected the man. "How are things at the lab?" he asked his brother.

"Not too bad. My staff and I are working on a surgery robot and I have a little something I'm doing on the side."

"Dinner," their mother called.

They all made their way to the dining room table where their mom had set out her best china, silverware and cloth napkins. Whenever Cedric asked about it, she always said every occasion they sat down as a family was a special one. Their father blessed the food and Cedric piled the grilled salmon, crab cakes, sautéed corn, mashed potatoes and steamed broccoli on his plate. Thank goodness he'd worked out earlier.

Over the meal, he and Jeremy caught their mother up on everything they'd told their father. Then Jeremy said, "I've been asked to speak at a robotics conference next year. In Madrid," he added with a huge grin.

"That's *wonderful*," his mother gushed.

His father nodded. "Yes, it is."

"Congrats, bro. That's big."

"Thanks. Madrid is on my bucket list and I'm going

to enjoy crossing it off. The conference lasts a week and I plan to get in as many sights as I can."

"Jeremy, you'll have to take lots of pictures."

"I will, Mom. Are you and Dad planning any more trips soon?"

His father set his fork on his plate. "As a matter of fact, we're thinking about doing a wine train tour in Napa and staying the weekend."

Cedric took a sip of his lemonade. "Sounds like fun." He wondered if Randi would like to take that trip. Outside of her favorite food being Mexican and the fact that she was the only woman to make him have back-to-back orgasms, he didn't know much about her personally. Then again, he'd never wanted to get that deep with a woman before. But for some unexplainable reason, he did with her.

After dinner, Jeremy volunteered to help his mother in the kitchen, while Cedric and his dad retreated to the family room. They chatted about the NBA and gave their predictions of who would win the championship.

"Dad, how did you know Mom was the one?" The words tumbled out of Cedric's mouth, shocking him in the process. If his father's expression was any indication, he felt the same.

"Well," he started slowly, "your mother was the only woman I'd met who matched my fire and drive. She encouraged me to follow my dreams and I did the same for her." He leaned back in his favorite recliner and a wistful smile spread across his lips. "She took my breath away every time she walked into the room. Her poise and grace, not to mention I thought she was the most beautiful girl I had ever seen. My heart would start beating faster and I'd be grinning like an idiot."

"Did she feel the same way?"

"Yes. She said she liked that I was straightforward about my intentions and didn't play games. I fell in love with her a week after we met. And she still makes my heart speed up when she comes into the room."

Cedric listened to the passion and love in his father's voice. In some ways, his father had described some of the emotions Cedric was beginning to experience. He didn't think he'd fallen in love with Randi, but what he felt went beyond just the physical. He enjoyed laughing and talking to her as much as he did kissing her.

"Is there a particular reason you're asking?"

"I'm not sure."

His father laughed. "Then I think you'd better find out. It would be a shame for some other fellow to take her off your hands while you're trying to decide."

Yeah, maybe he should.

Chapter 10

"This is the best steak I've had in *months*," Iyana said as she and Randi sat eating dinner Sunday evening. "Mine never come out this way. I either undercook it or burn it."

Randi laughed. "We all have our gifts, and yours is cooking like you were born in Mexico."

"I'm all in for food swaps." Iyana took another forkful of the meat. "How're things going with you and that hottie who was at your house?"

"He heard your comment, by the way."

Iyana's mouth fell open. "Are you *serious*?" She giggled. "Oh, well. It's not like he hasn't heard it before."

"No doubt." Randi still hadn't heard from him. She couldn't be mad, though. He'd set the parameters on that first night and she'd gone along with them. "But to answer your question, it's not. He canceled dinner the other night and when I asked about rescheduling, he said he'd

let me know. There was something in his tone that made
me think he was trying to find an out."

Iyana paused with her fork halfway to her mouth. "I
know you had a comeback."

Randi shrugged. "I just told him don't worry about
it. It's not like I didn't expect it to end. It was only supposed to be a short affair anyway."

"Yeah, but it turned into more than that for you, didn't
it?"

"Unfortunately, yes." She still couldn't believe how
fast Cedric had gotten under her skin. It usually took
weeks before the emotional part of her got involved in a
relationship. She'd naively assumed he would fall into the
same category, but she should have known by her initial
reaction to him that he would be different. "But it's okay.
I need to be focused on all these fires that keep popping
up, and working on getting into the ATF."

"The ATF? You didn't tell me about that."

"Oh, I didn't? I saw one of the agents I'd worked with
in the past at one of our task force meetings and he told
me about an opening that would be coming up in a few
months. It's not public knowledge yet, but I'm going to
start preparing for the exam and the fitness test."

"You've been working out since high school, and with
all you had to do to become a firefighter, I'm sure this
will be a piece of cake. It pays to know people."

"I hope so. It's still no guarantee I'll get the position,
but at least I have some time. How was LA?"

"A beautiful, sunny seventy-five degrees. It was too
bad I didn't get a chance to see any sights outside of the
sets. We started at the crack of dawn and ended when it
was dark." As they ate, Iyana talked about the grueling
but rewarding work.

"We should plan a trip."

"Ooh, count me in. I want to go to Disneyland and California Adventures."

Randi laughed. "How old are you?"

"What? Disneyland is for everybody. We haven't been since we were kids, and they have way more stuff now."

"That's true." And a couple of days away would help keep thoughts of Cedric at bay. She pushed her empty plate aside. "Universal Studios is there, too. We could make a weekend out of it and see everything."

Iyana reached for her phone. "Let me see how much tickets are." After a minute, she said, "We should probably go before June. Prices jump by twenty to forty dollars."

"I don't want to be that far away until we catch this arsonist. If it was only a couple hours away, I'd say let's do it next weekend."

"I hear you. Are you making any progress?"

"We thought so, but both leads turned up nothing." The fires were being mentioned more on the news and Randi made a mental note to call Brian tomorrow to find out if he'd heard anything else from the mayor's office.

"If anybody can figure it out, it's you, sis."

"I appreciate the confidence, because I don't feel it at all right now."

"Hey, my big sister is the best. Do like you always taught me—think outside the box. Don't just look at things in front of you, go deeper."

Randi grinned. "I can't believe you remember that. I said that to you when you were auditioning for your first part in high school." Many of the girls going out for the lead part in the school's spring theater arts production had chosen standard recitation parts, and Randi had told

Iyana she needed to stand out. And she had. Her love for the theater had expanded to include makeup, but Randi's sister still loved being on stage.

"Girl, I have that taped to my bathroom mirror. It's my mantra every day."

"I'm glad to hear it. Want dessert?"

"You'd better believe it. I ate light all day because I knew I was going to hurt myself over here. What are we having?"

"Ice cream sundaes." It wasn't until Randi had gotten home from the grocery store and started unloading that she realized what she'd done. Somehow those sundaes she and Cedric never got around to having had jumped from her subconscious to her shopping cart. Just like that, the rest of what happened that night came back to her in vivid detail. No other man had taken his time to kiss every part of her body as he had done. And that shower… She shoved the memories aside and took her dishes to the sink. "You want to make them now or later?"

"I'd better do it now. They changed the schedule and I have to be on set at five tomorrow morning, so I'll have to make it an early night." Iyana placed her plate and glass in the sink with Randi's.

Randi pulled out the ingredients and placed them on the counter. "I know you love brownies, so I baked some to go with your sundae."

"You are the best sister ever!" Iyana threw her arms around her, then clapped with glee.

"And you are the most *dramatic* sister ever."

Iyana bowed with a flourish. "Yes, I am." She straightened. "I think my phone is buzzing." She walked over to the table and came back with the cell in her hand. "Nope, it's yours."

Randi took it and saw Cedric's name on the display. She hovered her finger over the ignore button.

"Don't you do it," Iyana said. "Answer that phone. He might be calling to apologize."

"I doubt it." But she answered it anyway. "Hey, Cedric."

"How are you?"

"Fine." They had never engaged in this kind of nonsensical small talk and it felt awkward. "Is there something you wanted?"

"Actually, yes. I wanted to know if I can come by and talk to you tonight."

She closed her eyes. She wanted to say yes so bad but didn't think it would be a good idea. Five minutes in his presence and they'd be naked and in her bed. That would be the last thing either of them needed. "Tonight isn't a good time."

His sigh came through the line. "Then when?"

"Cedric, I think we should leave things the way they are."

"I don't agree."

"Why not? You're the one who wanted out."

"I never said I wanted out, Randi."

Randi paused. "You never said you didn't, either. Our last conversation ended a little abruptly, don't you think?"

"It did and I'm sorry."

Dammit! He wasn't supposed to say that. She glanced over at her sister.

"He said he's sorry, didn't he?" she mouthed. When she nodded, Iyana gave her the thumbs-up.

Randi rolled her eyes and turned her back. "I don't want to do this. We both knew what we had wouldn't last, so this is probably a good time to let it go." She struggled to get that last sentence out because, in reality, she didn't want it to be over.

"I agree that it started out that way, but I'd like to amend our agreement."

Her heart started pounding. "Excuse me? Amend it how?"

"I'll explain it to you when you have time to meet with me."

Randi banged her fist on the counter and put the phone against her chest. She groaned softly. Why was he doing this to her? Of course she wanted to hear what he had to say. Curiosity was definitely going to be the death of her. "I'll check my schedule tomorrow and let you know," she said, throwing his words back at him. She didn't want him to think this would be an easy fix.

"That's all I ask. Have a good night. And, Randi?"

"Yes."

"Thanks, sweetheart."

Despite her best efforts to remain unmoved, her insides melted like hot wax. She ended the call, tossed the phone on the counter and rubbed her temples. "I can't believe I caved."

"Hell, I can." Iyana cut a piece of brownie and placed it in her bowl. "I saw him, remember? You lasted far longer than I would've, and look on the bright side. You didn't cave completely. You told him you'd let him know."

"Yeah, but he said he wanted to talk about amending our agreement and—"

"And because you've always been the one who wanted an explanation for everything, you want to know."

"Exactly."

"Don't take too long to find out."

"Why not?"

"Because I want to know what the new agreement is going to be and how long it'll take you to actually cave after you hear it." Iyana pointed her spoon at her. "And you *will* cave. Any brother that gets you in the bed less than a week after meeting him has to be special. I don't care what you say, or him either, for that matter. There's more going on between you two even if you don't realize it. I saw the way he was looking at you."

"Whatever, girl." Randi had seen the way he looked at her, too. It made her feel like she was about to go up in flames. But then after that last round at his house last weekend, she thought she'd seen something else. It had lasted only a split second, but the look of tenderness on his face had seeped inside her. She knew then that Cedric would be dangerous to her heart. Now she was on the verge of opening herself even more. Randi prayed she wasn't making a big mistake.

Cedric took a deep breath and rang Randi's doorbell Friday evening. It had taken her three days to text him and during that time he'd been more anxious than he had at any time in his life. She opened the door and his heart rate kicked up. Something was definitely up with him. That had never happened in his entire adult life, so he couldn't chalk it up to some crush. "Hi."

"Hey. Come in."

"I was thinking we could go somewhere else to talk." Being behind closed doors wouldn't be a good idea, especially since he really wanted to kiss her. Instead of talking, he'd be trying to seduce her.

Randi seemed to read his thoughts. "I agree. Let me put my shoes on."

He came inside but kept his hands in his pockets and stayed by the door.

It took her only a couple of minutes, and they started out to the parking lot. "Where are we going?" she asked.

"Have you eaten dinner?"

"Yes," she said as she slid into the passenger seat.

He got in on the driver's side and drummed his fingers on the steering wheel. "It's not too cold, so we can go to that park around the corner or we can get dessert somewhere. I still owe you for that dessert we never had." Cedric slanted her a glance. He smiled inwardly at the slight hitch in her breathing, letting him know the attraction between them had not died down. It gave him confidence that she would be receptive to his plan. He had no idea how to approach the subject. This would be a first for him, and in hindsight, maybe he should have called one of his married cousins to get some pointers. "We can do both. Talk at the park first, then have dessert afterward. Will that work?"

"Sure. What exactly are we going to be talking about?"

"I'll tell you when we get to the park," he said with a wink and drove out of the complex.

She rolled her eyes. "I hope you're not going to waste my time."

So did he. It took less than five minutes to reach their destination and he hoped the park wouldn't be locked. Fortunately, it didn't close for another hour. They got out and started a leisurely stroll down one of the paths. Unable to resist, Cedric reached for her hand. They were content to walk without talking for a while. Finally, he said, "I'm sorry for the phone call and for canceling dinner."

Randi's steps slowed. "Are you saying that you didn't have to work, that you weren't busy?"

"No, I was plenty busy and didn't leave the office until after nine, but I should've gone to dinner and worked when I got home."

"I'm confused."

He laughed softly. "Join the club."

She pulled her hand from his. "Look, I—"

He faced her and placed his hands on her shoulders. "I know what I said in the beginning about this being just a physical thing, but somehow it's becoming more than that. I want to sit and talk with you, find out your favorite color, hear all about your dreams. I want to know all about you. That doesn't mean I don't desire you, because I do. Even now, I want to take you in my arms and kiss you, touch you, make love to you. I want to hear the sounds you make when I—"

She placed her hand over his mouth and took a quick glance around. "Okay, okay, I get it."

He smiled and kissed her hand. "What I want is to start over and get to know you and do all the things that couples do when they're dating. I want to be more than your bed partner."

"I… I don't know what to say. I'm not sure what I expected to hear, but that wasn't it."

"No?"

"No. I thought you were going to suggest we pick up where we left off."

"Oh, I want to do that, too."

Randi swatted him playfully on the arm. "Be serious."

"I'm very serious." He placed her hand on his growing

erection. "I've never been around a woman who makes me hard each and every time from just the sight of her."

"Serves you right. There's no telling how many women you've left wet and horny. I'm glad to be the one to give you a taste of your own medicine."

Cedric burst out laughing. He wrapped an arm around her shoulder and kissed her temple. "I don't know about you, woman." Her smile warmed him and he couldn't resist. He met her mouth in a tender kiss, exploring her at his leisure and wanting her to feel what he was trying to say. Mindful of where they were, he eased back, took her hand and continued their journey. "You still haven't said what you think of my proposal."

"I like you, Cedric. Honestly, I want to say yes, but I don't want to wake up tomorrow or the next day and find you've changed your mind. Then I'll get another phone call like the first one, canceling us. You still haven't explained why you did that."

"Fear. I've never had these kind of feelings for a woman, and I didn't know what to do with them."

"And you've figured out what to do with those feelings now?"

Cedric could still sense the fear lurking just below the surface, but not being with her would be worse. "I'm learning as I go, and I want to keep going with you. But only if you feel the same." He hesitated putting that last part out there, but a one-sided relationship wouldn't work.

She searched his face under the glow of the lamp. "I believe you. You are aware that men aren't supposed to make that kind of confession," she added teasingly.

"Yeah." His man card would be in serious jeopardy if anyone ever found out what he'd just said. "But for you, I'd say it again."

Randi turned away. "If I say yes, what happens next?"

"We seal the agreement with a kiss and go have some dessert." Her laughter rang out in the night and sounded like music to his ears. "What do you say?"

"I say you've got yourself a deal, Mr. Hunter."

Cedric captured her mouth again in a deep, searing kiss. "I can't get enough of kissing you." He touched his mouth to hers one last time and started back the way they'd come.

He drove to a nearby restaurant and they shared a dessert trio of chocolate soufflé cake, cheesecake brûlée and apple peach cobbler.

"So tell me all there is to know about Randi Nichols."

"Like what?"

"Whatever you feel comfortable telling me. Do you have a favorite color, holiday, vacation spot? Anything." She licked the melted chocolate off the back of her spoon and Cedric had to look away. She tempted him beyond reason.

"Let's see." She made a show of thinking. "I don't think I have a favorite color, but I tend to like darker colors like navy and black. Christmas has always been the best holiday because my mom, sister and I take a day or two to do all the baking, then we go to the spa and out to lunch to celebrate and bond." She ate some of the cobbler. "The only thing I'll say about a vacation spot is I'd rather be at the beach than in the snow. Give me a warm, sunny day anytime over the cold." She shivered. "I don't know how people live in those cold states."

He chuckled. "I'm with you on that one. Although, with the right person, the cold might not be so bad. Snuggling in front of the fireplace has its own appeal."

"Okay, yeah. I can see that. What about you? What are some Cedric Hunter facts?"

"We're pretty similar. Christmas has always been a big deal in our house, too. We either spend it at Lorenzo's or my parents' house here, or we all fly down to LA to spend it with my cousin's family."

"I remember you saying there were nine of you, not including parents. I can't imagine all those people in one place. The most we've ever had is nine. My dad's sister has three boys."

"It's a lot more now with just about everyone being married and having kids. Since we're all adults, everybody pitches in and helps with the cooking and cleaning." He opened his mouth to invite her to the next gathering and thought better of it. *You're getting way ahead of yourself.* He acknowledged liking Randi a lot, but taking her to meet his family was an entirely different story, one he wasn't ready to tell.

"If I was your mother, I'd make you all help, too. That's way too many mouths to feed." She shook her head. "What else should I know about you?"

Cedric thought for a moment. "I'd rather stay at home than go out partying."

Her surprised gaze met his. "Really? You seem so outgoing, I figured the club would be your normal hangout."

"You think I'm outgoing? When it comes to business, I have to be that way, but away from the office is another story." They polished off the remainder of the sweet treats. "Do you want anything else?"

"No, thank you. This was perfect. Just enough to taste without blowing my calorie count for the week."

He smiled and signaled the waiter for the bill.

Outside a few minutes later, Randi rubbed her hands

together. "Good grief, the temperature must have dropped by ten degrees while we were in there."

He hugged her close. "I'll warm you up."

She quickened her steps to the car and got in.

He hurried around to his side, started the engine and turned up the heat.

"Oh, and that little dessert doesn't make up for the one you owe me," Randi teased. "I want my make-your-own sundae and I like mine with either chocolate chip cookies or brownies."

Cedric laughed. "You can have your sundae and anything else you want."

"Anything?" She wiggled her eyebrows.

"Anything." A vision of her licking that chocolate off the spoon popped into his head. He planned to indulge in his own type of sundae. Yep, he liked this woman. *A lot.*

Chapter 11

Randi's phone rang at six on Saturday morning. She groaned and buried her head deeper in the pillow. "Please don't let it be another fire," she muttered. After a restless night, she'd finally fallen asleep two hours ago. Cedric had dropped her off at home last evening, kissed her with a passion that weakened her knees, then left. He'd said he wanted them to be more than bed partners, and with her growing feelings for him, the knowledge had made her happy. However, the parts of her that craved his touch didn't want *more than* to mean *instead of*. She groped for the phone on her nightstand and cracked open one eye. She saw her mother's name on the display and bolted upright in the bed. Her mother never called this early. "Hey, Mom. Is everything okay?" she asked as soon as she answered.

"Hey, baby. Of course. Why?"

She flopped back down on the pillows and released a

sigh of relief. "It's six in the morning, Mom. On a Saturday."

Her mother laughed. "Oh, sorry. Your dad and I are going on one of those turnaround trips to the Nevada state line and the bus leaves at seven. I wanted to check in with you before we left."

"You know you could've called from your cell phone on the bus, two hours from now." The ride usually took about three hours, but with the increase in traffic these days, it would most likely be longer.

"Please. I don't want all those folks hearing my business. Anyway, how are you? I talked to Iyana yesterday and she told me about all the fires. You think it's a serial arsonist?"

"We're not sure, but it's beginning to look that way."

"Well, you be careful out there."

Randi smiled. Her mother had said those words on Randi's first day as a firefighter and she continued to say them every time they talked. "I will. How's Dad?"

"He's good. Thinking about retiring in a couple of years. He said he's given the federal government over thirty years of his life and now he wants it back."

Randi chuckled. "I remember him saying that at year twenty-five. You know he likes bossing people around. He wouldn't know what to do with himself if he retired." Her father worked as a supervisor in the quality assurance division of a defense contracting agency.

"Exactly."

"What about you?"

"I don't know. I'd miss seeing all my babies grow up." She was a physician's assistant in a pediatric practice. "But enough about that. Iyana says you're dating someone?"

I'm going to strangle that girl. "Sort of. We met recently."

"Honey, you're either dating him or you're not. If you're talking about it being *sort of*, then something isn't right."

"We're dating."

"Where did you meet him? What does he do? Is he as good-looking as your sister says?"

"Goodness, Mom. You're grilling me like you did when I was sixteen." Her mother didn't respond. Randi sighed. "His name is Cedric and his is one of the construction sites that was set on fire. He and his cousin own the business and, yes, he's good-looking." Although Iyana's description of Cedric as being *fine* would be more accurate.

"You're investigating the fire and dating him?"

"Yes." She hoped her mother wouldn't lecture her about it being a conflict of interest. Randi continued to have mixed feelings about it herself. "But we agreed that he wouldn't ask me anything about the case when we're together and, so far, he hasn't."

"You're usually pretty cautious when it comes to relationships, so Cedric must be special."

Randi thought about their conversation the previous night. "Yeah, he is." She heard her father in the background. "Tell Dad I said hi."

Her father's voice came through the line. "Hey, baby girl. What's this I hear about you dating somebody? I need to come up there and check him out."

"Hi, Dad, and no you don't. At least not yet. We're still getting to know each other."

"You let me know if it gets serious, or if he breaks your heart. Either way, he'll get a visit."

"Yes, Dad," she said, shaking her head. "You know, I'm not a teenager anymore."

"Even more reason for me to check him out."

"Don't you guys need to get going? I don't want you to miss your bus." Randi and her sister were daddy's girls, and their father took protecting them to a whole other level when it came to men.

She heard his deep laughter. "Hey, you're still my baby."

"I know and I love you, Dad."

"Love you, too. Here's your mother."

"Okay, keep me posted on those fires and Cedric," her mother said when she came back on the line.

"I will. Have fun and I hope you and Daddy win lots of money."

"Me, too. Talk to you later."

"Bye." Randi placed the phone back on her nightstand and snuggled under the covers. She closed her eyes and tried to go back to sleep but kept thinking about Cedric and his proposal. He'd been forthcoming about his feelings for her, but she had held back, admitting only that she liked him. She more than liked him and would probably say she was falling in love with him. But no way would she tell him, not until she knew where the relationship was headed. For now, she'd take it one step at a time.

Randi shifted and tried to get comfortable but gave up after another ten minutes. She got up and went to the bathroom to brush her teeth and wash her face. Since she couldn't sleep, she decided to start a load of laundry, then get back in bed. As she sorted her clothes, a thought came to her. Smiling, she picked up the cell and sent Cedric a text. Just want you to know I didn't get any sleep last night and it's your fault. She didn't expect him to respond, but he'd see it when he woke up. Ten minutes later, the phone buzzed in her pajama pocket and startled her. Why was he awake at this hour? Maybe he had decided to go to work.

She read: Neither did I and it's definitely your fault. But I know the cure and I'm more than willing to do what it takes so both of us can get some sleep.

Laughter spilled from her. She dropped down on the bed and texted back: Is this one of those "I'm liable to show up at your house" things?

His reply came after a few minutes: I'll show up anywhere you want if it will put us out of our misery. Just say the word.

Randi responded: Word? What word?

She smiled and set the phone on her chest. She'd never even thought about teasing and flirting with another man the way she did with Cedric. He was the only man she'd felt comfortable showing her fun side. Why him? She still didn't know.

Her doorbell rang, breaking into her thoughts. Who in the world? She felt her eyes widen. *I know he didn't.* She scrambled off the bed, went out front and looked through the peephole. Sure enough, it was Cedric standing there in a pair of gray sweatpants and a fitted long-sleeved T-shirt. She opened the door.

Before she could utter a greeting, Cedric swept her off her feet and kicked the door closed. "You said *word.*"

"What?" Then she remembered the text. Randi burst out laughing. "What am I going to do with you?"

"I plan to show you." He strode purposefully down the hallway to her bedroom.

"I bet you do." And she was looking forward to every second.

* * *

Cedric woke up four hours later with Randi's naked body sprawled half on and half off his own. He couldn't remember the last time he'd had sex in the morning, mainly because he didn't do the morning after. He didn't sleep over at a woman's house and he certainly didn't have her over to his. Which made Randi an anomaly. Last weekend at his house, they had fallen asleep and didn't wake up until morning. Somehow, all the rules he'd had in place to govern his relationships were being broken one by one. The scary part was that it didn't bother him like it should. When he left his house that morning, he had planned to be gone for only an hour or so, but her texts had him changing directions and on her doorstep before seven. Cedric glanced over his shoulder at the clock sitting on her nightstand. It was well past noon.

His stomach growled. He hadn't eaten anything since dessert last night and he needed to find some food soon. He carefully shifted Randi, eased off the bed and went to the bathroom. She was propped up on the pillows with the sheet covering her when he returned. "Did you sleep well?" he asked.

Randi stretched and smiled. "It was the best sleep I've had in a week."

He slid under the covers next to her and pulled her close. "Glad to hear it."

"I didn't get a chance to ask when you got here because somebody was pretty eager, but how did you get to my house so fast?"

Cedric chuckled. "Hey, I didn't hear any complaints and you didn't have any problems keeping up. To answer your question, I was already out on my way to go running. After that first text, I changed my mind."

She turned her head toward him. "I have to watch what I say around you. One of these days, you're going to have me out in public doing something crazy."

"Probably not. I don't like having my business out in the open like that. Now, if there's no one around, that's a different story." They lapsed into silence for a short while. "What's on your agenda today?"

"Washing clothes and going to the gym for sure. I need to go grocery shopping, too, but I may wait until tomorrow. What about you?"

"Going over to the fitness center site to do some work and then, like you, heading to the gym to get a workout in. We should go together."

Randi shook her head. "I don't think so."

"Why not?"

"I've seen couples working out at the gym. They spend more time touching, kissing and prancing in front of the mirror than working out. When I go, I'm all business. I don't even talk unless I need a spotter."

He kissed the top of her head. "That makes two of us, so it shouldn't be a problem. My workout usually lasts about an hour to an hour and a half, but I can cut it short, if need be." He had been curious about her workouts ever since she mentioned them. With her history as a firefighter, they must be rigorous.

"Mine is about the same, and I'll probably go the whole ninety minutes today." She told him which fitness center she used.

"I have a membership to the same one and I can use any of the facilities. When Khalil's opens up, I'll probably cancel it and just go to his. It'll save me some money."

She sat up and stared. "You're expecting him to let you go for free?"

"Absolutely. It's free for all the family."

"Must be nice," she grumbled. "I wish I had a family member with a gym. The cost of this one keeps going up and up."

Cedric nipped her ear. "If you're nice to me, I'll put in a good word for you and get you a discount." Khalil would tease Cedric mercilessly when he found out he had changed his tune about the type of relationship he and Randi had. But at this point, he didn't care.

Randi grabbed a pillow and hit him across the chest. "That's blackmail. And I'm already nice to you. If I wasn't, we wouldn't be sitting here now."

Laughing, he snatched the pillow. "You're right, and I appreciate it." He flipped the covers back, scooped her up and left the bed. "We can shower, get some lunch— since it's way past breakfast—then we can go work out."

"What about you going over to Khalil's gym?"

"I can go on Monday." He placed her on her feet in the bathroom.

"You promised to take me over so I can see it. Remember?" Randi turned the water on and adjusted the temperature.

Cedric slowly ran his fingers up and down her spine. "We can do that, too. You want to go before or after we work out?"

"Before. After my workout is done, all I'm going to want to do is fall out." She got a couple of towels from the cabinet and placed them on the rack, then eyed him. "You are going to behave, right?"

He held up his hands in mock surrender. "All I can say is I promise I'll try." His body was already becom-

ing aroused from watching her bending and reaching. He
followed her gaze downward. "Hey, I'm a man standing
in the bathroom with a sexy and *naked* woman."

Randi shook her head and pointed a finger his way.
"Promise you'll behave, or you'll be showering alone."

"This time, and only because I'm starving." Two minutes into the shower, they both lost the battle of behav-
ing and ended up with her back to him as he entered her
from behind. He was so far gone, he was three strokes
in before he realized he had forgotten a condom, something he had always been fanatical about. He muttered
a curse, stumbled out of the shower to grab one off the
nightstand and rushed back.

Unlike earlier, this time was hard and fast. The warm
water flowed over his back as he thrust into her and he
tilted her forward for deeper penetration. Without missing a beat, she swiveled her hips and squeezed him with
her feminine muscles. He increased the pace and sent
them both over the edge, their blended cries echoing in
the space. "Girl, you make me lose my mind."

"That makes two of us," she said, her breathing erratic. "Now we need to wash up for real before this water
gets cold. I'm never taking a shower with you again. Oh,
and you'd better be glad you didn't get my hair wet."

Cedric laughed. "Hey, I know how you women are
about your hair. Why do you think I had you facing
away from the spray?" He gave her a quick kiss and they
washed up.

Later, as they sat eating in Bella Bru Cafe, Randi said,
"I didn't realize I was so hungry." She had eaten half of
her sandwich already.

"We did expend a lot of energy. I was thinking, since

we're doing the real dating thing, we should go out on *real* date."

"We have been going on real dates."

"Not really. You said the first one wasn't a date, we've eaten at home and we've gone to places like this one." He thought back and realized most of the time, the dates hadn't even been planned. "I'm talking about getting dressed up and going to a nice restaurant, one that requires reservations."

"It's been a while since I've done something like that."

"Good, then it's a perfect time. When is the next time you're not on call?"

"Wednesday through Friday."

Cedric reached for her hand. "Let's plan for Friday. I'll make reservations and let you know what time."

She smiled. "I think I'm going to like this *real* dating thing."

"So am I." More than he ever thought he would. Once they finished eating, he drove over to the partially completed fitness center.

Randi turned around in a slow circle. "This is huge, and there are two levels?"

He stared at her in her fitted performance T-shirt and those purple printed exercise leggings that clung to her every curve. "Yes. The administrative offices will be upstairs. He wanted to maximize the space on the first level." He pointed out where the pool and basketball courts would be, as well as the general layout.

"When will it be finished?"

"It's scheduled for June, but we might be able to get it done a couple of weeks early."

"Yeah, I need you to put in a good word for me. It's thirty minutes from my house, but I'm willing to make the trip. The good-friend discount will make up for the gas I'll be using."

He started to tell her he'd pick her up and bring her whenever she wanted, and pay for her gas, but he was supposed to be taking this dating thing slowly. And he didn't want to get too deep, too fast. Though in his estimation, it might already be too late. "I'll see what I can do. In the meantime, we'll have to use our current facility."

"Yeah, I guess so," Randi said with a little laugh. "And we should probably get going before I change my mind."

"I can't have you wimping out before you get to the ATF, so come on."

"There's no guarantee I'll get a position if it becomes available."

Cedric slung his arm around her shoulder as they headed back to the car. "You will." With her background as a firefighter and her confidence and determination, he had no doubt she'd get the job. They'd be a fool not to hire her.

On the drive, she asked, "How much of the work did you do on the fitness center, or did you just supervise?"

"Actually, I did quite a bit. I trust my crew, but Khalil is very particular when it comes to…well, everything, so I wanted to make sure his exacting standards were followed to the letter." Cedric left out the fact that he had done a few extra things for Khalil because Khalil made a point of ensuring his gyms accommodated people with all types of disabilities and offered reasonable and, sometimes, sliding-scale fees for membership. His cousin had a big heart and always said he didn't want money to be an issue for people who were trying to take control of their health.

"Look at that poor man," Randi said, changing the subject. "That just breaks my heart. I know the city is doing a few things to help, but I wish it was more."

He followed her gaze out the window to a homeless man huddled beneath a tarp. "I agree." Seeing the man reminded him of what his LA cousins had done. They'd renovated two closed-down hotels and turned them into transitional housing, purchased two buses—one outfitted for a mobile grocery store and the other a mobile shower—all for the homeless. Cedric had been thinking of doing the same on this side of the state. Every day he saw the growing population of homeless in Sacramento and, though he wouldn't be able to solve the problem, he could do something to ease the burdens of a few. He briefly wondered if Randi would be on board to help him if he floated the idea to her. He glanced over at the sadness reflected in her features and instinctively knew she would. They rode the rest of the way, both lost in thought. When they arrived at the gym, both headed toward the treadmills.

Randi punched in her program on the machine. "I do a fifteen-minute run to warm up before I hit the weights."

"Works for me." He did the same and started with a slow jog. He gradually increased the speed until he was at a full run. He knew Randi had to be in great shape, because whereas just about everyone else coming off the machines could barely catch their breath, she looked like she had been out for a leisurely stroll.

"I'll let you know when I need you to spot me." She sauntered off with a sexy sway of her hips.

They started their separate workouts and he couldn't help but marvel at her. Later, he searched the crowded area for her and spotted her over on a mat, planking with dumbbells and doing an alternating arm row. *Damn!* It was an impressive sight. Apparently, he wasn't the only one who thought so. He also saw a man smiling and trying to talk to her. For the first time in his life, Cedric experienced what he assumed must be jealousy. That was the only explanation for him wanting to stalk across the room and punch the man. He smiled inwardly at the death glare Randi shot the man, who finally took the hint and walked away. Cedric finished his third set on the leg press and moved to the pull-up bar, then the free weights for his shoulders and arms. He was returning the dumbbells when Randi gestured for him at the bench press.

As Cedric approached, he heard the same man from earlier say, "You look like you need a spotter, pretty lady."

Cedric folded his arms. "She has one."

"Yo, man, I'm sure there's some other woman you can help. The little lady and I are managing just fine."

Cedric dropped his arms and took a step.

Randi must have known things were about to get ugly because she said, "Cedric, can you add a hundred pounds, please?"

The man turned his stunned gaze on Randi. "You know him?"

"I do." She moved into position after Cedric added the weights. "Can you excuse us?" she told the man. "I need to get this done before my muscles cool off."

Cedric stood above her. "Ready, baby?"

She smiled. "Yep."

The man sent a glare their way and strode off. Cedric shook his head. "Do you always start trouble when you come to the gym?"

"Yep, always."

He chuckled and kept count. When she finished, he added more weight and they switched places. "I could get used to working out with you."

"That might not be such a bad idea. If nothing else, you'll keep the gnats away."

His laughter tumbled out of him and he almost dropped the bar.

She glanced down and smiled sweetly. "Problems?"

"Yeah. *You.*"

"I don't know what you mean," she said, innocently.

He glanced up at her sparkling eyes and felt himself fall a little harder. At this point, he couldn't stop it, even if he wanted to.

Chapter 12

"Did you and Cedric make up yet?" Iyana asked.

Randi wedged her phone between her shoulder and her ear while she transferred the load of clothes from the washer to the dryer. Because she had spent all Saturday with Cedric, she didn't get around to the laundry until Sunday afternoon. "Yes, we talked on Friday and he came over yesterday." Or showed up and put them both out of their misery, as he'd phrased it. She'd slept better last night than she had in weeks, so there must have been something to it.

"By the sound of your voice, I take it you're okay with the way things are."

"We actually decided to do something a little different. Instead of a friends-with-benefits type of relationship, it'll be a real one and we'll see where it leads." The part of her whose feelings were steadily growing was ecstatic about it, but her warier side still had some reservations.

"So he's officially your boyfriend now. I love it! Wait till Mom finds out."

"Speaking of Mom, I have a bone to pick with you." She went back to her room to fold the first load of clothes and put them away.

Iyana giggled. "My bad. But it's all good now since you two are really seeing each other."

"I have no idea how long this is going to last. We just made the decision. For all I know it could fall apart tomorrow, so I'd rather wait a few weeks before telling Mom and Dad. As it is, Dad started grilling me and asking me if he needed to come up and talk to Cedric."

She could imagine how that conversation would go. She had introduced only one man to her parents, and her father sat and glared the entire time. The words he'd spoken to her later came back: *I just don't get a good feeling about that man. Something's not right.* In hindsight, she should have paid attention because a month later, her ex decided he wasn't interested in a woman with such a dangerous job. However, Randi didn't think Cedric would have a problem winning her father over. His upbringing almost guaranteed he'd impress.

"I invited them to the screening of the latest movie I worked on and they said they'd come. It's two weeks from now. I hope you can come, too. And you might as well bring Cedric and get all the introductions out of the way."

Randi paused in folding the shirt in her hands. "No way, sis. I don't think so. We aren't at the meet-your-parents stage yet. I think I'm on call that weekend, but I'll come if nothing jumps off."

"Great. We need to go shopping. I need an outfit and I know you do."

"What are you talking about? I have nice clothes." She much preferred pants but had a few dresses stashed in the closet. It reminded her that she should start deciding which one to wear on her date with Cedric, because it would probably take the whole week for her to choose. She made a mental note to schedule an appointment at the hair salon, too.

Iyana snorted. "What passes for *nice* in your book looks closer to business casual. I'm talking red-carpet nice, you know, something with a little bling. Besides, now that you and Cedric are seriously dating, you're going to need some sexy dresses."

Randi sighed. The last time, Iyana had dragged her to malls from Sacramento to San Francisco and everywhere in between. They stayed out so long, Randi seriously considered spending the night in a hotel rather than driving the two hours back home. "Who says I don't have a sexy dress to wear?"

"Girl, I've seen your wardrobe. When is your next date with Cedric?"

"Friday," she mumbled.

"Oh, shoot. Let me get my calendar up. We're going to have to go sometime before then." There was a pause on the line. "Okay. I should be able to leave a little earlier on Tuesday and Wednesday. I'm probably going to have to start looking at some stuff online so I have an idea of what we're looking for ahead of time. We'll be power shopping. Which one works better for you?"

Randi sincerely wanted to say neither, but she'd tried that once and Iyana had showed up with an outfit that had alternating four-inch solid and see-through bands and was so short it barely covered Randi's backside. She had adamantly refused to wear it. As much as she would rather skip the whole ordeal, going would definitely be a better choice. "Wednesday, and *I'm* driving."

Iyana laughed. "That's fine. We'll only have two or three hours before the mall closes anyway, so you won't have to endure one of my shopping extravaganzas, dear sister. But, be warned, if you don't find anything, I *will* go back the next day without you and get something."

Randi groaned. "You are such a pain in the butt."

"But you love me," Iyana said in singsong.

"Yeah, yeah." Her cell beeped another call and she pulled the phone away from her ear to check the display. *Please don't let it be another one.* "I have to go. Work is calling."

"Okay. I hope it's not another fire."

"Me, too. Talk to you later." She clicked over to the other line and her heart sank as she listened. "I'll be there as soon as I can." Another construction site.

Thirty minutes later, Randi stood off to the side as firefighters battled the fully engulfed, nearly completed office building. By the size of the blaze, she didn't expect much of the complex to survive. She spotted Brian a short distance away and started in his direction. He glanced up and met her halfway.

"Hey, Randi."

"Hey. What do you have?"

Brian ran a hand over his blond hair. "So far, it's the same as the others—fire set at three different points, heavy scent of gasoline."

"We've got a serial arsonist, then."

"Yeah, and the mayor and the media are going to have a field day."

Spark of Desire

"Anybody hurt?"

"No. The building was empty."

"That's one good thing." She pulled out her pencil and sketch pad. "Let me get started. I'll catch up with you later."

He nodded and went back the way he'd come.

She began sketching. With the building being located on a main street, someone had to have noticed something. There was a fair number of cars on the road and it was only four o'clock—still enough daylight to see clearly. When she finished, she met up with the detective, and the two interviewed the people who had gathered. As with all the other fires, no one had seen anything or anyone suspicious. They stepped away to speak with the fire captain for a moment and he confirmed the similarities with the other fires.

"This guy must be Houdini," Brian said in frustration. "How is it that no one saw him coming or going in broad daylight?"

"I wondered the same thing. What about someone driving by? Even if they can't identify the person, we might be able to find out if we're dealing with one person or more."

"I'm planning to talk to the chief about possibly putting out a call through the media for witnesses." He turned at the sound of one of the officers calling his name. "Be right there."

"I'll let you know if I find something."

"Thanks." He hurried off.

Several minutes later, her phone buzzed. Randi pulled it out and saw a message from Cedric: The fire's on the news and I know you're there. Be careful and text me to let me know you made it home safely. She sent a quick reply, noting that she would. She put the phone back into her pocket. Those spaces in her heart that had been closed opened further.

"Did you get Randi flowers?"

Cedric glanced down at the phone sitting on the bathroom sink as he tied his tie. He had the speakerphone activated. He'd made the mistake of telling Jeremy about the date with Randi and the new direction of their relationship. "Of course." Or at least he would once he stopped at the store on the way to her house.

"What kind did you get?"

He paused, then said the first thing that came to his mind. "Roses."

Jeremy whistled. "That means it's getting pretty serious. I hope you didn't get red ones."

"Why?"

"Red roses mean deep love and desire. Unless that's the message you're trying to send…"

Deep love and desire? That was definitely not the message he wanted to send. He liked Randi, a lot, but he wasn't in love with her. He wanted to ask what color he should get, but he'd just lied about having the roses.

"Your silence says that's not what you want to say. If I were you, I'd go with pink—something that speaks to grace, elegance and admiration. Not love, but sweet. Now, if you're still trying to keep this casual, yellow will be your best bet. Those just say friendship or a 'hey, thinking about you' kind of thing."

Cedric had to admit he was impressed with his brainiac brother. Carrying the phone with him, he grabbed a pair of black loafers off the shelf in his closet and sat on the side of the bed to put them on. "Exactly why do you know all of this? Have you been buying flowers for women?" He'd bought flowers for his mother on her birthday and on Mother's Day, and his female cousins when they gave birth, but no other women. He didn't count that corsage from prom as flowers.

Jeremy laughed. "I've bought flowers for a few women, but I'm waiting on that special one to give those red roses. If you read anything other than books about construction engineering, you'd know this. And Google is your friend. Just look it up."

"Ha-ha, whatever. Get off my phone before you make me late."

"Have a good time. Oh, and can you drag this relationship out to at least October or November? I'm trying to keep from paying Zo that two hundred dollars."

The line went dead before Cedric could tell Jeremy what he could do with that damn bet. He picked up the phone and googled florists and saw that there was one still open a couple of miles from his house. He slipped into his suit jacket, picked up his keys and phone, then left. He did as his brother suggested and chose a bouquet of pink roses arranged in a crystal vase.

By the time he made it to Randi's house, his heart had started that familiar pounding. And when she opened the door to him, it nearly stopped. All he could do was stare. Her hair flowed around her shoulders and the light makeup she had on made her green eyes even more alluring. She wore a red off-the-shoulder long-sleeved dress that molded to every curve and stopped a good five inches above her knees. His gaze traveled slowly down her body to her bare legs and farther down to the sexy black sandals with one thin strap across the toe and one around the ankle. His arousal was immediate.

"Cat got your tongue?" Randi said with amusement.

Cedric finally found his voice. "Baby, you are *stunning*!" He handed her the flowers and brushed his lips across hers. "These are for you."

"Thank you, they're gorgeous. Come on in." She left him to follow. "I must say you clean up well, Mr. Hunter."

So did she. So well, in fact, that they were in danger of missing those reservations. He would never live it down if that happened. "Thanks." He couldn't take his eyes off her shapely bottom in that dress. "I sure hope I don't have to punch somebody out tonight."

She placed the flowers on the end table, then picked up her wrap and purse. "Why would you do that?"

"If a man so much as glances your way, there's going to be trouble."

She came and wrapped her arms around him. In her heels, she stood eye level with him. "That is the nicest thing a man has ever said to me." She gave him that smile he'd come to look for and placed a sweet kiss on his lips. "And so you know, the same goes for you. In this gray suit, you look like you just stepped off the cover of *GQ*. I'd hate to have to act up tonight if some woman starts smiling at you."

He chuckled. Her body pressed against his made it hard to think rationally. "Sweetheart, we need to leave this minute or we're going to miss dinner."

Randi hooked her arm in his and led him out the door. "Oh, no, we're not. I had to endure three hours of shopping with my sister for this date. We are going."

He threw back his head and laughed. "If it makes you feel better, I think it was totally worth it."

"Only slightly."

He shook his head and got them under way. When they arrived downtown, Cedric didn't even bother with looking for parking on the street and drove straight to the valet. He'd made reservations at Morton's The Steakhouse. It didn't take long for them to be seated and their drink order taken.

"You're still staring, Cedric," she said with a smile.

"I know. I can't take my eyes off you in that dress." He'd never seen her in anything aside from her jeans or casual clothes. He found that no matter what she wore, she exuded a strength, beauty and confidence he hadn't often seen. The server returned with their drinks and Cedric lifted his glass. "To one day at a time."

She touched her glass to his and sipped.

"I'm not asking for details about any of the cases, but how are you doing with all the fires? I know it has to be eating at you."

She set her glass down. "You have no idea how much."

"Don't beat yourself up. I believe you and the police are doing everything you can. I heard on the news they're saying it's a serial arsonist."

"Yes, and hopefully, someone who's seen something will come forward soon."

He could see the lines of frustration etched in her face and, not wanting to dampen the mood, turned the conversation elsewhere. "You mentioned having to endure shopping with your sister. You don't like shopping?"

Her smile returned. "I'm okay with shopping when I know what I want. I go in, get it and leave. Iyana, on the other hand, acts like shopping is a weekend excursion. Once, she had me all over the Bay Area—San Francisco, Oakland, Fairfield. We left at eight in the morning and didn't get home until almost midnight. When I shop with her now, *I* drive."

"Most women would think a day of shopping was heaven."

"I'm not most women."

"No, you're not." She had turned out to be very different from the women he'd dated, and in a good way. Cedric loved her directness and the way they bantered. He would never forget that semi phone sex. It had been all he could do not to leave the site that moment and drive over to her office. Their food arrived and over dinner, they continued to talk about everything and nothing. When it came time for dessert, he declined. "I owe you dessert, remember?"

Randi clasped her hands on the table and leaned forward. "Ooh, I can't wait. You didn't forget the brownies, did you?"

"I didn't forget anything." The things he planned to do with her and that chocolate syrup.

Randi placed her purse on the breakfast bar in Cedric's kitchen and slid onto a bar stool. She couldn't remember the last time she'd enjoyed a dinner date so much. She smiled, recalling his reaction when she opened her door. She'd have to concede Iyana this round. Her sister had told her Cedric wouldn't be able to take his eyes off her and Iyana had been correct. But then, Randi hadn't been able to stop looking at him in that charcoal-gray suit, either. When they'd walked into the restaurant, the heads of every woman turned. She couldn't blame them, and she'd had the supreme satisfaction of knowing he was hers. She observed him now as he removed his jacket and tie and draped them over a chair. He went about gathering the fixings for their sundaes.

Cedric placed a plate with brownies and chocolate chip cookies in front of her. "You can have one or both."

"Are these homemade?"

"Of course. You still doubting my cooking skills?"

"No," she said, laughing. "I figured you'd pick some up from the store. I didn't expect you to make them." Unable to resist, she removed the plastic wrap, broke off a piece of the brownie and popped it into her mouth. It had chocolate chips in it, just the way she liked. She tasted a cookie and found it to be as delicious as the brownie. "I'm having both." Randi reached for the bowl he put on the bar and added them.

"Do you want to warm them up a little?"

"Yes, please."

He put the bowl in the microwave for a few seconds, then brought it back. He pushed the ice cream toward her. "Vanilla, cookies and cream or chocolate."

Her eyes lit up. She added a little of the vanilla and cookies and cream and topped it off with chocolate syrup, whipped cream and four cherries. She found him watching her with quiet amusement. "What? I like the cherries."

"I didn't say anything." Cedric made himself one and sat next to her. "How is it?"

"It's so good, but I'm trying to be quiet so I can finish it." She saw the moment he understood the reference.

He chuckled. "Yeah, you're right. Keep the vocalizations down, baby."

"But when I'm done…"

"You can be as loud as you want."

A low pulsing started between her thighs and she

squeezed them together. Randi focused on eating her food, but the heat rising between them threatened to melt the ice cream and her. It didn't help, watching the way Cedric slid the spoon in and out of his mouth and the way his tongue swirled around the ice cream. She could barely finish hers. A few minutes later, she pushed the empty bowl aside and turned on the stool to face him. "You said I could have anything with my sundae. Well, what I want is you."

Cedric didn't hesitate. He hopped down and lifted her into his arms. "Grab that bottle of chocolate syrup. I hope you're ready."

"With pleasure." And yes, she was more than ready.

Chapter 13

Wednesday, Cedric finished the section of flooring he'd been working on in the gym and stood. Instead of installing the thinner rubber flooring like at Khalil's LA gym, he'd opted for the heavy-duty model that measured almost a half inch thick to provide extra cushioning and better durability.

Lorenzo came to where Cedric stood. "This is going to be nice when it's done." He took a few steps on the newly laid area. "Far sturdier. It'll stand up well to the weight of all the equipment. Did Khalil ask for it?"

"That's why I chose it, and no. It's a little upgrade I threw in." Cedric always went above and beyond for their clients, and even more so for family. He and Lorenzo started working on the next section. "Is everything just about cleaned up at the strip mall site?"

"Yeah. I called Preston before I left and he agreed to meet us out there tomorrow."

"Okay." They, along with four other workers, continued laying the floor and had made good progress by late afternoon. Confident the crew could handle the rest, Cedric and Lorenzo headed out. They had a late meeting with a land developer and then planned to stay longer to discuss finances.

At the office thirty minutes later, Cedric took a shower and changed clothes. Installing showers in their personal bathrooms had been one of his and Lorenzo's best ideas. They'd pitched the concept a few years ago when their fathers were still in charge, citing the need to present their best face to prospective clients, among other things. It hadn't taken long for the elder Hunters to see the benefits, as well. When Cedric finished, he walked down the hall to Lorenzo's office. His cousin had done the same and was pulling on a shirt.

"They here yet?"

"No." Cedric sat in one of the chairs across from Lorenzo's desk, pulled out his phone and checked his emails. He deleted the junk first and wondered how these people kept getting his email address. He came across one and instead of hitting the delete button, accidentally clicked on the link. It happened to be one of those Groupon offers, and as he read, he was glad he hadn't sent it to the trash. Cedric had been trying to come up with something unique to do for a date with Randi and he thought he might have found it.

"What are you smiling about? Did Randi send you some sappy message?"

He shot Lorenzo a look. "I know you're not talking about me when I've caught you damn near having phone sex with Desiree."

Lorenzo spread his hands. "Hey, what can I say. When it's good…"

"Anyway, no, she didn't. I happened to open this Groupon offer for glassmaking. I have no idea how they got my email address. Anyway, it says you can make a paperweight to take home. I've been looking for something cool for my next date with Randi and this might be fun."

"So you're all into this relationship thing now. I said you were going to go down hard."

"Who said anything about going down at all? We've only been going out about a month." Even as Cedric said the words, he knew they were a lie. He'd been falling from the moment he looked into her eyes.

Lorenzo chuckled. "Whatever you say. I think Desiree might like to do something like that."

"Yeah, especially since she's so creative." Desiree owned a bath and body shop in Old Sacramento and made all of her products.

"We could double-date like we used to in high school."

Cedric grinned. Those had been fun times. However, now it would have a far greater meaning. Although Lorenzo had already met Randi, that had been in a professional capacity. This would be considered introducing her to *family*, a totally different story. Was he ready to go that far? *Yes.* He checked the available dates. "Randi will only be available on weekends. Will Desiree be able to leave the shop?"

"I'm sure she can if she has enough notice. She's hired two more part-time employees, so that'll give her a little more flexibility."

They discussed which date would be best, and then Cedric sent Randi a text asking if she would be free. He didn't say where they were going because he wanted it to be a surprise.

The intercom buzzed and Lorenzo hit the button. "Yes, Tanya."

"Mr. Green is here."

"Thanks. Please escort him in." They both stood and greeted the prospective client. Lorenzo gestured him to the small conference table. "Please have a seat. Would you like some water, tea or coffee?"

"No, thank you." Mr. Green took a seat and placed a folder on the table.

Cedric and Lorenzo followed suit. For the next hour, Mr. Green outlined his vision for a three-story office complex, shared drawings, specifications and scope-of-work documents and discussed the bid-submission date. After seeing the man out, Cedric closed the folder. "Well?"

"Seems pretty straightforward. We have a little time to get the bid done, so we'll be able to decide if it's something we want to take on with everything else."

"I agree. I want to wait until I know for sure how much extra time the strip mall is going to take."

Several minutes later, Desiree poked her head in the doorway, and Lorenzo was up and across the room in a flash. "Hey, baby." He placed a kiss on her lips. "What are you doing here?"

Desiree held up a bag. "I knew you and Cedric were working late, so I brought dinner."

Cedric came over and kissed her on the cheek. "Thanks. How're things at the shop?"

"Good. You should bring Randi by sometime. You might find something to spice up one of those date nights."

He laughed. He and Randi had no problems in that department. A vision of him drizzling that chocolate syrup over her body and taking his time licking it off surfaced in his mind. No, they didn't have *any* problems.

"Ced, you should try some of the edible massage oil. And get the four-ounce size. You'll need it." Lorenzo wrapped an arm around his wife. *"Trust me."*

Desiree elbowed him and lowered her head in embarrassment.

"It's too late to be embarrassed now," Cedric said.

She thrust the bag at Lorenzo and tried to hide her smile. "You two eat before it gets cold. I'm going home."

"Thanks, sweetheart. I should be home by eight thirty at the latest. Oh, do you think you can get away from the shop next Saturday around one for about three hours? And before you ask why, it's a surprise."

She divided a glance between Lorenzo and Cedric. "What are you two up to?"

"Something good. I promise."

"Probably. I'll let you know tomorrow." She came up on tiptoe to kiss Lorenzo. "See you later." She hugged Cedric. "I hope I get to meet Randi soon."

"We'll see." His phone rang and he saw Randi's name on the display.

"That must be her," Lorenzo said to Desiree. "See the goofy smile on his face?"

Desiree giggled. "Leave Cedric alone. I'm glad she makes you smile. Hurry up and answer the phone. You don't want to miss the call."

Cedric shook his head, turned his back and answered. "Hey, baby."

"Hey. I got your text. I should be good to go for Saturday. What are we doing?"

"I can't tell you."

"What do you mean you can't tell me? How am I supposed to know how to dress or what to bring?"

"Casual, and you don't need to bring anything except your sexy self."

"You know I have ways of getting it out of you," Randi said suggestively.

"You can give it your best shot, sweetheart, but I'm not telling. I have a few weapons in my arsenal, too, so two can play at that game." He opened his mouth to say something else, but remembered he wasn't alone. "I'll call you when I get home later."

"Why didn't you tell me you were still at work? I'm sorry."

"You don't need to apologize. I'd take talking to you over work anytime." Cedric turned slightly and met the amused smiles on Lorenzo and Desiree's faces.

"Aw, see, that's why I like you," Randi said. "The next time I see you, I'll show you just how much. I'll talk to you later."

"Yeah, you will." He disconnected and noticed that the two were still staring at him. He pointed to the bag. "The food's getting cold. And I don't want to hear one word." He hadn't seen Randi since their Friday night date and all he needed was an excuse. They were supposed to be going slow, but that was feeling more and more like a losing battle.

No matter how many times Randi asked or how many erotic promises she made, Cedric wouldn't budge on the surprise. She glanced over at the smile on his face as he drove. "I can't believe you still won't tell me where we're going."

"You don't trust me?"

"I trust you fine." She'd said the words without thinking, but realized she did trust him, even though they had known each other only a short time. It usually took her much longer to let her guard down. She hadn't figured out why he'd been able to slip so easily beneath the barrier around her heart.

Cedric's eyes left the road briefly. "I trust you, too."

She focused her attention on the passing scenery. A few minutes later, he parked in front of a house in a South Sacramento neighborhood. "This isn't one of your family members' houses, is it?" Surely he wouldn't bring her over to meet them blind.

"No, baby." He leaned over and kissed her cheek. "I'd let you know if you were meeting my family. However, Lorenzo and his wife will be joining us. And she probably nagged him the whole way, too, because he didn't tell her, either."

Randi shifted to face him and narrowed her eyes. "What are you two up to?"

He laughed. "That's the same thing Desiree asked." He pointed. "There they are." He got out, came around to her side of the car and helped her out.

She observed the proprietary way Lorenzo held his wife and the look of adoration on his face as he listened to whatever she was saying.

Cedric and Lorenzo greeted each other with a fist bump, then Cedric kissed the woman on her cheek. "Desiree, this is Randi Nichols. Randi, my cousin-in-law, Desiree. And you've already met Zo."

"Good to see you again, Randi," Lorenzo said.

"Same here." Randi felt somewhat awkward seeing him in a nonprofessional capacity. "It's nice to meet you,

Desiree." Desiree stood a couple of inches shorter than Randi and had a beautiful face and easygoing smile.

Desiree reached out and hugged Randi. "I'm so glad to finally meet you."

The gesture caught Randi by surprise and she shot a quick glance Cedric's way. He merely smiled.

"Okay, you two," Desiree said. "Whose house is this and why are we here? The suspense is killing me."

Randi smiled. She liked Desiree. "Me, too."

Cedric grasped Randi's hand. "Come on."

They walked up the driveway and Randi noticed a sign on the side door that said "glass studio," with an arrow pointing toward the backyard. Cedric held the gate open for her and Desiree to enter first. A few people were milling around, looking at a variety of custom glass items, from goblets and pumpkins to vases and bowls. "These are gorgeous. Are we picking out pieces?" Randi picked up a blue goblet with swirls of black and white, marveling at its intricacy, then set it down.

"Nope. You're going to make something," Cedric said.

She whipped her head around.

He stroked a finger down her cheek. "You haven't said it, but I can tell this case is wearing on you, sweetheart. In your line of work, you see fire cause so much destruction. I wanted you to have a chance to see some of its beauty." He placed a sweet kiss on her lips.

Emotions welled up inside her so strong she couldn't utter a word. Randi never cried, but she was on the verge of doing just that and blinked back the tears that threatened to fall. She threw her arms around him, not caring that they had an audience. "Thank you," she whispered.

"You're welcome."

Lorenzo started singing, "I'm in the money..."

She divided a glance between him and Cedric.

Cedric said, "Ignore him."

A woman approached, smiling. "Are you here for the paperweight experience?"

"Yes," Cedric answered. He gave their names.

"Great. Follow me."

They crossed the yard and went into an area set up as a workshop. She introduced them to Sheila, the creator of the glass art. On one side of the workshop was a huge furnace with a sliding panel in the front. A bench with metal pipes resembling armrests bracketing each side sat several feet behind the furnace. To the right of the bench was a metal table. The other side of the space held two more metal tables and a cabinet with numerous small drawers.

"This is so cool," Randi said.

Desiree came and stood next to Randi. "I totally agree."

"I'm glad you like it," Sheila said. "If you're ready, we can get started on your paperweight. Which of you is making it?"

Cedric and Lorenzo pointed to Randi and Desiree. Lorenzo said, "They're both making one."

"Okay." Sheila led them to the cabinet and pulled out a few drawers. "We need to pick out some colors. Who's first?"

Randi raised her hand in excitement. She'd never done anything like this and had never considered herself to be very creative. She left that to Iyana. She moved closer and saw what looked like very thin, colored dry spaghetti or angel-hair pasta. "What are those?"

"Glass rods called cane. When you finish, the colors will be swirled in the paperweight."

Randi studied the variety of canes. "How about purple, royal blue, emerald green, black and…red?"

Using wire cutters, Sheila cut a few pieces of each color into two-inch lengths, took them to the table across from the furnace and arranged them in a pattern. She picked up a six-foot metal pole with a rubber handle and beckoned to Randi. Sheila slid the furnace panel open a few inches and Randi immediately felt the heat, even though she stood a good distance away.

"Wow, that's hot."

"Yep, about two thousand degrees. That's why I only open the door a few inches and stand five feet back. Now, grab the end of the blowpipe so you can gather some molten glass."

Randi handed her phone to Cedric. "Here. I need you to record this." Following Sheila's instructions, Randi tilted the pipe into the glass. A small blob of glass appeared on the end, then she withdrew the pipe.

"Randi, keep rotating the blowpipe so the glass doesn't cool, and come on over to the marver and pick up your color."

Randi rolled the glass in the rods and they stuck out like spikes. Sheila directed her back to the furnace and she placed the blowpipe just inside the door, rotating it and watching as the rods curled around the glass. They went back to the table and rolled the ball back and forth, then to the furnace to gather more molten glass. Randi repeated the process twice more. A big smile on her face, she glanced over her shoulder to where Cedric, Lorenzo and Desiree stood watching. "Are you getting all of this, Cedric?"

"Every second," he answered with a chuckle.

"Do you want to have the appearance of bubbles inside?" Sheila asked.

"Ooh, yes."

Sheila put the rod inside a pineapple-shaped mold, then gathered a little more glass. Next, she had Randi sit on the workbench and retrieve a ladle-like object from a bucket of water. Sheila laid the pipe on the bench rails with the glass in the block and guided Randi's hand as she rolled the pipe back and forth. Randi replaced the block in the water, got a pair of long tweezers called jacks and did the same thing. The paperweight glowed bright orange and yellow as the round shape took hold.

"All right, Randi. I'm going to finish it. Cedric, would you like to help?"

"Sure."

Randi traded places with Cedric, took her phone from him and watched in fascination as they completed the process. At last, Sheila stood and held the blowpipe vertically, still rotating it. She carried it over to a small table covered with layers of a heatproof material, where she rested the paperweight end of the blowpipe. After a few minutes, the glass cooled enough for Randi to see the swirl of colors and bubbles emerging. Sheila held the blowpipe up with the paperweight hovering, and with a cylindrical metal piece, tapped the pipe about six inches from the end. The paperweight dropped onto the cloth.

"Randi, there are some brands in that box. You can choose one if you like." Sheila used a blowtorch to heat the top surface and used the end of the metal cylinder to flatten a small area. She heated it again and gestured to Randi.

Randi selected a double heart and pressed it into the

glass. She smiled up at Cedric and he leaned down and planted a brief kiss on her lips.

"You did a good job," he said.

"Thank you. That was so fun." She couldn't get over the experience of seeing simple glass transformed into something so beautiful, and all by fire. Cedric had been right, and she would never forget this day. He'd given her such a precious gift and as she gazed up at him, she knew she had fallen completely in love with him.

Chapter 14

Monday evening, Cedric stuck his earbuds in, cranked up the music and started his run on the treadmill. Unlike the last time he came to the gym, tonight he'd be working out alone. He'd considered asking Randi if she wanted to come but changed his mind. She was back on call and he didn't want to chance their workout being cut short. His mind went back to Saturday and a smile curved his lips. Her show of emotion had taken him completely by surprise. She always seemed so tough, but the tears glistening in her beautiful eyes told a different story. He'd fallen a little harder in that moment. Cedric had asked Lorenzo to record it on Cedric's phone, while he did the same using Randi's. He'd played the video at least a half a dozen times since then. From her bright smile and sparkling eyes, to her biting her lip in serious concentration, he had been totally captivated.

The sounds of old-school R&B filled his ears and he

increased his speed. Several televisions were mounted from the ceiling, showing everything from sports to politics. Cedric scanned the monitors, checking the scores in the baseball game and the basketball playoffs. His gaze went to the next monitor and he momentarily froze, causing him to miss a step. He cursed under his breath and quickly recovered. He disconnected the music and listened to the news report. The mayor had held a press conference about the fires earlier in the day and the news was showing the replay. He saw Randi standing to the far side, and her expression said she clearly didn't want to be there. Cedric's ears perked up when he heard the mayor mention her name.

"…along with Detective Warner have been working diligently to bring the arsonist to justice and with new evidence, I'm confident this will be over soon."

He frowned. She had new information? He realized she couldn't divulge everything, but if they had evidence that would solve the mystery of who torched his site, he wondered why she hadn't mentioned it. Throughout the past month, it had bugged him to no end, and he still couldn't come up with one plausible explanation. He was tempted to call her right now for answers but decided to wait. Any way he asked the question might mess up what they had going. He'd have to approach the subject in a different way. Cedric reconnected his music and finished his run. Afterward, he went through his weight training workout.

By the time he finished and made it home, his muscles were damn near at failure, but he felt good. He showered, then took his dinner out to the sunroom. He'd warmed up leftover chicken fajitas from yesterday. As he ate, he went through the one hundred-plus personal emails he hadn't checked in almost a week. Most were junk, but one had to do with renewing his license. Cedric starred it and made a mental note to pay it tomorrow. He clicked on one from an old classmate who planned to relocate to Sacramento and wanted to know the best construction companies to work with. He hadn't seen the man in almost a decade, but they'd kept in touch over the years. Of course, Cedric would say his company topped the list, but he wasn't looking to hire at the moment. However, if they secured the bid for the office building, things could change. He placed the half-eaten fajita on the plate, wiped his hand and sent back a list of four good companies he knew off the top of his head. He polished off the remainder of his food and washed it down with a glass of water.

Cedric picked up his phone, scrolled through the recent calls and hit the button next to Randi's name.

"Well, hello, sexy," Randi said when she answered.

He chuckled. "Hello, yourself. What are you up to?"

"Oh, I'm relaxing in a tub filled with a ton of bubbles. What about you?"

He groaned. "In about a minute, I'm going to be on my way to your house to join you." Just thinking about sitting behind her in the tub, gliding the soap over her silky skin, made him hard.

She laughed softly. "Not that I would mind, but I'd probably be done by the time you arrived. Though, I could be persuaded to take another...just in case I missed a spot or something."

"Or something. Randi, you know I don't have any problems jumping in my car, and if you keep it up, you *will* be needing that second bath."

"Mmm, tempting, but how about we save it for another time?"

Cedric glanced down at his watch. If he left now, it would be close to ten when he got there. They both had to work in the morning and he had to be in Elk Grove by seven thirty. With traffic, the drive to the south side could take almost an hour. So, yes, they'd have to wait. He wanted to spend some uninterrupted time with her. These two- and three-hour snatches of time weren't doing it for him anymore. "Yeah, we'll save it." He turned the conversation to the news story. "I saw you on TV tonight."

Randi let out a low growl. "I wanted to muzzle that man. He made it sound like we were five minutes from finding this guy and that's not the truth."

"He mentioned something about new evidence, too."

"Again, I don't know where he's getting his information from. Detective Warner was as shocked as I was. Believe me, Cedric, if I find out something, I'll let you know."

"I know." He didn't know why he felt such relief. "Sounds like the mayor is trying to appease the media to get them off his back."

"Probably. I'm just glad they'll all be calling the police and not our office."

He heard water in the background. "Are you getting out of the tub?"

"Talking about this messed up my mood."

"I'm sorry. Let's change the subject and see if I can't get you back into the mood."

"What do you want to talk about?"

"How when we're in that tub together I'm going to take my time and wash every part of your body. Of course, after I'm done, I'll have to do an inspection to make sure I haven't missed anything. That could take at least an hour…or more." He continued to describe in detail what the examination would entail. The more he talked, the more aroused he became. Coupled with her soft gasps and moans, he was close to exploding. He had to stop now.

"Don't stop," she whispered.

"Baby, I have to or we won't be waiting." Cedric sucked in a couple of deep breaths and let them out slowly. "If I didn't have an early day tomorrow, I'd already be on my way."

"I know. I have a long day coming up, too. Otherwise, I'd be waiting at the door."

He didn't need to know that. "We need to get off this phone before both of us end up not sleeping tonight."

"But it would be *so* worth it," Randi said with a little laugh.

"Once again, you're skating on thin ice."

She laughed harder.

"I'll talk to you tomorrow. Enjoy your bath."

"Oh, I will now, thanks to you."

"Randi—"

"Good night, my love."

He went still. This was the first time she'd ever used any kind of endearment. He opened his mouth to ask her to repeat it, but heard the beep, indicating she'd hung up. Tossing the phone onto the lounger, Cedric leaned his head back and closed his eyes. He saw a cold shower in his future. And another long, restless night. Yet, he couldn't stop smiling.

Randi's head fell forward and she jerked herself upright. She took a hasty glance around to make sure no one had seen her. It was barely noon, but she was having a hard time keeping her eyes open. Her body had been in such an uproar after playing around with Cedric last night, she couldn't sleep. She'd awakened this morning pretty much the same way. If she planned to get anything done, she'd need a pick-me-up. She typically shied away from those energy shots, but not today.

At lunch, she went to a nearby 7-Eleven and purchased one. Because she didn't know how her body would react, she drank only half. It obviously helped, since she was able to stay alert for the rest of the day and complete two reports.

Late in the day, Marlon stopped by her desk. "Hey, Randi. I saw the press conference yesterday. The mayor must be pretty desperate to put that kind of exaggeration out there."

"Brian said he's going to talk to the chief about it. This is the last thing we need. You know the media is going to be all over us asking questions if we don't find this guy, like yesterday." She got angry all over again thinking about it. She hadn't wanted to attend the press conference in the first place. Having her face plastered all over the television screen was something she tried to avoid. Thankfully, she hadn't been standing directly on the podium with Brian, the police chief and fire captain. Randi thought she'd stayed out of the line of the cameras, but Cedric had seen her. Automatically, her mind went back to their conversation. She could still hear his deep voice in her ear describing how he intended to touch and kiss her. A touch on her arm shattered her reverie. "I'm sorry. What did you say?"

"I asked if you were okay. You seemed a million miles away."

"Oh, I'm fine," she said quickly. "Just thinking about the arsonist and hoping we'll catch him soon. How did court go?"

"Fine, I guess. Cross-examination is tomorrow." Marlon had been called to testify at a preliminary hearing in the city's charge against a manufacturing company that had ignored prevention codes and had its building go up in flames. He checked his watch. "It's almost five. You want to grab a bite to eat?"

In the past, Randi wouldn't have hesitated to say yes. They, as well as two or three other of their coworkers, typically got together for dinner once or twice a month. She didn't have any plans with Cedric tonight but didn't know how she felt going out to dinner with another man, no matter how innocent.

"Jada and Hiram are coming, but Pat had something to do. We're thinking pizza."

That made her feel better. "Sure. I need to make some copies, then I'll be ready." She completed the task and, after agreeing on a pizza restaurant, they all left in their respective cars.

Randi had barely finished her first slice when she got the call about another fire. Marlon's phone buzzed right after.

"So much for dinner," Marlon said. "Be sure to save me and Randi a couple of slices for lunch tomorrow."

Hiram snorted. "Hey, man. No promises. My wife has had me on this eating program with her and I swear she's starving me. This is the first time I've had food with flavor in a month, so you might want to take those pieces now if you want to have some."

Randi and Jada laughed. Randi reached over and grabbed another slice and put it on a napkin. There would be no telling how long they'd be out there tonight and she worked better on a full stomach.

Marlon did the same. "Ready?" he asked Randi.

"As I'll ever be."

On the drive, her phone rang. She engaged the Bluetooth. "Hello."

"Hey, sweetheart. Are you available for me to collect on that bath tonight?"

She groaned. "I wish. I just got a call and I'm on my way to a scene."

"Construction site?"

"I don't know yet. I hope not."

"Call me when you get home."

"Cedric, it could be one or two o'clock in the morning when I get in. I don't want to wake you up."

"I don't care what time it is, just call. I know you've been doing this for years, but I didn't know you then. I do now and I need to know you're safe. So humor me, please."

"I'll call." What else could she say? And she didn't ever remember him saying please.

"Thank you. Be safe."

"I will." That he cared so much about her safety made her love him all the more. Not once had he suggested she get another job, and although she knew he wanted to ask her for information, he respected her position enough not to do it. Maybe she could let herself hope.

When the fire came into view, her heart sank. Not only was it another construction site, but the paramedics had arrived. She prayed that someone hadn't died. Randi went through the customary drill. Later, she caught up with Brian and found out that a security guard had been injured but thankfully hadn't died.

"According to the guard, he was doing his customary walk around the premises and someone hit him in the back of the head. He's lucky the firefighters got here when they did, otherwise we'd be having a different conversation. We've got to catch this guy before someone gets killed," Brian muttered.

She agreed wholeheartedly. Just the thought of someone dying made her stomach churn. "Did anyone see anything?"

He looked down at his notes. "I got a vague description from a witness named Lawrence Steele. He remembers seeing a white male with dark hair, around five-nine or five-ten, wearing jeans. That's it. And he wasn't sure if the man was actually leaving the site. He only saw him walking fast."

"Well, at least it's better than nothing. Have you considered that the first fire in March might not actually have been the first? I'm going to check to see if there were any others before that time."

"I don't remember any offhand, but if you find something, let me know."

"I will." Randi searched for Marlon and spotted him several feet away, talking to the fire captain. "I'm going to check with Marlon to see what the fire captain is saying."

"Okay."

He went one way and she went in the opposite direction. Her conversation with Marlon confirmed what Brian had told her. Once the fire was out, she and Marlon combed the outside of the building for evidence—they wouldn't be able to go inside until tomorrow or Thursday when it was deemed safe. For now, they concentrated on determining the points of origin.

"Hey, Marlon. I think we've got another sign." Randi took several pictures of the still-smoking, half-burned wood, and documented the location. It was similar to the one found at Cedric's site, but this time the word *pay* was clearly visible.

Marlon squatted next to her and shined his flashlight over the area. "Looks like the same color paint, too."

The paint signature hadn't yielded any results in the area the last time. Brian had mentioned widening the search, just in case it had been purchased somewhere else. However, so far, nothing had come up. It took them another three hours to gather all the preliminary evidence, then Randi dropped it off at the office so it could be delivered to the lab in the morning. She didn't make it home until almost two.

She headed straight for the shower and washed off the smell of smoke. It was the first time she'd been the lead on a serial case, and not being able to solve it had her beyond frustrated. Right now, however, all she wanted to do was fall into bed and sleep for a day. She flipped the covers back, slid between the cool sheets and sighed tiredly. Her eyes closed.

A moment later, Randi's eyes snapped open. *Cedric.* She really didn't want to wake him up, but she had promised. Reaching for her cell, she made the call.

"You home?" came the sleepy greeting.

"Yes. You should've just let me call you in the morning, instead of waking you up in the middle of the night."

"We've already had this conversation, baby. It said on the news someone was injured. How are you doing with all this?"

"I'm frustrated as hell that we can't find one solid lead to get this guy. Every piece of evidence that has some potential ends up being another dead end. It's almost May and this has been going on for two months."

"I can imagine you're pretty frustrated. I won't lie and say I'm not just as anxious for this to be over, because I am. I'd feel a whole lot better not having to worry about whether this idiot is going to go after another one of my sites. But I believe you'll find that one piece you're looking for."

"I'm glad one of us is confident. Right now, I'm not feeling that way." She couldn't believe she'd told him that. Randi rarely gave voice to her doubts or uncertainties, unless she was talking to her family, but lately, she seemed to have no problems opening herself up to Cedric.

"Sometimes, I feel the same way when I start a new project. I wonder if I'll be able to build it to whatever the specifications are or if the developer will be pleased with the finished product. I think these moments of fear and doubt go with the territory in any career, but as my dad always told me, as long as you do your very best, the rest will follow."

"Your father sounds like a special man."

"He is, and so is my mom. I consider myself blessed to have them."

She could hear the love and admiration in his voice and wondered if she would ever get a chance to meet them. "I feel the same about my parents." They fell silent for a moment. "I should let you go back to sleep. Thanks for talking to me."

"Are you going to be okay? If you need me to come hang out with you, I will."

His offer tempted her oh, so much. "No, I'm fine, but I appreciate the offer. I'll call you tomorrow."

"Okay. But if you change your mind, promise you'll call me."

"I promise. I… Good night, Cedric."

"Good night, sweetheart. Sleep well."

Randi held the phone against her heart. She had come so close to telling him how much she loved him.

Chapter 15

Cedric: Will you go away with me next weekend?

Randi: I'd like that. Where are we going?

Cedric: Lake Tahoe. The temps are still a little cool in May and the nights colder, but I'll keep you warm.

Randi: Count me in! Just let me know when we're leaving.

Cedric: I'll pick you up Friday around 7:30. Hopefully, some of the traffic will have died down by then.

Randi: I can't wait.

That had been a week ago and the conversation had stayed with him. Cedric sensed the simple bachelor lifestyle he'd always enjoyed changing in a big way, and he still was unsure how he felt about it. Yet he'd invited her to his private getaway. When he and Lorenzo first floated the idea of building homes in Lake Tahoe, Cedric had been adamant about not bringing any women outside of his family to his sacred space. Now he was breaking that rule. He seemed to be breaking all of them with Randi.

Shaking his head, he refocused on his task. Cedric worked alongside his employees out at the strip mall site, trying to shave at least two weeks off the delayed schedule. The early May temperatures had warmed up considerably, many of them hitting the eighties. With the longer days, he hadn't left once in the past week until almost seven, and more than half of his staff volunteered to stay overtime with him. The long hours had cut into his time with Randi, but then she'd been working just as many, if not more, hours. She'd even been going in on weekends. He recalled their middle-of-the-night conversation after the last fire. Her vulnerability had tempted him to drive over, despite her telling him she was okay. He'd wanted to wrap her in his arms and whisper that everything would be alright. He still did, only there hadn't been time. They needed this time away from the madness, and he was looking forward to their weekend.

Cedric checked the time. Today, he planned to leave on schedule. Cedric hadn't seen Randi in over a week and he missed her. For a man intent on staying single for the rest of his life, the admission was staggering. He'd forgotten to ask her about stopping by tonight, so he made a mental note to text her when he got back to his office. He finished working on the frame that would replace one of the damaged walls.

"Lana, I'm headed back to the office."

Lana poked her head from around the other side of the wall. "Okay. I'll let Carlos know. He went to pick up that order of nails." Carlos was the project foreman.

"Thanks." He stripped off his gloves, answered a few

questions from the workers, then left. When he got back to the office, he stopped at his assistant's desk to pick up his messages.

"There's only a few here. Lorenzo took care of the rest."

"Thanks, Loretta." He sifted through them as he walked to his desk and saw one from Preston, wanting to know if there had been any updates on the case. Cedric sighed. *I wish.*

He lowered himself into his chair and sent a text to Randi first, asking if she'd be home tonight, then picked up the phone to call Preston. "Preston, it's Cedric."

"Hey, Cedric. Can you hang on a second?"

"Sure." He heard muffled voices in the background. While waiting, he went through the rest of his messages. Most were from clients who had questions on their various projects, but nothing urgent. His hand froze on one from the McBride brothers. They were notorious for wanting to make extensive design changes midstream. He and Lorenzo had implemented steep costs for any late-stage alterations and, so far, the brothers hadn't asked for more.

"Sorry," Preston said, coming back on the line. "How's it going?"

"We're getting the framing redone on the damaged areas and should be done in two weeks. I got your message, and the police are still searching for the arsonist."

"It's been all over the news, and the mayor's saying they're close."

Cedric scrubbed a hand down his face. "I think the mayor is playing politics. I spoke to the fire investigator and they're still following leads, but they don't have anything yet."

Preston muttered a curse. "You don't think this guy is going to come back a second time, do you?"

"I don't, and I've hired a security company to do regular patrols." It was another expense they hadn't accounted for. However, Cedric and Lorenzo deemed it necessary. Neither of them wanted Preston to decide to take his business elsewhere. They had also agreed not to mention anything about the message left by the arsonist.

"Sounds good. And just so you know, aside from this hiccup, you do good work, so I don't plan to pull out."

"I appreciate that, Preston. We'll do everything we can to keep the delays to a minimum."

"Thanks. Talk to you soon."

Cedric hung up, leaned back in his chair and closed his eyes for a moment. A wave of fatigue hit him. He needed to get a good night's sleep tonight. In his twenties, he'd had no problems putting in extensive overtime, but his body was letting him know those days were long gone. As Randi had pointed out, he was closer to forty than not.

"So, you're sleeping on the job now?"

He rolled his head in Lorenzo's direction and sent him a hostile glare. "At least I'm not sitting on my ass in an office all day."

Smiling, Lorenzo crossed the room and dropped down into a chair. "Oh, then you're daydreaming about Randi?"

"No, I am not. Remember, I've been putting in twelve- and thirteen-hour days for the past week, so I haven't seen her since we went to the glassblowing place."

"All the more reason you'd be sitting here thinking about her. By the way, that was a good call. Desiree can't stop talking about her paperweight."

"Randi seemed to enjoy it, too." Her reaction surfaced in his mind, along with the myriad emotions that had gripped him. Her tear-bright eyes and whispered thanks as she hugged him had opened places in his heart he never knew existed. Cedric had gotten caught up in her excitement and it had him contemplating what to do next to make her happy.

"I don't think that adequately describes Randi's response. By the way she jumped all over you, I'd say she more than *seemed* to enjoy herself. She's in love with you."

Cedric frowned. "What are you talking about? She's never said anything like that."

Lorenzo shrugged. "Maybe not in words, but the way she looks at you says so. And you're in love with her, too."

Cedric sat up straight. "I—"

Lorenzo held up a hand. "If you're going to start lying about your feelings, you can save it. Don't forget I've known you all your life, and I do mean *all* your life. You have never done the things you've done for Randi with any other woman, and she's not the only one with stars in her eyes. I've watched you with her. You're falling hard, my brother."

Cedric slumped back against the chair. "I know," he finally admitted. "I don't understand what the difference is between her and any of the other women I've dated. It's not like there wasn't chemistry with them."

"That's the thing about love, you don't always understand." Lorenzo chuckled. "It's scary as hell because you feel like you're in a car with no brakes and about to go over a cliff."

"Yeah." His cousin had described exactly how Cedric felt. As hard as he had tried to keep from falling for Randi, he couldn't stop the sensations from taking over. It still scared him. "What am I supposed to do?"

"Let it happen, Ced. Randi is an intelligent and beautiful woman. I know you were happy with being single—so was I—but trust me when I tell you, finding that one special woman is worth every risk you're going to take."

He weighed Lorenzo's words. What if things didn't work out between them? Where would that leave Cedric? He didn't know anything about heartbreak because he hadn't been in a relationship that wasn't wholly physical.

"I know what you're thinking. You're wondering what happens if it doesn't work out, but you can't go into it with that mind-set. If you do, you'll be setting yourself up for failure because you won't give yourself completely. I tried that, remember? It doesn't work."

Cedric's cell chimed. He checked the display and read the message from Randi: I'll be home around 6p. If you want dinner, let me know. I owe you more than a salad. J

He typed back: See you at 6:30 and I'm fine with salad as long as it comes with kisses.

Lorenzo laughed and stood. "That smile on your face says you're going to have a good evening."

"Yeah, I am." What else could he say? "Before you go, I got a message from the McBrides. Any idea what they might want?"

"I hope they're not trying to make any more changes. I'm seriously considering not taking on any more of their projects."

"I hear you." In Cedric's mind, not all money was good money, especially if it interfered with their other contracts. "I'll call them tomorrow."

"You taking off soon?"

"As soon as you get out of my office. I need to go home and shower."

Lorenzo just shook his head. "I want my money."

Cedric smiled but didn't comment. At the rate he was going, he would definitely be paying that $200. He didn't see himself holding out until the end of the year or the end of the summer, for that matter. He was ready to lay his cards on the table and tell Randi he was in love with her over the weekend. Lorenzo seemed to think she felt the same, but if she didn't, she would by the time they made it back to Sacramento on Sunday. He planned to make sure she was falling right with him.

"Hey, Randi. Hang on a minute."

Randi groaned and rolled her eyes. *If one more person calls my name...* She had been trying to leave the office for the past fifteen minutes, but there had been one thing after another. As it stood, she should have been gone forty-five minutes ago, and if she didn't leave soon, she wouldn't have time to take a shower before Cedric arrived. She was anxious to get their weekend started. The thought of two days with no interruptions had her almost jumping for joy. She turned to her co-worker. "What's up, Dena?"

Dena waved an envelope in the air. "This is for you. It came to me by mistake."

"Thanks." The front had her name on it in big, bold letters. She assumed since it didn't have an address, it had come from somewhere in-house. Hopefully, it contained the information she had asked for on any previous construction site fires that had occurred in the past year. She stuck it in her bag. "See you on Monday." She

hurried out of the building and to her car before someone else stopped her. Blessedly, no one did.

Traffic was still a nightmare and it took her almost
double the normal time to get home. Randi stopped to
get the mail from her box and dumped it in her bag. She
threw up a wave at a neighbor and rushed inside. She
tossed the mail on the counter before grabbing some
cheese and crackers from the kitchen to stave off the
hunger and continued to her bedroom. Thankfully, she
had already packed and only needed to add her toiletries.
She finished her snack and went to take a quick shower.

When she finished, she still had a few minutes, so
she made half a turkey sandwich. It would take at least
two hours to get to Tahoe and she figured Cedric would
want to head straight there, instead of stopping for food.
Two bites in, her cell rang and she retrieved it from the
counter, where she'd left it plugged in to the charger.
"Hey, sis."

"Hey, girl. What are you doing on Sunday? Since
Mom and Dad are going to be here, I thought we'd go
out for brunch somewhere."

Randi had completely forgotten that her parents were
going to be there for the weekend. She'd had to opt out on
going to the premiere tonight because she hadn't known
what her schedule would look like and Iyana had needed
to get the tickets early. "I'm going to be out of town and
I'm not sure what time I'll be back. It definitely won't
be in time for brunch. What time are they flying out?"

"They aren't leaving until Monday. And where are
you going? The better question would be *who* you're
going with."

"I'm going up to Tahoe with Cedric," she said around
a bite of her sandwich.

"This is getting pretty serious."

"It feels that way, but he hasn't said anything aside from wanting us to take things one day at a time." It had been on her mind since last night when Cedric came over. After dinner he'd given her the most sensual bath she had ever had in her life. When he made love to her, there had been something different in his kiss and in the way he touched her. She couldn't put her finger on exactly what, but she'd felt it. She hadn't told her sister about Cedric's surprise or how it made her feel, and didn't have time to get into it tonight. "Cedric will be here in about ten minutes, so I'll call you when I get back. If it's not too late, I'll stop by."

"You might as well just bring Cedric because you know Dad is going to want to meet him, especially when I tell him why you can't come."

"More like grill him," Randi mumbled, popping the last bit into her mouth. Though she was an adult, Randi didn't like to flaunt certain aspects of her relationship in front of her parents and considered asking her sister not to mention the whole out-of-town thing. But she'd never made a practice of lying to her parents and wouldn't start now. That left another problem. Introducing Cedric to her father might give Cedric the impression she was looking to take the relationship to another level. "I don't know if that's a good idea. I don't want Cedric to think I'm trying to rush him into something more serious." Just because she had fallen in love with him didn't mean he felt the same.

"True, but like I said, Dad most likely won't take no for an answer. You can bring him here or I guarantee you he'll come to you."

"I know. Anyway, I need to go."

"Have fun."

"I plan to. Talk to you on Sunday." She thought about what Iyana had said. Randi knew her father would be full of questions if she chose not to bring Cedric over. She couldn't decide which would be worse—Cedric thinking she was pushing him toward the aisle or her father questioning Cedric like a prosecutor going after a witness on the stand. Neither situation appealed to her, but she had two days to figure it out.

She threw the napkin away and went to make sure she had everything ready. Cedric arrived a few minutes later and she could only stare at him. Her gaze roamed over his handsome face. He looked good in anything he wore, but somehow, the jeans and silk pullover tee made him even sexier. He unleashed his full-dimpled smile and her pulse skipped. He leaned in for a slow, sensual kiss that made her senses spin. "Hi," she finally managed.

"Hey. Ready?"

"Yep." She pointed to her bag on the floor by the door.

Cedric leaned down and picked it up. He held her gaze intently. "I missed you." He kissed her once more, took her hand and led her out to the car.

He'd missed her? The way he'd stared at her made her breath stack up in her throat.

"I checked the traffic before I left and we should make good time. There were a couple pockets farther up the hill, but hopefully, they'll be cleared up before we reach that area."

"As long as I don't have to drive, I'm not worried about the traffic," she said with a laugh. "I'm just going to make myself comfortable over here in the *passenger* seat and let you handle the road. Oh, and I'm sure with all those rules about how to treat a woman, at least one of them has to do with me not driving."

He chuckled. "There might be a rule like that, but I won't have any problems breaking it if you keep talking smack."

Randi laughed. She reached over, turned up the music and danced in her seat. "I'm not talking, I'm dancing to the music." She settled in the seat and as the miles passed, the tension she'd been carrying started to drop away in waves. She had no idea she was falling asleep until she felt a touch on her arm.

"Wake up, sleepyhead."

"Are we almost there?" Randi sat up, bleary eyed, and surveyed her surroundings. Not seeing anything resembling a hotel, she frowned. "Where are we? There aren't any hotels here." She saw only a handful of cabins. All sat a good distance apart but had a clear view of the lake.

Cedric laughed softly. "That's because we're not staying in a hotel." He helped her out of the car and gave her a quick kiss.

She remembered Tahoe had several cabin-lodging properties. This one seemed to be a newer development. She followed him up the driveway and across the wide covered porch to the front door. He unlocked it and gestured her in. Randi didn't know what she expected, but it certainly wasn't the elegantly decorated living room. Comfortable black leather furniture, modern lighting and gleaming wood floors hardly qualified as rustic. "Wow, cabins have come a long way." She ventured left and entered a full kitchen filled with modern appliances and a table that seated six. Cedric came in a moment later carrying several grocery bags and placed them on the counter.

"As soon as I bring everything in, I'll give you a tour."

She turned his way. "You've been here before?" It shouldn't have bothered her that he might have brought some other woman here, but it did.

"Yep."

Randi waited for him to elaborate, but he disappeared around the corner. Her curiosity would have to wait. Minutes later, she heard the front door close and he stuck his head in the kitchen.

"Okay, that's everything. Come on."

He led her through the two-story cabin. Two smaller bedrooms, each with its own bath, were on the lower level, while the master bedroom took up the entire upper floor. It had a sitting area with a fireplace and a private balcony with what she knew would be an incredible view of the lake. The bathroom reminded her of the one at Cedric's house. "This is really nice. How did you find this place?"

Cedric fit himself behind her and wrapped his arms around her. "I built it."

She spun around. "This is *your* house?"

He nodded. "The other two belong to Lorenzo and my brother, Jeremy. Jeremy bought his land a couple of years ago and asked me to design him a cabin. Zo and I decided to do the same before someone else bought up the rest of the land."

A perfect place for an intimate getaway, she thought grimly. "You must come up here a lot."

"No. I finished it just before winter last year and this is the first time I've been here for pleasure, instead of work."

Relief flooded her. "Thank you for inviting me to your special place."

"A special place for a special lady. Are you hungry?"

Still trying to process his statement, it took her a moment to answer. "Um, no, but I'm freezing. Do you have anything hot to drink?"

"I have just the thing." He turned on the fireplace, then adjusted the thermostat. They went back downstairs to the kitchen and he dug through the bags. He held up a tin. "Hot chocolate."

Randi smiled. "Too bad we don't have the stuff to make s'mores. That would make it perfect."

"Ah, but I do, and I have a fire pit where we can roast the marshmallows."

"You sure know how to start a weekend."

Cedric winked. "You ain't seen nothing yet, baby. As a matter of fact, I know exactly how to make it even better." He trailed kisses down her neck. "And I can warm you up much better than hot chocolate," he murmured.

She wholeheartedly agreed. *He* was the best hot chocolate she'd ever tasted, and she forgot all about being cold the moment his lips touched her skin.

"So, do you want the hot chocolate, or...?"

"I'll take the *or* for two hundred, Mr. Hunter." He swept her into his arms and strode up to his bedroom. He placed her on the bed and followed her down, his mouth connecting with hers. His hands were everywhere, heating her up from the inside out.

Cedric lifted his head and held her gaze. "I hadn't planned to do this tonight, but you make me lose control."

She reached up and caressed his face. "That makes two of us."

"I need to tell you something."

Randi studied his serious expression and her heart

started pounding. Was he having second thoughts about their relationship and wanting to go back to their original arrangement? She had promised herself she wouldn't settle in a relationship. Not sure she wanted to know, she asked the question anyway. "What is it?" The words came out far softer than she had intended.

A slight smile curved his lips. "I love you," he said simply.

Her heart pounded harder and faster. "You what?"

"I love you, Randi. You're everything I never knew I wanted. Falling for you has probably been the scariest thing that's ever happened to me, but it's also been the best. And I'm going to do all I can to make you fall right with me."

She stared at him, stunned. His passionate confession and tender expression were her undoing. Every emotion she had been trying to hold back rushed to the forefront, overwhelming her. She needed several seconds to form a reply. "I'm already there, Cedric, falling with you." What looked like relief washed over his face and he pressed his mouth against hers in a kiss so achingly sweet, tears stung her eyes. With a sensual smile, he took his time stripping away her clothes, touching and kissing each part of her body as he bared it.

"You take my breath away." Cedric resumed his quest, pausing to suckle and tease her breasts, before moving lower to part her legs. "Every part of you turns me on—your mind, your spirit…" His head dropped between her thighs and his tongue grazed her core.

Randi gasped and her hips flew off the bed.

"Your smile, every part of your beautiful body, your eyes…"

She moaned and shivered as his fingers probed her

slick, wet folds. She arched against his hand, riding out his wicked rhythm. The pressure built and bolts of pleasure tore through her as she screamed his name.

He stood, removed his clothes and donned a condom. "Are you warm yet?"

"Getting there, but I'm still a little cool." In reality, she was on fire and only he could quench it.

He lowered his head and slid his tongue between her parted lips at the same time as he eased his shaft inside her. He thrust in and out with long, deliberate strokes. His hand roamed over her body as he whispered tender endearments.

"Cedric," she called on a ragged moan. He rocked into her over and over, varying the length of his strokes, but keeping the same languid tempo. Randi wrapped her arms around his broad back, clutching him tighter. "I love you."

He increased the pace. Their groans and cries intensified until they convulsed together. "You're mine," he whispered.

All-consuming sensations spread throughout her body, electrifying her nerve endings and leaving her weak and dizzy. She wanted to be *his* for the rest of her life.

Chapter 16

On the drive home Sunday afternoon, Cedric couldn't stop smiling. He hated to admit it, but his cousins had been right. *This being-in-love thing isn't so bad.* And she loved him, too. The past thirty-six hours with Randi had been incredible, and he wished they could have stayed a little longer. Despite the cool temperatures, the sun had been shining and they'd enjoyed quiet time sitting on the beach, the porch or the balcony off his bedroom. They had also finally gotten around to making the s'mores and hot chocolate. Of course, the chocolate had tasted much better on her. Randi's voice broke into his thoughts.

"I had such a great time this weekend." She sighed contentedly. "I wish we could've stayed longer."

"I was just thinking the same thing. Maybe we can come back soon."

She laid a hand on his arm. "I'd like that." A few seconds later, she said, "I've been trying to come up with a way to tell you something, so I'm just going to say it."

When she paused, Cedric briefly glanced her way. "What?"

She met his gaze. "My parents are in town and my dad wants to meet you. My sister mentioned us dating."

He refocused on the road and sighed. He loved her, but meeting her parents meant moving to a whole new level. Then again, he now knew where he wanted this relationship to end up—the one place he always said he would never go. "That's fine. Where are they staying?"

"At my sister's. We can stop by on the way to my house, if that's okay."

"Works for me."

"I have to warn you, my dad can be pretty intense."

"I'll be fine." Or so he hoped. He'd never done this before and almost wished he had more time so he could ask one of his cousins what to expect. It was probably for the best, though. His family was already going to tease him mercilessly. He didn't need to give them any more ammunition. He could do this. All he had to do was tell the truth. He loved Randi and that should be enough. By the time they made it to Iyana's house, he was confident he could win them over.

"We're not going to stay long because I have to get myself ready for the week and I know you do, too."

"Do you want to get some dinner after we leave here?" he asked as they walked along the path leading to her sister's unit.

"Can I have a rain check? I need to do laundry and a few other things before it gets too late." She rang the doorbell.

"Of course, sweetheart." He kissed her.

"I guess the two of you didn't get enough of each other this weekend," Iyana said when she opened the door.

Randi jumped back and Cedric chuckled.

"Come on in. It's good to see you again, Cedric."

"Same here." Iyana stood a couple of inches shorter than Randi and had a beautiful round face. Whereas Randi's eyes were green, hers were a mixture of brown and green. Before they took two steps into the house, Randi and Iyana's parents appeared. Their mother smiled and Cedric knew instantly what Randi would look like in twenty years, and where she had gotten her green eyes. Her father, on the other hand, wore a scowl Cedric figured was supposed to be intimidating. He smiled inwardly.

"Hi, Mom and Dad," Randi said, hugging each of them. "This is Cedric Hunter. Cedric, my parents, Andrew and Debra Nichols."

Cedric extended his hand to Randi's father. "It's very nice to meet you, Mr. Nichols." He repeated the gesture with her mother. "I see where Randi gets her beauty from."

Mrs. Nichols laughed. "Oh, he's a charming one, Randi."

Randi shook her head and smiled. "Yeah, I know."

They all went into the living room and before Cedric could sit down good, Mr. Nichols asked, "Where did you meet my daughter?"

"A fire at one of my construction sites."

His brow lifted. "So you work in construction? How long have you been with the company?"

"I've been there since I could hold a hammer in my hand, but I didn't officially start working there until I was sixteen. My cousin and I assumed ownership of our family's construction business a little over a year ago."

"I see. And what are your intentions toward Randi?"

Taking Randi's hand, Cedric spoke to her father, but his eyes never left hers. "I intend to love and protect her for as long as she'll have me." Okay, so *that* wasn't what he'd planned to say. He was supposed to say something like they were still getting to know each other and he'd treat her with the utmost respect. But now he'd laid all his cards on the table.

Her father grunted.

Mrs. Nichols patted her husband's hand. "Oh, that's enough, Drew." She smiled Cedric's way. "I'm so glad my baby found someone like you."

"If I ever find a man who looks at me like that…" Iyana said, wistfully.

Everyone laughed and it broke the tension. Cedric told them a little more about his family and company.

"We need to get going," Randi said about twenty minutes later. "Cedric has an early morning tomorrow."

Smiling, Cedric stood and helped her up.

Mr. Nichols came to his feet. "It was really good to meet you, Cedric, and I hope to see you again soon."

"Same here, sir." He shook the proffered hand. "Mrs. Nichols, it was a pleasure." Instead of shaking his hand, she gathered him in a warm embrace.

"The pleasure was all mine."

They said their goodbyes and headed back to the car. "Well, how did I do?"

"This is the first time my dad has ever smiled at a guy I was dating. Did you mean what you said?"

"Every word, baby." He drove out of the lot and went toward the freeway.

"Where are you going? I only live a few minutes away."

"I figure since it's meet-the-parents day, you might as well meet mine. I don't want to be the only one on the hot seat."

Randi's mouth fell open. "You…" She punched him in the arm. "You can't just go over there and say, 'surprise.'"

"Sure I can. Watch me." He burst out laughing at the stunned look on her face. She didn't need to worry, his mother was going to love her. She didn't say another word for the rest of the drive.

When they arrived, she got out of the car and fidgeted with her clothes and hair. "Do I look okay?"

"Why are you so worried? You look beautiful." Since his parents weren't expecting him, he didn't use his key but rang the doorbell instead. Randi stepped behind him as if trying to hide, and he smiled.

"Cedric. I didn't know you were coming by," his mother said when she opened the door. "Come in, honey." Her questioning gaze met his.

"Hey, Mom. I didn't know I was coming until a few minutes ago. I have someone I want you to meet." He stepped aside. "Mom, this is Randi Nichols." His mother didn't even let him finish the rest of the introduction before she grabbed Randi's hands and pulled her into the house. Randi turned his way and he shrugged.

"Oh, my goodness. Please, come in. I'm so happy to meet you."

"It's nice to meet you too, Mrs. Hunter."

"She's a doll, Cedric."

She took Randi past the foyer and living room to the family room, leaving an amused Cedric to follow.

"Reuben, look who's here. And this is Randi. Isn't this wonderful?"

His father set aside the newspaper and came to his feet. "Randi, it's lovely to meet you."

"It's nice to meet you, Mr. Hunter."

He gestured to the sofa. "Please have a seat." He turned to Cedric. "I'm glad to see you got everything straightened out, son."

"So am I. Mom, Randi and I are dating, but can you not call everybody in the family tonight to tell them?"

She feigned innocence. "I wasn't going to call everybody."

"Uh-huh. Randi, don't let that innocent look fool you. She's been waiting for I don't know how long for this moment. My entire family is going to know I brought you here before we make it out of the driveway."

Randi laughed. "It's okay. My mom is probably going to do the same thing."

"See," his mother said, "she said it's okay. This is what mothers do. How did you two meet?"

They ran down the same information they'd shared with Randi's parents and the fact that Randi used to work as a firefighter.

"I applaud you, Randi. We women can do whatever we put our minds to. Forgive me, I was so excited about meeting you I forgot to offer you anything. Would you like something to eat or drink?"

"No, thank you."

"We can't stay," Cedric said. "I just wanted you to meet Randi and to let you know that you've gotten your wish."

His mother's brows knitted in confusion. "What wish?"

"That I'd find someone." He brought Randi's hand to his lips and placed a kiss on the back. "I did and I'm in love with her." Cedric had never seen his mother rendered speechless, but his announcement had done just that.

"And I love him, too," Randi said, smiling at Cedric.

Apparently, that was all his mother needed to hear because she started crying. "I'm so happy. *Hallelujah!*"

Cedric's father shook his head and chuckled. "I'm glad you found your special girl, Cedric."

Cedric focused his gaze on the woman who had come into his life and turned it on its head. "So am I, Dad." They chatted a few minutes longer, but when his mother started talking about lunches and spa days, Randi's shell-shocked face told all. "Ah, Mom, we'll have to talk about this another time," Cedric said. "I need to take Randi home."

"Oh, okay. But I expect you to bring her to dinner next week."

"We'll let you know." He grabbed Randi's hand, said a hasty goodbye and hustled them out of the house.

On the drive, Randi said, "Your mom was a little excited."

"Sorry about that. I should've warned you. You're the first woman I've introduced to them, so she's going to be a little over the top for a while. All my other cousins are married and she'd been on me and Jeremy."

She laughed. "Well, my mom does the same. I guess it's a mama thing."

"I guess." As he'd predicted, his parents loved her. Just like him. He was reluctant to leave once they made it back to her place. Waking up to her for the past two mornings had him really considering spending the night.

He carried her bag inside and placed it on the chair, then followed her to the kitchen.

"You want something to drink?"

"Nah, I'm good."

She got a glass of water and came to the breakfast bar where he stood. "I don't know how I'm going to sleep by myself tonight. I kind of like snuggling next to you."

Cedric did, too. He'd awakened several times to find her sprawled across his body, her arm draped around his middle. In the past, he'd always avoided lingering after his encounters because intimacy was never the goal. With her, he found he enjoyed that almost as much as the physical parts. "I can always stay the night."

Randi laughed and flipped through the mail "Yeah, but I don't think we'd get too much sleep."

"That's the point," he said, nuzzling her neck.

She stiffened and gasped

"What's wrong?"

"I... This came for me at work and I thought it was some information I requested."

He glanced over her shoulder and read the letter. Someone was warning her off the arson case. It didn't have a signature. "I don't like this."

"Neither do I. Why would they send this?"

"We need to call the police and I think you should let someone else handle the case."

She rounded on him, her eyes blazing. *"Excuse me? I will call Detective Warner and let him know, but this is my job and I'm not handing it off to someone else."*

"No, you could get hurt."

"Cedric, I went into burning buildings for over six years. This is not even close to being that dangerous.

And if I'm able to get an agent position within the ATF, I'll be in far more intense situations."

"Baby, look." He couldn't take it if something happened to her.

"No, *you look*. You don't get to tell me how to do my job."

He took a deep, calming breath. "Randi, I'm not telling you how to do your job or saying you need to find another one. I love you and I just don't want anything to happen to you."

She snorted. "So, if I told you I didn't want you to climb another ladder or scaffold, would you do it?"

"That's different."

"Is it really? You could fall off the damn thing and get hurt, too, or even killed. But I wouldn't ask you to stop doing the job you love. Yes, what I do comes with risk, but it's *my* choice. If I get a similar case down the line, am I supposed to say, 'Sorry, I can't take it, it's too dangerous'?" She folded her arms and narrowed her eyes. "Is this another one of those chivalrous rules you grew up with? I thought you were all for women doing whatever job made them happy."

"What? No. I am." Cedric ran a frustrated hand over his head. Obviously, he wasn't explaining himself well. He reached for her and she pushed his hand away. "Randi—"

"You said you admired me for doing what makes me happy. That has to include me staying on this case. I need to know that you can deal with my choice."

He remained silent. If he said yes, it could mean her getting injured or killed. However, if he said no... Their eyes held for a long moment, then she turned away.

"I see. I love you, Cedric, but I don't know if this is

going to work. Maybe we both need to take some time and figure out what we really want."

"I already know what I want—*you*."

Tears filled her eyes. "But that means having all of me, not just the safe parts. And I don't think you're ready for that right now."

He opened his mouth to tell her he was ready, but she held up a hand.

"Just go, Cedric. Let's not make this any worse than it is."

"Randi, I—" She shook her head. He sighed. "No matter what you think, I do love you." He placed a soft kiss on her lips and walked out. In less than ten minutes, his world had come crashing down and he had no idea how to fix it.

The next few days went by in a blur. Randi had called Brian Sunday night after Cedric left and turned over the letter. After that she'd cried herself to sleep. Instead of things getting better as the days passed, they had gotten worse. She missed Cedric so much. She totally understood his concerns because they mirrored her family's. But her family had learned to respect her career choice in spite of those fears. The fact that Cedric didn't answer her question about being able to deal with this aspect of her job had solidified her decision to end the relationship. If he had issues with one letter, he certainly wouldn't be able to take it if she got a position with the ATF. By Friday, the hurt hadn't lessened, but she tried to bury her heartbreak and focus on her job.

Randi had finally gotten the information she had requested on previous construction site fires from the lead investigators and had been surprised to find three others.

Although the fire reports were available on the database, oftentimes the investigators kept additional notes. She always did in case she was called to testify in a case. The earliest incident was almost a year ago, but she'd ruled that out as being connected. That fire had been caused by a space heater left on by one of the workers. Randi read through the report on a second one that happened in October and found a few similarities, but nothing concrete. Because of the timing, it could have been some Halloween prank. The third one happened around Christmas and seemed to have a few more markers, particularly the fact that it had three points of origin. She had a meeting with Brian in an hour and would update him on what she'd found.

Randi was so engrossed in reading that it took her a moment to realize her cell was buzzing. She picked it up and saw Cedric's name on the display. Her finger hovered over the accept button for a couple of seconds before she hit Ignore. She closed her eyes to block out the pain. She couldn't talk to him right now. Forcing her emotions down, she refocused on the report in front of her. Or at least tried to. After reading the same sentence three times, she set it aside, got up and went outside to clear her head.

It was eleven in the morning, but the early May temperatures had already risen to near eighty. They were going to be in for another hot summer. She stared up at the sky. She'd thought nothing could compare with last year's breakup, but she was dead wrong. In hindsight, she realized she hadn't really been in love back then. True, she'd experienced some level of melancholy for a short while, but nothing like she felt now. She would probably end up talking to Cedric at some point, but she just wasn't ready because it would only remind her of a love she couldn't have. He'd called and texted every day and she had ignored them all. She hadn't even bothered to read the texts or listen to the messages, but she couldn't make herself delete them, either. Randi inhaled deeply and let the breath out slowly. She repeated the process twice more. Usually, it helped, but not this time.

Her cell buzzed again and she hoped it wasn't Cedric calling back. She sighed in relief upon seeing Brian's name on the display. "Hey, Brian."

"Hey, Randi. I know it's a little earlier than our scheduled meeting time, but I'm just down the street."

"Actually, now works fine." She needed as many distractions as she could get. "I found some information on the other fires that might be of interest."

"Good. See you in a few minutes."

Randi went back to her desk and gathered the two reports. She had highlighted the key information to make it easier to find.

Brian arrived ten minutes later and they sat going over what she'd found. "I'd like to talk to the owners to find out if they've had any employee problems. Want to take a ride?"

"Sure." She locked her desk and followed him out to his car. As he drove off, she checked the addresses of the companies. "One is in the Del Paso Heights area and the other one in Roseville." Her stomach clenched. She double-checked the address to make sure it wasn't near Cedric's office and relaxed when she realized the two offices were nowhere near each other.

"Let's start here and work our way out."

She rattled off the Del Paso Heights address and he input it into the GPS. "Have you found out anything about that letter?" Contrary to what she let on, it had rattled her.

"Not sure how your name came up, but I think we have a leak. The only thing I've found so far is that someone told the media you have a critical piece of information that's linked to the arsonist."

"The paint?"

"I don't know. They didn't report any specifics. Apparently, the story ran on the news late Thursday night."

She'd missed the news that night because Cedric had come over. An image of them in her tub rose in her mind and she pushed it away. "So, if he'd seen it, he could've easily dropped off the envelope on Friday."

"Bingo. The lab didn't find any fingerprints, so there's not much we can do. As far as we know, he doesn't have your home address, but just in case he does, I can see about getting a squad car to drive by a couple times a night."

"That's not necessary. My complex is gated." However, Randi would be taking extra precautions when she went in and out of her place until they caught this person.

Brian parked in front of the first office and they went inside. He introduced himself and Randi and flashed his badge. "Is Mr. Barton in? We'd like to talk to him about the fire at his site in October."

The receptionist's nervous gaze darted between Brian and Randi. "Just a minute." She lifted the receiver and made the call. "He'll be right with you."

A man came toward them shortly afterward. He was short, stocky, fortyish and balding. "I'm Craig Barton. We can talk in my office." They followed him the way he'd come and into a cramped workspace. "Have a seat. You wanted to talk about the fire?"

"Yes," Brian said. "The report indicated that it might have been arson."

"It did, but the police haven't been able to find out much else. Have you found something?" He paused. "Do you think it's connected to the ones happening now?"

"We don't know. Around the time of the fire, had you had problems with any of your employees?"

Mr. Barton leaned back in his chair. "Not at all. And I haven't had any since then. I actually had to hire a few day workers to get that site back on schedule."

Randi listened as Brian asked the man a few more questions related to the employees and competition with other companies. In the end, they were no closer than they had been before arriving. They thanked Mr. Barton and went to the next site. She and Brian ended up having to wait twenty minutes while the owner finished up a conference call.

"Mr. Lockett will see you now," the assistant said, gesturing them into the office.

Mr. Lockett stood and extended his hand. After the introductions, they all sat.

Brian started with the same line of questioning.

Mr. Lockett didn't have to think long before he nodded. "There was this one guy, Tommy Glaskins. We finished a project two weeks before Christmas and I had hired some extra workers to get it done on time. They all knew there was a possibility it was only a one-job offer, but Tommy thought he'd be the exception because he's the cousin of one of my project managers. When he didn't get picked up, he threw a fit. Came in, started yelling, flipped a chair. Said I'd regret it. I threatened to call the police and he left. Two days later, I walked out of here late in the evening and found my car covered in paint."

"What color?" Randi asked.

"Gray."

She and Brian shared a look.

Brian leaned forward. "When did the fire happen?"

"About a week later. I'd swear he set that fire, but without proof, there was nothing I could do."

Because there had been cigarette butts found at the site, the fire hadn't been definitively ruled arson, but Randi's gut was now telling her otherwise.

"Do you have the contact information for Mr. Glaskins?" Brian asked.

"I can ask my assistant to dig it up. Do you think he might have done it?"

"That's what we'd like to find out."

Mr. Lockett called his assistant and asked her to bring in the information.

Randi jotted down some notes. "Mr. Lockett, has anyone called asking for references for Mr. Glaskins?"

He drummed his fingers on the desk. "As a matter of fact, I got a couple of calls around the beginning of the year, and then another one about two weeks ago. I couldn't tell you the names of the earlier companies, but I should have a record of that recent one because I was out of the office when they called and my secretary took a message." When the assistant came in with Tommy's information, Mr. Lockett asked her to bring in the message file.

Armed with the information, they left. They'd need to call all the owners of the recently damaged sites, including Cedric, and ask about Tommy Glaskins. That was one call Randi wasn't looking forward to making.

Chapter 17

"Since we're in Roseville, we can stop over at Hunter Construction and see if Mr. Glaskins's name rings a bell," Brian said as they got back into the car.

Randi's heart sank. She'd wanted to avoid seeing Cedric for as long as possible. But she couldn't very well say that to the detective. "Okay." With any luck, he'd be out of the office and Lorenzo could answer their questions. Then again, she knew Cedric and Lorenzo were close, and he more than likely would know what had happened between them. *This is just great. Reason number two hundred and fifty why I should have just ended it after that first date.* The closer they came to the office, the faster her pulse raced. Randi gave herself a pep talk. They'd be in and out in a few minutes and she and Cedric wouldn't be alone at any point. She could do this. Only she hadn't counted on the effect seeing him again would have on her. Cedric was talking to his assistant when

Randi and Brian walked up, and when his eyes locked on hers, it took everything inside her not to launch herself into his arms.

"Detective Warner, Ms. Nichols, how can I help you?" Cedric asked.

Brian stepped forward. "Do you have a few minutes?"

"Sure. Let's go into my office. Loretta, we'll finish up after."

Cedric led them inside and closed the door.

Before Randi could sit, he was there, pulling out her chair. His body brushed against hers and the contact was just enough to remind her how much she wanted his touch.

He rounded the desk. "Is this about the fire?"

"Yes." Brian's cell rang just as he opened his mouth to elaborate. He glanced down. "I need to take this. It shouldn't be more than a minute." He quickly left the office.

Randi tried to avoid looking at Cedric and pretended to focus on the notepad in her hand.

"How are you, baby?" Cedric asked quietly.

She lifted her chin. "Fine."

"I'm not."

She saw the pain and misery in his eyes and didn't want to be moved.

"I miss talking to you, touching you, kissing you…"

"Cedric, please don't," she whispered, barely holding it together.

"Loving you."

She was a heartbeat from breaking down and willed back the tears threatening to fall.

"I need to talk to you, Randi. Do you know how hard it's been not holding you in my arms? Five days is a long time to be without you. Please, ba—."

Brian came back into the room.

Randi breathed a sigh of relief. Had that phone call lasted one more second, he might have caught them in a serious lip-lock. Cedric saying *please* had her damn near ready to jump across the desk. She was just that close to succumbing.

"Sorry for the interruption. Mr. Hunter, do you recall interviewing a Tommy Glaskins sometime this year?"

"Not offhand. But I did hire two people around the beginning of March." Cedric turned toward his computer. "I can check my appointments." He pressed a few keys and studied the screen. "Yes, he's on here. I didn't hire him because his reference indicated he might be a hothead. I usually make a notation on everyone I interview, in case they try to circle back around sometime in the future. Do you think he's the one who set fire to my site?"

"We're not certain." Brian stood. "Thanks for your time. I'll be in touch if I find out anything else."

Cedric rose to his feet and shook the detective's hand. "Thanks." He extended his hand toward Randi. "Ms. Nichols."

Randi hesitated briefly, knowing she couldn't refuse. "Mr. Hunter." He clasped her hand gently and stared intently into her eyes.

"Thanks for all your help."

She attempted to pull away, but he held on a little longer before finally releasing her hand. She read the plea in his eyes. "You're welcome." She turned and walked out without looking back.

Randi drove straight to Iyana's house after work. She'd texted her sister after leaving Cedric's office to make sure she'd be home because she needed to talk to someone. She'd toyed with calling her mother, but her mother would go straight to her father and that's the last thing she wanted right now.

Iyana opened the door and pulled Randi in. "I've got the wine already poured."

Randi smiled for the first time in five days. "Maybe you should bring the bottle." She dropped down on the sofa and leaned her head back. "This has been the worst week of my life." Everything reminded her of Cedric—a song on the radio, the hot chocolate in her cabinet, the gym—*everything*. Her sister came back, handed her a glass, then sat next to her. Randi immediately took a huge gulp.

"Have you talked to him yet?"

"No, but I had to go to his office with Detective Warner today." *I miss talking to you, touching you, kissing you...loving you.* His words came back in a rush. She set the glass down and the tears she'd been holding back came in full force. "Why is this so hard?"

Iyana hugged Randi. "Just like you told me once, it's hard because it's your heart. But your situation is different from mine. Cedric still loves you, sis. He's worried about your safety and I can't be mad at him for that. I truly believe you two can work this out."

"I don't know. What if it happens again? I want to work for the ATF and I'm not going to give up my dream."

"Who says you'll have to? I bet Cedric is kicking himself right now. When you saw him, how did he act?"

Randi refused to say because she knew her sister would probably pick up the phone and call Cedric herself.

"You're not talking, so I guess that means he's as miserable as you." A smile played around her mouth. "You really ought to call him. I'll set it up, if you like."

"No! There's no telling what kind of trouble you'd start."

She shrugged. "Just trying to help. I want you to be happy, Randi, and I know Cedric is perfect for you."

"I'll think about it."

Iyana took a sip of her wine. "I wouldn't wait too long. You don't want some other sister to snap him up. You're lucky we're sisters, otherwise I might've had to do a little hip swivel past him."

"You are outrageous." Randi recalled the jealousy she'd felt when she thought he'd taken another woman to his cabin.

"I know, but I'm serious. Remember how they made those pro and con lists on *Why Did I Get Married?* You should do the same."

Randi didn't need to make a list to know the pros far outweighed the cons. She picked up the phone.

Friday evening, Cedric sat in Lorenzo and Desiree's family room as miserable as he'd ever been. They had invited him and Jeremy over to cheer him up, as Desiree had put it. The only thing that would lift his spirits was getting things straight with Randi. He couldn't eat or sleep and his concentration had dropped to an all-time low. He hadn't made any headway on anything since she walked out of his office earlier.

"I caught a glimpse of Randi today when she and the detective were leaving. She looks as pitiful as you. When are you going to talk to her?"

Cedric didn't even lift his head. "Zo, it takes two people to talk. I've called, texted and was this close to begging today." He snapped his fingers for emphasis. "The detective came back before we could really talk."

"And her career?" Jeremy asked. "You know she's right about your job being just as dangerous. Remember that time you fell off the ladder and fractured your ankle?"

Cedric scowled at his brother. "Whose side are you on?" He didn't need to be reminded. He'd been seventeen at the time and one of the ladder rungs had snapped. The only saving grace was that Cedric had been just four feet from the ground.

"Yours. If you love her, you've got to decide what's more important—living your life without her or supporting her career choice and having her by your side forever."

The thought of her being harmed in any way caused a churning in his gut. "She wants to be an ATF agent. I googled it and I'm not sure how I'd handle her basically doing what police officers do."

Lorenzo stretched. "Then you need to let her go."

Cedric stared at his cousin incredulously. Just the thought made his heart clench. "I can't."

"Then you know what you need to do. Love requires risk. Are you willing to take it?"

"Ced, Mom is crazy about Randi and she said she's never seen you so happy. I haven't, either."

Randi did make him happy. He buried his head in his hands. He couldn't lose her.

"When you're ready to win her back, I have something guaranteed to help." Desiree handed Cedric a small gift bag.

Lorenzo chuckled.

"What is it?" Cedric asked. He read the label. "Massage oil?"

"Yep. It warms when you rub it in, gets even hotter

when you blow on it, and it's edible," she added with a wink. "How do you think I got your cousin back when I almost messed up our relationship because of my fears?"

Jeremy burst out laughing. "You think you can whip me up some of that when I find my woman?"

"Sure. Just let me know."

Cedric kissed her cheek. "Thanks." It was a nice gesture, but as it stood right now, he didn't know if he'd ever be able to use it.

She patted his arm and left the room.

Jeremy pulled out his wallet. "Zo, I hate to admit it, but you were right." He laid two $100 bills on the table.

"Thanks," Lorenzo said with a wide grin.

Cedric pushed to his feet. "I'm going to go."

Lorenzo walked him to the door. "I hope you two can work it out."

"So do I. See you later." He sat in his car minutes later, deciding what to do. He really didn't want to go home. He used to crave the silence of his house, but now he wanted to fill it with Randi's laughter.

Cedric started the car. He backed out of his parking spot just as his cell chimed a text. When he saw Randi's name, his chest tightened. He was almost afraid to read the message. Can you meet me at the park near my house in 30 minutes? He typed back one word: Yes!

He had to constantly watch his speed as he drove. In his rush to get to the park, he'd found himself going almost fifteen miles over the speed limit twice. To keep from possibly getting a ticket, he set the cruise control.

Cedric spotted her car as soon as he turned into the lot. She must have seen him because she got out and leaned against her door. He parked next to her and it took all his control not to haul her into his arms and kiss her. "Hey."

"Hi."

Not able to resist, he gathered her in his embrace and held her close. She rested her head against his shoulder. Neither of them spoke. Having her in his arms again felt good, and he sensed his world tilting back into position. At length, he released her. "Do you want to go for a walk?"

"Yes."

He entwined their fingers and they started down the path in companionable silence. Because he was the one to mess things up, he had to be the one to fix them. "I'm sorry."

"So am I. I know you're concerned, and I love you for it. When I decided on this career path, I knew there were risks. I could even die. It's not something I take lightly, and I try to do everything I can to remain safe." Randi stopped walking. "I want you to be part of my life, Cedric, and I want my job, too."

His hands framed her face. "I know that, and I want you to do your job. I'll be worried, but to have you, I'll swallow my fears. I'll even help you study and work out for your ATF exam, because I think you'll make a damned good agent. I don't care what you do as long as at the end of the day, you come home to me."

She searched his face. "Are you saying…?"

"I'm saying I love you and I want all the parts of you." She still looked skeptical. "I need you in my life, Randi, and I'll do whatever it takes to keep you with me. I never imagined I'd find someone like you and I can't give you up. I *won't* give you up, not without a fight." He heard her cell ring and groaned inwardly. She still hadn't answered him. Randi stepped back and answered her phone. From the bits and pieces he could gather, he knew this conversation was going to be put on hold.

Randi finished the call and pocketed the phone. "I have to go. There's a lead on the arsonist."

She studied him, seemingly gauging his reaction. "Go catch this guy and be safe." They reversed their course and headed back to the parking lot. "Can we have dinner tomorrow?"

"Yes."

When they reached their cars, he held her door open for her. "Call me when you get home, no matter how late."

"I will. And Cedric?"

"Yeah, baby."

"I love you and I need you in my life, too." She gave him a soft smile.

Cedric returned her smile and the pressure in his chest eased. He gave her a quick kiss and closed the door behind her. He waited until she'd driven off before getting into his car. Maybe he'd get to use that massage oil after all.

Chapter 18

Randi arrived at the same time as Detective Warner and three other unmarked police cars. He'd asked her to park half a block away in a strip mall lot. She got out of her car and met him halfway.

"What's going on?"

"I tracked down the owner of the construction company Mr. Lockett gave us, the one who called him just recently for a reference for Tommy Gaskins. The owner has two building sites, and I've had undercovers staking out both. I got a call saying that the same man has passed by this site four times."

"Did he have anything with him, like a paint can?"

Brian shook his head. "No. It looks like he's just casing the joint. If he comes back, we want to be ready."

From where they were parked and with the days being longer, the sun had just begun to set and they had a clear view of the construction site. She trained her eyes on the area and prayed they could end this tonight.

More than an hour had passed when Brian asked, "I was meaning to ask you, did something happen between you and Mr. Hunter today?"

She should have known he'd pick up on the vibes. Randi faced him. "Yes. Love happened."

His eyes widened. "You and...? When did that happen?"

Randi chuckled. "I thought you were a detective."

"I am, but according to the women in my life, I'm clueless when it comes to matters of the heart," he said with a laugh.

She rolled her eyes. "Men."

Their laughter was cut short when Brian's cell buzzed. "Yeah." He listened and nodded. "We're on our way." He pocketed the phone. "Showtime. He's around the back trying to cut the fence. Stay behind me."

Randi got her Ziploc filled with gloves out of her car and stuffed it into her pocket. "Okay." They crossed the street and after checking their surroundings, Brian unlocked the gate with the key given to him by the owner. Four other officers joined them, and Brian silently gave them orders. They crept around to the opposite side of the building.

Brian took a quick peek. "Looks like he's painting something," he said, his voice barely audible.

The sign. At least they'd get the paint this time and she could compare it with the other samples.

Once everyone was in position, Brian gave the go command. The officers converged on the man and Brian, with his gun drawn, said, "Drop it! Stand up slowly and keep your hands where I can see them."

Randi observed the action from her spot around the corner. The man didn't look like he wanted to comply with the order, and Brian repeated his command. After a few tense moments, the man slowly got to his feet. Before any of the officers could move, the man tried to make a run for it. One of the officers tackled him less than ten steps in. Randi shook her head. Once the man had been handcuffed and led away, she approached and squatted next to Brian.

"This looks like all the same gear he used at the previous fires." The paint, gasoline, lighter and the wood painted with the complete message: *You'll pay Arnold.* It was finally over.

"I'm going to go talk to him," Brian said.

He left Randi to collect the evidence. She donned her gloves, took several photos, then drove her car carrying her equipment over and carefully packaged and labeled everything. When she finished, she checked in with Brian and left to drop the samples off at the office.

Randi made it home just before eleven. She was anxious to talk to Cedric but decided to shower first. Once she'd settled on her bed, she called him.

"Hey." Cedric had picked up on the first ring. "How did it go?"

"We caught him."

"Thank goodness. Do you know why he was doing it?"

She didn't see any harm in telling him. It would most likely make the news. "From what we can gather, he was doing it for revenge. He'd been let go from a construction crew just before Christmas. That's when he set that first site on fire. Then he went after every one of you who turned him down for employment."

He muttered a curse. "So now I need to start checking for crazy in a person's background when I'm hiring? I'll keep these details to myself until you say it's okay to share."

"Thank you." It had never crossed her mind that he wouldn't keep her confidence.

"How are you doing?"

"Better now that things are getting straightened out between us. I was miserable," she confessed.

"That makes two of us."

Though they were on the right track, she still needed to be sure he understood everything he was signing up for. "We need to talk about what's going to happen if I'm able to get on with the ATF."

"There's no *if* about it. You will get on with them. And you're right. I did some research and I know you'll have to go through extensive training."

"You did?"

"Of course. This is your dream, sweetheart, and I'm going to do everything I can to help you make it come true."

Randi had thought she couldn't love him any more than she already did, but his words filled her heart until it nearly burst out of her chest. "I appreciate that, Cedric. You realize the training is in Georgia, and it'll be about six months for both parts."

"I saw that. It means I'm going to rack up a lot of frequent-flier miles."

She laughed. "I don't know how I'm going to last that long without seeing you whenever I want. This week seriously tested me."

"You and me, both. Things weren't right between us this week, but when you leave for Georgia, that won't be the case. You'll be taking my love with you and that'll get us through. That and technology," Cedric added with a little chuckle.

"*Yes*, for real!" Thank goodness for texting, email and especially videoconferencing. Hearing his voice was good, but she needed to see him, too. "So, we're going to do this?"

"If you mean us staying together, then yes. I'm in this for the long haul. I told you earlier I need you in my life, but I also want you there. Are you with me?"

"All the way." Randi scooted down in the bed and smiled.

"I can't tell you how happy I am to hear that. I know this is jumping the gun a bit, but since we're talking about the future, do you think you'll want to have children? Will you be able to, as an agent?"

Children means he's really thinking long-term. "I do want them and, yes, I can do both. What about you?"

"I'd never thought about it, honestly, because I always envisioned myself staying single. I'd planned to be the cool uncle to all my nieces and nephews. But I can see myself being a dad."

She giggled. "Well, you'd better get on it. You are pushing forty, you know."

"I see you're back to skating on thin ice again. You know what happens?"

Yes, she did, and she'd love every second of the consequences. They talked well into the wee hours of the morning and when she hung up, Randi knew she'd finally found the man she would love for the rest of her life. And she hadn't had to settle for anything less.

"I need to blindfold you," Cedric said as he and Randi stood in his driveway.

Randi cut him a look. "Um, we've never done blind-folds before."

He sighed with exasperation. "Can you behave for five minutes? That's not what I'm talking about." At least not at this moment. "This is for the surprise, so humor me."

"Oh, alright."

He tied the scarf around her head. "Is it too tight?"

"No."

He waved his hand in front of her face and held up three fingers. "How many fingers?"

"What? I can't see your fingers."

"Good." Cedric took her hand and led her inside the house.

"This is so unnerving," Randi said with a laugh.

"We're almost there." They had gotten off the phone at five and he'd been so excited about his plans that he was up and out the door after less than four hours of sleep. He'd rest tonight. They both would. He guided her through the kitchen and through the sunroom to his back-yard. "Ready?"

"Come on, Cedric. The suspense is killing me."

He released the blindfold.

She gasped. "Oh. My. *Goodness!*" Her hands came up to her mouth and she slowly walked over to the blanket he had placed on the grass.

He had covered the blanket with pillows, a low table with a setting for two and a vase full of red roses—the darkest and biggest ones he could find—with scattered rose petals around the outside. "Do you like it?"

"Like it. I love it." She threw her arms around him. "I love you, I love you."

"I love you, too. We'll have dinner in a little while,

but first I have something for you. Actually, I have three gifts for you."

"Does one of them include us going back to the glass studio?" Randi asked with a wide grin.

Cedric chuckled. "Not this time, but I hope you'll like them as much. Have a seat." He waited until she was comfortable, then lined the boxes up in front of her. He'd used the same-size box for each gift. He pointed. "This one first."

She carefully removed the ribbon and paper and lifted off the lid. Inside, he'd placed a jewelry box. He noticed her hands shaking as she opened it. "Oh, Cedric. It's beautiful. So do you have the one with the key?"

He'd purchased a pendant with a small lock on it. He took it out of the box and draped it around her neck. "No. We don't need a key. This symbolizes our unbreakable love and my forever devotion."

Randi kissed him. "You're seriously ruining my reputation." She swiped at the tears falling from her eyes. "I don't ever cry."

"As long as they're tears of joy, I don't mind." He wiped away the lingering wetness from her cheek. He vowed to never make her cry tears of sadness again. "Okay, this one next." In his mind, she was taking too long to open the box. He wanted her to hurry up and rip the paper off. Her hands flew to her mouth when she finally opened it. Cedric eased the box from her hand and opened it. "From the moment I looked into your beautiful eyes, I knew you'd change my life. At the time, I just didn't know how much. I want to help you reach all your dreams and be your safe haven, to speak when words are needed or share the silence when they aren't." He brushed his thumb across the lock pendant. "I want to live inside the warmth of your heart forever. Will you marry me?"

"Yes," she choked out.

He slid the ring onto her finger. "I wanted to have something created special for you." He'd chosen a flawless diamond solitaire surrounded by red diamonds. "Something that matches your unique fire and spirit."

"This is the most beautiful ring I have ever seen." She held her hand up. "I love you so much."

"I love you more. But you have one more gift to open."

"I can't imagine what would top this. You're spoiling me."

"I plan to spoil you for the rest of our lives." He wanted to always be the one to put a smile on her face and a sparkle in her eyes

"Massage oil?"

"Yep. You said you like chocolate and so do I, so…" Desiree had given him chocolate- and strawberry-flavored oils and he'd been anxious to see if they did what she said. He put a little of the chocolate-flavored oil on his fingertip and rubbed it across her lips.

"I thought this was a massage oil."

Cedric wiggled his eyebrows. "It is. And it's edible." He blew softly and alternately licked and sucked it off. She moaned and locked her mouth on his. He kissed her down onto the blanket.

"I hope it'll be like this with us forever."

"It will be, baby. Forever."

Epilogue

One year later

"What are you doing?" Randi asked, laughing.

"I'm carrying you over the threshold, what does it look like?" Cedric kicked the door to his cabin closed behind him and went straight to the bedroom. He had never been so glad to leave a party in his life. When she came down the aisle toward him wearing the sexy strapless white gown, it was all he could do to stand still. He'd been mesmerized by every sway of her hips. As soon as it was appropriate, he'd hustled them to his car and driven straight to Tahoe. They would spend one week here, then the second one in the Bahamas. His baby loved the beach and he'd take her to every one of them if he could. He placed her on her feet and just stared at her. "Do you know how much I love you?"

"I hope it's as much as I love you." She brushed her

lips across his. "The first day we met I would've never imagined us being here like this."

He recalled how he had behaved. "Yeah, I acted pretty rude."

"You did, but you've more than made up for it."

"I'm glad."

Randi walked out to the balcony and stood at the rail. "It's so beautiful."

"And so are you," he said, coming to stand behind her. "Are you disappointed about the job?" The ATF position she had been eying hadn't come through because the person who had planned to retire decided to stay on another year. Cedric had mixed feelings. Her not leaving gave them extra time together.

"A little, but I'm not worried. Jason said he's still going to put in a good word for me whenever it becomes available. He said he was impressed with my work on the arson case. I didn't realize he'd paid that much attention, with it being local."

"Of course, he paid attention. You were great. I guess it's true that it's all about who you know."

Randi glanced at him over her shoulder and smiled. "I guess so."

"Speaking of who you know, Desiree sent us a little present."

She laughed. "Desiree's presents are trouble. And the other reason I'm glad we have more time."

Cedric went still. "What are you talking about?"

She turned in his arms. "Let's just say the result of all her *presents* will make his or her debut in about seven months."

He felt as though his heart stopped and started up again. "Wait, are you saying…are we having…?"

"We are. You're getting kind of old and I don't want you leaning on a cane while you're trying to play catch with our child."

"I'll show you old." He backed her into the room.

"I was hoping you'd say that."

Cedric threw back his head and laughed. With her there would never be a dull moment. His bachelor days were over and he couldn't be happier to change his tune. He'd found a new song—a love song—that he would sing for the rest of his life.

* * * * *

But…*he is fine*. She let her gaze roam over his features, his strong hands, his chiseled jaw, his dark brown eyes and his lean frame.

He was hard lines and smooth brown skin, and her fingers itched to sketch him, to put his beauty on canvas. He was dressed in a navy blue tailored suit with a white shirt underneath and dark brown leather oxford shoes. She couldn't keep her eyes to herself. His style was professional but chic. But there was also a kind of sexy nerd aura to him. *Ooo wee.* She resisted the urge to fan herself because she suddenly felt warm, hot actually.

Aria had a thing for men who could outsmart or outmaneuver anyone. The smarter, the better. And when she fell, she always fell hard. But inevitably it didn't work because the men she'd dated always tried to change her, or mold her into an image fit for their world. After Holloway, she'd made a vow to never get into a relationship with another man who wanted to put her into a box. But she could still enjoy the view and appreciate a man who looked like he was molded from a precious metal. Myles definitely fit the bill.

She smiled to herself and glanced up to find Myles staring at her, a tiny smirk on his lips. He'd caught her checking him out. *Oh. My. God.* Her cheeks heated and she wanted to sink into her seat a little.

There was never a time when **Elle Wright** wasn't about to start a book, already deep in a book or had just finished one. She grew up believing in the importance of reading, and became a lover of all things romance when her mother gave her her first romance novel. She lives in Southeast Michigan.

Books by Elle Wright

Harlequin Kimani Romance

It's Always Been You
Wherever You Are
Because of You
All for You

Visit the Author Profile page
at Harlequin.com for more titles.

ALL FOR YOU

Elle Wright

To my mother, Regina, you are missed.

Acknowledgments

Without God, I would be nothing.
I thank Him for being everything to me.

To Jason; my children, Asante, Kaia, Masai;
and the rest of my family, I love you all BIG. There are
so many of you, I can't name everyone. But you know
who you are. I learned long ago that you don't have
to be blood to be family. That couldn't be more true.
I appreciate the time, the talks, the hugs, the tears…
everything. I thank you all for your unwavering support.

To my lit sis, Sheryl, thank you.
I don't have to tell you why. You already know. Love you!

To my agent, Sara, I thank you for believing in me.

To the Kimani Family,
thank you for your encouragement.

I wouldn't be on this journey without all of your love
and support. Thank you for being #TeamElle!
You all mean the world to me!

Dear Reader,

It has been such an honor to write for Harlequin Kimani. Thank you for taking this journey with me.

The last of the Jackson brothers really gave me a hard time. Myles. He was so intense, so serious. I couldn't wait to open him up a little. Except he was much more complex than I ever imagined and nothing like I expected. I'm really glad that I saved him for last.

All for You taught me lifelong lessons, revealed things within myself that I was too scared to face. Everything that Myles deals with is something I've dealt with. It's easy to ignore the voice of your passion for practical. It's so easy to go to a job and not feel like you're doing your *work*. Your work is what makes you happy and satisfied. It should never feel like a chore, like an obligation. I hope you can listen to your voice and focus on your work.

Thank you for everything! I hope you enjoy the ride!

Love,

Elle

ElleWright.com

@LWrightAuthor

Chapter 1

"Who the hell wears dress shoes and slacks to sip and paint?" a gruff but friendly voice joked.

Dr. Myles Jackson paused in the doorway to the paint studio, Cocktails and Canvas. All of his siblings were inside. "Shut the hell up." He glared at his identical twin brother, Ian. "Can I get in the door first?" he grumbled.

Myles tried to ignore the chorus of chuckles from his siblings, but the laughter grew louder and more obnoxious by the second. Even his "date" had joined in. *Strike one.*

When everyone quieted down, Myles introduced the woman by his side to his siblings. All of the Jackson clan and significant others were in attendance tonight. It was a tradition to celebrate birthdays with each other, and it was his sister-in-law Avery's big day.

If he didn't love Avery so much, he would have gone home, locked himself in his music room and worked out on the keys the tension that had set in after a long day at the hospital. His piano and the music he made on it was his safe space, his therapy, his salvation. The notes had called to him for as long as he could remember. And he made it a point to play every single day.

Myles greeted the beautiful birthday girl with a hug. At five months pregnant, Avery had the glow that often accompanied pregnancy. He smoothed a hand over the soon-to-be new member of the family. "How are you?"

Avery groaned. "Busy and tired."

"You should be tired. You're all over the place." She had two hit televisions shows on the air, after all, and a new development deal with NetPix, the popular streaming platform taking the world by storm with its original programming.

"OMG, I love *The Preserves*," his date screeched. "I'm loving the Lucky and Kat story! And where did you get your bag? It's not even on sale for the public yet!"

Myles glanced over at the woman he'd brought with him to the paint party. The entire time he'd been with her, she'd talked his ears off during the drive there— about clothes, about shopping, about handbags. As if that wasn't bad enough, the high-pitched decibel at which Tina spoke made him want to jump out of his own car. He should have known better. No date his father had ever set him up on was worth his time or effort. Tina was the daughter of one of his father's closest business associates, and Myles had been briefed on the importance of this date.

His father, Dr. Lawrence Jackson, had planned to open an exclusive cosmetic surgery practice in their hometown of Ann Arbor. Tina's father was the city planner in charge of approving the development of the land earmarked for the building.

Avery grinned. "It was a gift from the designer."

Tina screamed.

If Myles heard another *OMG* or *Seriously* again, he might just fake a migraine and take her home before dinner.

"Bruh." Ian approached him with a questioning stare. "Who the hell is that?"

"Dad."

"Ah… No further explanation needed."

"Don't start," Myles muttered. He didn't need another lecture about their father's exacting demands of them. "It's not the time."

Ian held up both hands in surrender. "Hey, I'm not saying a word. I've already made myself very clear on the subject."

For years, Ian had been urging Myles to tell their father to step off, but Myles had yet to take him up on the advice. He was pretty sure his brothers thought he was scared of his father. But it was just the opposite. Despite his demanding and bougie ways, Dr. Law, as they called his dad, had his respect. The man was a gifted surgeon and professor. He traveled the world teaching his patented techniques in top medical centers. He could only hope to be as formidable a doctor as his father.

Myles thought about his many patients and the pile of charts awaiting him at work. He rarely took time off, but he wouldn't miss Avery's celebration. And family was important to him. He glanced around the room. Ian had ventured off to join his fiancée, Bailee. His older brother Drake was cuddled in the corner with his wife, Love. Avery and his uncle-brother El were chatting with another couple near the food table. Although El wasn't their biological brother, he'd been raised like one of them, hence the moniker uncle-brother. Myles's date, meanwhile, was… Making duck lips and taking selfies.

It was unfortunate to actually meet someone who cared nothing about anything that wasn't a designer whatever. The prognosis was grim. The chance of a second date was highly unlikely.

Myles strolled over to the food table, made a small plate of chicken wings, grapes and cheese. He popped a cube of Colby Jack into his mouth, followed by a grape. He checked his watch. Dinner was hours away, and he'd forgotten to eat today.

The studio was set up with three lines of rectangular tables. Each table had six easels already set up with blank canvases. A worker was walking around pouring paint onto white plates while another set cups of water and sets of paintbrushes near each station.

He made his way to the table and took a seat. A small hand reached out and snagged a grape off his plate. "Hands out of my plate, Mel."

Mel grinned when he met her amused gaze. She shrugged. "You know I can't resist. You're so OCD."

He ignored the comment. Myles had never been diagnosed with obsessive-compulsive disorder, but his siblings had always joked with him about the particular way he did things. Everything had a place, he didn't like people to touch his food, and he always washed his hands every time he touched someone else's bare skin. "What's up?"

Mel smirked. "Where did you get your date? Myles, she went to high school with me."

That got his attention. *Strike two.* Mel was only

twenty-four years old, nine years younger than him and Ian. *Damn.* "She's not my date. I'm doing Dad a favor."

"Look at her." Mel pointed toward the window where Tina was checking out her butt in the storefront reflection. "She's not smarter than a fifth grader. You're a freakin' surgeon, big brother."

He chuckled. Mel was one of his favorite people in the world. He still remembered her at six years old, running through the garden screaming that she was going to marry Lil Wayne. Myles had been there for every big event in her life, from preschool graduation to dance recitals to swim meets to prom to college graduation. She'd recently made the decision to forgo medical school and attend business school in New York City. It was a huge decision, especially considering they were all expected and groomed to follow the family tradition of attending the University of Michigan Medical School. He would miss her, but he was so proud of her.

"You're silly." He nudged her, like he'd always done.

She placed a hand on his leg. "I'm so serious. She's ridiculous."

Myles smiled at his little sister, noted the concern in her big, brown eyes. "I'm fine."

"Are you? Because I can't leave town in good conscience without knowing that my brothers will be all right."

"Mel, you've been MIA for years now."

She laughed. "I have not. I've been trying to be great, living my best life." Mel clapped and did a chair twerk, while singing the chorus to the popular song that seemed to play on the radio every time he turned it on.

Myles groaned. *I hate that damn song.* "What time does this thing start, anyway?"

At that moment, a woman rushed into the studio. "I'm so sorry. I had an important phone call from my manager. But I have great news," she told Avery.

He watched as Avery hugged the woman. Mel jumped up and joined the other ladies who had crowded around her. His sisters huddled in a circle while the mystery woman whispered something to them. Soon the ladies let out a loud cheer and hugged her.

His brothers approached the table, talking about the Detroit Pistons and their losing streak. El clasped his shoulder, unfazed by the halfhearted head nod Myles gave him in return. Because all Myles could see, all he could focus on, was *her*.

She wore ripped, black skinny jeans and a loose-fitting black tank. The multicolored sleeve tattoo on her left shoulder was intricate, with detail that he wanted to study. He'd never been attracted to women with ink, but this woman seemed to call to him on a primitive level.

Leaning to his left, he asked Ian, "Who is that?"

Ian glanced up. "That's Aria Bell. She is part of the ladies group."

"What ladies group?"

"Bailee, Avery, Love and Mel have been going to some ladies-night-out group. The purpose is sisterhood, since none of them have actual sisters."

Myles let his gaze travel from Aria's long, black waves with cherry-red highlights down to black sandals with red, painted toes. "Is she the instructor?"

Ian shrugged. "I think so. I don't know. Why?"

"Nothing."

Ian shot him a quizzical look. "Aren't you on a date?"

"Shut up."

Aria walked to the front of the room, and the women

joined their significant others at the tables. Tina slid into the seat next to his, and he forced his gaze away from Aria, shooting the social media queen a polite smile.

"Hey!" Aria jumped onto the podium and spun around to face them. "I'm Aria, the owner of Cocktails and Canvas. I apologize for being late, but I trust that my staff has been helpful. I see that you're ready to paint the Detroit skyline with me tonight. Can I see a show of hands for everyone who's done a sip and paint event before?"

Myles gaped when Drake raised his hand right along with the women in the room.

"You're holding out on us, bruh," Ian said.

Drake hugged Love. "Date night."

Instead of continuing the playful insult party, Ian backed off and peered down at his fiancée, Bailee. Less than three years ago, Myles and his brothers had been single and loving it. Well, except for El. And slowly all of them had settled down and turned their attention from work, women and freedom to marriage, family and date nights. Drake had started the chain reaction when he went to Las Vegas with Love to attend her family reunion and woke up married. El followed when he nursed a very sick Avery back to health and healed her heart in the process. Then, surprising them all, Ian's one-night stand had turned into forever.

Since then, most family events had shifted into set-Myles-up parties. But he wasn't interested in a hookup. He dated when *he* wanted to. When he settled down, it would be on his own terms. Until then, he'd enjoy the single life a little longer. *Maybe with the lovely Aria.*

Aria continued her spiel, telling the room more about her business, her love of art and the painting process for the night. They spent several minutes preparing the canvas by using stencils to trace the skyline. Then they got started on their masterpieces. Aria walked them through each stage of the painting, starting with the background.

"This is fun," Tina said, sweeping her paintbrush across the canvas. "I've never been to one of these parties before. I always thought it was weird."

Myles let out a heavy sigh and prayed no one asked Tina to elaborate.

Unfortunately, it wasn't his lucky night because Love asked, "Why?"

"Because it's boring. Who wants to sit around painting when you can go clubbing or shopping? Plus, I'm not a fan of art or paintings. Most are weird, anyway, and make no sense. I prefer pictures."

Myles checked the time on his watch. Tina babbled on about the ugly woman in the "one painting in the movie *Annie*" and the "stupid disfigured man surrounded by blue that used to scare her when she was a little girl." He wanted to stuff a bunch of grapes into her mouth to shut her up. The more she talked, the worse it would be for him later when his siblings blazed on him for bringing her in the first place.

Across from him, Love clutched invisible pearls while Drake stared at Tina slack jawed. Myles glanced at Mel just in time to catch the hard roll of his sister's eyes. Melanie smirked and mouthed the words *fifth grader* to him before returning her attention to her own painting. Mel's face never could hide her emotions.

Next to him, Ian burst out in laughter, not even trying to disguise his amusement. "Nice, bruh."

Massaging his temples, Myles shook his head. Only a few more hours.

"Myles, I have to go to the little powder room," Tina whispered.

He stood and pulled her chair out for her. Once she exited the room, he turned to his family. Multiple sets of eyes stared back at him. "What?"

"What could you possibly have in common with someone who is a ding-a-ling?" Love blurted out.

Myles opened his mouth to respond, but nothing came out. Because Love liked everyone. Love was nice to everyone. Evidently, that art comment had tipped his loving sister-in-law to the dark side.

"See!" Mel shouted, smacking her palms on the table. "I told you. Even Love said it."

"I think we should leave Myles alone," Bailee announced. "Obviously, he needs help finding a date," she added under her breath.

"Really, Bai?" Myles asked. "I thought we were cool."

His twin's fiancée shrugged. "Hey, I'm just sayin'..." She stuck her tongue out at him.

"What she's saying is, Dad should be the last person to pick your dates." Ian turned to him. "It's time to put a stop to that."

"Okay, everyone, can I have your attention?" Aria said, drawing his focus back to her. "We're going to work on the Detroit River now." Tina chose that moment to rejoin the group. "We're going to use varying shades of blue and a little purple to bring out the detail in the water, give it a realistic quality. But in order to make purple, I want you to take a little bit of the red paint and mix it with blue."

Tina gasped. "Wow! I didn't know red and blue made purple! I have to post this on my page."

Aria paused, her paintbrush midair. Her incredulous gaze met his. "Oh, damn," she muttered.

"What?" Mel deadpanned.

Love tucked a strand of hair behind her ear and looked away from him. "This is awkward."

Myles punched both of his fists against his thighs, hoping to relieve his growing frustration with Tina, with his family, with the entire situation. But especially with himself. Ian was right. He'd spent far too much time being the good son, the one who didn't rock the boat, the Jackson who did what was expected. No more. *Strike three.*

Myles walked into the restaurant later, loosening his tie. Sip and paint was finally over, and Tina was safely at home. The hostess led him to the private dining room El had reserved for Avery near the back of the building. He'd run into a few paparazzi outside, one of the downsides to having a famous Hollywood producer in the family.

Inside the glassed-in space, his family sat around the table laughing and drinking. When he entered, they all paused mid-conversation.

"What's up?" He took a vacant seat next to Mel. "What did I miss?"

"Where's Tina?" Mel asked.

"At home. I dropped her ass off." The room erupted in a round of applause. Myles couldn't help laughing at their antics. "Y'all get on my damn nerves."

El clasped his shoulder, giving it a squeeze. "Good job, bruh. You didn't disappoint me. Tell my brother to stay out of your love life."

Ian slid a shot glass full of what Myles hoped was tequila. He needed a drink. After he'd dropped Tina off at home, she'd tried to entice him with sex. When he'd turned her down, she went crazy, calling him all sorts of names he'd never heard of but attributed to her age group. Then, after she did a weird neck roll and flicked him off, she stormed into her father's house. Because, yes, she still lived with her parents.

After he took the shot, Myles motioned to Ian to refill the glass. "Thanks, bruh."

They were at the newest night spot in downtown Ann Arbor, a restaurant that had recently been featured in *Food and Drink Magazine*. Located on Main Street, the restaurant had three different levels of privacy and experience. The private dining room El had reserved was on the third and top floor.

Known as one of the best areas to live in the country, Ann Arbor had established itself as a place to meet, a place to be and a place to grow. It was home to the University of Michigan, a melting pot of different cultures, and a large city with a small-town feel. Myles had lived in the area for more than half of his life.

Outside the floor-to-ceiling windows, he watched people mill around, enjoying the setting, the nightlife and the June breeze. He'd seen a change in the area over the past several years. More and more businesses catering to the growing millennial population had set up shop in the downtown area, offering a wide variety of experiences from art galleries to wine bars to medical marijuana dispensaries. Although, he'd spent several years in Las Vegas as a child, he couldn't call any other place home.

"Are you good?" Ian asked.

Myles nodded. "Yeah, I'm all right. It's been a long day."

"Anything interesting happen at work today?"

Myles and his brothers all worked for Michigan Medicine, formerly known as the University of Michigan Health System. Being a surgeon for one of the nation's leading medical and research institutions was an honor. He'd worked hard in school, put in many hours of studying to become who he was today. Nothing and no one could take that away from him. But if he were being honest, his schedule had been wearing on him. He'd gone straight through undergrad to medical school, then through residency to a competitive and demanding fellowship. Now he was poised to open up a private cosmetic surgery practice with his father, one of the most sought-after plastic surgeons in the world. And Myles couldn't help feeling unfulfilled.

"I'm tired," he admitted. "Work seems to get busier every day. My patient load is picking up, and the new practice logistics have taken a lot of my time."

Myles hadn't intended to mention any of this to his twin. It wasn't too long ago that he and Ian had argued over the control their father had on Myles's life. As they'd grown into adulthood, each brother had carved out his own niche in medicine, going against Dr. Law's plans for their lives. When El became an emergency psychiatrist instead of a plastic surgeon, it had seemingly set off a chain reaction of rebellion in his brothers. Drake followed, declaring cardiothoracic surgery as his specialty. Ian had never enjoyed plastics, preferring to help patients beyond the walls of the hospital. His twin had spent over a year volunteering for organizations such as the American Red Cross and, most recently, Doctors Without Borders. It wasn't until Ian realized that he wanted to marry Bailee that he'd decided to stay close to home and become a trauma surgeon.

That left Myles with the sole responsibility of carrying on their father's legacy. It wasn't something he took lightly. And it wasn't something he *didn't* want to do, despite what his family thought. While his father had turned his focus toward the more lucrative aesthetic aspects of the practice, Myles had chosen to concentrate on the reconstructive facets of his specialty. He wanted to improve the function of the body by correcting impairments caused by traumatic injuries, burns, disease, and congenital or developmental abnormalities. For some of his patients, the difficulties they faced due to abnormalities often lead to depression or worse. Helping his patients obtain true quality of life, after a corrective surgery, was extremely fulfilling for him.

"When you say you're tired, are you talking medicine? Or Dad? Or both?" Ian bit into a buttered piece of bread.

Shrugging, Myles said, "Everything. I don't know, I just feel unsettled, like my life isn't mine." *It never has been mine.*

Things had been strained between all of them and their father, but lately Ian and Dad had come to an understanding of sorts, which led to more improvements in all of their relationships with Dr. Law. In recent months, his dad had attended several family events and had actually had fun and interacted with the family, dropping his all-business approach for fleeting moments. There was a long way to go, but it made Myles hopeful for more lasting change in the family dynamic.

"I told you it—"

"I don't want to get into a deep conversation here, bruh. I just…needed to get that out."

Ian eyed him for a few moments before he sighed. "Okay."

He knew it took a lot for his brother to drop the subject. They were both stubborn as that damn day was long. But he appreciated his brother's acquiescence, even though he was sure Ian would bring it up again sooner rather than later. It was just the nature of their relationship. Still, he couldn't say it bothered him, because his twin brother was his best friend, the only person who knew mostly everything about him and never judged him.

Before Myles could share the wild end to his "date" with Ian, he was rendered speechless yet again by the lovely woman approaching the table. Aria Bell had just joined the party, and Myles's night had just looked up.

Chapter 2

"Shit." The pain had intensified over the last several minutes. Aria should be used to it by now, but she wasn't. "I feel faint." She gasped. "I think you're doing it too hard."

"Don't move," Brent ordered, smacking her butt with his free hand. "It's possible that you become more of a crybaby with each tattoo, Aria."

She let out a tiny giggle, followed by a growl. "Shut it. It hurts."

"Almost done," he murmured.

The low buzz of the tattoo gun was the only sound in the room for several more minutes as Aria's best friend, Brent, finished the design she'd created. Soon Aria felt a soft washcloth against her side.

"All done?" she asked, unable to hide her excitement at seeing her newest tattoo.

"You're all set." Brent helped her up off the table, and she hurried to the full-length mirror he kept in his shop.

From the moment she'd met Brent during her junior year in high school they'd been inseparable. They'd bonded over their love of art, ink and horror movies. He was the one person she felt comfortable being herself with. And even when she moved to New York City to pursue her art after high school graduation, he'd remained one of the most important people in her life.

Aria took in the intricate details of the phoenix now lining her side. Her friend was a genius, and the only person she'd ever trust with a tattoo gun. "You're amazing, Brent." The orange, red and black design was perfect, just as vivid as the painting she'd created for her upcoming exhibition at the Charles H. Wright Museum in Detroit, Michigan.

It was the culmination of a career that had seen devastating lows and amazing highs. Aria's work as a professional artist spanned over a decade, and she had worked hard to get to this point. She'd spent hours in her studio creating paintings that she hoped would transcend time and evoke emotion in the observer. She'd presented her work in over thirty-five galleries, exhibitions, and other venues or mediums, including television and print. Her latest collection had received rave reviews from respected curators around the nation, with offers to show in several galleries. And it was an honor to exhibit in one of the country's greatest museums of African American history.

Tears threatened to spill as she met Brent's smiling eyes in the mirror. She swallowed past the huge lump that had formed in her throat. "Thank you," she whispered.

"No, thank you for letting me do it." When she'd asked him to do the tattoo, she'd expected Brent to balk at her request to duplicate her own painting on her body. But he'd surprised her when he told her he would give it a try. It had taken a few sessions, but the finished product was worth the hours in the chair.

"You're the only one who could."

Brent had chosen not to pursue art in the way she had, but he created wonderful works of art every day as the owner of InkTown Tattoos. Although his parlor was located in Ann Arbor, next to her studio, the title of his shop was a play on their hometown of Inkster, Michigan.

She twisted her body, still in awe over his work. "I'm so glad I'm back. Missed you." Aria had recently moved back to Michigan for a change of scenery. Twelve years in Manhattan had taken a toll on her art and her life. She'd hit a wall creatively. So, when Brent mentioned wanting to purchase a new building for his shop, she started making plans to move. She approached Brent with the idea to partner with him on the purchase of the building, and now they were sitting in the newly renovated space that housed both of their businesses.

Although she'd spent years honing her craft, she was ready to give back to the community, to teach art to others. Cocktails and Canvas opened to rave reviews a little over two months ago, and she couldn't be happier. Next, she'd realize her dream of opening an art school.

Brent pulled out his cell phone and winked. "Missed you, too." Aria lifted up her arm, stretching so that Brent could take a pic of the design. He snapped a few photos. "But you're seriously cramping my style with the ladies. For some reason, they don't believe me when I tell them we're just friends."

Aria laughed and shoved him playfully. "Which is a

good thing, because that last chick you brought around should have stayed where you found her."

Brent owned a duplex, and had offered Aria the smaller unit next to his until she found a permanent place to live. It had only been eight months and she was ready to move. She loved Brent and didn't mind living close to him, but she needed more space.

Over the last several months, she'd seen countless properties in Ann Arbor and other surrounding suburbs like Ypsilanti and Canton, but she'd yet to settle on anything. The only thing she knew for sure was she wanted to purchase a home with enough square footage for a dedicated art studio where she could work.

"Don't play me." He pointed at her. "I can't help it if I'm irresistible."

"Yeah, whatever. Don't you ever get tired of the bachelor life? Beer, takeout, women. And repeat. Every day."

Brent had never had a hard time finding a companion, with his lean body, long dreadlocks and dark skin. Women from all around made throwing themselves at him a sport. They couldn't really go anywhere without him being propositioned.

"Hey, I love my life. Beer is good. So are women and takeout," he said with a shrug. "Besides, you're one to talk about romantic choices," he continued.

"Is that what they're calling booty calls now? Romantic choices?" She laughed when he threw a towel at her.

"Maybe if you found a romantic choice, you wouldn't be walking around in sweatpants and fluffy slippers all the time when you're at home."

"Ha ha. I'm not dating anyone right now. My focus is on my career."

He frowned, staring at her until she fidgeted under his pensive gaze.

"Stop looking at me like that," she said. "We're not talking about my love life. But seriously, Brent, you're so intelligent. And you look good. You can do much better than the women you're dating. It's just like the paint party I did for Avery last week. Her brother in-law was fly. He's a surgeon, very intelligent, intense… But then he brings an airhead who didn't even know that red and blue made purple."

Brent barked out a laugh. "Who over the age of ten doesn't know that?"

She smacked her palms on her legs. "Exactly."

The room descended into silence for a moment before Brent said, "Aria, are you going to tell me what happened with Holloway?"

"No, I'm not. We're not having this discussion."

He approached her and tipped her chin up to meet his concerned gaze. "Listen, I'm glad you're back. But I'm worried about you. You spent years building a life for yourself in your favorite city, and all of a sudden you pack up and move. I understand your parents are here, but—"

"You're here."

He waved a dismissive hand. "Whatever. I know how to book a flight and come see your ass." He instructed her to hold still.

Sighing, she let him place the plastic wrap over the tattoo to cover it. "I know. But, really, there is nothing to talk about. I came home because it was time."

Holloway had been her boyfriend for three years. They'd met when he offered to set up a show for her at a prominent gallery in Harlem. He'd done a lot to help her career early on in the relationship, but Aria soon realized his intentions were never really pure. He'd stolen earnings and art from her. Not only was he a thief, he was a lying cheater who'd paraded a string of women around the city while she'd been holed up in her studio working. Even though it wasn't the deciding factor in her move, she couldn't deny the drama with him had contributed to the stress that had marred her last year and a half in New York. But no one needed to know the sordid details of their breakup. Holloway Gray was in her past, and no longer a factor in her life.

"Fine. I won't push you. I never have." He gave her shoulders a reassuring squeeze. "But I want you to know that I'm here for you whenever you're ready to talk about it."

Pulling him into a tight hug, she burrowed into his warm embrace. "Thanks, babe. I love you for it."

"I love you, too. And if I need to use my fists on that asshole, I'm more than willing."

She pulled back and smiled up at him. "That's why you're my bestie."

He rolled his eyes. "Ugh, I hate when you call me that."

Giggling, she asked, "What should I call you then?"

"Homie. How about that? Better yet? Brent? That's even better. This is why you need some girlfriends. I'm so glad you joined that ladies-night-out group."

When Aria moved back to Ann Arbor, she'd met up with Avery Montgomery, a friend she'd worked with on occasion. Avery had invited her out for dinner one evening and introduced her to her sisters-in-law. Since then, they'd done several activities together, from winery tours to movies. Aria truly enjoyed the budding friendships. All of the women were a hoot and fun to be around.

"I'm glad, too," she said. "I especially love that they are so down-to-earth."

Avery produced one of Aria's favorite television shows, but never flaunted her fame. When they got together, they didn't discuss work or celebrities. The focus was to let loose, to have fun and to cultivate a sisterhood. Conversations were thoughtful and timely, not portentous or formal. There were no petty rivalries or shady overtones in the group. All of them, despite being married or related to one of the wealthiest families in Ann Arbor, and successful in their own right, were straightforward, fun and genuine women of color. And Aria felt blessed to have connected with them.

"I get to pick the next activity," Aria announced. "Tattoo party?"

He shrugged. "Maybe. If you hook me up with Mel."

She sliced a hand in the air. "Not a chance. She's a good girl. I don't want you loving and leaving her like you do everyone else."

"I should be offended, but I'm not." He chuckled. "She's fine as hell, though."

Aria smiled. "She's beautiful. But off-limits to you, homie." Her phone buzzed in her purse. She pulled it out and rolled her eyes. "It's my mom."

He busied himself sterilizing his equipment. "What does Mrs. Bell require of you now?"

There was no love lost between her best friend and her mother. The two had never gotten along, most likely because Brent didn't give a damn about appearances. Because of that, Elizabeth Bell had never ceased to point out all of Brent's flaws to Aria.

Aria waited until the phone stopped buzzing. "She invited me for Sunday dinner. I've been avoiding it."

"Somehow I'm not surprised." The sarcasm in his tone was unmistakable.

Her parents lived in the township of West Bloomfield, which was about thirty-five miles from Ann Arbor. It was also one of the most expensive places to live in the Detroit metropolitan area. Louis and Elizabeth Bell had successfully moved on up since their days in Inkster. After serving as Chief Judge for Inkster, her father had made the transition to the Michigan Court of Appeals. Currently, he was on the newly elected governor's short list for the Michigan Supreme Court.

Although Aria was proud of her father, the fervor surrounding his possible appointment had created a rift in the family. Long story short… Her mother wanted her father to go for it. Her father? He didn't need the job to feel like a success. He'd worked hard all of his life and was ready to slow down a little.

Aria spent a few minutes composing a text to her mother, deleting and retyping many times before she settled on the right wording. The last thing she wanted was to leave the door open for more communication. The simple one-line response, I'll be over within the hour, should be sufficient enough.

Once the text was sent, she dropped her phone back into her handbag. After walking over to the mirror, Aria reapplied her lipstick and ran her fingers through her curls. "It's time I stop avoiding this." She turned to him. "You wouldn't want to come with me, would you?" She waggled her eyebrows.

He shook his head. "Hell, no. But you can bring me

back a plate. Especially if the cook makes that slappin'
chicken dish she made last time."

The Bell's personal chef, Celeste, was one of Aria's
favorite people in the world. The older woman had been
with their family since their Inkster days. Celeste had
started as a part-time housekeeper and cook, and now
lived with Aria's parents.

"I'll be sure to sneak you a plate, okay?" Aria said,
grabbing her purse and walking to the door. "I'll call
when I get home."

"I want a divorce."

Aria met her father's hard glare across the dinner
table. Louis Bell hadn't said anything during the stilted
Sunday dinner, but she never expected those would be
his first words.

Her gaze traveled from him to her mother, who continued to spoon the tasteless macaroni and cheese onto
her plate. Apparently, they'd given Celeste the night off,
because dinner tasted like her mother's bland cooking.

Mrs. Elizabeth Bell had always been one to ignore
the obvious, choosing to only focus on things that suited
her own agenda. Aria had spent many of her childhood
days and nights attending political fund-raisers and other
high-society events in the state, giving fake smiles, playing hostess and shaking sweaty palms. She'd competed in
beauty pageants, participated in cotillions and served on
her mother's auxiliary groups for various organizations.
It was actually during one of those dreaded fund-raisers
for the Detroit Institute of Arts that Aria discovered her
love of visual art.

"Did you hear me, Elizabeth?" Louis asked, setting his fork down on his plate. "This has gone on long enough. We're not doing each other any favors."

Elizabeth shifted in her chair, picked up the bottle of merlot and nearly filled up her wineglass. It was the first sign that her mother was actually bothered by the turn of events. *Because a lady never pours more than five ounces at a time into a wineglass.* It was a lesson that had been instilled in Aria since she was old enough to pour wine.

"Louis, this isn't the right time to discuss this," Elizabeth said.

"When is the right time?" Louis pushed his plate away from him.

Aria wondered the same thing. Her parents had faked happy couplehood for years. They'd been hanging on by a thin string since she'd turned Tween. Now, at thirty-one years old, she considered it a blessing that one of them wanted to end the charade.

"You've been avoiding me for weeks," her father continued. "And when I finally get you to agree to dinner, you invite Aria."

Aria frowned. "Dad, what are you talking about? Don't you live here? Since when do you have to set a date to talk to Mom?"

"I moved out three weeks ago, Aria."

Her eyes widened. "What? Why didn't either of you say something?"

Aria had talked to both of her parents multiple times in the past three-week period. At no point did either of them let on that they weren't residing in the same house. Even when she'd arrived for dinner, nothing in the house seemed off or out of the ordinary. Both parents were seated in their normal spots, doing normal things—her father working in the office, her mother complaining about everything, neither of them acknowledging the other. Everything felt like it did since forever.

Growing up in the Bell home had been pretty drab and dreary. Aria was extremely close to her father, but she had always clashed with her mother. For years, she'd hoped to get a little brother or sister, if for no other reason than it could have lightened her load or lessened the mound of expectations her mother had for her. She hadn't been lucky in the sibling department, but she'd managed to make it through her childhood. Sure, she had a standing appointment with her therapist every first and third Friday of the month, but she had carved out her own niche in life.

"Aria, can you give us a few minutes alone?" Her father asked, offering a sad smile. "I'll explain everything later, sweetie."

"Okay." Aria swallowed, dropped her napkin on the table. "I'm going to just head home."

"Stay right where you are, Aria," Elizabeth ordered.

The no-nonsense tone with which her mother always addressed her pissed her off most days. But Aria knew heartbreak when she heard it. It was written all over her mother's face. And despite her own complicated relationship with her mother, she wanted to be sensitive to that. With a heavy sigh, Aria stood. "Mother, this is not a conversation I should be involved in. It's between you and Dad. It's best that I leave."

"No, you're not leaving." Elizabeth finished her wine and poured another healthy glass. "We're having Sunday dinner as a family."

Another few minutes of tense silence followed, with Aria still standing and her parents glaring at each other.

This isn't awkward at all. "How about I go into the kitchen and give you two a minute?"

Aria didn't give her mother time to respond. She simply grabbed her plate and rushed into the kitchen, leaving her parents alone.

It felt like the freakin' twilight zone. Her parents rarely fought. Hell, they barely raised their voices around her. Yet, it wasn't a shock her father wanted out.

For several minutes, she didn't hear a peep from the other room. No raised voices, no glass breaking, no furniture moving. In fact, it was so quiet she wondered if they were still in the dining room. A few minutes later, she heard a loud scream. The piercing sound startled her, and she jumped up from the bar stool she'd perched herself on and ran back into the dining room.

Standing in the archway, with angry tears streaming down her flawless face, her mother yelled, "Get out of this house, Louis. You've made a fool of me."

Her father stepped forward, arms suspended in mid-air. Aria wondered if he would pull her mother into a hug, to comfort her. Instead, he let his arms fall to his side. "I've never been unfaithful, Elizabeth. I've always treated you with respect. I've taken care of you. But I'm tired, Liz. I'm tired of coming home to a wife who doesn't show me any type of affection unless we're in public. I'm sick of begging you for quality time. We've lived in this loveless marriage for far too long. And I don't want to do it any longer. Life is too short to waste it being unhappy."

"I can't believe you're doing this to me," her mother said. "What will everyone think?"

A tear fell down her father's face, and Aria's heart broke for him. "I had hoped that you would tell me that

I was wrong, that you do love me, and that you want to work on this marriage for *us*. I guess that was too much to hope for."

The man in front of her had sacrificed so much for them, and all he wanted was the love of his wife. Her life would have been so different had it not been for her daddy, her personal dragon slayer. He'd bought her first set of paintbrushes, set up a makeshift studio in their attic, attended all of her shows and supported her in every way that mattered.

Unable to hold herself back any longer, Aria ran to him and hugged him tightly. She hoped he could feel her love for him—she needed him to know that she cared about his feelings. When his arms finally wrapped around her, she knew he got it.

"Love you, sweetie," he murmured into her hair. "Love you so much."

"I love you more than all the pennies in the world, Daddy." Aria's eyes filled with tears. As a child, they'd have little "I love you" battles, each of them coming up with outlandish ways to quantify their love for each other.

"I love you more than the grains of sand on every beach in the world."

She giggled. "I know."

"We'll do lunch soon."

Nodding, she murmured against his shirt, "Okay." He still smelled like a mixture of soap and trees. His scent was as comforting now as it was when he'd read to her until she fell asleep at night.

He pulled back and pinched her cheek, like he'd done for as long as she could remember. Then, he turned to her silent mother. "Liz, you spend so much time wearing a mask, putting on a front to people I couldn't care less about. I love you. I really do. But I want a divorce. My lawyer will be in touch."

Then he was gone.

"I'm sorry you're going through this," Aria said after a moment. "I love you both."

Her mother tugged on her shirt and lifted her chin high. "No need to apologize. I expect you to still attend the fund-raising tea next Sunday at the club."

"No, I'm not going, Mother. Did you even hear Dad? Do you even care?"

"This is between me and your father."

"You brought me into it when you invited me here for dinner, knowing that you had personal things to discuss with him."

"I can handle your father."

Aria crossed her arms. "Obviously, you can't. He's gone."

"He'll be back." Elizabeth let out a heavy sigh. "In the meantime, I see no reason you can't still attend the tea. Everyone is expecting you."

Before Aria could protest further, her mother pivoted on her heels and walked out of the room without another word.

Chapter 3

Aria walked into the Afternoon Delight Café in downtown Ann Arbor and scanned the small but bustling dining area. When she spotted Mel seated in a corner booth, she headed over to her.

"Hey," Mel said with a wide grin.

"What's up?" Aria dropped her bag into the booth. "I'm glad you were able to find an empty booth. I'm starving. Be right back."

The popular café, famous for its omelets, huge pancakes, deli sandwiches and stellar service, was crowded as usual. On Saturdays, the line to get in often extended down three storefronts.

Ann Arbor had grown since Aria used to sneak to town with Brent for the Top of the Park Summer Festival or the Ann Arbor Street Art Fair when they were teenagers. The art scene had always appealed to her, and she'd briefly considered attending University of Michigan for her undergraduate degree before she'd decided on New York University. The cultural and social atmosphere in the city was why she'd jumped at the chance to open up a business in the area. The rent was incredibly expensive, but there weren't many places in the world that gave her the feeling of living in a city and a small town at the same time.

Aria didn't need to see a menu to know what she wanted. The Quiche Lorraine was calling her name. She walked up to the counter to place her order before rejoining Mel at the table. The server had just dropped off a plate of Eggs Benedict and raisin toast for Mel.

"Looks delicious," Aria said, placing a hand over her grumbling stomach. "I feel like I haven't eaten in twenty-four hours." Technically, she hadn't had a meal since yesterday morning. Yesterday, she'd held a private party for a group of adorable little ten-year-old girls and then spent the rest of her day in the studio, finishing up her latest painting and organizing the space.

"Girl, we've gone over this before. If you can't remember to eat on your own, set an alarm on your phone. Use the technology available to you." Mel took a bite of her food and groaned. She pointed her fork at her plate. "I swear, I always expect my food to be bad one day and it never is."

"I know," Aria agreed. "I haven't had a bad meal here yet. And I come here at least once a week."

They laughed. It felt good to meet a friend for breakfast. Art was such a solitary task that Aria used to go days without talking to another human being, especially during the first few years after she'd graduated from college. Aside from Brent, she'd never really been good at maintaining friendships. During college, she'd been cool with her roommate, but once she moved out into her own space, communication between them slowed down and eventually stopped. Yes, she'd met wonderful people, talented artists, but she was hard-pressed to think of someone who had made a lasting impression or connection to her. Brent had been spot-on when he'd encouraged her to accept Avery's initial invitation to dinner and a movie all those months ago.

The waitress set Aria's quiche down on the table several minutes later and refilled their coffee mugs. While they ate, they chatted about a little bit of everything, from sports to fashion to hair color. When Aria first started attending the ladies-night-out group, she'd immediately bonded with Mel. The youngest Jackson sibling was set to move to New York City and attend Aria's alma mater for graduate school. They'd spent a lot of time talking about the city, the social scene and the university.

Aria was happy for Mel. It took a lot of guts to leave the safety net of family and friends to start something new. But she knew Mel was up to the challenge.

"So, I'm admittedly nervous," Mel confessed. "September is not that far off, Aria. What if I can't hack it?"

"Stop, Mel. If I could survive and thrive at the age of eighteen, you can at twenty-three. Besides, you have everything you need to make it in the city—money, a support system, intelligence and common sense. The rest will fall into place."

Laughing, Mel said, "You're funny. But you're right. I do have all those things." Mel had mentioned a close family friend who lived in the city had offered to hold an apartment in a new development for her. She'd already won half the battle. Finding an affordable and nice residence was a huge victory.

"I'm excited for you. And I'll definitely come and crash at your pad when I have to go back for work."

"Definitely." Mel doctored her new cup of coffee, adding two creams and three sugars. "Speaking of work… Are you excited about the exhibit in a few weeks?"

She nodded. "And nervous."

"I think it's pretty kick-ass, though. I can't wait to see your collection."

Aria made it a point to keep her work private until it was time to show. The only person she ever shared works in progress with was Brent. Her experience with Holloway had left a sour taste in her mouth when it came to sharing her art.

"It's my most personal work to date. I poured everything into it."

The *Metamorphosis* was a study in black female identity. She wanted women to see themselves in her work, to identify with her own struggle to rise above adversity. Aria had used techniques she'd learned during her undergraduate curriculum, her master of fine arts, her sabbatical to South Africa and her time in Paris. The collection included acrylic and oil painting as well as images made using other nontraditional materials such as felts and glitter. The centerpiece of the exhibit was her best painting, the self-portrait she'd created four years ago. The thought of showing something so personal terrified her, but she'd held that work in her private studio for years and it felt timely and necessary and poignant to include it.

"I love when you talk about your art, Aria." Mel smiled at the restaurant employee who'd just appeared to take away their plates. "You get this glow in your eyes. I want to feel like that about something that I created."

She studied her friend. "Is that why you didn't go to medical school like your father wanted?"

"That, and I hate blood." She giggled. "I've never been able to stomach the hospital. I don't like needles, and I'm a big crybaby. There's no way I'd be able to tell a patient that they were going to die. The paramedics would have to carry me out on a stretcher the first time one of my patients passed away."

Mel had shared a little about her family trajectory to med school and her decision to not follow in her father's footsteps. From what Aria gathered, Mel's father was a control freak who didn't take kindly to his children forging their own paths. It was something she could relate to because of her own mother.

It had been over a week since her father's divorce proclamation and her mother had yet to bring it up again. She really was hell-bent on denying it had ever happened, in typical Elizabeth Bell fashion. Aria had joined her father for dinner last night at his new house. For the first time since she could remember, her father seemed at peace in his space. She could tell he was still heartbroken, but his resolve was strong. He'd made a decision and he would stick to it. And her mother would continue to mask her pain and relationship woes to the public.

Living with a parent who made everything hard had taken its toll on Aria. She knew what it was like to push back against tradition and expectations. It took her moving away to assert some independence on her life, and she had no doubt that Mel would soon realize she'd made the right decision stepping out of the box her father tried to keep her in.

"So, basically, you have identified your strengths and weaknesses," Aria mused. "That's a good thing."

"Chile, I know. I'm not like my brothers. They are so calm under pressure."

Aria thought about the Jackson brothers. She'd met all of them and had spent a little more time with El because of Avery. They all had different personalities, but she could tell they took their jobs seriously and enjoyed what they did. "I can definitely see that."

"You haven't spent much time with them because they're always working, but I hope you get to know them better. They're good men to have in your corner."

"I'm sure they are."

Mel gasped and waved wildly to someone behind Aria. "Ooh, Myles is here. Myles!" Aria swiveled in her seat just as Myles approached their table. Mel jumped up and gave him a quick hug. "Have a seat?"

Aria met Myles's gaze and smiled politely, giving him a small wave. "Yes, join us."

Myles slid into the booth, next to Mel. "I'm not staying. Just here to pick up breakfast. I have a meeting with the city planner in half an hour."

Mel rolled her eyes. "Oh, God. You're really going through with the private practice, huh?"

"You know the answer to that," he said.

Aria took a moment to study the "serious" twin, as the ladies had dubbed him. She'd only met him once, at the paint party weeks ago. During that short time, she'd immediately judged him based on his date. The woman at the party was a lot on the airhead side, and Aria had no use for men who dated based solely on looks. Because that had to be the only reason he'd brought that woman to the party.

During the sip and paint, they hadn't said much to each other, but watching him with Mel made her rethink her original opinion about him. It was obvious he loved his sister. He paid attention to her, listened intently to her babble on about a variety of topics in a short time span. Being an only child, she'd often wondered how it would have felt to have a wise, big brother to warn her against the pitfalls of life or bounce ideas off. With Brent, they'd pretty much wandered blindly into the wilderness of life together and had made plenty of mistakes.

But…*he is fine*. She let her gaze roam over his features, his strong hands, his chiseled jaw, his dark brown eyes and his lean frame. He was hard lines and smooth brown skin, and her fingers itched to sketch him, to put his beauty on canvas. Dressed in a tailored, navy blue suit with a white shirt underneath and dark brown leather oxford shoes, she couldn't keep her eyes to herself. His style was professional but chic. There was also a kind of sexy nerd aura to him. *Ooo-wee*. She resisted the urge to fan herself because she suddenly felt warm, hot actually.

Aria had a thing for men who could outsmart or out-maneuver anyone. The smarter the better. And when she fell, she always fell hard. But inevitably it didn't work because the men she'd dated always tried to change her to fit into their world. After Holloway, she'd made a vow to never get into a relationship with another man who wanted to put her into a box. But she could still enjoy the view and appreciate a man who looked like he was molded from a precious metal. Myles definitely fit the bill.

She smiled to herself and glanced up to find Myles staring at her, a tiny smirk on his lips. He'd caught her checking him out. *Oh. My. God.* Her cheeks heated and she wanted to sink into her seat a little.

Fortunately for her, Mel didn't seem to notice and

continued to tell Myles about the latest Bailee and Ian wedding updates. In the meantime, he hadn't broken eye contact with her. He studied her like she was the latest surgical technique, like he wanted to master her. She swallowed, scratched the back of her head.

"So, anyway, I love the fact that they decided to keep the wedding small," Mel said. "I just wish they'd chosen a summer wedding."

He shrugged, still eyeing Aria. "I don't know, Mel. At least, they're doing the ceremony in New Orleans."

Aria couldn't help but smile. She'd heard the love story of Ian and Bailee during one of their outings. The newly engaged couple had met in a dark bar, in a French Quarter hotel. Usually, those types of meetings led to hot sex or mace in the face. Well, in Aria's experience anyway. But their story was the stuff romance-movie dreams were made of. Hot man, beautiful woman, one-night stand, then forever. She'd swooned while listening to it, so she could only imagine how Bailee felt to live it.

"I know. At least, we'll get a reprieve from the Michigan winter for a week."

He chuckled, the sound warming Aria like hot chocolate on a nasty, rainy day. With whipped cream. A waitress brought his carryout bag and an empty mug over to him. She filled the mug with coffee, winked at him and then disappeared into the kitchen.

"Myles, do you know her?" Mel asked.

He shrugged. "I eat here a lot."

"Whatever. She was flirting with you."

"She wasn't."

"Oh, please." Mel looked at Aria. "Wasn't she flirting?"

Aria tilted her head and bit down on her bottom lip

before nodding reluctantly. Wait a minute... *Am I flirting, too?* She stiffened in her seat and finished off her coffee. Clearing her throat, she finally said, "Yep, she sure was."

Grinning, Mel added, "I bet your food is extra good today. She probably even gave you an extra piece of raisin toast."

Myles barked out a laugh. He had a beautiful laugh, one that made Aria feel some type of way, like she wanted to giggle or melt into the booth. It had been a long time since she'd felt it, too. But she wouldn't name it because that would make it real. Attraction. She was attracted to Myles.

"Are you busy on June 24?" Mel asked Myles.

He shook his head slowly. "Not that I know of. Why?"

Mel gestured toward Aria. "Because I want you to be my date to Aria's exhibition opening."

He watched her over the rim of his mug. "What type of art?" he asked.

Aria shifted in her seat. "I've dabbled in several different types of visual art, but my first love is oil painting."

"Isn't that awesome?" Mel said.

"It definitely is." His eyes flicked down to her lips, then back up. He set his mug down and leaned forward. "What's the subject?"

"Me, mostly. Black women empowerment, life, love, struggle. The exhibit is sort of based on my life."

"Nice. I'll definitely be there. I'd love to see your work."

"Great." Aria wasn't sure why her voice came out all breathy and soft, but it did. "I appreciate the support."

He stood and mussed Mel's hair. "I better get going." He met her gaze again. "Good seeing you, Aria."

Aria clasped her hands together. "You, too."

He leaned down and kissed Mel's forehead and made his way out. Aria tried not to watch his retreat and failed miserably. When she looked at Mel, her friend was eyeing her curiously. "What?" Aria asked. "You're staring."

"Just making sure."

She asked, "Making sure...?"

"I didn't imagine that you were checking my brother out."

So, Mel wasn't as oblivious as Aria had hoped she was. "I should probably get going, too. I have work to do."

A slow grin spread across Mel's face. "Okay. I know a brush-off when I hear it. I should probably head to work myself."

Aria pulled a few bills from her wallet and set them on the table. "I'll call you? I might need your help narrowing down my outfit for the opening. Maybe we can check out the new restaurant near the mall afterward."

"Sounds like a plan." Mel hugged her. "Talk soon."

"Did you miss me?"

Myles smiled as he entered the patient room. "Of course, I did." He leaned down and placed a soft kiss to the forehead of one of the most important people in his life. "I hear you've been giving the staff hell."

The older woman grinned. "Always."

"I thought I told you I didn't want to see you back here in the hospital, Ms. Pennie."

Penelope Kemp had been a constant presence in his life for years. He often credited her with saving his life, clearing away the clutter that accompanied so much of his childhood.

"Oh, hush," she said, with a dismissive wave. "You don't tell me what to do."

He tilted his head. Drake had texted him during their meetings with the city planner to let him know that Ms. Pennie had arrived in the emergency room a few hours ago. She'd recently been diagnosed with breast cancer and was recovering from a fairly straightforward lumpectomy and a course of radiation treatment. According to her chart, she'd presented with shortness of breath, persistent cough, and pain in her chest and arm. He gave her a quick once-over and noted the swelling in her arm.

"I'm the boss, today, Ms. Pennie."

"You're never the boss of me, Myles Jackson."

He pointed at her. "That's Dr. Jackson to you at this moment." He laughed when she glared at him.

"Whatever boy. And when are you going to bring a beautiful woman in here for me to meet? Your brothers have all settled down. It's your turn."

Same talk, different day. Ms. Pennie didn't have any children, and he was the closest thing to a son she had. Myles shook his head and sighed. "I'm not looking to settle down anytime soon. But trust me, you'll be the first to know when I am."

"Any new prospects?"

Myles thought about Aria. Technically, she wasn't a prospect, but he hadn't been able to get her out of his head since the first day he'd met her. Seeing her that morning at Afternoon Delight had made it worse. But there was no way in hell he would say any of that to

Ms. Pennie. She'd have his wedding planned before to-morrow.

He took a seat near the bed. "So, what's going on?"

Ms. Pennie explained the pain she felt, and Myles jot-ted down notes on his tablet. She wasn't his patient, but he would make sure she was taken care of. "I probably should have opted for the mastectomy," she admitted.

Myles didn't respond. They'd discussed her options many times before her surgery. He'd recommended the mastectomy, but even in her older age, she couldn't fathom not having a breast and had chosen another route.

"Do you think the cancer has spread?"

He glanced up at her then. The sheen of tears in her eyes, the fear shining back at him made him feel help-less. Because he didn't know what to tell her. The doc-tors had run a series of tests to rule out metastasis, but he hadn't looked at the results, even though she'd granted him written permission to do so as her power of attor-ney and patient advocate.

He picked up her hand and squeezed. "I don't know. But I'm going to choose to think positive, like you al-ways tell me to do."

"Finally." She burrowed into the mattress. "I finally said something that got through to you."

She said a lot that got through to him. Once, Myles had cried for hours because he kept hearing notes in his head. He was probably around five years old. Every time he would listen to music, the sounds in his head grew louder and more persistent, almost like they became a part of his soul. One day, he'd sat down at the grand piano and started to play. His life changed forever that cold December morning. He'd tapped the ivory keys until he'd perfected the Christmas tune he'd been listening to.

For years, he would sneak into the piano room and play, mostly by ear. It wasn't until he met Ms. Pennie one summer that he started to make sense of the music in his head. Although they didn't live in Michigan for much of his childhood, they'd stayed summers with his mother's family there. Ms. Pennie lived in the house across the street. She'd worked as a music teacher and saw something in him without him even articulating anything to her.

The first summer, she'd asked him to visit her at her house and he'd gone without hesitation. She'd watched him play that day, studied him. Then she offered to teach him how to do more. Of course, he'd accepted the invitation and went to see her every day at five o'clock. She'd taught him about notes. Every good boy digs football and FACE. The mnemonic that he'd repeated over and over again to memorize the different notes of the treble clef. He'd learned about rhythm and pitch, texture and tempo. Practicing scales, triads, seventh chords and key signatures replaced television and video games. While his brothers were running around, hiding in the woods and building forts, he was reading books on composition and technique and studying a wide range of musical genres from Beethoven to Debussy, Miles Davis to Duke Ellington, Ray Charles to Billy Joel.

Myles had never really looked forward to anything. But he found himself excited about summer vacation every year. Eventually, his lessons with Ms. Pennie progressed to music theory and logic, chord progressions, combining elements to make melodies.

At thirteen, Myles composed his first original song. He still remembered playing it for Ms. Pennie and the look of pride on her face. She encouraged him to keep going, keep perfecting the sound. And he had never stopped reading, writing, thinking music. Even when he made the decision to attend medical school, to become a surgeon, music was never not a part of his life. It was something he kept to himself, though. Only a handful of people knew how much it truly meant to him. He'd only played in public a half dozen times, most recently for his good friend's wedding.

He felt a strong hand squeeze his, bringing him back to the present. Glancing up, he met Ms. Pennie's knowing eyes. "Where did you go?" she asked.

"Just thinking about you and everything you taught me."

"Myles, my sweet, sweet boy. I've never been more proud of a student than I am of you. Not only are you a gifted musician and composer, you're a skilled surgeon and a caring man. I'm going to be fine. Remember, think positive."

He blinked, willed away tears that had threatened to fall. Nodding, he said, "I know, but…" He swallowed. "Just so you know. I can never repay you for being exactly what I needed back then. I'm not sure where I would be if I hadn't met you."

She shot him a watery smile. "You'd be just fine, boy. You didn't need me."

"I'm serious, Ms. Pennie. I wouldn't be who I am today if—"

"Everything you are today is because of your courage, your willingness to take risks."

Myles was smart enough to know he wouldn't win this argument. He never did. Ms. Pennie knew about his childhood. The piano in the house was just for show, because none of them were allowed to make music on it.

He'd learned that the hard way one fateful day. But Ms. Pennie had never asked any questions or made judgments. Years of lessons, time spent at the piano, and she'd never charged him or made him feel like he owed her anything. She simply loved him and proved it every single day.

Ms. Pennie caressed his face with a shaky hand. "I love you, son."

He smiled. "I love you, too."

Chapter 4

The Charles H. Wright Museum, founded in 1965, held the largest permanent exhibit on African American culture. Among the collections were the *Blanche Coggin Underground Railroad Collection*, the *Harriet Tubman Collection* and an exhibit honoring the life of the Queen of Soul, Detroit native Aretha Franklin. And now, it held *Metamorphosis: A retrospective of life and love*. The artist? Aria Bell.

Myles had spent several minutes studying the art and the artist. Both were beautiful, fascinating, colorful and emotional. The more he observed both, the more she and her work intrigued him. It made him want to get to know her, to find out more about her inspirations. All of his siblings were in attendance to support Aria. The museum had put on a program to honor Aria and her contributions to the art world. He was impressed by her commitment to visual arts, to her own work. At the end of the program, the curator introduced her. Instead of a long speech, she'd given a short, moving talk about the power of art to tell stories, transform and inspire change. Aria had given honor to those who had inspired and shaped her worldview, to those who had taken time to teach and push her to create. As she'd spoken, he thought about his own connection to music. In so many ways, they were the same. His music, her paintings.

"She's amazing," Mel whispered. "I knew she was talented, but I had no idea how transformative her work was."

Above them, a painting called *Aria's Metamorphosis* hung. The description was just the title and date created. Different shades of reds, blues, purples and greens made up the background, but in the middle was a face. Her face. One side was smooth, like a porcelain doll, with clear skin and straight hair. The other side was textured, colorful. The hair on the wild side was almost floating, snaking around the canvas like vines. It was stunning. And he couldn't stop staring at it, speculating on its meaning. He knew what it meant to him, but he wondered what she was thinking when she'd created it.

"It's beautiful." Myles didn't have to turn to Mel to know she was watching him. He could feel the weight of her stare on him.

"The colors…it's almost three-dimensional."

Myles swallowed. "Like the artist," he murmured. He turned to meet Mel's pensive gaze. "Don't read too much into that, little sister."

She smiled. "Hard not to, big brother. I've seen the way you look at her."

Shrugging, he said, "She's a beautiful woman. But I don't know her."

"You could get to know her."

Myles had thought about the concept of "getting to know" Aria since he'd met her. But something always stopped him from asking her out. He'd seen her several times since the sip and paint, but they'd only shared superficial conversation. Even at Afternoon Delight, when he was seated so close to her that he could smell the hint of jasmine on her skin and see the flecks of gold in her brown eyes, they'd really only talked about things that didn't matter, safe subjects that wouldn't challenge their worldviews.

He tore his eyes away from his sister and peered back up at the painting, at Aria. "We're very different. I'm sure we have nothing in common." Except he instinctively knew he was wrong. *His music, her art.*

"Sometimes opposites make the best soul mates. Look at Bai and Ian. Completely different, hopelessly in love."

He snickered, thinking back to Ian and the way Bailee seemingly dropped into his lap. As happy as he was for his brothers, he hadn't fooled himself into thinking the same would happen to him. His life wasn't a romantic comedy. "A fluke," he responded dryly. "It's not an everyday occurrence."

"True, but look at Love and Drake, El and Avery… Life isn't a fairy tale, yes, but it can be fulfilling, and you can find love."

Mel had always believed in fairy tales, true love against all odds. He suspected that had a lot to do with the protective bubble they'd wrapped around her from the moment she was born. His sister was a princess of sorts. They'd kept her from a lot of pain, hidden so many of life's trials from her.

For years, she didn't realize that their father had spent years having an affair with Drake's mother, while married to Myles and Ian's mother. Mel didn't know that Dr. Law had never been faithful to her own mother, his current wife. She had no idea that Dr. Law had offered to pay Avery off if she left El or that their father tampered with Drake's career to get him away from Love until both relationships were on solid ground.

In hindsight, he figured they should have let her experience the trials and tribulations of real life, but they couldn't bear to dim the light always present in her doe eyes. He hoped that she always believed in possibilities.

"I'm not looking for love, Mel."

"I'm going to hook you two up. She's single, you're single. You're both attractive. And she's smarter than a fifth grader."

He laughed, pulling his sister into a hug. "Stop. Am I ever going to live that down?"

"Never," she said.

They continued their tour through the exhibit, checking out the various paintings, looking for meaning in the colors and forms. The final painting was breathtaking, a phoenix rising from the ashes. He'd seen similar renderings on T-shirts and in print media, but the phoenix in Aria's picture wasn't a bird-like creature. It was a mythical, beautiful brown superhero. It was her, nude and floating midair. It was her, with her thin waist, long legs, full breasts and majestic, massive wings of flames behind her. At the same time, long feathers covered her breasts and her core. The fire flared from her skin and her hair, sparked from her fingertips. Smoke billowed in the background. There were cracks on her skin, battle wounds. But it was her eyes—red, burning and bright— looking at him, that held him mesmerized. The painting was so vivid it felt animated, like he could reach out and feel the heat of the flames. He felt pain, struggle, redemption and victory.

"Wow," he whispered. He wasn't sure which painting spoke to him the most, the first one or the last. But both evoked palpable emotions.

"I know," Mel said. "I bet Love is in heaven right now."

Myles smiled, scanning the room for his sister-in-law. He spotted her over by the first painting, noticed Love wiping tears from her eyes as she stared up at the portrait. Across the room, near the entrance to the room, Aria stood watching everyone as they reacted to her art.

His gaze roamed over her tall, lean frame. She was lovely in every way. From her black leather boots to her wild, colorful hair. But it was her smile—genuine and bright—that stopped him in his tracks. He felt like he'd caught a glimpse of a priceless treasure, glimmering like gold. The only problem? It wasn't shining on him. Instead, it was directed at some other man.

Aria hugged the man, who'd never been far from her the entire night. Myles had noticed them together right away. They were comfortable with each other, but he couldn't put his finger on who he was to her. Were they friends or lovers? Coworkers? Was the man with the dreads her agent?

"Let's go over and talk to Aria?" Mel pulled him toward the entrance.

By the time they made it over to them, Avery and El

had joined them. They were all smiling now, chatting excitedly about the work.

Aria's smile didn't falter when he approached them, though. Instead, she met his gaze full on. "Myles, I'm glad you came."

"You're amazing." He pretended not to notice the look Avery and Mel exchanged, and figured they'd talked about him and the possible love connection Mel had previously mentioned to him. "I'm glad I came, too."

Aria averted her gaze for a moment before returning it to him. "Thanks. Brent, you know Mel. This is her brother, Myles."

"Ah, the serious twin," Brent mused. "I've heard about you."

Briefly Myles wondered what Brent could have heard about him when he had no clue who this guy was. But instead of racking his brain with the possibilities, he held out his hand and gave Brent some dap. "Good to meet you. I'm guessing you already met my brother Ian, the fun twin."

Aria laughed, and Myles memorized the melody. "That's funny. Is this your way of confirming you're no fun?"

"He's fun," Mel responded—a little too loudly. "He's so much fun."

Myles looked down at Mel and pleaded with her to stop with his eyes. Apparently, she got the hint because she closed her mouth and walked away. Turning to Aria, he simply said, "I'm fun enough. But if you'll excuse me, I'll let you get back to your guests."

Myles had always been known as the twin who never really let loose. Ian had always been the one people wanted to be around, the star football player, the brother who wasn't afraid to jump into the water with clothes on. Although Myles played baseball all through school, enjoyed going to games and other social events with his brothers, he'd always preferred being alone with his music or working. It had never really bothered Myles to be known as the serious twin. Until now.

As the event wound down, Myles found himself back before the first painting. He examined the surface, imagined how Aria had looked while she created it. How was it possible that she'd captured something so real, so raw?

"It's my favorite."

Myles turned to find Aria standing next to him, peering up at her own work. *When did she get here?*

"It was my capstone project in my undergrad program. I spent weeks in the studio staring at a blank canvas. I didn't want it to be ordinary, but I wanted it to mean something."

"I'd say you accomplished that goal."

"I hope we didn't offend you back there, calling you the serious twin."

"No. I'm not easily offended. And it's the truth. I am serious, and Ian is fun."

She bit her lip. "Still, I just hope it didn't come off like an insult."

"Is Brent an artist, too?"

"He is." She smiled. "A tattoo artist. He owns Ink-Town Tattoos."

"The business next to Cocktails and Canvas?"

"That's the one. We're partners. He's actually the person who convinced me to move back to the area."

Myles turned his attention back up to the painting. He wanted to ask her if Brent was her man but decided to keep his mouth shut.

"What are you working on now?" he asked, wanting to keep her there with him for a little while longer.

"I'm showing at the University of Michigan Museum of Art for Black History Month, so I'm finishing up the installation for that space. And I'm also working on something for Avery."

"Sweet. Must be exciting."

"I can't deny it's been rewarding to be recognized for my work. I set my goals high, and I feel honored to be in this space." They stood in silence for another moment before she asked. "You keep staring at the painting."

"What can I say, it speaks to me?"

"What is it saying?"

Somehow, this conversation, this interaction was more intimate than he'd expected. And if he admitted how this picture made him feel, it would change things between them.

"Probably not what you intended," he said. "Art means different things to different people. That's the point, right?"

"I'd like to hear what you think. How does this painting speak to you?"

Myles peered up at the masterpiece and thought of a safe answer, one that wouldn't generate more questions. "She has two sides. One side conforms to rules imposed on her and the other side makes the rules. One side represents creativity, while the other represents conforming to others' expectations. One side is sweet, the other is wild. One part of her is dying."

"Why?" she asked.

He glanced at her out of the corner of his eye, noted the tremor in her hand as she gripped her throat.

"Why do you think that?" Aria said.

"Because she's being swallowed up by the dream of freedom. Which is a good thing. But the desire to please, the need to be what people expect never really goes away." And he knew it all too well because he'd lived it himself. "This painting...it's the only one that doesn't have a price tag on it."

"It's not for sale."

He turned to her and found her studying him with a curious expression on her face. "Why not sell it?"

She shrugged, offering him a small smile. "Because it's mine. It's me. It reminds me of where I came from and where I'm going. And it belongs on my wall."

"That's understandable."

A woman walked over to them and whispered something in Aria's ear. Once the woman was gone, Aria turned to him. "I'm sorry. I need to go handle something."

"Certainly."

She hurried off across the room to where an older man was waiting. Myles watched as Aria shook the man's hand and led him over to one of the paintings on the far side of the room. Making his way back over to the *Phoenix*, he glanced down at the placard near the base of the canvas.

Myles pulled out his phone and typed a text. For the first time in his life, he was going to follow his gut and make an impulsive decision.

Aria walked into the Charles H. Wright Museum the next morning. The opening had been a huge success, and she'd agreed to meet her agent to discuss the business of art, more specifically, whether she was able to make any sales.

Stella was chatting with the curator of the museum, when she entered the exhibit. Once she spotted Aria, she grinned. "We just sold the *Phoenix*."

"Really?"

"Really." Stella held up her phone. "The transfer went through minutes ago."

As elated as Aria was to sell a piece of her artwork, the *Phoenix* meant a lot to her. Early on in her career, she would cry each time she'd sold a piece. It was hard to let them go. Still, she'd soon realized that she couldn't keep every single painting. The purpose of creating was to share.

"How exciting!" Aria said. She stepped up to the painting in question, ran her thumb over the edge. "I'll miss this one."

"Well, you'll always have the ink on your side to remind you of her."

Stella had taken a chance by signing Aria a little over a year ago, after the debacle with Holloway. She'd helped her through the breakup and the subsequent investigation, and proved to be an invaluable ally and someone Aria considered a friend.

"Did we get asking price?" Aria said.

"We sure did."

"That's even better. Who is the buyer?"

"Actually, he's still here. I told him you were on your way, and he wanted to meet with you."

Aria craned her neck around, scanning the immediate area for people. The room was empty. Turning to Stella, she asked, "Did he say what he wanted to meet with me about?"

"No, but he's a hottie. I noticed him at the opening last night."

Aria tried to picture the men in attendance. She'd made it a point to talk to each person who came so it could be anyone. "Young or old?"

"Young."

"Another artist?"

Stella shook her head. "No. Definitely not an artist."

"Definitely not," a male voice from behind her said.

It wasn't just anybody's voice, and the raspy sound of it made her stomach do an odd flip. She turned slowly and met the amused eyes of Myles Jackson.

"Myles."

"Aria." He stepped closer. "Hi."

"Hi," she breathed. "You bought one of my paintings?"

"I did."

Stella stepped in. "And we're so elated that you loved the *Phoenix*. And we appreciate your understanding in keeping it here at the museum until the exhibit is over."

It wasn't uncommon for art buyers to purchase a piece of art and allow the artist to keep it for showings. And since that particular work was important to the overall collection, Aria appreciated that Myles was willing to leave it there.

"Yes, thank you," Aria said.

"I'm going to leave you two alone." Stella squeezed Aria's arms before she left the room.

"You look surprised that I would purchase your work." He approached her until they were standing mere inches apart. Too close.

Aria retreated back a few steps. "No, I knew you loved my signature piece because we talked about it."

One of the things that had stuck with her from last night was the conversation with Myles. When she'd asked him to tell her why *Metamorphosis* spoke to him, she'd expected… She didn't even know what she'd expected. But she certainly hadn't thought he'd speak on it so eloquently. Normally when people tried to explain her paintings, it came out practiced, almost like they'd opened a textbook and read up on words to use to describe artwork. But Myles… He was so spot-on it felt like he'd split her open and squeezed her heart.

"I loved this one, too."

"I can't thank you enough. Your support means a lot to me."

"No need to thank me."

"No, seriously. Myles, the painting is not cheap."

"I'm aware of that."

She giggled. "I guess you are. Stella told me you wanted to meet me. So, I thought the purchaser was someone I didn't know."

"Last night wasn't a good time to discuss your work. You had to entertain your guests."

She took a seat on a bench, and he followed her, sitting next to her. "What did you want to discuss?"

"I'll admit I have a keen interest in the art, but I'm also intrigued by the artist."

Aria blinked. "The artist?" she croaked. "Me?"

"You."

"As in my creative process?"

"That, too."

She let out a slow breath. *Damn.*

"Have dinner with me?"

She frowned, still unable to believe this turn of events. Myles Jackson had just asked her out to dinner. On a date. Just the two of them. Admittedly, she was attracted to him. He'd stoked something in her that she hadn't felt in a long time. *Maybe forever?* But…could she date him? They didn't have anything in common. He was so buttoned up, and she was not. It would be over before it started. And what would they talk about exactly? Her art could only keep the conversation going for so long before it became stilted.

"Aria?" His voice was soft, calm.

She shook her head. "I'm sorry. I guess I'm just confused. You asked me out."

"For dinner." His lips quirked up into a sexy half smile. "How is that confusing?"

"I…um. I can't go out with you."

"Are you seeing someone else? The man at the exhibit?"

"Brent?" Aria laughed. "He's like my brother."

"Good. Let me take you out."

She jumped up and paced the floor. "I'm not sure that's a good idea. You're Myles. I'm friends with your sisters. I'm not sure—because I've never really had girlfriends—but I think that's against the Girlfriend Code or something."

"Yeah." Myles tapped his chin. "That's not a thing."

"Okay, but it would be awkward with them if—"

"It's dinner. Not a wedding."

"But we're so different."

He stood and walked toward her. "So different that we can't eat a meal together?"

Aria couldn't help it. She laughed. "You're funny."

"I don't think anyone has ever told me that before," he said to her, shoving his hands into his pockets. "I am the serious twin."

When he chuckled, she shoved him playfully. "You got jokes."

He barked out a full laugh then. "Only with you."

For some reason, she believed him. And that little admission made her want to say yes even more than she already did. "I'm not surprised often, Dr. Jackson, but you really shocked me today."

"Why? Is it so hard to believe I'd want to take you out?"

"Actually, yes. Like I said, we're very different."

"Is this your way of telling me no?"

She tilted her head and assessed him. She was sure it would be a mistake to do anything with him alone. Especially with the way her nerve endings were sparking to life in his presence. Oh, and the heat that had coated her insides at the sound of his voice. But she surprised herself when she said, "Lunch? Saturday."

He smiled. "Okay. Lunch."

Aria pulled out one of her business cards and scribbled her personal phone number on the back before she handed it to him. "Call me and let me know the time and place."

"I'll call you and let you know what time I'll pick you up on Saturday for lunch."

"You're pretty stubborn, huh? I can't meet you there? Saturdays are really busy for me at the studio. I'm thinking it would be better if I can just meet you at one of the restaurants near there."

He sighed. "Fine. You win. We'll meet for lunch on Saturday."

"Good."

"Good." He searched her eyes, and for a moment, she thought he was going to kiss her. Instead, he simply smiled. "See you soon."

Then he was gone.

Chapter 5

"I need some advice, Brent." Aria eyed the outfit hanging in the back room closet of the studio. It was her signature "date" look—ripped jeans, leather jacket and revealing cami. She'd pair it with kick-ass high-heeled sandals. Sexy but comfortable.

"What kind of advice?" Brent took a seat on the couch. When they'd renovated the studio, they'd added a living space in the back, because both of them spent so much time in the building. There was a television, a computer with two huge monitors, and a mini workout area with a treadmill and free weights. "Why are you staring in the closet?"

She nibbled on her thumbnail. "I'm going on a lunch date today."

Aria had spent the entire week thinking about her date with Myles, going over the reasons she said yes and why she should have said no. The only conclusion she could come up with was…curiosity. He seemed to debunk all of her early theories about him, that he was straitlaced and work focused, and she'd damn near fallen in strong like with him after his explanation of her painting. There was nothing sexier than a man who loved and appreciated art. Especially *her* art.

"A date? Finally?"

She picked up a pillow and threw it at her friend. "Be quiet. There's nothing wrong with focusing on myself."

"Is that what you were doing?"

She glanced at him through the mirror. He dipped his hand into a huge bag of chips and pulled one out. "Yes. I chose to concentrate on getting settled here and putting out this work."

"Gotcha."

She hated him. *Not really.* Sighing, she walked over to him and plopped down on the couch next to him. "Can we at least pretend that you're supportive and not simply trying to point out what I don't want to face?"

"Ha! Well, at least you admitted it."

"Seriously. Advice?"

He bit down on a chip and held out the bag for her to take some. She grabbed a handful. "Fine. What type of advice? And who is your date?"

"Myles."

He choked, and she patted his back. Hard. Brent pushed her hand away. "Okay, okay… Are you trying to kill me?"

"Brent." She folded her arms across her chest. "Please."

"I'm sorry. I'm just surprised. Why Myles?"

"Because he asked me out. And he's pretty funny. And he bought the *Phoenix*."

"So, he bought a date with you?"

Aria stuffed her mouth with chips. Her best friend had only said what she'd thought initially. How convenient that Myles bought a painting and then asked her out the same day, after he requested a "meeting" with the artist. It all seemed suspect.

"Hey." Brent rubbed her back. "Chew that food and stop avoiding this."

Swallowing roughly, Aria took a few sips of water from her bottle on the side table.

"So, you've thought about the possibility?" he asked.

She nodded. "Yep. Pretty much." She lifted her legs up and rested her chin on her knees. "But at the same time, he doesn't seem like he would do that. The entire exchange felt sincere. And I could have said no."

"Do you like him?"

Aria shrugged. "Kind of."

"So, what's the problem? Besides the obvious."

"See!" Aria gripped Brent's shoulder. "You see the obvious reasons why this isn't going to work, right? He's so different, too buttoned up. They call him the 'serious' twin, for goodness' sake."

"And he's exactly the type of man you said you didn't want to date anymore."

Aria dropped her head, picked at a stray thread on the cuff of her pants. Her mother had paraded a lot of men in front of her every time she came home for a visit, and all of them were like Myles—professional, intelligent, respectful. Until she agreed to give them a chance, that is. They'd spout all kinds of frilly love stuff about being attracted to her beauty as well as her brains. They'd wine and dine her, tell her how her personality put her above the rest. Then, as soon as she got comfortable, they'd slowly start making suggestions. Straighten your hair or wear this dress or paint your nails pink instead of blood red. Eventually, they'd ask her to reconsider her dreams in favor of a more acceptable career—like fund-raising, nursing or stay-at-home mother.

And the sad part? Even after she'd put her foot down and told her mother to never try and hook her up again, Aria found herself dating the same sort of men. *I guess I have a type.* Holloway was the last of the trust fund babies. Well, the last of the fake trust fund babies. Because he was broke and he'd latched on to her when he'd seen promise and dollar signs. Why the hell would she put herself right back into the same situation for Myles?

She leaned into Brent, letting him wrap strong arms around her. "I'm not telling you not to date him. I just need you to not hide your head in the sand about your reasons."

"It will be fine." Her statement was more for her than for Brent. "He's a nice guy. He's connected to my friends. And it's just lunch."

"Was that your idea?"

"Hell, yes. Lunch is during daylight hours, doesn't last long and won't ruin the rest of my day if it doesn't go well. I can go and see what he's talking about, eat a free meal, and come back here and work."

Brent laughed. "You're crazy. So, what's the advice you needed? Seems like you have it all figured out."

Aria stood and walked back over to the closet. "My outfit." She pointed to the items in question hanging there. "Should I change, or keep on what I'm wearing?" Currently, Aria was comfortable in camouflage joggers, a black T-shirt and black Roche Ones. "I mean, it is technically a date. Shouldn't I walk in lit?"

Brent frowned. "I thought we said we wouldn't have

these sorts of conversations now that you have some girlfriends. Why don't you call one of them and do what y'all do?"

"I can't."

"Why?"

"Because they're related to him. And—" she scratched her neck "—I haven't told them about it."

"Wow, so I must have missed the memo. I didn't know this was a secret date."

"Shut up and answer the question."

"The fact that they're related to him should prompt you to talk to them more. They have more insight into what he likes."

"But you're a man."

"Yeah, a man who doesn't want to date you or kiss you or do you."

Aria's mouth fell open. "Should I be insulted?"

"No." He stood and walked to the closet. Sighing, he pulled out the outfit, peered at it, then put it right back where it was. "Keep on what you're wearing?"

"I'm not exactly sexy in this outfit."

"Listen, I can't speak for Myles, but I know a little about men and their thought process." He gripped her shoulders, looked into her eyes. "Don't take this the wrong way—you're beautiful—but chances are he didn't ask you out because you dress like a minx."

Aria pouted.

"Don't give me that look," he continued. "All I'm saying is, he obviously likes your everyday look."

The corner of her mouth lifted up. "Really?"

"Absolutely. And I can kind of see why—in a first-cousin type of way."

She laughed, pushing him away. "You get on my nerves. I guess I should take that as a compliment."

"You definitely should, because it is."

Aria hugged Brent and placed a kiss on his cheek. "Have I told you how much I love you?"

"So many times I've lost count."

"I probably should put on makeup."

He frowned. "Every. Day. Aria. No. Makeup. Aria."

She really did love her bestie, but... "Lip gloss?"

"Fine." He shrugged and took his bag of chips. "I have an appointment in five. Have fun today."

"Thanks." She picked at her hair in the mirror. "I will try."

"Don't do anything I would do."

"No chance of that happening. Like I said, lunch, daylight, short."

A little while later, Aria walked into the local Applebee's for lunch with Myles. He was already seated at a corner booth. As she approached the table, disappointment crept up on her when she noticed his attire. It was noon, on a Saturday, and he was dressed in a suit. And she was...not.

That mere fact only cemented in her what she already knew. This date would probably be their last. There was no way they could be anything more than friends.

"Hi." She stopped at the table.

He glanced up and smiled. "Hi." He stood, gave her a polite hug and a kiss on the cheek, and waited until she slid into the other side of the booth. "I'm sorry. I was checking my emails."

Aria let her gaze roam over his face. *Oh, my God.* It was a tragedy that she had to end this before anything could start. Because Dr. Myles Jackson was ridiculously hot. He looked so good in that suit her inner nasty-girl was practically begging her to take him for a spin. Still, she wished he'd worn something a little less formal, like just a button-down shirt and a pair of jeans. *Damn it.*

The waitress came and took her drink order. Once the young woman was gone, Aria leaned forward. "Before this goes any further, I…let's talk." Myles leaned forward, too. So close their arms were touching. *Damn it. He smells* good. And it wasn't just his scent. His hair, his skin, his eyes, his hands… Everything about him seemed to make her feel a little crazy and a lot confused by her strong reaction to him. "Because I have questions."

As if he lived to torture her, he blessed her with his sexy ass smirk. "What do you want to know?"

She wanted to know what he looked like with his clothes off, but she would never see that. Swallowing, she tapped her finger on the table. "I've been trying to come up with a reason."

"A reason why…?"

"You asked me out. I have to know why."

He stared at her with narrowed eyes. "This again?"

"Yes. It's just… I think I'm confused because I'm not sure I'm your type."

Myles leaned back, took a sip from the glass of water in front of him. Aria looked at the glass sitting just off to her left and considered mimicking his action but felt like that would be petty. A few tense seconds later, he resumed his former stance. "What makes you think I have a type?"

Aria sighed. "Because at the studio, you came with a date. Tina. The woman who didn't know that red and blue made purple? I'm not trying to be judgy, but… I'm nothing like her."

* * *

Myles couldn't believe this turn of events. He'd waited all week to see her again, to talk to her. He'd agreed to lunch, not dinner. He'd even agreed to meet her at Applebee's. And he *hated* Applebee's. And now this woman was questioning his… Hell, he didn't even know what this was.

But he'd been trained to remain calm under pressure, to not react. He took a deep breath and met her questioning gaze again. "Tina wasn't a real date. I took her out as a favor. For my father."

She winced. "Oh."

"Right. So, to answer your question. I don't have a type. And I don't play games. I asked you out because I find you to be extremely beautiful and smart and fascinating."

Her mouth fell open, and a pretty blush crept up her neck. "Oh," she repeated.

Myles liked that he made her nervous. He wanted to see if her blush reached other parts of her body. "I understand why you would think that, though. About Tina."

"I'm sorry. I… It's just that we're so different."

"How so? Because you keep saying it."

She pulled her arms off the table and rested her hands in her lap. "Can I be honest?"

"Please do."

"You're a surgeon. You seem like you like order, routine. I'm an artist. I work when I'm inspired. I don't punch a clock to create."

"But you have to punch a clock to run your business."

"That's just a part of what I do, not who I am."

"So, tell me who you are?"

She tilted her head and assessed him. The skepticism

and interest in her brown eyes was unmistakable. He
wanted to tick off numerous reasons their perceived differences didn't matter in the grand scheme of things.
Because now? He was pretty sure she would be his before the end of the month. Some people would call him
cocky, but he thought of it as confident. His instinct had
never failed him yet, and his gut told him that the connection burning hot between them wouldn't be doused
any time soon.

A few moments passed before she leaned forward
again. "I'm someone who has worked hard to get where
I am. I've fought for my career and my way of life. And
I'm at a point where I'm not going to date just anybody
so I can post my relationship status on Facebook. If I'm
going to invest my time and energy into a man, I want to
be respected and valued as a woman."

Myles couldn't take his gaze off her. The more she
opened up to him, the more he wanted her. His pulse
thundered in his ear as he waited for her to continue talking. But he decided to throw another card on the table,
in the hopes it would build trust.

"I won't pretend to understand how it feels to be you.
I can only tell you my truth. I asked you out *because* of
those things. Because I could see something in you, feel a
connection when we talked. I thought it would be good to
explore it. But I'm not always right." He *was* right about
her, though. But he wouldn't push her. "Sometimes huge
differences can't be overcome. If we leave here and you
feel that is the case, then we'll just be cool. Friends."

She relaxed in her seat. "Okay."

He held his hands up at his side. "No pressure. We're
good?"

Aria blessed him with a smile, and he swallowed hard.

That smile knocked him off his square every damn time. "We're definitely good."

The waitress brought Aria's drink to the table and they quickly placed their lunch order. Several minutes later, they were eating. They talked about her work, why he purchased the *Phoenix* and what he thought it meant. She admitted that his explanation of the *Metamorphosis* had made her curious enough to accept the date initially.

"You didn't like me when we met, did you?" he asked.

"Why would you say that?"

He shrugged. "I saw the way you looked at me that night."

Aria pointed her fork at him. "That literally had nothing to do with you. Well, it had something to do with your date."

He barked out a laugh. "Tell me how you really feel."

"Hey, you asked. But the day had been one meeting after another. Good news, but I was exhausted."

"You're from Michigan, right?"

She set her fork down and wiped her mouth with her napkin. "Yeah." She nodded. "My father served as the District Court Judge for Inkster."

"Really? Is he still there?"

"No. My mother never wanted to be there in the first place. He eventually moved to a federal court. When he switched jobs, we moved."

"Yeah, I actually lived in Las Vegas as a young child."

Her eyes widened. "Really? I love Vegas."

"It's all right."

"Oh, come on. Nonstop lights and action and people... so much inspiration. So much fun."

"Like I said, it's all right. I like it here better."

"Why?"

"For one, I like the change in seasons. And I actually enjoy Ann Arbor."

She hummed. "It is nice here. I'm glad I came back."

"You're stunning."

She dipped her head, scratched the back of her neck. "Thank you, but you don't have to tell me that."

"I do. I don't say anything that I don't mean."

"I can believe that."

"So, if you believe that, then you can believe me when I say you're so beautiful."

"Myles…" She twirled her napkin around her thumb.

"Just accept the compliment, Aria."

"Fine."

"Finally!" He pumped his fists.

"If you can tell me that, I guess I can admit that I think you're fine as hell."

He laughed. "Well, that's good to know."

"So, why aren't you taken? All of your brothers are married, settled down."

Myles hated that question. It seemed as if everybody in his life was taking bets on his love life. "I don't know. I definitely don't sit around wondering when my turn is coming. I work a lot. There are things I want to accomplish in my career."

"And you don't think you can find love while working toward those goals?"

"That's not it. My brothers have successful careers *and* happy home lives. But I'm not in a rush. It's been a long time since I've been with someone."

She shot him an incredulous glance. "Oh, please. Now, that's hard to believe."

"What? Why is that so hard to believe?"

"Because…you're hot and a doctor. I'm sure there are plenty of women who want to be your *one*."

"Not any women I want to be with."

"How long has it been?"

He snorted. "Um… January?"

"January?" She smacked her hands on the table. "That's not a long time. Try two years."

He blinked. "Two years? You haven't been with anyone in that long?"

"I was just saying…some people go that long without sex. January was just five months ago."

As they finished their lunch, Myles attempted to formulate a game plan in his mind. Would she balk at another date so soon? Or should he play it cool and casual?

Once he paid the bill, he walked her to her car. She walked ahead of him a little, giving him time to check her out. She wore camouflage pants and a black T-shirt. The fact that she'd chosen comfort over revealing was sexy as hell. He'd hoped she would come as herself and not some made-up version of what she thought he wanted. Just one more thing that made him want to see her again.

Refreshing, fun, hilarious… Those were all words that had run through his mind during lunch. His life had been so hectic, so busy. And she'd made him laugh, she'd challenged him. He wanted more of that.

Standing in front of her car now, she smiled. "Lunch was nice. I'm glad I came."

"Any chance you'll let me take you to dinner?"

"Myles, I—"

He reached out, brushed his thumb over her cheek and pressed his fingers to the pulse point behind her ear. "I think I figured it out."

"What?" she whispered.

"The problem. Somewhere along the line, I think you got confused. Maybe you think because I'm the serious twin, I'm the lame twin."

She opened her mouth to speak, but then closed it again.

"Maybe that's why you see us as different? Is that right?"

The steady beat of her heart pounded against his fingers. *Confirmation.* His phone buzzed in his coat pocket, but he ignored it.

"Are you going to answer that?" Her voice was as soft as her skin felt to his fingertips.

Myles shook his head. "You didn't answer my question."

"I guess, I..." Aria swallowed visibly, dropping her gaze. "I think..."

I'm in trouble. Because, in that moment, all he wanted was her lips on his. He couldn't take it anymore. He'd told himself to wait it out and let her set the pace. But he wanted her.

Then her eyes were on his again, watching him. *Is she going to push me away, make up an excuse to leave?* But instead of pushing him away, she wrapped her arms around his waist and pulled him closer. A heartbeat later, her lips were on his, kissing him. Myles had never been lost in someone before, so consumed by a woman that he couldn't think straight. But there was a first time for everything because that was exactly how he felt. He'd set rules for his life at an early age, and he'd never wanted to veer from his path. Until now. Aria Bell was a game changer.

Finally, breaking the kiss, he leaned his forehead against hers. "So... Is that a yes...for dinner?"

She dropped her head on his chest, giggling. "It's a date."

Chapter 6

"Any luck?" Brent asked, walking into the studio the following Monday.

Aria sighed, her eyes focused on the blank canvas in front of her. The same blank canvas she'd been staring at for two days. She shook her head. "Nope. I don't know what's wrong with me."

"You're whipped."

Her head flew around to face him. "Stop. That would imply that I've actually had sex in the past year."

During lunch with Myles, she'd slipped up and admitted it had been two years. It had been way too long since she'd been with someone. But she'd also been too engrossed with work to meet anyone that she'd been attracted to. Until Dr. Myles Jackson ensnared her with his dark eyes and sexy smile.

"I'm telling you, you haven't been right since the date with the doctor," Brent said. "You're distracted."

"Not true."

He shot her an incredulous look. "Yeah, right. You forget, I saw you after the date."

Aria thought back to Saturday afternoon, after she and Myles kissed so long and so hard and so good, right in the middle of the Applebee's parking lot. It felt like they were the only two people there. In that short time, with one kiss, her world seemed to tilt on its axis. Because he was nothing like she'd expected. She didn't know what to expect. The only thing she knew for sure was...*shit*. He'd mastered the art of kissing.

It had been days since she'd seen him, but she couldn't stop thinking about him. She still felt the heat of his hard body against her, smelled his cologne as if he was sitting next to her. Aria could still taste him.

"Aria?" Brent waved a hand in front of her, drawing her from the memory.

She jumped. "Huh?"

"You agreed to another date."

"I did." Which was totally against her plan to eat lunch and let him down easy so as to preserve the relationship with her friends. She absolutely should have turned him down. Because he wasn't right for her. There were too many "not right" boxes he checked off. He was zipped up. She was free and easy. He was tightly scheduled. She was spontaneous. And, most important of all... Girlfriend Code. *Hello.* She loved hanging out with his sisters. Getting involved with him could definitely jeopardize her newfound friendships. Still, she'd agreed to see him again. For dinner. And after dinner. "But I'm going to cancel." *No, I'm not.*

When she met Brent's gaze, she knew he knew she

was lying. He walked over to her and squeezed her shoulder. "Have you talked to him?"

"Not on the phone. We texted." Multiple times a day. She wouldn't tell Brent that little tidbit.

"Listen, it's not the end of the world. So, you're attracted to him. Feel it. Besides, you have something to celebrate."

Aria smiled up at her best friend. He was right. The bid she'd put on a house had been accepted. She would finally have her own space again. "I know, right?"

Her Realtor had called her with the news a few hours ago. Aria had fallen in love with the house on sight and had hoped she'd be able to purchase it. In less than a month, she would be a homeowner, and her relocation would be complete and permanent. At least for now.

"It's not the end of the world." Brent stood behind her, arms folded over his chest. "It doesn't make you less human to be attracted to someone."

"It's not that. I just don't think it's right, you know? I still feel like I'm setting myself up for more heartbreak with him."

"Why? You told me that he seemed sincere, and not like you expected."

"Still… He could be playing me."

"I give up." Brent lifted his arms in surrender. "This is why you need to talk to a woman. Because men don't sit here and analyze and pick and overthink something so simple."

"I'm not being unreasonable. He's rich, he's organized, he's a workaholic. And there's a part of him that I fear he'll never let me see."

That was the other part that bothered her. Yes, they'd talked about his work and his family, but he was still pretty closed off. The dress clothes and buttoned-up vibe seemed more like a defense mechanism than a fashion choice, a way to keep people from seeing the real Myles. She'd realized that too late in her last relationship, how a man's outward appearance could be like armor, protecting him from anyone who wanted to pierce through to see the real person underneath. She wouldn't make that mistake again.

She shook her head, not knowing how to articulate that without sounding weird. "Forget it. I'm just going to cancel. I'll explain that I'm not in a space to date right now. I can use the house as an excuse. I need to concentrate on moving and working. And let's not forget that I have a bigger reason for moving back to Michigan."

Opening the studio was great, but Aria's ultimate goal was to start an academy, a school that focused on bringing art to inner-city kids who would not normally be exposed to such programs. Aria had completed a dual graduate program in art education and fine arts. She wanted to give children the gift of expression, creative freedom.

"How can I forget? You know I'm all about that dream of yours. I can't wait to see it come to fruition."

Picking up a paintbrush, she dipped it into the shade of red she'd mixed when she arrived at the studio and flung it onto the canvas. Without another word, she stroked the canvas, happy to be painting and not staring. Her best friend walked away, knowing time alone in her element was exactly what she needed to clear her mind.

Hours later, Aria emerged from the back room, intent on grabbing something to drink from the corner store and maybe a Greek salad from the family diner next door. When she exited the building, she froze.

Myles stood there, leaning against his car and smiling at her. "Hi."

"You're here?" she said.

"To see you." He stood to his full height and walked toward her, his eyes never leaving hers.

Aria forgot about canceling dates and hidden agendas. She couldn't think of any reason she shouldn't go out with him.

"I figured I'd stop by to see you, take you for a walk. Show you that I can be spontaneous."

The fact that he'd come to see her in the middle of the day, when she knew he would normally be at work, made her feel special. Because one of the things she'd assumed was a deal breaker with him was the inability to be spontaneous, to go against the grain, let loose and do something unexpected. And yet, he'd surprised her. Again.

She looked down at her outfit. She'd spent the last few hours working. Her worn jeans had fresh paint spattered on them, and her oversize shirt hung off her shoulders sloppily. And she was sure her hair looked like a hot mess.

"I'm not suitable for people today," she said.

His brown eyes raked over her body, from her clunky work boots all the way up to her eyes. His perusal was so thorough, so slow, it felt like he'd stripped her bare. "You look beautiful."

No one had ever gazed at her like he was right now. His heated gaze made her feel warm, safe, beautiful and sexy. She shifted on her feet. "I didn't expect you. Come on in."

He followed her back into the studio. "I missed you." Her gaze dropped to his lips. He'd just gotten there, and she was already imagining him kissing her, holding her. "I've been painting." *Get it together, Aria.*

The corner of his mouth quirked up into a smile. "I think I figured that out."

She couldn't pull her eyes away from him. He really was a work of art. If he had any physical imperfections, she couldn't tell. Because everything about him was perfect to her. He smelled clean, like soap and sanitizer. Leaning in a little, she took a whiff.

He pulled back. "Did you just sniff me?"

The question shook her out of the Myles trance she'd been in and she backed away, tugging her shirt down. "No," she lied. "I think I'm getting a cold."

He traced her lips with his forefinger. "Your mouth... There's a fleck of paint." His voice was gruff, dangerous.

Aria pulled a handkerchief from her back pocket and wiped her mouth. "Still there?"

With hooded eyes on her mouth, he licked his lips. "No. You got it."

"Where are we going?"

His eyes snapped to hers. "Huh?"

"You said you were taking me for a walk?"

"Oh, yes. Let's go."

"You still haven't told me where we're going? I should change."

He shook his head. "No need to change. You're fine the way you are."

Aria smoothed a hand over her hair, hoping she didn't look like Medusa, ready to terrorize the modern world. "If you say so."

Myles held out his hand. "You ready?"

"For what?"

"To come with me."

Aria knew his statement was so much more than what he'd said. *Am I ready to go with him?* Against all of her reservations she slipped her fingers into his, and tried not to moan at the warmth and strength of them. Yes, she had a thing for hands.

A little while later, they were walking through the park, strolling leisurely and eating Italian ice. It was a perfect summer day. She dipped her spoon in her cup and sampled the mango-flavored treat. "This is so good. Thanks for bringing me here."

"No problem."

"Why did you? I already said yes to dinner."

He bumped into her softly. "I just wanted to make sure you weren't going to cancel on me."

She laughed. Loudly. "I was really close to canceling," she admitted.

"I'm not surprised."

"I'm sorry."

"What for?"

"For being so weird. I just have a lot of baggage." She glanced at him out of the corner of her eye. "It's not your fault, though."

"You mean, it's you, not me."

Aria giggled. "You crack me up."

"I try," he murmured. "So, have you changed your mind? About canceling on me?"

"Pretty much." She stopped and turned to him. "But I have a request."

He stepped into her, staring into her eyes. "What's that?"

"Take me somewhere that means something to you. I don't want to go to some stuffy, expensive restaurant. You want to know me? Show me you."

He sighed, like he was considering her condition, and nodded. "You got it."

Smiling, she started walking away. "Good. Then, I'll make sure I'm ready and waiting when you pick me up Friday night." As they neared the studio, she let her gaze roam over him. Today he wore another suit, black with a light gray shirt and tie. "Can I ask you a question?"

"If I said no, would you listen?"

"Probably not."

He chuckled, eating a spoonful of his strawberry Italian ice. "Then, shoot."

"Do you always dress in a suit and tie?"

"Is that a problem for you?"

She shrugged. "I'm just curious. Every time I've seen you, you've been dressed formally. Even at Applebee's on a Saturday. If I'm being honest, that does give me pause. Because I'm not so formal." She made a show of looking down at her outfit. "See!"

"I dress casual sometimes," he said. "Usually when I'm not working. And I work a lot."

"You said that before." They reached the studio door, and she unlocked it, stepping inside. Brent didn't appear to be in the building, which was a good thing because she didn't want to answer any questions. Once inside, she tossed her empty cup into the trash. "Do you ever feel overwhelmed with work? Need a break to let loose?"

"Not normally. Until now."

Suddenly nervous, she forced her eyes straight ahead, to the wall on the other side of the room. Because if she looked at him, she would lose the battle of wills she'd waged in her head from the moment he'd shown up in front of her place of business.

"Aria," he whispered, approaching her.

She let out a slow breath. "Yes?"

He didn't speak, didn't finish his thought. He just stared, like he wanted to simultaneously save her and spank her, like he wanted to worship her. *Damn.* She wanted that, too. Which was unfathomable, really. They'd shared only one kiss. It was one perfect kiss, but still. She wanted to give in.

Swallowing, she turned to walk away, far from him and his intense eyes and hard body. But he reached for her hand, pulling her closer, back to him.

He traced an invisible pattern with his thumb over her palm, sending sparks of electricity through her body. *That's it, I can't take it anymore.* Aria wasn't some high school girl crushing on the star football player. She was a grown woman, capable of not sounding desperate and needy for male attention. This was no big deal. He was only a man, and she had plenty of experience dealing with men.

"Myles," she mumbled. "You can't do this."

When his lips turned up into that sexy smile, she exhaled. He was doing this on purpose, tempting her, and her body ached for his touch. "Do what?"

"I don't know. Whatever you're doing."

She felt the rumble of his laughter against her. "Looking at you?"

Unable to stand being so close to him any longer, she put her hands up to his chest and backed away. "I can't… I can't think." She sucked in a deep breath. *Or breathe, apparently.*

He gripped her wrists and pulled her back to him again. "Then, don't. That's a good thing."

"Is it?" Her eyes dropped to his lips.

Myles leaned forward, nibbled on the corner of her mouth. "It is."

His lips weren't even fully on hers and she felt weak in the knees. He was so close, so male. "You're teasing me."

"Am I?" He traced her bottom lip with his tongue before he dipped it into her mouth.

She gasped, gripping his shirt in her fists. Any protest that could have been forming died on her lips when he finally kissed her. *Oh my.* His mouth applied the perfect amount of pressure. This wasn't an average kiss. It was…more. With every kiss, every nip, he was stealing something from her. A low moan escaped her lips as he ravaged her mouth. He was the fan and she was the flames. His hands were everywhere—on her waist, her behind, in her hair.

With his mouth still pressed to hers, he pulled her toward the couch in the corner. He fell back onto the cushions once they reached their destination and pulled her on top of him. *Oh my, he's good.* She straddled his lap and frantically unbuttoned his shirt. She traced his hard chest and abs with her fingers, reveling in the feel of his skin. She wanted to create a mold of his amazing body, paint the lines of his handsome face. And she hadn't even seen him naked yet. He was a work of art.

He bit down on her neck gently. "Aria," he groaned.

"Myles." She rocked her hips into him as the ache in her belly intensified. "We shouldn't be doing this."

He gripped her hips, holding her still. "If you're not ready—"

"Shit. Aria!"

Aria froze when she heard Brent's booming voice. "Oh, no." She slid off Myles and hit the floor with a loud bump. Then she jumped up. "Brent, it's not what you think," she shouted.

Brent's hands were over his eyes. "What the hell are you doing? Oh, I'm traumatized." He mimicked a gag. "I'm going to be sick."

"Oh, shut it," she yelled.

"This is the studio, a place of business. No sex."

She crossed her arms. "It's my studio," she huffed. "Go back to the shop." Aria glanced over at Myles, who was watching her, amusement in his eyes.

"I can't believe you, Aria." Brent paced the room, muttering a string of curses. "This is a nightmare."

"Nothing happened. And Myles was leaving." She tugged on Myles's arms, but proved too shaky to move him. He finally took pity on her and stood. "You're going," she told him.

"I am? Why? And didn't you say he was like a brother to you?"

"Because it's against God's plan for me to see her in this position," Brent said.

"Brent! Shut up." Aria pushed Myles toward the door. "You have to go back to work."

"No, I don't," Myles said.

"Okay, but you have to go somewhere else."

"Aria."

She stopped, peered up at him. *God, he looks so good.* "I'll call you."

Myles caressed her face and kissed her possessively. When he pulled back, he said, "I'll go. But I need to make something very clear. Us?" He gestured between them. "It's happening." He brushed his mouth over hers again and then walked out.

"Where have you been?" Ian asked, sliding into Myles's booth in the hospital cafeteria.

Myles dropped a french fry on his plate and glared at his twin. "Minding my business."

"Wow." Ian leaned back, studying him. "What the hell is your problem?"

"Nothing," he grumbled.

Except he did have a problem. And her name was Aria. It had been a day since their impromptu walk and make-out session. She'd yet to call him, though. Which made Myles grumpy and irritated. Top that off with his father riding him about business and a shift at the hospital that prevented him from banging out his frustration on his piano, and Myles was downright pissed.

"Bruh, talk."

He closed his eyes and sighed. "No."

Myles and his brothers never talked about women in an *I need some advice* type of way. Well, he'd never *asked* for advice. Usually, one of them would just point out if another one of them was acting like a punk or making a stupid decision.

"Is it Ms. Pennie?" Ian asked, concern in his eyes.

"No."

Myles had checked in with his music teacher just before he headed to the cafeteria. Ms. Pennie had developed radiation pneumonitis, which was caused by radiation therapy aimed at the chest or breast. The doctor had prescribed a steroid and she had been able to go home last week. Myles was thankful the cancer hadn't spread.

"That's good." Ian gulped his water. "Dad?"

"I'm not talking," Myles said.

"You're not talking about what?" El said, joining them with a tray of food.

Annoyed, Myles muttered a curse. "Nothing."

"Myles is in a mood," Ian told El.

"Ah. Is it my brother?" El bit into his burger.

When El was a kid, Dr. Law had already graduated from college, married and left home. His grandparents weren't really around, so Myles's father took El in and raised him with them.

"No."

For years, Myles had listened to his brothers tell him he needed to stop letting his father run his life. He didn't need another round of that. While they'd pushed back against Dr. Law, Myles had chosen to chill. He and his dad didn't have a bad relationship. He wouldn't say it was a typical father-son relationship, either, but he was okay with that.

Myles learned a long time ago to keep private things that really mattered to him. While his father knew he played, he'd purposefully kept his music to himself because he knew Dr. Law wouldn't understand. And Myles didn't feel like hearing the lectures about making money and career moves. He just wanted to live his life with some peace.

Nonetheless, his life was anything but peaceful right now, and it was all because he'd gone home yesterday horny and frustrated. He wanted Aria, thought he'd made some headway with her, but she'd literally pushed him out of her studio when Brent walked in. Which meant one of two things—something was going on between Aria and Brent, despite what they said about each other, or Aria was ashamed of Myles. Maybe.

He rubbed his forehead. "I asked Aria out," he blurted out.

El and Ian stopped, food midair.

"Artist Aria?" El asked, setting his burger back down on his plate.

"Yes," Myles grumbled.

Ian grinned and pointed at El. "I told you. I should have bet you. Wait until Drake hears this."

"Is that why you're scowling?" El opened his bottle of water. "Did she say no?"

"No," Myles responded.

"Are you going to give us more than one-word answers?" El asked.

Myles glared at his uncle-brother. El was an emergency psychiatrist, and it was in his nature to try to shrink people. He pushed his tray away from him. "No."

"Well, nice talking to you, bruh." El laughed. He tipped his chin in Ian's direction. "He's got it bad."

"I've never had to work this hard for a date," Myles announced. "And just when I thought she was on board, her friend comes in and she basically flips out."

"What friend?" Ian leaned forward.

"The guy that was hanging around her at the opening."

El cocked a brow. "Brent?"

"Yes," Myles growled.

El laughed. "They're just friends. Nothing going on there."

"And you know this because...?"

"I know Brent," El said. "And Avery told me."

Myles guessed he should feel better. But he didn't know how to feel. In a matter of weeks, Aria had turned his life upside down, had him going to Applebee's and out for walks in the middle of the day. That wasn't him. He was all schedules and work and women who didn't require much effort. Even still, he'd wanted to do those things. With her. He didn't mind Applebee's or Italian ice because he was with *her*. And it infuriated him that he didn't know how she felt.

Yes, she wanted him. He could tell that she was attracted to him. Attraction was fleeting, though. It went with the moment, with too much to drink or with the weather. The chemistry was strong, obviously. But the fact that he couldn't go a day without thinking about her or imagining her smile told him that it was more than that for him. Which was ridiculous, since they hadn't even gone out on a real date.

He blinked, shaking his head as if it would clear his mind. When he glanced up at his brothers, they were staring at him, mouths open. Frowning, he asked, "What?"

"Wow," Ian said. "You do have it bad. Welcome to the club."

Without a word, Myles picked up his tray and left.

As he hurried toward the surgical wing of the hospital, Myles pulled out his phone. Scrolling through his contacts, he paused when he saw Aria's name and debated whether he should call or text or just let it go. It bothered him that she hadn't called when she'd said she would. *When did I turn into that guy?*

Show me you.

Her words repeated in his mind on an endless loop. Could he do that? Honestly, he'd struggled with it. The reason he always remained calm and disciplined had everything to do with the way he managed to keep people and their problems at arm's length. Showing Aria who he was could potentially threaten that peace he tried so hard to hold on to. Was it worth it?

Sighing, he typed out a text. Still waiting on that call.

The little dots bounced around the screen immediately and he smiled, picturing her face as she tried to figure out how to respond. They hadn't known each other long at all, but he felt like he understood her, like they were two sides of the same coin.

Yesterday, it had taken everything in him not to pick her up, carry her out of the studio and take her home. So he could show her just how real the connection was. Their make-out session was unexpected because he really hadn't gone there for that. At the same time, it was undeniable. She was so perfect. Soft in all the right places, responsive. He didn't want to push her, and he wanted her in a way he'd never wanted any other woman. Still, there was something about him that made her hesitate, like she didn't believe it, believe *him*.

Finally a text came through. I'm sorry. Good news, though. I haven't canceled our date yet.

Myles chuckled and typed out a quick response. That is good news.

How should I dress?

Like you.

One of the things he liked about Aria was that she wasn't afraid to be herself. She dressed how she wanted, styled her hair for her. She marched to a beat that she'd created for herself. Something about that appealed to him. When she'd strolled out of the studio yesterday before their walk, he could barely catch his breath. Paint everywhere, hair wild and free, clunky old boots, and she was still the most beautiful woman he'd ever laid eyes on.

Myles was a realist. He'd never waxed poetic about anything or anybody, yet he couldn't seem to help himself with Aria. That was why he knew this would happen. He just had to be patient.

I hope you know that flattery doesn't really work on me.

Myles fired off a "sad face" emoji and barked out a laugh when she responded with a gif of a woman winking at him. Just sayin'.

I'm just speaking the truth.

Okay. I'll dress like me. And I'm looking forward to seeing you.

Myles knew what that meant. She'd thrown down a gauntlet of sorts with her "show me you" request, and answered. Friday. See you soon.

Have a good week.

He made a decision in that moment to share a part of himself he'd never shared with a date. Friday, he'd bring Aria into his world.

Chapter 7

Myles walked into the studio Friday evening. Aria had texted him earlier and asked him to pick her up there because she had a class late afternoon and wouldn't have time to go home and change. Brent was seated on a chair, talking on the phone. When Brent noticed him, he told Myles that Aria would be right out.

Myles nodded and waited. He heard Brent talking to someone he assumed was a date because Brent had told the person on the line to be waiting for him with no clothes on at the door when he got there.

Brent ended the call and stood, approaching him with his hand outstretched. "What's up, man? Aria is in the back trying on too many outfits to count."

Myles gave him dap. "I told her to dress like her."

The other man shrugged. "I told her the same thing. But…women."

Shoving his hands in his pockets, Myles laughed. "My sister is the same way. Never satisfied with the first outfit."

Brent studied him silently.

Never one to shy away from anyone, Myles met his stare straight on. "Aria is perfect the way she is."

"Definitely. It took her a long time to get to the point where she believed it, and there are still times when I have to remind her." It was obvious Brent cared about Aria and wanted to be sure Myles wasn't going to disrupt her life. "Listen, Aria is family, since we were kids. I've seen her hurt too many times by men with agendas. If you're pursuing her as some sort of project or because of some pre-midlife crisis, don't. Hurt her, and I'll hurt you."

Myles tilted his head. The threat coming from Brent was unmistakable, but it didn't make him angry. If anything, it made him respect the other man. He would say the same thing to anyone who would date Mel, and he was glad Aria had someone who had her back. "I can respect that. I feel the same way about my sister. Just so you know, I asked Aria out because I like *her*, not for any other reason."

"Myles?" He turned to find Aria standing in the doorway to the room, a smile on her face. She stepped forward, and he didn't miss the glare she shot Brent's way as she neared him. "Don't mind Brent. He's just—"

"Looking out for his friend," Myles interjected. "I would do the same for Mel."

"That's right, Aria," Brent said, as he headed out of the room. "Have fun."

Once they were alone, Myles paused a minute to take her in. He'd expected her to come out in jeans and a colorful blouse; instead, she wore a short red halter dress and strappy sandals. Her hair was loose, flowing in deep waves down her back. The purple highlights she'd worn the last time he'd seen her had been replaced by bright red streaks. But it wasn't the dress that drew his attention—it was the ink on her left arm, running underneath the fabric of her dress. He wanted to twirl her around, peel off her dress, so he could see every inch of her. *Simply stunning.*

She peered up at him, a soft smile on her lips. Aria didn't wear a lot of makeup, which he liked. Her face was smooth, natural. Her eyes were bright. His hands itched with a need to touch her, so he reached out and trailed his fingers down her cheek, loving the way her eyes fluttered closed.

"You look…"

"Like me," she whispered.

He smiled. "Like you. You're beautiful."

She averted her gaze as a blush worked its way up her bare shoulders and neck. He watched her face, transfixed. He found himself cataloguing everything about her, memorizing the lines of her face. The studio was bright, and he noticed a blue ring around her irises. In that moment, he knew his life had forever changed.

Tearing his eyes away from her, he asked, "Are you ready?"

Nodding, she said, "I am." She pulled at his shirt. "You didn't wear a suit."

Myles had chosen to dress in a pair of jeans and a black shirt. "No suit tonight."

"It's ridiculous how fine you are." Her eyes widened and she clamped a hand over her mouth. "Oh, my God. I can't believe I just said that out loud."

She dropped her head onto his chest. He wrapped his arms around her and kissed the top of her head. "I'm glad you did." He pulled back, held out his hand to her. "Let's go."

Baker's Keyboard Lounge was a Detroit staple. Myles remembered convincing Ian to snag fake IDs so they could get in when they were younger. The jazz club had a rich history of showcasing major acts from the region, around the country and abroad. Aria had asked him to show her who he was, and he figured this was the perfect atmosphere to do so.

When they arrived, he led her into the dining room. The hostess, Jackie, smiled and greeted him by name. She escorted them to a secluded booth near the back of the place. The main room was small, and there was no dancing. Just people ready to listen to good music. This particular night, a friend of Myles was headlining.

Once they were seated and their drinks were ordered, Aria turned to him. "You brought me to a jazz club."

He wrapped an arm around her. "Yes, I did."

The bar was packed as usual. Purple uplighting set the romantic, intimate mood. People were seated near the stage, eating and drinking. The music was loud and lively, and Myles felt right at home. He always did. Although he was classically trained, jazz was his first love. The first jazz song he'd ever played was "In a Sentimental Mood" by John Coltrane and Duke Ellington. He'd spent hours listening to Coltrane, Davis and Ellington. Other artists like Oscar Peterson, Vince Guaraldi and Herbie Hancock also shaped his own music. The sound of fingers tapping keys, the blare of the trumpet, the pulse of the drums and the smooth sound of the sax had always made him feel alive.

"What is it about this particular place that represents you?" Her eyes searched his, looking for something he wasn't sure he wanted her to see. "The music, the food?"

He sucked in a deep breath. "Music is everything to me."

She smiled. "Do you play?"

Nodding, he said, "Yes."

"What do you play?"

"Piano, mostly. And a few other instruments."

Once again, Myles was hit with the most beautiful smile he'd ever seen up close. His stomach roiled as desire shot through his body.

"I have to say, that's pretty amazing. Why do I get the feeling you don't share that with many people?"

"Because I don't."

Aria picked up his hand, offering him comfort and understanding with that one motion. "I get it. I'm extremely private about my art. I don't show anyone my work until it's complete. Except Brent. And even then, it takes a long time for me to get to the point where I want to sell something."

"Music is something that's mine," he confessed softly. "It has offered the gift of expression. It has inspired me and comforted me. It's my drug, my therapist and my friend. It's my life."

Myles swallowed, surprised he'd admitted that to her. But he knew she'd understand. She'd get it. Because art was like that for her."

"That's beautiful," she whispered, leaning closer. Her eyes dropped to his lips. "Music for you, is like my art for me."

"It is."

Time seemed to slow to a standstill. He couldn't talk, he couldn't think. Because she was too damn close. Her smell, her voice, her hand in his. Despite the bustle of activity around them, it felt like Myles and Aria were the only two people in the room. Was it possible to want her even more? During the car ride down to Baker's, which was about forty-five miles from Ann Arbor, Myles had been struck by the emotion that had churned within him simply because she was near. Her scent had wrapped around him like a tight glove, and he'd wanted to touch her, to kiss her until she couldn't think about anyone but him. He wanted to see that dazed, hooded gaze in her eyes. The one she'd had at the studio.

"Aria, I feel like I need to say something before we go any further."

She frowned. "Why? Myles, if you're going to tell me you have a girlfriend or something like that, I'll kill you."

Myles laughed, brushed his thumb over her chin. "No. I don't do drama and I'm not a cheater."

"That's good to know."

"But here's the thing. There is something about you that I can't ignore. I felt it at the sip and paint, even though you barely looked my way. I felt it at the opening, when I looked at your work. I felt it on our walk and at your studio. I feel it now. If that's too much for you, let me know. Please tell me it's not, though. Please tell me it's not just me?"

She placed a finger over his lips, and he kissed her fingertip before he sucked it into his mouth. Slowly. Aria swallowed visibly. "Damn, that was hot."

He laughed.

Aria pulled her finger from his mouth and shifted in

her seat to face him. "And to answer your question. It's not just you."

Myles leaned in and circled her nose with his before he brushed his lips against the corner of her mouth. "Good."

A waitress arrived with their drinks, interrupting the heated moment. Aria turned and tasted the classic mojito she'd ordered. The low moan she let out a second later went straight to his groin. Damn, he wanted her.

"This is delicious," she said.

Myles watched, sipping on the beer he'd ordered as she perused the menu. Once they had placed their orders, they settled back into the booth. They listened to the music in comfortable silence.

"Are you familiar with the musicians onstage tonight?" she asked.

"Martel Pierce, the guitarist, is a good friend of mine." He brushed an errant piece of hair from her face. "We've known each other for years."

"That's sweet."

"I'll introduce you. He usually stops over between sets." Absently Myles reached out and tugged her closer. When she giggled, he said, "You were too far away." And he needed her close to him, in more ways than one.

She leaned forward to grab her drink, and he studied one of her visible tattoos. Skimming the back of her neck, he traced the outline. Aria turned her head a little, gazing at him over her shoulder. "Do you like tattoos?" she asked.

"I like yours."

"Do you have any?"

He nodded, dipping a finger under the halter strap and tugging it down slightly so he could see the rest of it. *It couldn't be.* It was. Even in the dim lighting, he recognized the design. A near-exact replica of Aria's *Metamorphosis.* "It's your painting."

Aria bit down on her bottom lip. "Brent did it years ago. I wanted a permanent reminder of it, and he's the only one I trusted to do it justice. He's brilliant with a tattoo gun."

He pressed his mouth to her shoulder, right over the tattoo. "It's beautiful." He turned her chin toward him. "You're stunning, Aria."

"Myles, you're intense," she whispered. "You make me feel... I don't even know how to describe it. But I like it."

"Good."

Dinner arrived, once again interrupting the moment. Aria dug right in, biting into a chicken wing with gusto. "Oh. My. God. This is off the chain."

Chuckling, Myles said, "I have to say, the food never disappoints."

"It reminds me of Celeste's fried chicken. I've never been able to perfect it."

"Who is Celeste?"

"Our housekeeper-slash-cook."

Curious, Myles wondered about her family. They'd only talked in general terms. He knew her father was a successful judge, but she hadn't mentioned much about her mother. He got the gist that they didn't get along, though. "You cook?"

"I try. Honestly, I'm not that great at it. But my macaroni and cheese is slappin', thanks to Celeste. She tried to teach me how to make lasagna and smothered pork chops, because those are my favorite dishes. Needless to say, I didn't get the hang of it. Oh, I miss eating her food."

"I take it you don't see her often."

"No. I don't get by my parents' house much. And I don't see that changing any time soon."

"Why?"

"My relationship with my mom is kind of strained. Always has been. And recently my father filed for divorce, so the tension in the family is at an all-time high."

"I know how that feels," he admitted.

"My mom had a promising career in media before she got pregnant with me. Then, she gave it all up to be a wife and mother. Sometimes, I wonder if that's the reason why we never got along. Or worse, if that's the reason why I felt like I would never be good enough for her."

Myles recognized the look in her eyes. He'd felt that rejection so many times in his life, from his mother and his father. It was yet another connection between them, another thing they had in common. Dr. Law wasn't a great father. And his mother... She had been at home barely enough to be a good mother. Yet, he'd spent most of his life chasing the approval from his father, wanting the nurturing from his mother. It was a good thing he had his music, his siblings, Ms. Pennie. He would have gone crazy, otherwise.

"What about your father?" he asked.

"I love my father. He's the best. But part of me feels guilty. Because if I hadn't shown up, he would have been free from my mother. And maybe happy?" She shrugged. "And that was super heavy. I'm not even sure why I told you that."

"You can talk to me."

"This is a date. We are supposed to be flirty and sexy. Not serious and sad and retrospective."

"Isn't this part of it, though? Getting to know each other?"

"True. But enough serious talk. We need to get this date back to lighter ground."

"Fine. I have a question for you. When you're not painting, what do you like to do?"

"I love horror movies, dominoes, and taking care of my plants. And I like—" She sucked in a deep breath at the hunger displayed in his eyes. Her gaze dropped to his mouth.

Myles hooked a hand around her neck and pulled her to him, brushing his lips over hers before deepening the kiss. He explored her leisurely, enjoying her soft moans. She was sweet, warm. The mixture of seasoning, mint and lime on her breath drove him crazy with need. It was a first for him, showing such a public display of affection. But he couldn't stop himself. Pulling back slowly, he watched as she licked her lips.

"Sorry," he said.

With her hands against her cheek, she nodded. "No need to apologize. That was…nice."

He smirked and turned back to his plate. They spent the rest of the evening talking about his music and her art, favorite horror flicks and basketball. Myles found out that Aria was a huge football fan and loved the Detroit Lions, she'd just purchased a home, and her favorite song was "I Want You" by Marvin Gaye.

Martel did join them for a few minutes during his break but couldn't stay because his girlfriend was in the house. He did promise to invite them back for his next performance, and asked Myles to play, as he always did.

It was sometime during the third set that Aria leaned closer and peered up at him. "Thanks for bringing me here. I'm having a ball."

"Does this mean you'll go out with me again?"

Aria giggled. "On one condition."

He cocked a brow. "And what is that?"

"You play for me." Myles froze, tension taking over his body. Aria must have noticed because she sat up and turned to him. "What's wrong?"

"Nothing," he lied.

"Myles, we've had a great date. I've learned your favorite scary movie is *Halloween*, that you think you can beat me in dominoes, and—"

"I can beat you in dominoes."

"We'll see," she chirped. "I know about your affinity for cheesecake and that you love seafood. But I feel like that's only a small part of you. If your music is like my art is to me, then I've only scratched the surface tonight. And I want to know more."

Myles was speechless. Aria was right. He'd shared some things, but not everything. She'd already shown him her. It was his turn to really deliver. "Come home with me," he said.

"To what?"

"Not to sleep with me if that's what you're worried about. But I want the record to show that I wouldn't mind if you did."

"Myles, I—"

"Aria, come home with me so I can show you me. The rest? We'll play by ear."

Myles unlocked his front door and gestured for Aria to enter his home first. He lived in a newer neighborhood on the north side of Ann Arbor. The inside of his house was modern, but there wasn't much furniture. However, the view off the back of the house was amazing, overlooking lush trees and a man-made lake. Aria's fingers itched with the urge to paint it. It had been a while since she'd done a landscape.

"This is gorgeous." She felt him walk up behind her. Through the glass, she noted the way he leaned in and closed his eyes as if he'd smelled something so beautiful. Grateful that she'd remembered to wear her favorite perfume, she turned to him and gripped the front of his shirt in her hands.

Myles devoured her with his stare, and it made her feel reckless. Because she shouldn't want to sleep with him this soon. But she did. And it scared her. At the same time, she didn't want to let fear keep her from seizing the day.

They'd had one delicious make-out session in the studio, and she knew it wouldn't take much for her to abandon her no-sex-on-the-first-date rule. Because the last time that happened... Yeah, she didn't want to think about that nightmare experience. But over the last few days, she'd dreamed of him while she was asleep and daydreamed about him while awake. And she wanted those dreams to be her reality. Sooner rather than later.

Things were moving too fast, though. *Weren't they?* This was too new. *Right?*

"What's on your mind?" he asked, brushing her hair off her shoulders and pressing a kiss to her right one.

A wave of uncertainty washed over her. "Just thirsty," she lied, rolling her eyes at the lame fib.

He walked to the refrigerator and opened it. "Wine? Or beer?"

"What kind of wine?" She joined him at the fridge.

"Mel brought over this moscato." He pulled the bottle out, holding it up for her to see. "I have a bottle of merlot over on the counter."

Aria pointed at the bottle in his hand. "I'll have a glass of the white."

He grabbed a glass from the cabinet. The kitchen was gorgeous—dark cabinets, dark wood floors and state-of-the-art stainless steel appliances. As Myles poured the wine in her glass, she scanned the family room off the kitchen. A huge television was mounted to the wall, and a large sectional sat in the middle of the room. She wondered if he had a lot of company.

A moment later, Myles handed her the full glass and she took a sip. "You're not going to drink with me?"

"I'll get something later." He laced his fingers in hers and led her through the house to a closed door at the end of a hallway. He turned the knob and opened the door.

Aria followed him inside, gasping at the sight in front of her. A grand piano sat near floor-to-ceiling windows. There were three keyboards of various sizes in one corner, five guitars hanging on hooks against a wall. There wasn't much seating, only a love seat against the wall, a stool and a chair. Off the room was an enclosed sound booth.

"This is amazing, Myles." She walked around the huge room. Brushing fingers over the turntable in another corner, she glanced at the album sitting there. Duke Ellington and John Coltrane. "I haven't seen one of these in so long."

His eyes were on hers and she explored the room. "I found it for a steal. It plays well, too." He walked over to her and put the needle on the vinyl. "In A Sentimental Mood" blared through the surround sound speakers.

Aria smiled as memories of summers, her father's vintage Mustang and licorice assaulted her. "This song is everything."

"It's my favorite song," he told her. "My favorite piece to play."

She turned to him. "Play for me?"

Myles sat at the piano, his fingers immediately playing the melody. With his eyes closed, he continued to play along with the song. But Aria wanted to hear only him. She lifted the needle off the record.

Her stomach tightened as Myles put his own spin on the song. The music coming from the piano was lovely, full and rich, deep and powerful. His face, though... She could tell he was in the moment, becoming one with the music, opening himself up to her with each note.

Aria felt tipsy, and not because she'd finished her wine. Her glass was still half-full. It was all Myles. Setting her glass on a table, she walked over to the piano, slid onto the bench next to him and let his music seep into her soul.

By the time he played that last note, Aria was on fire. The room descended into silence and he dropped his forehead to the piano. A few minutes later, he turned and looked at her, his head still resting against the lid, like it was his salvation. But the way he was gazing at her? He stared at her like she felt it, too. Like he was just as confused as she was. Like he wanted her to give him the answer to let him know that what they were feeling in that moment was right.

"I'm not crazy," he murmured.

She smiled, shaking her head.

"This happened?"

Aria swallowed, but before she could respond, she felt his hand slide between her thighs, resting there, as if waiting for her to give him permission. He sat up, brushed his nose up her neck to her ear.

"Aria…" He pressed his mouth to her pulse point, and she shuddered. Her eyes fluttered closed at the sound of her name on his lips.

"Myles." Her voice sounded foreign to her own ears, with a different tone than she normally used.

"Are you going to let my hand go?"

Aria blinked and looked down. She hadn't even noticed that she'd closed her legs, trapping his hand. She shook her head slightly.

He chuckled in her ear and she melted into the bench. "I want everything. I want to know what makes you happy or sad. I want to know what makes you angry and what makes you want me. I want to explore you, study your movements, memorize the sound of your voice so I can play it on my piano. Worship you."

"Yes," she breathed, finally letting her legs relax. "Please."

Aria knew they were speeding past the point of no return. The line she hadn't wanted to cross so soon seemed to be in the rearview mirror. And she didn't care. She just wanted him to make the ache go away. When she felt his fingers graze her core, she moaned. But his hand didn't stay there long. No, it disappeared in the next moment and strong hands gripped her waist, lifting her up and setting her on the piano in front of him. The sound of various notes pierced the air, echoing in the room. He kissed her stomach.

"Myles," she whispered.

His eyes were on hers, a question in them. "Do you want me to stop?" He inched her dress up slowly. Sensations overloaded her, thrilling her with the anticipation of what came next. "Do you want me to stop?" he repeated.

Aria swallowed. Time-out for overthinking everything. Tonight, she was going to give in. "No."

"Can I have you, Aria?"

"Yes," she groaned.

"Say it," he commanded softly, his voice a low rumble.

"You can have me." Her hips started moving of their own accord as he rubbed her through her panties. His touch was featherlight and slow. So slow she wanted to scream. Or cry.

"Good," he whispered.

He bit the inside of her knee, and his tongue grazed the spot he'd bitten. He kissed and nipped at her inner thighs as he worked his way up.

"Oh, my… Myles, please. Just…" Aria let out a frustrated sigh. "I'm really ready for you to have me."

The sound of his laughter sent waves of pleasure straight to her core. "You're really ready?"

"Definitely ready, and—" Before she could finish her sentence, she felt and heard the fabric of her panties give way as he ripped them from her body. "Oh. Damn, I just bought those panties."

"I'll buy you another pair," he assured her right before he sucked her clit into his mouth. Aria cried out in response, panties forgotten. Because… *Oh, my.* Even if she could form a coherent thought, she didn't want to. She wanted to concentrate on the delicious orgasm building in her. *Shit.* She was coming—on a piano. The orgasm buzzed through her, setting her ablaze and wringing her dry.

Myles didn't give her any time to recover, though. He pressed his mouth to hers, sucking on her tongue until she groaned. Or was that him? Lifting her up into his arms as if she weighed no more than a piece of paper, he carried her through the house to his room.

The loud boom of a kick against a door sounded, and seconds later she was falling into a pillow-top mattress. She let out a delighted yelp as he crawled up over her body, placing wet kisses along her calves, her knees, her thighs, her quivering belly, her breasts, her collarbones, her chin and finally her mouth.

Oh, yes.

"So beautiful," he murmured against her lips.

"Myles," she breathed. Aria felt like a live wire, as if she could blow at any minute. It was electric. He was exactly what she needed.

He smiled down at her. "That's right. Myles. Just remember who's making you feel this way." He nipped her chin.

"I won't forget." She unbuttoned his shirt and pushed it off, tracing the tribal tattoo on his shoulder. "Take your clothes off."

He made quick work of stripping and sheathing himself with a condom. Aria was speechless, in awe of his physique. The artist in her wanted to pause and sketch him—with charcoal pencils, of course. But…her body wanted him inside of her more than she wanted to immortalize him.

Soon he was lying against her, his erection pressed against her core. Aria sucked in a deep breath as he entered her, slowly. They stayed like that for a few minutes, eyes on eyes. Myles's eyes closed as he began to move. No more flirty banter, no more jokes, no words at all. Only skin against skin, teeth, low moans, lips and sweat.

Myles let out a low curse and picked up the pace. Aria met him with urgency as her body seemed to open up for him in a way it had never done before. She was going to come. Again. But she wanted to prolong this slice of bliss, she needed to feel it longer. Except…her orgasm didn't want to wait. It crested within her, stealing her breath and zapping her strength—and maybe her sanity—as it took her over. Myles followed behind her, groaning her name over and over again.

And as the last tremor flowed through her body, Aria knew… *I'm in trouble.*

Chapter 8

"That tickles." Aria giggled.

Myles traced the outline of the tattoo on Aria's side. "This is…wow." He'd spent several minutes admiring her ink, taking in the intricate details of the images and the vivid colors. "And Brent did this?"

"Yes," Aria breathed.

He kissed the small of her back, then brushed his lips over the swell of her lovely behind. She was lying on her stomach, her legs bent at the knee and her chin on her hands. After they'd made love, he was supposed to be grabbing them a snack before round two, but when he'd turned on the bedside lamp, he'd noticed her tattoos and had to give them a closer look.

"How long did it take?" he asked.

Aria glanced at him over her shoulder and arched a brow. "Which one?"

So far, he'd studied the replica of the *Metamorpho-*

sis on her upper back and shoulder. On her side was the *Phoenix* tattoo. She had a line of butterflies on her right foot and a gerbera daisy on her wrist. Behind her ear was a dream catcher, and several stars in a pattern over her wrist.

"All of them."

Aria smiled. "Brent is a perfectionist, so it could take anywhere from thirty minutes to several hours over multiple days."

Myles hated to think of Brent touching her skin, even if it was innocent. He'd keep that to himself, though. "Which one was your first?"

She turned onto her back and held up her wrist. "This one. It was Brent's first design. He practiced on me. Since then, he's touched it up, but it's pretty much the same."

Once again, Myles resisted the urge to growl at the mention of Brent's hands on Aria. "Do you plan on getting more?"

"Maybe." She shrugged. "I do want one on my stomach."

Just then, Aria's stomach growled. He laughed. "Hungry?"

Covering her face, she said, "How embarrassing!"

"Don't be."

She peeked at him through her fingers. "That was definitely not sexy."

He smirked. "On the contrary, it was very sexy."

"Stop."

Myles got up and slid on a pair of sweatpants. Grabbing a shirt from one of the drawers, he handed it to her and watched as she put it on. Twenty minutes later, they were in the kitchen, Aria sitting on the kitchen island and Myles on one of the stools.

She dipped her hand into a huge bag of Cheetos, pulling out three and biting into one of them. "I didn't peg you as a cheese puffs type of guy."

He wasn't. Mel spent a lot of time at his home and they were hers. Myles didn't eat much junk food, so he didn't keep it in the house. "I'm not," he admitted, sticking his hand into the bag of Lay's potato chips they'd cracked open.

"I love chips," Aria said, snatching one of his chips from him. "And ice cream. So good."

Frowning, he asked, "Together?"

Aria nodded. "Of course. It's yummy."

"I've never heard of that before."

"You should try it."

"How about I just take your word for it?"

She laughed. "You're hilarious."

"So you keep saying."

"I'm serious." She eyed him. "You've definitely surprised me. More than once."

Myles squeezed her knee. "How so?"

"You just do. I love your home, and the music room… wow. This is so different from the Myles I first met."

Myles had spent a great deal of time and money getting the room just right. Over the years, he'd collected equipment for the studio, instruments, books on music and sheet music. He'd purchased his house because he wanted to be able to play without disturbing neighbors. The neighborhood was a new development in Ann Arbor, with several custom-built homes being completed every month.

"Thanks," he said. "I spend a lot of time in there."

"I bet you do. If you're anything like me with my studio, it's your second home."

Aria got it. That room was so much more than a room. It was a safe haven for him. He could spend hours in there and not leave even to eat. Showing her the room, playing for her… He'd opened himself up to her in ways he'd never thought possible. Myles hadn't known Aria long, but he felt comfortable with her. Somehow, he knew that he could trust her with that part of himself.

"You play beautifully," she continued. "Thanks for sharing that with me, because I know it was hard for you."

He feathered his fingers over her calves. "When did you decide to show your art to the world?"

The corners of her mouth turned up into a wide grin. "In high school, I painted an abstract of an eye."

"An eye?"

"Yes. I don't know why I chose that particular image for my project, but I did. My teacher loved it so much, she entered it into a local competition. I won. That was all the confirmation I needed."

"Do you still have the painting?"

She shook her head. "No. I gave it to my teacher when I graduated from high school. She was retiring and it was my gift to her. She cried. Since then, she's been a huge supporter of my work. She came to my first gallery showing."

"Nice."

"Have you ever considered pursuing a career in music?"

Myles had always been content to keep his music private. Lately, though, he'd wondered what would happen if he tried to do more. "I can't say I've always thought about it. But I have recently."

"Is it because of your medical career?"

He thought about that for a moment. "Not really. I've worked hard at both. I like what I do."

"But you don't love it."

I don't. "I don't hate it." Working at the hospital wasn't something he dreaded on a daily basis, so he knew it hadn't been a mistake to go to medical school. He knew he was lucky to have work that engaged him intellectually, even if it didn't fully complete him. But he was aware that being a surgeon alone wouldn't sustain him forever. He knew he needed something else.

"Maybe you can do both. One day. Celeste would always tell me that we all have gifts that have the potential to change our lives and the lives of all of our friends and family, and even strangers. That's why, even on my worst days, I paint. Because I want to bless others."

Myles had heard the same thing from Ms. Pennie and his siblings forever. He shrugged. "I don't know."

"I didn't plan to sleep with you tonight." Her eyes widened as if she hadn't meant to say that out loud. She bit into a cheese puff and muttered something he couldn't make out.

Smiling, he took a sip from a bottle of water. When he'd brought Aria home that evening, he thought they'd have a glass of wine, maybe talk about her art or his music before he showed her his music room. He had not expected her to end up in his bed so soon. Some day, yes. Now, no. "I never expected this," he said.

"I can't say I regret it, though. I was worried I would, but I don't."

He stood, parting her thighs and stepping between them. "I feel the same." He dipped his tongue into her mouth, loving the taste of her.

She wrapped her legs around his waist. "Dr. Jackson, are you trying for a repeat?"

"Of course, I am. That was always the plan. I just had to feed you first."

Aria's head fell back as she laughed, and he took the opportunity to place wet kisses over her shoulder blade and up the long column of her neck. Her giggles turned to a low moan, and finally she whispered his name. "You're killing me," she said.

"So good," he murmured against her skin.

Myles couldn't get enough of her. He'd never ached to kiss or tease or taste a woman before. She was so responsive, so ready for him. He felt her, hot against his growing erection. He cupped her breasts in his hands, loving the way she pushed into his palms. Unable to stand the barrier between them any longer, he pulled his shirt off her and took one pebbled nipple into his mouth, sucking greedily until she cried out.

Aria pushed his sweats down. "Please," she whispered. "Stop teasing me."

"Say it," he commanded, brushing his fingers against her sex and rubbing her clit with his thumb. "Tell me you want me again."

"I do," she breathed, lying back against the granite. "I—"

The loud buzz of his phone against the countertop broke the haze of desire, and Myles muttered a curse. He'd been so distracted by her that he'd forgotten his phone all evening. It had been sitting on the counter since they'd been at the house.

Aria's eyes popped open and she turned her head toward the sound, a frown on her face. "What time is it?"

Myles didn't care. Not when he was two seconds away

from being inside her again. He leaned down and kissed her belly. The phone buzzed again. "Shit," he grumbled, picking it up and peering at the screen. After the buzzing stopped, he noticed that he'd missed ten calls.

Aria sat up and kissed his jaw. "Is everything okay?"

He scrolled through his calls, noting that most of them were from his brothers. Something must be going on. Myles turned to Aria. "I should probably get this." Stepping back, he pulled his pants up while Aria tugged his shirt back on. He dialed Ian.

"Where the hell are you?" Ian said when he picked up.

"Minding my business," Myles countered. "What's up?"

"It's Ms. Pennie."

Myles's heart fell. "What happened?" Out of the corner of his eye, he saw Aria leave the room. "Is she…?"

"She's fine," Ian assured him. "But she's back in the hospital. She took a fall. The housekeeper called the ambulance and they rushed her here. They're running tests."

Myles closed his eyes and let out a heavy sigh. "Okay."

"She's asking for you."

"I'll be there as soon as possible."

Myles ended the call. He'd told Ms. Pennie to take it easy, but he had a feeling his pleas to rest fell on deaf ears. The older woman was determined to remain independent. It had been hard just to get her to hire a live-in housekeeper to help her out, but he was glad he'd convinced her to hire Sharon. The two women got along well and had even become friends.

The home Ms. Pennie had lived in since Myles had known her was one of the largest in the upper-class neighborhood his parents once lived in and too much for her to take care of by herself. She'd finally agreed to hire help, and he was glad that he'd insisted. He didn't want to think about what would have happened had Sharon not lived there.

"Are you okay?" Myles turned to find Aria standing in the doorway, fully dressed. She shifted on her feet. "It's just… You look stressed."

"I'm sorry. I need to go to the hospital."

"Patient?"

He wanted to tell her about Ms. Pennie, but he couldn't bring himself to talk about it. The cancer had not spread, but the thought of her hurting herself, of her being alone made him sad. That woman was more to him than a music teacher, and life without her wasn't something he wanted to think about. Swallowing past a lump that had formed in his throat, he said, "Family."

Aria approached him, concern in her eyes. She reached out and pressed a hand to his heart. He held it to his chest and let her presence comfort him. "I'm sorry. Do you need anything?"

"I just need to go to the hospital."

She offered him a sad smile. "Okay. I understand. Take care of what you need to take care of. I can call an Uber."

He shook his head. "No. I'll drive you home."

Myles hurried to his room to get dressed and took Aria home. The car ride was quiet, but not uncomfortable. When he pulled up at her place, he put the car in Park and turned to her.

Aria dropped her head, twirling her purse around her finger. "Thanks, Myles. I had a great time."

He reached out and turned her head to face him. "I did, too. I'll call you."

"Okay."

Leaning forward, he brushed his lips against her temple before he placed a lingering kiss to her mouth. When he pulled back, Aria brought her fingers up to her lips and opened her eyes slowly. "Talk to you soon."

Before he could come round to open her door for her, Aria did it herself, wordlessly slid out of the car and ran to her door. Seconds later, she was inside, and Myles was on the road to the hospital.

Myles wasn't even in the room and Aria swore she could smell him. She blinked in an attempt to will the persistent thoughts of him away. Yet, as she stared at the blank canvas in front of her for the fourth day in a row she couldn't get him out of her head.

Is it possible to want him even more? One unforgettable night together should have cured her insatiable desire for him. But, no. Her brain power was solely focused on him. Sex. That damn word and everything associated with it had stolen her creativity.

Myles's brand of love nearly made her lose all of her control and beg him for more. The forget-your-name sex that people waxed poetic about in books and movies. That make-you-wanna-holla lovemaking that stuck to her bones like a good meal. It made her want to call in sick, to put every painting on hold and cancel all of her shows. Because she just wanted to be under him, over him or in front of him. And yet, it wasn't just the physical attraction that drew her to him. It was him, their connection. Everything about him, from his music to his smile to his sense of humor. Aria enjoyed discovering a side to him that she knew wasn't on display for just anybody. It made her want to find out more about him.

Maybe it's because our night was cut short. He had

to leave right in the middle of what could have possibly been an even better session than the first, right on the countertop. The call from the hospital had put a damper on the evening. He was nice, he was sweet and caring. A gentleman. He'd driven her home, given her a beautiful kiss and promised to call her. *Then he didn't.*

She wasn't one of those women. *Hell, no.* She hadn't gone into this with the expectation that they were doing anything more than dating. But she'd stared at her phone for the last hour, even when she tried not to. No calls, no texts.

It had been days since they'd talked, and Aria couldn't figure out if he was giving her the brush-off or he was simply busy. At this point, she had no choice but to accept that he probably hadn't enjoyed that night as much as she did. She'd complained to Brent about it so much in the last three days that Brent had banned her from talking about Myles for the next twenty-four hours.

Aria knew his job meant a lot to him and had told herself not to be disappointed when the call didn't come through. But when he'd shared with her that it was a family issue, she had hoped he'd tell her more. Not that he owed her any explanations, because he didn't. Still, she wanted to know what had made him look so sad. She wanted to know him.

Frustrated, she pulled out her charcoal pencils, grabbed the pastel paper she kept on hand and hoped her mojo would return. With sweeping movements, she traced an outline of a portrait, content with her choice to abandon the paint for the afternoon.

Several hours later, Aria stared at her masterpiece and found Myles's eyes staring right back at her. Seriously?

She'd drawn *him*? Irritated with herself, she flung the paper hard, watching it float to the ground.

She grumbled a curse when the bell chirped, signaling someone was entering the building.

"Aria?" a voice called from the front of the studio.

Sighing, Aria stood up and shuffled out of her private studio into the public area. There were no classes scheduled today, so she had no staff there. When she noticed Bailee and Avery up front, she smiled.

Aria greeted them both with hugs. "What's up? I didn't expect you."

"We were in the area for lunch and figured we'd stop by and see if you wanted to grab something to eat."

"I wish I could, but I'm swamped here," Aria lied. Going to lunch with Myles's sisters wasn't the best idea. Especially since she was having a hard time *not* telling them that she'd even gone out on a few dates with him.

"Girl, you look like you need food. And I checked the schedule online. You have no classes today." Bailee gestured toward the door. "Come on. Let's hang out."

Aria frowned. "I'm so serious. I'm the only one here today, and I need to get something down on canvas. Can we schedule lunch for next week?"

Avery looked up from her phone, where she'd been typing something. She searched Aria's eyes. "Are you okay?"

"I'm fine." Aria crossed her arms over her chest and blew a stray hair from her face. "Just busy and preoccupied."

All week, Aria had read the posts in their ladies' group thread on Facebook with interest, hoping to find out what family issue had happened with Myles. But none of the women had mentioned anything sad or important happening. Which meant he was more than likely giving her the brush-off. Yet, Aria had a hard time reconciling that with the man who'd pursued her so relentlessly. Sure, she'd given it up on the first date, but she'd never expected him to ghost her. *Why did he do this to me?*

"You've been quiet in the group, too," Bailee said. "Are you sure you're good?"

"I'm dating Myles," Aria blurted out before she could stop herself. "I mean. I went out on a few dates with him."

Bailee and Avery stared at her, mouths open and eyes wide with surprise.

"We went out." Aria paced the room, flailing her arms around. "To lunch at Applebee's, then on an impromptu walk around here. Then, he took me to Baker's Keyboard Lounge for dinner and jazz. We went to his place, and…" She swallowed. "He played for me. Then, he got this call from the hospital and took me home and I haven't heard from him since."

"What?" Bailee said. "He ghosted you?"

Avery patted Bailee's shoulder. "Stop, Bai." She approached Aria and squeezed her arms. "Let's order lunch in here. Okay?"

Aria nodded. "Okay." As much as she hadn't wanted to burden them, she felt a weight lift off her as they surrounded her with their support and affection.

Half an hour later, Aria, Avery and Bailee were seated in her private studio, eating Chinese. They'd dined in relative silence for a few minutes when Bailee set her carton of orange chicken down on a nearby table.

"I'm sorry, I can't not talk about this," Bailee said. "When did you decide to go out with Myles?"

Aria stared at her shrimp-fried rice, using her fork to turn over one shrimp after another. "A few weeks ago, after the exhibition. He bought the *Phoenix*."

With wide eyes, Avery asked, "Seriously?"

Nodding, Aria said, "Yes. He asked me out. I agreed to lunch. He's very charming. He was different."

"And lunch turned to dinner?" Bai asked. "At Baker's?"

"Yes. And before that, he showed up here and took me on a walk, bought me Italian ice."

"You got busy with him." Avery sipped on her tea. "What night was this?"

"Friday."

"Friday," Avery said. "That's the night Ms. Pennie went to the hospital."

"Oh, yeah," Bailee agreed. "Ian had been trying to reach him all night. We were there for hours, waiting with her."

Hope crept into Aria's bones at the possible excuse for not reaching out. If this Ms. Pennie was important to Myles and she was in the hospital, that was an understandable reason for his silence. *Maybe.* "Who is Ms. Pennie?"

Avery and Bailee exchanged glances. "She's a friend to the family. Myles is extremely close to her."

"Have you seen him?" Aria asked. "Is he okay?"

Bailee nodded. "I saw him yesterday. He's okay."

When Bailee didn't say anything else, Aria sighed. "Good to know. Thanks for telling me."

"Aria, don't assume that he's avoiding you." Avery patted Aria's leg. "Myles is not like the other brothers. He's very private, and often retreats within. I've been around them for years, and I have never seen him react to anything. I'm surprised he played for you, because he doesn't do that usually."

"That's what he told me." Aria stood and stalked over to the trash can, pitching her food inside. "But this isn't okay. It's not cool for him to sleep with me and then just fall off the face of the earth."

Bailee jumped up and approached her. "I don't think that's what he's doing."

"You don't know that," Aria countered. "I get it, though. He's your family and you want to defend him. But I can't. Granted, it was my fault for sleeping with him so fast, but he's wrong as hell."

"I agree." Avery joined them. "He should have called."

"Exactly." Aria started cleaning, picking up pieces of paper off the floor, throwing away empty cartons of food and a stale bag of chips. "I should have followed my first mind with him, and I didn't. My bad. I won't do it again."

"Aria, stop." Bailee pried a balled-up piece of paper from Aria's fist. "Myles isn't a jerk. He might be closed off, but he wouldn't hurt you on purpose." She looked at Avery. "You know that."

Avery shrugged. "I know that. But he still messed up."

"You're not helping," Bailee muttered.

"She's only saying what I've already thought a million times since we went out." Tears welled up in her eyes and Aria cursed her emotions. "I get it, though. I'm not his type. He probably was attracted to me because I was different."

Avery shook her head. "Now, I'm going to have to step in. As wrong as Myles is, I don't believe that he would do something like that. I *do* believe that you should talk to him."

"You definitely need to speak with Myles," Bailee agreed.

"What's the point?" Aria flopped down on the couch. "I've been through this before. There is always some guy who is attracted to my seemingly wild side, who wants to be with me to scratch an itch. At least, Myles isn't after my money or fame." She shrugged. "That's something."

Bailee sat next to her. "Why would you say that?"

Aria wondered if she could confide in these ladies. Really confide and tell them about some of her past struggles in relationships. Yes, she'd talked her issues out with Brent, but he was right when he mentioned she needed girlfriends to bounce things off. Because there were some things that, as a man, he would never understand.

"It seems impossible considering I haven't known him long at all, but I really liked him." Aria sucked in a deep breath, surprised that she'd said it out loud. "After every warning sign, after all of my reservations, I find myself thinking about him all the time."

Avery sat on a table across from her, a soft smile on her face. "That's beautiful."

"No, it's not. Because I shouldn't want him. He's everything that I told myself I wouldn't do again. I've spent a lot of years in relationships with men who pretended to love me for me but, in the end, wanted to change me. Or they realized that I'm not who they would want to bring home to their families. I can't do that again."

"Do we know that's what Myles is doing, though?" Bailee asked. "You're making a decision based on one thing. For all we know, he could have just had a really bad week. Maybe he didn't want to bring you into it?

Maybe it slipped his mind to call? We can't assume that
he's decided you're not who he wants in his life."

"Bai is right." Avery leaned forward. "Myles is one
of the good guys. That much I know. I can't say he's not
an idiot for not calling, but I know he wouldn't take ad-
vantage of you like that."

The weird part was, Aria felt that in her bones. Still,
the evidence, the radio silence over the past week all
pointed to one thing. As good as he seemed to be, he
was inconsiderate. If he was at work or dealing with
Ms. Pennie and had forgotten to call her, she didn't see
that getting better. If anything, once they got to know
each other and become more comfortable, it would most
likely get worse.

"I don't know. He's a contradiction. And it confuses
me." Aria jumped up and walked to the far side of the
room. With her hands on her hips, she whirled around.
"It kind of makes me contradict myself. I don't even
know if that makes sense because I'm all over the place."

"What about him is a contradiction?" Avery asked.

"Because, like I said, he's everything I shouldn't
want."

"Why, though?"

Aria froze, turning over the many ideas swirling
through her head. She chose her next words carefully.
"He plays beautiful music. So beautiful, I was overwhelmed with emotion listening to it. But he won't pursue his passion. I suspect it's because he's bogged down
with obligation. Don't get me wrong. I know that feeling, because I've lived it myself. But at the end of the
day, how would I fit into that narrative?"

"Maybe you're exactly what he needs to propel him
forward onto a different path." Avery smacked her palms

against her legs. "But I'm still trying to figure out why that's a reason to not want him? If you like him, why not feel it? Why not go with it and try to make something work? Even if there's a risk. What if it works out and you're happy in the end?"

"He's a doctor. A surgeon, for goodness' sake. He's rich. On paper, he's everything my mother tried to force on me. He's exactly the type of man who she would want me with. I've been there and done that before. I shouldn't do it again."

At the same time, Myles drove a freakin' Jeep when he could drive a Benz. His house was in a regular neighborhood. It wasn't a mansion on a hill. Yes, he had money, but he didn't flaunt it. He never made her feel like he thought he was too good for her, like the parade of men her mother brought around her.

Myles had admitted to her that he took his lunch to work most days. When he admitted that he didn't like Applebee's, she'd expected him to tell her he liked to dine at some highbrow, expensive restaurant. But he really just preferred Chili's.

"I don't know what to do with this," Aria said.

Avery nodded. "You like him, despite your differences. And that scares you."

"Yeah. Because every time he reveals something personal to me, it's not what I expected. And that makes me want him even more. Oh, my God. It makes me fall for him a little more every time. And then he doesn't call, and I'm left with this feeling of being a fool for even opening myself up to someone I knew I shouldn't be with in the first place."

"Okay, I get it." Bailee crossed her legs and smoothed her skirt. "Ian is totally the opposite of me. Just being with him gave me the courage to make lasting changes because I watched him pursue his passion despite what his father expected. I'm more like Myles. I was comfortable—to a certain extent—following a set path, basing my life choices on what everyone wanted for me and not what I wanted for myself. What if you're his perfect half, the person who completes him, the woman who pushes him to follow his dreams? What if he's that balance for you?"

"What if he's not?" Aria asked. "My last relationship was awful. He used me, stole from me and blamed me when I left him. He told me that I was not good enough for him to bring home to his mother. He told me time and again that I needed to change. It was abuse, but not physical. Because every time he hurt me or belittled me, it felt like a punch to the face. But I fought for it, for him. For years. Until I decided that I didn't want to live like that anymore. Then, I left. And now I'm here, falling again for someone who may not be able to give me what I deserve."

"But why?" Bailee stood and approached her. "You're jumping way ahead here, Aria. You haven't even had a discussion with Myles. Why are you at the point of the relationship when it burns to the ground already?"

"Because I already feel exposed. I already feel like a fool. This week with no communication from him tore me up inside. One night together, and I'm checking my phone every minute for a text. Hell, no. I'm not doing that again."

Avery sighed. "But Myles is not your ex."

"You're right. He's not. He's so good. He's gentle, loving, and he made me feel safe. So safe that I let him make love to me on our first official date. And right now, I'm remembering all the promises I made to myself to not let a man make me feel so weak again. I remember how long and hard that fall was when I lost myself in a man who wasn't good for me. Even if Myles has a good excuse for not calling me, I'll always be waiting for the other shoe to drop. And that makes me crazy. I'm scared to want him, because I know it will be easy to fall in love with him. And that scares me even more. Because one day he might wake up and realize that I was just a phase, that I don't fit into his world, that I wasn't worth as much to him as…"

Aria didn't complete her thought because she wasn't ready to put it into the atmosphere. The simple fact was her feelings for him were like a blazing, uncontrollable inferno that would burn her to the ground if she let herself succumb to them. Myles had the potential to destroy her.

"Aria—" The bell above the front door chimed, interrupting Avery.

"One second. I'm going to lock up." Aria hurried to the front and stopped in her tracks when she saw Myles standing there.

Chapter 9

Aria stared at Myles, standing in her doorway as if it was a regular day, as if he hadn't given her the cold shoulder for almost a week. Suddenly, anger replaced the melancholy that had taken over her life for the past several days.

"What are you doing here?" she asked, folding her arms over her chest.

"Can we talk?" Myles asked, his voice so soft she almost thought she'd imagined it.

"I think you said everything you wanted to say with your lack of communication over the last week."

He inched closer. "I'm an idiot. I didn't think. Things spiraled out of control at work and I… There is no excuse."

Aria felt her anger slip at his words. He didn't try to argue with her, he didn't try to make her feel she was unreasonable. He just admitted he was wrong. Which was all new to her.

Avery and Bailee chose that moment to come out from the back. "Myles?" Avery said. "You're here. About time," she mumbled.

Myles frowned. "Yes. What's going on?"

"We're leaving." Bailee hooked an arm in Avery's. Turning to Aria, Bailee mouthed, *Call me.*

Seconds later, the ladies were gone and Aria was alone with Myles. He stepped forward. "Don't," she said, her voice firm. "I'm not sure who you think I am, but I think we need to get some things straight."

"I agree."

"I'm not the type of woman who sleeps with men for the hell of it."

"I know that."

"I don't treat sex so casually. For you to be with me and then disappear like you did is unacceptable."

"You're right."

Aria sighed. "I can't do this."

"I'm sorry." Myles started toward her again, and her heartbeat thundered in her chest as he neared her. "I should have called. I should have done anything other than what I did." Now, standing in front of her, he traced her jawline with his finger. "Aria, I told you I didn't expect this. But you probably thought I meant I didn't expect to sleep with you."

"Isn't that what you meant?"

He shook his head. "No. I meant I didn't expect *you.* I didn't count on you breezing into my life and changing things."

"How so?"

"From the first moment I saw you, I wanted more. I

can't explain it, it's not rational. I've never been one to pursue any woman. I never had to. And I don't know what to do with that."

"Why didn't you call me? I was worried about you. You looked so sad when you got that call."

"I wanted to call. Multiple times I picked up the phone, dialed your number, but—"

"But you didn't."

"No. I didn't. I don't have a good reason, only regret. I wish I had handled things differently."

She poked him in the chest. "I do, too."

"Can you forgive me?"

She wanted to forgive him. She wanted to throw her arms around his neck and let him take her in the back. But she wouldn't do that. One thing she'd learned about herself over this was that she wasn't ready. Obviously. Bringing baggage and old insecurities into a new relationship wasn't a good idea under any circumstance. "Maybe."

His gaze dropped to her mouth. "Please," he whispered.

"Even if I can forgive you, I think we should just be friends."

Myles leaned back. "Really?"

"It's not you. It's me. I'm just not ready to date someone. I don't want to have expectations of you, and I'm not ready to meet your expectations. It's better if we take a few steps back. Friends is good. This way I don't have to be waiting for a call from any date. If I see you, I see you."

"Ah." He smirked. "Just friends, huh?"

Aria backed up and patted him on his shoulder. "Yep."

"Okay. I can be a good friend."

Aria eyed him skeptically. "Really?"

"Yeah." He rubbed his hands together. "You know, it's kind of good that you want to be friends. Friendship is a great start to a relationship."

She wondered why he had that gleam in his eye. *He's up to something.* "Right. Except in this case, we'll continue to be friends."

"Right. Just friends. Which means you can't kiss me."

Immediately, Aria's focus shifted to his full lips. Kissing him in that moment was all she wanted to do. But she'd laid down the rules. For *her* sanity. "I don't want to kiss you," she whispered.

"You're sure?"

Aria nodded, leaning forward. "Very sure." Her heart was beating so loud and fast she felt it in her throat. "No kisses."

He bent lower, ran his nose down her cheek. "None. At all."

Damn. He knew exactly what he was doing, looking all good, unnerving her. She placed her hands against his chest and pushed back to put some space between them. "So, we're in agreement. I have to..." Aria had failed at sounding unaffected by him so she pointed toward the back. "Get back to work."

"Fine, Aria. I'll talk to you soon."

"Yep. Sure."

Myles turned and walked out, and Aria slumped against the wall. She smacked her forehead with her palm. *Good job, Aria.*

A week later, Aria received lunch delivered to the studio with a note. "Hope you enjoy lunch, friend." She opened the bag to find a chicken gyro with a small Greek salad on the side. Smiling, she inhaled the sandwich. *Yum.*

Aria couldn't wait to dig in to her lunch. Thanks to the stellar work of her real estate agent, she'd closed on her new house early. Brent had convinced her to hire movers instead of doing it herself, so in just one day, the company had cleaned out her storage unit and delivered all of her belongings to her home. They'd worked until the wee hours of the morning setting everything up, and then she'd come in to the studio to work. Tonight would be her first night in her own place, and she was ecstatic.

She bit into her gyro and groaned, silently sending up a prayer of thanks for her *friend.* Picking up her phone, she texted Myles. Thanks for the lunch. Friend. It's so good. #Greedy.

His reply came in seconds. Ha. You're welcome. Enjoy your gyro, Aria.

She tossed her phone onto the couch. Every day since she'd told him they should be friends, he'd sent her a gift to the studio. The first day, he'd ordered a kale-and-spinach smoothie from her favorite place. It had shocked her because she hadn't recalled telling him how much she loved that particular flavor. He'd even remembered to substitute the banana for strawberries.

One day she'd arrived at the studio to find a beautiful vase full of peach dahlias and peonies. Aria had immediately started a new painting inspired by her flowers. It had taken her much of the day and the next to complete it. But it was going in her next collection.

After a long day at the studio, she'd been surprised when one of Myles's interns stopped by with vanilla ice cream and potato chips. She'd eaten every bit, along with the doughnuts from Washtenaw Dairy he'd had delivered yesterday. Not only was Myles being unfair, he was contributing to her weight gain.

"I need to go to the gym," she murmured to the empty room.

Brent poked his head in. "What's up?"

She smiled at him, gyro midair. "Hey."

"You have company."

Hope bloomed in her belly at the possibility it could be Myles, and she chided herself mentally. They were friends. Just friends. *That's all.* "Who is it?"

"I thought I'd come see my baby girl." Her father entered the room.

Aria jumped up and ran into his arms. "Daddy! You're here."

He wrapped his arms around her and squeezed. "I figured I'd come check you out." He kissed her brow when she pulled back. "I missed you."

She hadn't seen her father since opening night of her exhibit. After years of working year-round, he'd taken a much-needed extended vacation to the Maldives. Just seeing the many pictures he'd sent her via text made her heart swell. He'd deserved the break.

"Daddy, how was the trip?" She took a seat on her stool.

"It was amazing. I have never spent so much time simply resting and relaxing and sightseeing."

"I'm just happy you enjoyed yourself. The pictures were lovely."

"You should definitely put it on your bucket list, sweetie."

Aria smiled at her father. "I will."

"I figured I'd drop by and take you to dinner. So that we can catch up."

She studied her father. He'd always seemed larger than life, fearless. But she knew he was hurting over the deterioration of his marriage. Picking up his hand, she squeezed. "Are you okay? I spoke with Mom last week. She told me she signed the papers."

Her father nodded. "Yes, she did. When I returned from my trip, my lawyer showed them to me."

According to her mother, the settlement had been fair and there was no reason to contest it. Aria had made her peace with the divorce, though it still angered her that her mother had treated the entire separation as nothing more than a trip to the grocery store. Every time she'd seen her mother, there was no emotion in her face or her tone. It was almost like the divorce was happening to someone else.

"I'm sorry, Dad. I know you're hurting."

"I'm just fine, sweetie." He scanned the room. "I've been thinking, though. If you wouldn't mind taking the day off, I could use your help picking out decor for my place."

Aria grinned. "I'd love to spend the day with you, Daddy. And I can shop for my new house, too. By the way, I want you to see it."

"Sounds good to me."

Aria spent the rest of the afternoon with her father. They walked downtown and visited several little shops along the way. By the time they'd finished, her father had picked up several items for his new home and Aria enjoyed seeing him smile. After she'd given him a tour of her house, he'd invited her to dinner.

Seated across from her father at Real Seafood Company Ann Arbor, they discussed her art and her plans for the rest of the year as far as exhibitions were concerned.

"I missed the deadline for the Art Fair this year, but I do plan to go. Want to join me?"

"I'd love to, but I'm in court most of the week."

The Ann Arbor Street Art Fair took place every year in July. It was one of the largest fairs in the nation, and she considered it a must-see for every art lover. Ann Arbor literally transformed into one huge exhibit, closing off segments of major streets for the four-day event. Artists from around the world displayed dynamic pieces of art, in categories such as mixed media, sculpture, painting and photography. Live performers served as entertainment for attendees. Aria remembered attending when she was a teenager and falling in love with the atmosphere. She'd vowed to be a featured artist there one day.

Unfortunately, it wouldn't be that year. Aria had been so busy with the move and opening Cocktails and Canvas that she'd missed the cutoff to apply for a vendor booth. The process was extremely competitive, with thousands of artists applying for a coveted slot. Several of her friends did make the deadline, though, and she couldn't wait to go and see what they'd come up with.

"Aw, well, maybe I'll pick you up a piece for your housewarming."

"Just make sure it's not too wild. You know I like subtle."

She giggled. "I know. I promise I'll behave."

Their waitress approached their table and took Aria's dessert order. Cheesecake was the perfect nightcap. Once the server left, she glanced up and noticed Mel waving at her from near the front of the restaurant. And her friend wasn't alone.

"Oh, no," Aria mumbled.

Her father frowned and turned toward the door. "What's wrong?"

"Nothing," Aria lied, just as Mel reached their table—with her brothers in tow. Every brother. Including Myles.

"Aria!" Mel hugged her. "It's good to see you."

"You, too." Aria plastered on a wide smile. "Mel Jackson, this is my father, Judge Louis Bell."

Mel greeted Aria's dad with a hug. "It's so good to meet you finally. I've heard a lot about you."

Louis smiled at Mel. "Nice to meet you."

"Hey, Aria," El said, giving her a quick embrace."

"What's up, El?"

The other brothers greeted her in quick succession. Aria glanced up at Myles before turning back to her father. She pointed to each of the brothers as she introduced them. "This is Drake, El, Ian, and…Myles. They're surgeons at Michigan Medicine."

Her father exchanged handshakes with the brothers. "Good to meet you. You wouldn't happen to be any relation to Dr. Lawrence Jackson, would you?"

Drake nodded. "He's our father."

"Really?" Louis nodded, too. "I've played several rounds of golf with your father. We both serve on the advisory board for Detroit Neighborhood Revitalization Foundation."

"I didn't know that, Daddy," Aria said. Again, she looked up at Myles, who was watching her intently. She shifted in her seat. "That's great," she said loudly, as if this were the best news in the world. *Why did I just yell that?* She was mortified at how her voice had boomed in the quiet room.

"It's great work," her father replied. "Over the years,

the city has seen an influx in new business and residents."

Although Louis had lived in Inkster for much of his childhood, his parents were from Detroit. He'd resided off Seven Mile Road for the first six years of his life and had spent a lot of time in the city.

"What are you guys doing here?" Aria asked. "Where are Love and Avery?"

"It's siblings dinner," Mel said. "We do it semiannually, just us. Ian missed the last one, and we thought we'd move it up because I'm moving next month."

Aria nodded. "That's cool. Daddy, Mel is moving to New York and attending the business school at NYU for her graduate degree."

Louis raised an interested brow. "That's good. You definitely want to ask Aria about New York. If I wasn't sure she was born and raised here, I would think she grew up in Brooklyn."

Aria laughed. "Daddy, stop." She took a sip from her drink and peeked at Myles again. Yep, he was still watching her.

Her father chatted with the brothers Jackson about their careers and Ann Arbor for a few minutes, while Aria tried not to look at Myles again. Except she couldn't keep her eyes off him. In her defense, though, she hadn't seen him since she'd told them they should be friends. Talked to him, yes. Laid eyes on him, no.

He looked so good she wanted to bite him. And since she remembered every bit of their night together like it had happened that morning, she knew he wouldn't mind. Dressed in dark jeans, a stark white shirt and a blazer, he definitely deserved the attention he was getting from many of the women in the restaurant. Attention that made Aria want to fight someone, anyone. *My control is slipping.*

Louis Bell could definitely command attention, because everyone was engrossed in what her father was saying about the state and lending a helping hand to those in need. Aria cared about people in need—she just couldn't concentrate with Myles standing so close.

Soon the hostess interrupted them to let the Jackson clan know their table was ready. In a few short moments, they said their goodbyes and left her with her father.

Aria exhaled slowly, closing her eyes.

"Aria?"

She glanced up at her father, who was eyeing her curiously. "Are you okay?"

"Sure," she said. "Do you mind if I take my cheesecake to go?"

"I'm okay with that. But I'm a little concerned about you."

"I'm fine, Dad." She turned to find Myles staring at her from his table, that damn sexy smirk on his face. "Thanks for dinner."

"Tell me, is Myles something to you?"

Aria blinked. "What?" She scratched the back of her head. "Why would you ask me that?"

He shrugged. "Because I noticed a few things."

"Like what?"

"How you introduced him when he came over."

Aria struggled to recall the introductions. "I don't think I said his name any differently than the others."

"And then there was the staring."

She placed a hand over her chest. "Me?"

"And him."

Sighing, Aria leaned back in her seat. "Okay. We went

out on a few dates, and I recently told him that I just wanted to be friends."

"Friends don't look at each other like that."

"Dad, I'm not ready to be with anyone. I just want to focus on my business and my art. That's it." She sliced a hand through the air.

He leaned forward, taking her hand in his. "Aria, I know you've been through a lot. I know it can be terrifying to trust again after heartbreak."

"It was so hard," she breathed, brushing a lone tear that had fallen. "Which is why I think it's best to kind of chill for a minute."

"I understand the need to protect yourself. I remember what it was like to be young and falling for someone. I know what it's like to lose someone you hold so dear. There were bad times, but the good times... Those were priceless. Even though we're divorcing, I wouldn't trade those moments for anything in the world. And I want that for you. I want you to fall in love with someone who loves you for you. But the only way that will happen is if you're open to it. So, don't close yourself off. Any man would be lucky to have an Aria."

Aria chuckled. "Daddy, you're amazing. I love you so much. Thank you."

He patted her hand. "Now, let's get out of here."

She placed her napkin on the table. "I need to go to the restroom."

"I'll make sure your cheesecake has extra strawberries."

Aria stood and walked toward the bathroom hallway. Lost in her swirling thoughts, she barreled into a wall. Only it wasn't a wall. It was hard muscle. And it smelled good. *He* smelled good. Slowly she lifted her eyes.

Myles smirked. "Hi."

"Hi." A smile formed on her lips. "I'm sorry I ran into you."

"That's nothing to be sorry about. You feel good." One of his hands slid around her waist. "You look good."

Aria gasped. "Thanks."

"Aria…" Her name on his lips made her feel warm all over. She'd missed his voice. "We should talk."

"We've talked."

"Text is not talk."

"I can't do this." She backed away. "My dad is waiting for me. I have to go."

"Aria, wait." He grabbed her wrist, pressed his fingers to the pulse point.

"You always do that."

He frowned. "Do what?"

"When you touch me, you measure my pulse." She shook her head. "I don't know what that means. Or even if you realize you're doing it. But it drives me crazy."

"In a good way?"

The best way. "I don't know."

"Please, can we talk?"

Aria couldn't take it anymore. Being Myles's *friend* seemed next to impossible because she didn't have platonic feelings for him. Imagining her *friend* naked, imagining him kissing her and making love to her was not appropriate behavior.

She paced back and forth in the short hallway, not even caring if she looked unhinged or even slightly deranged. Muttering to herself, she turned over every reason she had for hitting the pause button on them, and none of them made any sense to her now. All of them were just excuses to walk away. Because she wanted him in a way she'd never wanted anyone, and she needed to let herself feel it.

Stopping in front of him she searched his eyes. "Myles?" His eyes were on hers, watching her so intently she felt it all the way to the tips of her toes. *Forget it.* She caressed his face and pulled him to her, kissing him. Hard.

His lips, his soft moans, his hands… *Oh, God.* But they were in a public place so she reluctantly broke the kiss. Then she turned on her heels and walked into the restroom.

Aria took a few minutes to compose herself before she emerged from the bathroom. Myles was gone, and she hurried to her father. On her way to her table, she glanced over at Myles, who tipped his glass to her with a gleam in his eyes.

Smiling to herself, she fired off a text with her address to him. Then, she sent another one. Meet me at my house at 10. Friend.

Chapter 10

"Hey, boy." Ms. Pennie smiled at Myles as he entered her bedroom. "I was wondering if you were going to stop by."

Myles greeted her with a kiss to her temple and set a bag on her bedside table. "I brought dinner."

Ms. Pennie peeked in the bag. "Thanks so much."

He watched Ms. Pennie prepare her fish by cutting it into tiny pieces, like she'd always done. "How are you feeling today?"

She shrugged. "I'm good and tired."

After her fall, her doctors had ordered an entire battery of new diagnostic tests to ensure the cancer hadn't spread to her bones or her brain. Once they ruled out metastasis, Ms. Pennie had been released home with a referral for physical therapy and strict instructions to stay off her injured leg as much as possible.

Myles had hated to leave Aria after their night, but he

had to be there for Ms. Pennie, just as she'd always been there for him. In hindsight, he realized he should have told Aria the truth or at least called to check in with her, but he'd done what he always did when the stress of life was too much. He worked, then went home and played until his fingers were sore. As a result, he'd hurt Aria.

He'd been in a haze of routine and hadn't snapped out of it until he'd received a terse text from Avery telling him he'd messed up—in a not-so-polite way. He'd dropped everything and raced to the studio to see Aria, to apologize for treating her as if she didn't matter. Because she did.

"Boy, what's wrong with you?" Ms. Pennie dipped her fork into her coleslaw. "You seem distracted."

"I'm fine, Ms. Pennie." He smiled and sat on the chair next to the bed.

"I need you to stop worrying so much about me, son. I'm fine. Old, but fine."

"I know. But I can't help worrying about you."

"I tripped on an old shoe. That's why I fell. But I do have something I want to run by you—I'm going to put the house on the market."

Myles's eyes widened. "What?"

"I don't need this much space anymore. I haven't given private lessons in years, and it's a lot of upkeep. Roaming those empty halls just seems to highlight the simple fact that I'm alone."

"You're not alone, Ms. Pennie. I'm here."

She waved a dismissive hand. "You're a doctor. I don't expect you to check on me every single day. Besides, I need you to get a wife so I can die knowing you're being taken care of."

"Don't say that." He folded his arms over his chest. "That's not funny."

"I'm not laughing." Tense silence filled the room for a few moments. "Anyway. What do you think?"

"I think it's smart. On both fronts."

"Good. I'm ready to travel and see things I've never had a chance to see. Who knows, maybe I'll find a nice beau and get my groove back."

"I didn't need to hear that." He shook his head when Ms. Pennie burst out laughing. She was never one to hold her tongue. Sex talk wasn't off-limits in her opinion. To him, it was like talking to his parents about it.

"Ha! I knew that would get to you, boy." She set her fork down. "I will need your help with the sale."

Myles nodded. "Anything you need. I can call my Realtor and ask him to take care of everything."

"Thank you."

She finished her dinner, while he watched her. Ms. Pennie had stayed in her home so long because she loved it. The house had been built in 1939 and had undergone several renovations over the years. It was prime real estate in the city, located in one of the best neighborhoods in Ann Arbor. Selling it should be no problem, but he hated that she felt she needed to. He understood why, though. Too much house for one woman.

"So, have you met any nice women?"

Myles chuckled. "There you go. We're not talking about me right now."

"You know I have to ask." She bit into her roll.

"Every time I see you?"

Ms. Pennie cracked up, tossing a piece of bread at him. "At least, I'm consistent."

"Well, you'll be happy to know I have met someone I like."

Like was a strong word for him when it came to

women. He didn't throw the word out there often, or at all. Yet, somehow, he felt it wasn't big enough. The word didn't encapsulate everything he felt for Aria. He wasn't crazy enough to think he'd fallen in love with her after one date and one night of sex, but he knew it was…more.

Myles glanced at his watch. Nine o'clock. In one hour, he'd be at her house and he hoped they could move past this faux friend thing.

"You like someone?" Ms. Pennie arched a brow. "I don't think I've ever heard you use that word before about someone you're seeing."

"That's because she's not like anyone I've ever spent time with."

Ms. Pennie smiled. "Tell me more, boy. Don't hold back."

Myles started from the beginning, telling her about their meeting at the paint party and ending with him playing for her at his house. Because she didn't need to know anything beyond that point.

"Wow. You played for her?"

"I did."

"How did you feel?"

Myles glanced up at the feeling, recalling the night in question. The music, Aria… Mixing the two together was intense, but it felt right. For years, he'd kept his music separate from everything. For the first time, he didn't mind merging his music with his relationship.

"Good."

"I'm so proud of you, son. I always told you to share your gift with others. Maybe you can take over for me and teach. There are so many children who would benefit from your expertise."

Over the years, Ms. Pennie had encouraged him to

pick up her business of private lessons. He'd always balked at the idea because he already had such a busy schedule.

"No, I'm okay with things the way they are." *For now.* Something told him his status quo was about to change very soon, though. "Back to the subject at hand. I enjoy being with Aria. She's beautiful, intelligent, and she gets it. She understands why my music is so important to me because her art means so much to her."

"That's good." Her chin trembled. "I'm so happy to hear that. Now, I have to stay alive so I can hold your babies."

Myles frowned. "I told you to stop with that death talk. You're not going anywhere."

"I know, I know. I want to meet this woman."

He smiled. "I hope you can soon. I'm supposed to meet her in an hour."

Ms. Pennie gave him the once over. "And you're wearing that?"

Myles's gaze dropped down to his outfit, then back to Ms. Pennie. "Wh-why? What's wrong with my outfit?"

"Nothing. It just dawned on me that you're not wearing a full suit. I'd say this woman is already doing wonders for you."

He barked out a laugh. "You're funny."

She shooed him out. "Go ahead and leave. I wouldn't want you to be late for your date."

Myles stood and kissed her brow. "I'll see you tomorrow. If you're feeling up to it, maybe I can take you to the Art Fair. At least down Main Street. I don't want you out walking in the hot weather for too long. Plus, if this year is like the last few years, it'll rain."

"That would be nice. You know I love to go."

"I do." And he'd always taken her. It was a tradition that he'd like to keep going because he knew she looked forward to it.

"Maybe you can bring your Aria, so I can meet her."

"Don't get ahead of yourself."

"Boy, bye. See you tomorrow?"

"Definitely."

Myles knocked on Aria's door right at ten o'clock. She opened the door as if she'd been running. Her hair was wild, and her cheeks were flushed. She'd changed into a long, flowing kaftan with a colorful African print. *Beautiful.*

"Hi," she breathed.

"Hi." She stood still for a moment, her eyes on his. He wondered if she'd changed her mind about him coming over, because she made no move to invite him in. "Are you—?"

"Come in." She motioned him inside.

He shoved his hands in his pockets and walked into the house. He scanned the living area, noted the bold colors on the walls, sculptures lining the shelves. Several paintings sat against the wall on the hardwood floor. There was no furniture in the room, just an area rug.

"Thanks for coming," Aria said from behind him.

Turning, he smiled. "Thanks for inviting me. You have a nice place."

The smile that greeted him nearly took him out, it was so beautiful. "Thanks. I still have a lot to do, but I'm happy that I had kind of a blank slate to put my own spin on the house. We painted a few days ago and I like the way it turned out. Now, I just have to fill it up with furniture."

He walked around the room slowly, studying each piece of art. "You didn't bring furniture with you from New York?"

"Not really. I brought a few pieces, but I wanted to start over."

He stopped, pondered her words. There was so much he wanted to know about her. She'd hinted at failed relationships in her past, but he sensed her last one had done the most damage.

"Did you want a glass of wine? Or a beer?"

Shaking his head, he turned to face her. She stood near the door still, shifting from one foot to the other. He inched closer to her.

Aria held out her hand, halting him in his tracks. "Before we go any further, I have to say this. I'm kind of goofy. Maybe some people would call me neurotic. I live in my head. For years, my only friends were my Barbie dolls because my mother insisted on entering me in every beauty pageant she could, and I didn't like being around the girls I competed with. Brent was the first friend I had that actually had a pulse." She let out a nervous giggle. "I spent years building a hard exterior just to deal with my mother and her lofty expectations. I left home because I knew I'd suffocate if I stayed. This is not to say that I never let my guard down because I did—a few times. It never ended well for me.

"When I moved back, I told myself I wouldn't get involved. I told myself that this move was about my career. I needed to reset. Then I met you, and it felt like you saw me. You understood my work, you made me laugh, you pay attention to the small things that are really big to me. There's something so…" She sighed heavily. "So innate, so natural in our connection. It scares me. I didn't want it. And when you didn't call, I told myself this was my out, that I could walk away knowing that you weren't shit and I was right to not want it."

He laughed. "Really?"

"Really. But here's the thing. Even though it hurt that you didn't call, I'm kind of glad you didn't. Because it gave me a chance to really think about what it is that I want. Bottom line? I convinced myself that it would be easy to walk away from this." She motioned between them with her hand. "But it's not easy to turn my back on something that feels so right. So, you tell me. Am I imagining that this could be more? More than sex, more than ice cream and chips, more than oil paint and sheet music?"

Myles brushed a stray hair out of her face. The woman in front of him was fearless, even though she couldn't see it. The plea in her eyes, the sincerity in her words... She was being so open and honest with him he wanted to give her everything she needed. "You're not imagining this. It's not just you."

She dropped her head and let out a shaky breath. "Good."

"Can I say something?"

Aria lifted her head slowly. "Yes," she whispered.

"It never bothered me to be referred to as the serious twin—before you. I'm not spontaneous. I wear suits because I'm comfortable being uncomfortable. Because it makes me better, sharper. The only friends I have are my siblings and their spouses, and I've always been okay with that. I live in my head, too. I never had Barbie dolls, but I had instruments that served the same purpose. I've never let my guard down to anyone who wasn't my family. But there's something about you that makes me want to."

Aria sucked in a deep breath. "Myles, I… I lost my words." She giggled.

He leaned his forehead against hers. "I've thought a lot about how I handled things. I don't want you to ever feel like you don't matter. I have a lot to learn about relationships, but I want to try. Because the alternative isn't something I want to imagine."

She gripped his jacket and tugged him closer. "Okay. You can kiss me now."

Myles didn't need another invitation. His lips were on hers, his hand was fisted in her hair, and he was kissing her with everything he had. She tasted like cheesecake and strawberries, smelled like oranges and snow.

"Need you," he murmured against her lips. "Now."

"So, does this mean you don't want anything to drink?"

He lifted her in his arms. "We can drink later, baby."

"In that case, I have a really nice countertop in the kitchen."

Laughing, he hurried to the kitchen and set her on the granite. He pulled her gown up and off, flinging it behind him. He expected to rip her panties off again, but she was gloriously naked and ready for him. "Perfect," he grumbled against her ear before he nipped her lobe with his teeth.

Aria pushed his jacket off and started on his buttons. Myles's skin seemed to heat up from within with every brush of her knuckles against his chest. "Screw it," she mumbled, before she ripped open his shirt, sending buttons flying everywhere.

He didn't have time to react to the fact that she'd ruined his shirt because she unbuckled his belt, unbuttoned his pants and pushed them off.

"I'm sorry about your shirt," she said. "But you had on too many clothes."

Their lips met again in a frantic kiss. He couldn't stop touching her, committing her body to his memory.

"Condom," he grunted. "In my wallet."

She groaned, falling back against the countertop. He stumbled when he tried to step out of his jeans, which were pooled at his feet, nearly taking an "L". He yanked his wallet from his back pocket and pulled out a condom. He sheathed himself quickly and pressed his erection against her core.

"Now, Myles," she whispered.

He thrust into her hard, enjoying the soft purr that burst from her lips. He closed his eyes to center himself. She felt so good, so warm. He moved slow at first, letting her get used to him again. He wanted to take his time with her, worship her the way she deserved. But then...

"Harder," she whimpered. "Take me. Harder."

He let out a low curse, then picked up the pace. They moved to a rhythm all their own, slow and fast. Myles was unraveling. The way she said his name, a mixture between a moan and a whimper. The feel of her legs gripping his hips. The sight of her beneath him, writhing under him. He didn't think he could last much longer. He was so caught up in her he couldn't think straight.

Myles pressed his thumb against her sensitive nub, rubbed her until she gasped for air. "Aria." He dropped his head to her breast, bit down on her nipple. "Let go."

Aria came then, shouting his name over and over again. And he followed her, coming so long and hard he had to grip the countertop to remain standing. Once the tremors subsided, he picked her up and slid to the floor, on top of her gown.

Aria took his bottom lip in her mouth, nibbled on it before pulling him into a slow, lingering kiss. Then she wrapped her arms around his neck, hugging him tightly. She brushed her lips over his ear. "Thirsty now?"

He laughed. "Definitely."

"Beauty pageants?" Myles massaged the ball of her foot, sending shivers of awareness right to her core.

They were seated on the bed, facing each other, with only a thin sheet draped over them. Myles leaned back against the headboard. Her bed was her first and best big purchase for her home. The pillow-top mattress made her feel like she was floating on a cloud and she loved that it was adjustable. She'd had to buy a custom-made headboard, but it was worth it.

Aria dipped a potato chip into her ice cream and bit into it, letting out a low moan. Not only did Myles rock her world in more ways than one, in multiple positions, he'd surprised her when he'd run out to the local twenty-four-hour Meijer around the corner to grab ice cream and chips when she awoke with a growling stomach. He'd also brought back breakfast, having noticed that her refrigerator was bare.

"Yes," she grumbled. "It was pretty much the worst time of my life. Caked-on makeup, full-length sparkly gowns and a fake smile is not my idea of fun. But my mother liked to have something to talk about to her friends."

His hands inched up her calf. "I'm sure that was torture for you."

"It was ridiculous. When I left home, I didn't wear a dress for two years. I kept having flashbacks."

Myles laughed. "What changed? Because you look damn good in a dress."

She shot him an amused look. "You like that look on me, huh?"

"I don't think I've ever seen a look I didn't like on you."

Aria's face burned at his sincere tone. "Do you have to work tomorrow? I mean, today." She glanced at the clock—2:33 a.m. Usually, she'd be neck deep into a painting, but she could admit this was a better way to spend her evening. Aria was a night owl. She preferred evening activities because she found her level of creativity was heightened once the sun went down.

"I have to be at the hospital at six."

Aria raised a brow. "That's early. Don't you need to get a little sleep? I don't want you operating on some patient without your beauty rest."

"My first surgery isn't scheduled until noon. But I have to do rounds in a few hours."

She piled a mound of ice cream on a big chip. "I don't know how you do it. I hate mornings."

"Not a morning person?"

"God, no." She tipped her head up and dropped her treat into her mouth. "If the world sees me before ten o'clock, everyone should run for cover. I'm a monster."

"I don't mind the mornings when I'm not working. But the hospital is crazy right around eight."

"I know. I had to go establish care with my new doctor and couldn't find a parking spot easily. I ended up doing valet."

"It's worth it," he agreed.

She eyed him. He didn't look tired. There were no bags or dark circles under his eyes. But she wondered if he'd just learned how to mask his weariness. "Have you ever taken a vacation?"

"What?"

Aria picked up the gallon of vanilla ice cream and set it on the bench at the foot of the bed. She ate a chip before she closed the bag and put it next to the ice cream. "You're so devoted, to your job, to your family. Don't you ever get tired of being bogged down by obligation? When was the last time you did something for yourself?"

He arched a brow, and she knew what he was thinking before he could articulate it.

"Other than me, of course," she joked with a playful roll of her eyes. "When was your last trip out of this area?"

He squeezed her knee and shrugged. "It's been a while, maybe January? I visited Ian in New Orleans."

Aria had learned from Bailee that Ian had done a stint in Doctors Without Borders. "I love New Orleans. Did you have a beignet?"

He shook his head. "No, but I ate a lot."

"Well, you must go back one day just to visit Café du Monde. You won't regret it."

"I'm sure. Love tells me that all the time."

Powdered dough and confectioner's sugar were the first things she'd bonded over with her new friends. They all liked dessert. After every outing together, they'd stop at some place and order multiple desserts with many spoons.

"I'll be sure to grab one when we go back for Ian's wedding."

"Good."

"What are you doing next week?"

The change in subject jarred her a bit and she met his waiting gaze. "Which day?"

"Any day."

"Does this mean I have to wait until next week to see you again?"

He grinned, a wicked sexy-as-hell smirk that she felt all the way to her toes. "Not at all. The Art Fair is next week, and I planned on going out one day. Are you exhibiting?"

Shaking her head, she brushed the hairs on his leg. "I missed the deadline. But I definitely planned on going out. I invited my father, but he can't make it. And Brent is offering Art Fair specials, so he wants to be in his shop."

"Come with me?"

"Sure."

"I want you to meet someone."

"Who is that?"

"Her name is Penelope Kemp. We call her Ms. Pennie. And she's important to me. I told her all about you and she can't wait to meet you."

Aria's heart swelled. She knew about Ms. Pennie from Avery and Bailee, but he'd never mentioned her. Not when he'd apologized, not in any of the texts he'd sent, not last night when he'd opened up to her about some things.

"I never told you this, but she's the reason we had to cut our first night together short," he continued. "She took a hard fall and had to be rushed to the hospital."

"And you had to be there."

"Yes, I did. She recently went into remission. Breast cancer. I was worried that she might have a recurrence. It's been a tough few months."

Squeezing his hand, she said, "I bet. I'm so sorry to hear that."

"I don't really do this."

She frowned. "Do what?"

"Talk."

"We don't have to. If you're uncomfortable."

"Actually, I'm not."

She leaned back on her elbows and peered up at him. "I'm listening."

"When I was a kid, I wasn't allowed to play in the house. We had a huge, expensive grand piano that I couldn't touch. But, for as long as I can remember, I've heard notes in my head."

Aria could relate. Her fingers had itched to draw since she could hold a crayon. "That's pretty cool."

"I guess. I thought I was crazy for a while. But Ms. Pennie took me under her wing and started to teach me to make sense of the notes."

Aria hummed. "So, she's your teacher?"

He nodded. "The best teacher I could ever have. She changed my life."

Aria noted the affection in his eyes and his voice when he talked about Ms. Pennie. "Awesome. My father once told me that good teachers don't give you the answers, they guide you on your pursuit to find the answers. I've had a few who've inspired me to take my art to levels I'd never even dreamed of." She laid her head against the mattress and peered up at the ceiling. "When I think about how art has changed my life, it makes me want to give that gift to others."

He chuckled softly. "Ms. Pennie just said something like that to me today."

"See. Good teacher. That's why I want to open an art

school. I want children who don't have access to art in their school to be able to create." Myles was quiet for a moment, and Aria perched herself back up on her elbows and eyed him. He was staring at her. "What?"

"Nothing."

"You think I'm crazy."

"For what?"

She shrugged. "I don't know. When I tell people I want to open a school, they tend to think I'm being self-important or setting my goals too high."

"I think you're amazing."

"Oh, God, you have to stop making me feel all mushy." She giggled. "I'm already hot for you."

Myles laughed. "You're silly."

Aria ran her fingers over the hair on his legs. "Anyway, I'm glad you have Ms. Pennie. We all need someone like her in our lives." She'd been blessed to have her father and Brent, and couldn't imagine life without people who'd encouraged her to dream big.

"We're extremely close. She tells me I'm the son she never had."

"I love it. I'd love to meet her."

"Just so you know. I've never introduced her to a woman before."

Her eyes widened. "Never?"

"I've never wanted to."

"Hmm." She tapped her chin. "What if she doesn't like me?"

"I'd say the chance of her not liking you is very small. Besides, what's not to like? You're beautiful, in every way. She'll love you."

She pointed at him. "You do realize that you don't need to sweet-talk me anymore. I'm already a sure thing." Aria burst out laughing when he gripped her legs and pulled her to him. He crawled on top of her, resting his body against hers.

Myles brushed his lips against the column of her throat, over her jawline and finally against her mouth. There was no tongue or teeth, no frantic pawing at each other. Just their breaths mingling, his nose brushing hers, his soft groans in her ear. At this point, they'd shared many kisses, but this one… It was sweet. Soft. And it had just ruined her for anyone else.

He pulled back and searched her face. "Sure thing, huh?" he asked, placing a kiss to her pulse point.

"You did it again." Aria barely recognized her own voice in that moment. Probably because she was drowning with need for him to make love to her again.

"Did what?" he murmured against her sensitive skin.

"Your lips are on my pulse point," she breathed, tightening her legs around his waist.

His low chuckle felt like a balm against her body, and she wanted to burrow into him like he was a warm blanket on a cold day. "Aria," he whispered.

"Yes."

He rested on his elbows and kissed the tip of her nose. "Don't ask me something you already know the answer to."

Aria pinned him with a gaze, stared into his brown eyes. She read the desire in them, the need. He wanted her, but there was so much more within their depths. It felt more important than eating or sleeping or breathing. Instinctively, she knew things had changed. She'd felt the shift earlier, and it was more pronounced now.

She had so many questions. She thought she knew why, but she didn't want to assume that his feelings for her were already as strong as hers were for him. The ball of sensation in her gut squeezed, shooting sensations through her body. She felt both weak and strong, tormented yet happy.

"Tell me," she urged him.

The corner of his mouth quirked up into a soft smile. "Not yet. However, I will tell you that I'm done talking." He pressed his hard length against her core. "I'm taking now."

Then he kissed her, right as he pushed inside her. And Aria was lost.

Chapter 11

The next week, Aria worked on her house, her business and her dream. Now that she was officially a home-owner, she could shift some of her focus to the school she wanted to open. In her spare time, she'd looked at empty schools and buildings that would serve her purpose. Brent had helped her scout out locations, and she'd even contacted an architect to get a feel on how much renovation costs would be.

Myles had been working long hours at the hospital, and they'd barely seen each other. He'd managed to stop by and bring her lunch one day during the week, and he'd surprised her last night with a spontaneous date to a Detroit Pistons game. Other than that, they'd relied on FaceTime, phone calls and texts to communicate.

It felt good, though. To let herself explore the attraction that seemed to burn hotter and brighter by the day. They'd talked for hours about everything and found they had so much more in common than she'd ever thought possible considering she once thought their differences were too big to overcome.

During the game, he'd cheered loud when they scored and cursed even louder when they messed up. *A man after my own heart.* Aria preferred football, but she loved seeing him let loose in public.

Myles had confessed that Ms. Pennie wanted him to teach music, and she'd encouraged him to consider it. He had too much talent to not pass that on to someone.

Her phone buzzed on the table. Picking it up, she smiled when she saw Myles's picture flash across the screen. "Hi," she answered.

"Hey." The low rumble of his voice warmed her.

Will he always have this effect on me? She hoped so. "What's up?"

He sighed. "I was hoping to have the afternoon off, but I have a surgery that I have to scrub in on. With my father."

Myles hadn't talked about his father much, and she didn't push. She'd already heard from Avery that Dr. Law was an ass on his good days, and she could definitely empathize. Her mother was the same way. When her mom found out she'd gone to dinner with her father, she'd accused Aria of taking sides. It was the first time the woman had shown any emotion about the divorce, and it wasn't even directed at her father, but her.

"Is that a bad thing?" Aria asked.

"Not really. I always learn from him."

"Okay." Aria missed him, but she didn't want to come out and just say it. For some reason, that felt too deep for her. They were in a happy bubble, getting to know each other, and she didn't want to mess that up with any heavy, emotional stuff. She blurted out, "I want to cook for you."

"You do? But you said you didn't cook. Should I eat before I come?"

"Ha ha. You got jokes."

Myles laughed. "Just kidding with you. What do you want to make?"

"It's a surprise." To her, too. Especially since she hadn't seen the inside of a grocery store since she'd moved into her house. "Can you make it at eight?"

There was silence on the line for a moment and she assumed he was checking his calendar. *My little organized man.* "I should be able to do that. I'll bring dessert."

"Sounds like a plan."

Later, Myles arrived promptly with a cheesecake in hand. She cheered and took the confection from him. "Yum. You're the best." She sniffed the box.

"Hi, to you, too." Myles raised a brow.

"Oh." She stood on the tips of her toes and kissed him twice. "Hi." He wrapped his strong arms around her waist, nearly crushing the cheesecake. "Wait!" She set the dessert down on a small table near the door and hugged him.

He lifted her in his arms and placed a proper kiss to her lips. One that made her want to rip his clothes off and ride him all night.

Myles set her on her feet. With a frown, he asked, "Is dinner ready?"

Aria felt heat creep up her neck. Yeah, so dinner was a fiasco. She'd tried to make shrimp Alfredo because he had told her he loved it. Big fail. Huge! The shrimp had burned, the sauce was lumpy, and the spinach she'd sautéed tasted more like salt and oil than green vegetables. "So, about dinner…"

"What, Aria?"

"I sort of…ruined it."

He laughed. "I had a feeling I should call first. Just to make sure I shouldn't bring food and not dessert."

Aria picked up the cheesecake. "No, dessert is good. I improvised on dinner. We're good."

He followed her into the kitchen. "You're sure. I can run back out to grab something."

She waved a hand in dismissal toward him. "No, you're good."

At least, Aria had set the mood. She'd lit candles and asked "Alexa" to play the John Coltrane station. Jazz floated through the house, courtesy of her surround sound speakers.

"Have a seat at the table?" she said, nodding toward a newly purchased set. "I'll bring dinner over."

Myles took a seat as he was told.

"Wine?" She held up a bottle of merlot.

"Sure. Want me to pour?"

"Nope. You just sit there and look fine." Aria filled two glasses with wine and handed him his glass. They toasted to improvisation.

He held up the dominoes on the kitchen table. "I guess you're finally ready to let me beat you."

"In your dreams." She winked. "I figured it would be a nice way to decompress. You had a busy day, and so did I."

"What did you do?"

"I worked a little at home, then at the studio. Me and Brent met with an architect."

"What for?" He stared at her over the rim of his glass. "Are you renovating the studio already?"

"No. I just wanted to get an idea of how much it would cost to renovate this building I saw the other day. It's an old school in Inkster. I think it would be a perfect location for an art school."

When Aria was thinking about locations, Inkster had been the first city to pop into her mind because there was no high school in the town. The state had dissolved Inkster Public Schools in 2014, and the children were split among several other surrounding districts. Bringing an art school to the area would be an amazing investment in the futures of so many children.

Often, art and music were the first programs to be cut when state funding of schools decreased, and Aria wanted to fill in the gap. Funding such an endeavor would take time. Hiring qualified teachers and staff, buying necessary supplies, and transforming a building into an oasis for her future students wasn't going to be cheap. She didn't expect the school to open for another few years, but she wanted to at least secure the building.

"I plan to take my dad there next week, so he can see it." She pulled a platter from her cabinet and transferred the new dinner to the large plate. "I think he'd approve."

"Is the building abandoned?"

"Not yet. It's actually functioning as a charter school. The owners have decided to close it."

"How are you handling funding?"

"Looking for investors." Avery's best friend, Jessie, ran Avery's foundation and had given her very helpful tips for raising the money. "I'm thinking of enlisting the help of some of my colleagues and having a silent auction to help raise the money."

Aria had been in the art world long enough to have made many connections. She was sure she could get people to donate to the cause. It would take some planning, though.

"That's a good start. I'd like to see the building."

She looked at him. "Really?"

"Yes. If you don't mind."

"Of course, I don't mind. Maybe we can go there after the Art Fair tomorrow?"

"That works."

She set the platter on the table and immediately burst out in a fit of giggles at the shocked look on Myles's face. He glanced down at the plate, then back at her. She bit her lip. "See! I improvised. Grilled cheese and french fries."

Leaning back in his chair, Myles laughed. "You're crazy. Good thing I like grilled cheese sandwiches."

Aria handed the waitress her menu, then glanced over at a smirking Myles. "Don't say anything."

Myles laughed. "Hey, I'm not saying a word."

When Aria had bitten into her grilled cheese sandwich earlier, she'd quickly realized one thing. Wheat bread was not her thing, and she'd only bought it because Myles didn't eat white bread. Plus, she'd used the wrong cheese. Cheddar cheese, not the processed American cheese that she loved. She couldn't figure out how that happened. And because of her oversight, she wasn't able to enjoy her dinner. After two bites, she couldn't do it anymore.

Myles had taken one look at her and suggested they save the grilled cheese for another time, when she could show him all the ways white bread and processed cheese were superior to the healthy stuff. He'd promptly stood and told her to grab her purse because they were going out for dinner.

"I'm so embarrassed," she said.

He placed his hand on top of hers. "Don't be. I'm happy you wanted to cook for me."

Cooking for anyone had never been high on her list of fun things to do. Long ago, after several kitchen disasters, she'd accepted the fact that she wouldn't master a stove. It was a hard pill to swallow back then because Celeste had been such a role model for her. She'd wanted to be like her, able to whip up tasty meals with ease. Celeste didn't need recipes or measurements. The older woman instinctively knew how much salt or sugar or garlic went in every dish. Aria, on the other hand, needed to measure everything, and still wasn't guaranteed a good dinner.

"I wish it had turned out better."

"This is nice, too."

She turned her palm up and linked their fingers together. "It is." Myles glanced at something over her shoulder and muttered a curse. "What's wrong?"

"My father is here," he said.

Aria froze, resisting the instinct to pull out her compact and make sure her face and hair were suitable. It was something she would have done if her mother had shown up. She hadn't realized she did it until Brent had pointed it out to her years ago.

Myles slipped his hand from hers just as Dr. Lawrence Jackson approached their table. Aria looked up at the imposing man. She'd seen pictures of him when she'd Googled Myles weeks ago. The man was definitely handsome, with smooth mocha skin, a salt-and-pepper beard and mustache, and a tall, lean frame.

"Myles," Dr. Jackson said.

"Dad," was Myles's one-word reply.

Dr. Jackson gave Aria the once-over but didn't speak. Instead, he asked Myles, "Is this why you've been avoiding my calls?"

"I just saw you today. In surgery."

"We have business to discuss."

Myles sighed heavily. "I'll make time next week."

The intimidating doctor turned his attention back to Aria. "And who is this?"

She blinked. The similarities between her mother and Myles's dad were astonishing. Elizabeth Bell had been known to be a dismissive snob and had treated many people the same way Dr. Jackson was treating her.

Myles spoke for her. "Dad, this is…Aria. A friend."

Her eyes flashed to Myles, hurt that he'd downplayed what was obviously more than a friendship. She tamped down her emotions and reached out to shake his father's hand. "Nice to meet you."

"A friend, huh?" Dr. Jackson mused. "Good."

Did he just say "good"? Like she wasn't worthy of being more than a friend to his son. Her body tensed, and heat flushed through her. Memories of previous relationships with men who'd told her she was good enough, only to later demand she change to be more suitable for their world, assaulted her.

"I expect to hear from you, Myles," Dr. Jackson said. "We have a short timeline to get everything done."

Myles didn't answer his father. He simply nodded. There were no goodbyes or even a fatherly hug. Dr. Lawrence Jackson just walked away, along with Aria's appetite.

She stood. "I'm ready to go."

Myles frowned. "Why? We haven't eaten yet."

"I'm not hungry. Take me home."

Aria headed toward the door without another word.

Back at her house, she kicked her shoes off and headed toward the kitchen. Myles followed her.

"Are you going to ignore me forever?"

She poured herself a large glass of wine and gulped it down. "It's tempting," she replied, refilling her glass.

"Aria, I—"

"I'm not sure how I feel about that interaction with your father." She took another sip of wine before she set the glass back on the countertop. "Scratch that, I know exactly how I feel. You introduced me as your friend, like I'm nothing more than a casual acquaintance."

"Aria, will you let me explain?" He stepped forward and she held up a hand, signaling him to stop where he was. His shoulders fell. "My father is—"

"I don't care who your father is!" she yelled. "This isn't about him. This is about you. And me. This is about the fact that you downplayed our relationship. You acted like I'm nothing to you."

Myles frowned. "You don't get it."

"Really? I think it's pretty clear."

"If you'd just let me talk," he grumbled, "maybe you would understand."

Aria shook her head. "You know what? Maybe you should go."

"I'm not leaving."

She shot him a hard glare, crossing her arms over her breasts. "Fine. Tell me how I should take this. Why didn't you tell your father that I'm more…?" She swallowed over a hard lump in her throat. "That I'm your girl, that we're together."

He reached out and swiped a tear that she didn't even realize had fallen. "Aria."

"No. Are you ashamed of me?" Her chin trembled, which made her angrier. With herself for letting him make her feel like this. With him for making her question her value.

"Hell, no." His voice came out like a loud boom, and Aria retreated backward in response. *He is pissed.* "Why would you say something like that?"

She was pissed, too. "Because you dismissed me!"

"I didn't dismiss you. I protected you."

"From what? From your father?"

"Yes. You don't know him. And I didn't want him to insert himself into our relationship like he's done with everyone else in my family." He let out a slow, exasperated breath. "Meeting my father as my girlfriend would have made you run far and fast."

"Why?"

"Because he's not a nice man. He's cold, calculating and manipulative. He's everything you thought I was. Aria, I just found you." He caressed her face, searched her eyes. "I'm not ready to lose you."

Aria backed out of his hold, grabbed a bag of chips and her glass of wine, and walked over to the patio door. She slid it open and stepped outside. The night air centered her, made her feel normal for just a moment. Because nothing about this situation was normal for her. She took a seat on one of the wicker chairs and set her glass on the table. Myles joined her moments later.

"My father wasn't easy to love," he said. "He... Hell, he wasn't here. He worked all the time. And my mother was so busy pretending to be the perfect wife and mother that she forgot to be one."

Aria rocked in her chair silently. Their experiences were so similar it was uncanny.

"It's funny because all of my brothers…" He continued, "We had one person who stood in the gap for us, someone who provided that nurturing we needed to adjust."

She closed her eyes. "Ms. Pennie."

"Yes."

She looked at him then, studied the profile of his face as he stared out into the dark. "So, your brothers had a Ms. Pennie?"

"Yeah, they did. Drake had Love's mother. Ian had Dr. Solomon and his family."

Aria knew Gloria, Love's mother. The older woman had joined them on one of their ladies group outings. She was a hoot. She also knew Mia, who was Dr. Solomon's daughter and Ian's best friend. "What about El?"

Myles tapped his fingers against the table. "El would disappear and go to church when we were kids. I suspect his nurturer was there."

She stared down at her bare feet. "Your parents sound like my mother. I think that's why I got so upset. She was… I don't know." She hunched a shoulder. "She was *her*. My father always told me to love people where they're at. So I learned to never expect more from her. If that makes any sense."

"It does."

"The older I get, the more I know I'll never be the woman she wants me to be."

"You're okay with that?"

"Yes." She snickered. "Don't get me wrong. It would be nice to have her support, and even her approval to some extent. But I don't need it. Because the woman she wanted me to be was some Stepford wife whose sole existence was finding a husband, having kids and maintaining status."

"My dad is the same way. He always made these rules for us, required us to be part of his society. Whether that meant taking part in formal balls, playing sports or being available as an escort to his friend's daughters. Aria, my life wasn't easy. My father forbade me to play my music. He would have never supported my lessons with Ms. Pennie, which was why she did them secretly at no cost. My way to cope was to fly under the radar. I didn't get in trouble, I excelled at school and at baseball. I followed the family path."

"And you're okay with that?" she asked, throwing his question back at him.

"Oddly, I am. When I went to medical school, I was doing it for him. But I found that I actually like the work. It's not a chore. My brothers and Mel... They don't get it. They think I'm doing this solely for my father."

"You're not?"

He shook his head. "I'm not."

He picked up her hand and kissed the inside of her wrist, holding his lips to her pulse point. "I'm sorry I hurt you, because that wasn't my intention. Everything about this feels right to me. *You* feel right to me. I'm not ashamed by you, I'm in awe of you."

Aria's pulse raced against his fingers. He'd just melted her with his words. In a minute, she might be a puddle on the floor. In a minute, she might be in love with him. If she wasn't already.

"I hate that your mother doesn't realize how badass you are." He brushed his lips against her palm and up her arm. "Your career is pretty amazing."

Aria smiled. "How would you know? You've only seen one collection."

"Google."

"You researched me?" She'd definitely looked him up, stalked social media for him only to find that he didn't have a single page anywhere.

"Yeah. I did."

"Okay."

"Okay, what?"

"I forgive you." He dropped his head onto her arm, and Aria ran her fingers over the back of his neck with her other hand. "Myles?"

He lifted his head, stared into her eyes. "Yes?"

"You're pretty badass yourself. It's a shame your father doesn't realize it." She stood from her chair and climbed into his lap. He wrapped his arms around her and burrowed his head into her neck.

"Thank you," he murmured against her skin.

"Myles?"

"Yes, Aria."

"Thank you."

Chapter 12

Ann Arbor was jam-packed with people from all around, browsing displays, eating carnival food and fellowshipping with friends. The sun burned hot, but Myles didn't notice. All he could see was Aria. She hadn't stopped smiling since they'd arrived an hour ago.

She'd printed out a map of the many booths and then led him around to those she'd starred in red ink. Today, she wore black shorts that showed a little too much of her legs, a pink tank and a pair of black-and-white Chuck Taylors. One word. Adorable. He wanted to eat her up.

As they strolled down Main Street, Aria waved at a few artists and stopped to talk to others. Many vendors had congratulated her on her exhibit at the Charles H. Wright Museum. While they were there, Aria was invited to show her work at several galleries including the Museum of Contemporary Art Detroit, or MOCAD.

Aria had taken and handed out business cards left and right. And had even managed to talk to one of the board members of the Ann Arbor Art Fair. He was pretty sure she'd have a booth next year.

They stopped at the Food Court for lunch. A live band played original tunes while people danced and sampled food from the various trucks. Aria ordered a huge corn dog, cheesy fries and a large lemonade. Myles bought sausage and peppers and a bottle of water.

"Want to sit?" she asked.

He nodded.

They found a table near the stage and took their seats. "Fry?" she asked.

He snatched one from her plate and popped it into his mouth. Greasy foods weren't his thing, but there was something about carnival food that made him want to eat everything in sight. "Good."

She dipped her corn dog into some ketchup. "This is great. I'm sorry Ms. Pennie couldn't be here."

Myles was sorry, too. That morning, he'd dropped by her house to pick her up, and she'd told him that she was in a lot of pain and didn't think she should go. He'd thought about calling Dr. Kirk to ask if he should bring her in, but before he could suggest it, Ms. Pennie had told him to "mind your own business, I'm fine." He knew a losing battle when he saw one, so he didn't fight her. He'd check on her later.

"I hate that she couldn't be here," he said. "I know she's disappointed."

"Is she okay?"

"She's still in a lot of pain from the fall."

"So, it's not the cancer."

Myles had shared more about Ms. Pennie with Aria

over the last week. "No. The doctor has confirmed she's still in remission."

"But you're still worried."

Although it wasn't a question, he answered her anyway. "I am."

Ms. Pennie and Sharon had started packing up the house slowly but surely. His Realtor had agreed to put it on the market, but there was some work that had to be done before it was listed. Myles had hired painters and a landscape artist. He'd even gone over to the house and helped clean out the attic while Ms. Pennie barked orders.

Aria placed her hand on top of his and squeezed. "That's normal. She's like a mother to you. I would be worried, too."

He sighed. "Right. The problem is, I know she's good. I saw the reports. There's no need to be so worried."

"Listen, medicine is one thing—an emotional connection is another. Your brain knows, your heart feels. That's all there is to it."

Myles dropped his head and she hugged him to her, offering him a comfort only she could give. He wrapped his arms around her waist. "Thank you," he mumbled.

"I have an idea," she said. "Does Ms. Pennie have any dietary restrictions?"

"Not right now."

Aria hopped up and pulled him to his feet. "Let's take the fair to her."

An hour later, he knocked at Ms. Pennie's door with Aria by his side. He could hear Ms. Pennie cursing him out through the door.

"I told you not to come back here, boy!" The door swung back. "And—" The curse died on her lips when

she noticed he wasn't alone. "Oh." She smiled and held
the door open. "You brought your friend. Come in. What
brings you my way?" Ms. Pennie had turned on her nice
voice, as opposed to her pissed-at-Myles voice.

He held up the bag of greasy food. "Brought you
lunch. Ms. Pennie, this is Aria."

Aria hugged Ms. Pennie. "It's so good to finally meet
you. I've heard so much about you."

Ms. Pennie ran her fingers through her hair. "It's
about time he brought you to meet me. But I wish he'd
told me ahead of time. I'm in the process of packing,
and I could have cleaned up a bit. And combed my hair."

"You look lovely," Aria said. "And you should see
my house."

The grin that spread across Ms. Pennie's face made
him smile. She looped an arm through Aria's and led
her to the sunroom. "I would say we can go outside on
the patio, but it's hot as hell outside."

Aria giggled. "I love it. A woman who tells it like it
is. I'm the same way."

Ms. Pennie turned to Myles. "I like her already. You
betta do the right thing, boy."

"All right now, Ms. Pennie," he told her.

Elbowing Myles not so subtly, Ms. Pennie said, "I remember when I used to wear short shorts. You couldn't
tell me anything back in those days."

Myles covered his face, shaking his head. "Ms. Pennie."

"I'm serious, boy," the older woman continued. "I
used to get a lot of male attention back in my prime."

Aria laughed. "I bet you did."

Ms. Pennie winked. "See." She pointed at Aria. "She's
a keeper."

They spent the rest of the afternoon with Ms. Pennie. At one point, Aria had even started packing up boxes with her as they chatted about the weather and Avery's television show, *The Preserves*. Myles noticed the ease with which Aria interacted with Ms. Pennie, and it endeared her to him even more.

He couldn't keep his eyes off Aria. For the first time in his life, music and work didn't hold his undivided attention. And that meant one thing. *I'm in trouble.*

"Can you tell this boy that he needs to play more?" Ms. Pennie asked after finishing off her lemonade." And in public?"

Myles groaned. "Ms. Pennie. Please."

"No, son. It's time you get out of that box you put yourself in and share your gift."

"I agree, Ms. Pennie," Aria said with a shrug. "He's so talented."

"Can we not talk about this?" he asked. "We're having a nice afternoon."

Ms. Pennie ignored him and talked directly to Aria. "He's always been closed off. He keeps his music private because of his father. I know it."

Aria tilted her head, observing him. But she didn't say anything.

"I wish that damn Lawrence would just leave the kids alone."

Gotta love how she still called them kids when all of them were over thirty with the exception of Mel. "I'd rather not talk about my father, Ms. Pennie."

"Ah, fine." She rolled her eyes. Hard. "Whatever."

"Glad to see you're feeling better," he said.

"I just love you, boy. I want the best for you."

Myles knelt next to her. "And I love you, too. But we

don't have to do this every time I see you, ya know. We can just chill and talk about other things."

Ms. Pennie caressed his cheek. "I wish you could see how special you really are."

Aria squeezed his shoulder and he froze. He hadn't even realized she'd moved from her spot on the other side of the room. "He is special, Ms. Pennie."

He peered up at her and mouthed, *Thank you.*

Ms. Pennie yawned. "I'm so tired."

Myles fought the warring emotions battling for dominance in his heart. On one hand, he knew better. The lab tests and the imaging studies had confirmed the cancer was indeed in remission. But his heart didn't want to know a life without her.

He smoothed Ms. Pennie's gray hair back and kissed her cheek. "We're going to let you rest." Myles held out his arm, and Ms. Pennie looped hers through his and stood. He walked her to her room.

"You didn't have to do this, Myles." Ms. Pennie squeezed his biceps. "Sharon will be back in a few minutes. She just had to run a few errands."

"I wanted to."

Inside her bedroom, she shuffled over to the bed and sat down on the edge. She peered up at him, a watery smile on her face. "You mean so much to me, boy. Thank you for being you."

"I don't know any other way to be."

"That girl down there is perfect for you, two sides of the same coin. I think she will help you to live a little, to take chances. That's all I've ever wanted for you."

"I wish you'd stop talking to me like you're dying. You still have plenty of life left to live."

"I'm not dying. I just want to see my favorite person in the world happy."

Myles smiled. "I'm happy. Thanks for caring."

"All right. Now, get out. Go spend the rest of the day with your Aria."

My Aria. Myles liked the way that sounded.

"Domino."

"Shit," Aria shouted. "Not again."

He shrugged. "Hey, I can't help it if you suck."

Aria stuck her tongue out at him, and he laughed. "I can't help it if you suck," she mocked in a high-pitched, annoyed voice. "I have never lost this much in my life. I think you're cheating."

"How?"

She held a lone domino up to the light as if she were inspecting it. "I don't know. But something is not right about this situation."

Chuckling, he turned over the dominoes and motioned to her to shuffle them. God, he hadn't laughed this much in years. It felt good. *She* felt good. After they'd left Ms. Pennie's house, they had returned to his place. He'd promptly stripped her naked and made love to her on his living room floor.

Once he'd fed her, she'd challenged him to a game. Myles had warned her of his skill level from the beginning, but she talked a lot of smack. He had no choice but to shut her up by beating her. Three times.

Aria muttered a curse under her breath, something about cheaters and cocky know-it-all players.

"Sore. Loser. That's what you are."

She leaned back in her chair. "What can I say, I hate to lose."

"I hate losing, too. That's why I don't do it."

She threw a kernel of popcorn at him. "You're impossible."

"And you have no game plan, you just jump right in."

Her mouth fell open in mock offense. "Are you saying I don't know how to strategize?"

"Yep."

"Ugh, you make me sick." She tapped the table. "Pick your bones."

He picked his pieces and waited for her to do the same. The game started with him slamming the double six tile on the table.

Aria groaned. "I quit."

"You've been quitting since we started," he joked.

She studied her set and made her move. "I had a really great time today."

"Me, too."

"Ms. Pennie is a doll. Thanks for taking me to meet her."

He pinned her with his stare. "Thank *you* for making her laugh. She's had a rough year."

"Can I say something?"

Myles sat up straight. "Go ahead."

"I wish you would reconsider your stance on your music. Even if you don't want to play for audiences, you could make a world of difference for that little boy who, like you, hears the notes in his head and doesn't know what to do with that. You can definitely make an impact."

Myles thought about his childhood, about the way he'd lived his life up until now. What she said made sense to him, and he couldn't help thinking about the ways he could make a difference to a kid who struggled like he did. "You think so?"

"I do. And the good news is, you don't have to stop being a doctor to be a musician. You can still perform surgery and play, or even teach music. I feel like you think you can't do both, and that's not true."

It wasn't that he didn't think he could do both. Myles knew he could. But the act of playing in public, of opening himself up like that to strangers, made him feel vulnerable.

"Just…think about it," she said.

He nodded. "I will." Then, he set another tile on the table. "Now give me twenty-five!"

"No!" Aria jumped up on the table, crawled the short distance to him and kissed him. Hard.

Shit. He pulled her into his lap. "What was that for?"

"I'm not giving you another point. But I am ready to give you something else entirely, something more satisfying than a losing streak."

He nipped her chin. "I can't say I'm opposed to that particular game plan."

She giggled and sucked his bottom lip into her mouth. Someone groaned. He just wasn't sure if it was him or her. "Then, let's play."

"What's up, bruh?"

Myles gave Ian dap and took the seat across from him. "Nothing much."

The one-line text he'd received from Ian that morning, telling him simply to "check in" had prompted lunch today. It had been a while since they'd spoken, longer than they'd ever gone without talking in some capacity. Myles knew he had to come through. So, he'd texted Aria and asked for a rain check on lunch.

"You've been MIA," Ian said.

"Busy." Myles took a bite of his sandwich.

"Busy with work? Or Aria?"

"Both," he said through a mouth full of food.

"We're back to one-word answers, huh?"

Myles laughed. "Can I chew my food first?" He sipped from his water bottle. "I'm good. Aria is…good."

"So, this is serious?" Ian grinned.

Myles wanted to confide in his brother. They'd shared so much through the years about everything. He wanted Ian to know how much Aria had changed his life in just a short time. He called it Life after Aria, because there was a stark difference between now and how he'd lived before he met her.

She'd pointed out things he'd never seen or even bothered to try to see before. She talked and dreamed in vivid colors, which was good. Because he could believe in her dreams. Aria loved with everything in her, and he wanted to live up to that. They hadn't said the words yet, but they'd been moving at warp speed toward them.

"I didn't think it was possible," Myles admitted. "To care for someone like this."

"How?" Ian asked incredulously. "You saw how it knocked all of us out for the count. And I distinctly remember you laughing at me."

When Ian went crazy over Bailee, they'd all shared a laugh at his twin's expense. "Look at you now, though. You're about to marry a beautiful woman."

"And I'm happy. Go figure. Even Dad has come around some."

Myles groaned. "He's come around to you, and Drake and El. He's still the same asshole to me."

Ian frowned. "What happened?"

Myles told Ian about how Dr. Law had acted with Aria. "She was pretty upset."

"As she should have been." Ian threw his napkin at Myles's chest. "You messed up."

"I know. But you know how Dad is."

"He's only like that because you tolerate it."

Myles opened his mouth to argue and then closed it. Ian was right. He'd never told his father to step off.

"I told you a long time ago that you needed to nip this in the bud, sooner than later," Ian said. "Stop traveling along the path he set for you and blaze your own trail. You'll be happier for it."

"Once and for all, this is my path. I like what I do."

"But you want to do more. Do it. If you want to focus on your music for a while, do it. If you want to write songs, go for it. Don't let obligation keep you from it. Now, tell me how you fixed things with Aria."

Myles finished the story, telling Ian about the conversation at Aria's house later. "She's...everything, bruh."

And he meant that. Aria had offered him acceptance, understanding. She'd offered him a way out of his bleak existence, the daily routine of work, home, music. He didn't need to spend hours in his studio because it made him feel anything other than the weight of his obligations. Because she'd awakened something in him that he'd never felt before. He didn't have to fake or front for her. He could just be him, because she wanted the man he was. With her, he didn't think about work, he didn't care what his father thought of him. He just wanted to be with her, to create with her...to love her.

"I didn't expect it," Myles said.

They both knew what the "it" was, because Myles had seen Ian fall fast and hard for Bailee. He'd watched

Drake slowly realize that his life didn't work without Love. When El admitted that Avery was the one for him, they'd all given him their blessing. Now it was his turn. And he couldn't say he wasn't enjoying every minute of the time he spent with her, getting to know her, learning what made her tick.

"No one ever does," Ian mused. "Just don't make any grand gestures before I get Bailee down that aisle. She's liable to blow any day."

Myles cracked up. "Shut up, bruh. Bailee is good."

"You don't sleep with her. This wedding business is for the birds. I'd rather just do it without all the formality."

For the most part, despite the access to money, none of them were flamboyant. They didn't floss for people or buy expensive brands just to prove they could. Maybe because they'd watched their parents do that all of their lives? More likely because they'd realized early on that money couldn't buy peace of mind. Spending time with each other, building relationships instead of destroying them, and helping others in need had been shared goals between them.

"What happened to eloping?"

"She's calling it an elopement, but the guest list keeps expanding by the day."

"Well, you have to give her what she wants."

Ian nodded. "And you know I will."

"But it couldn't be me," Myles said.

"Drake wants to plan the bachelor party."

Myles finished his sandwich, balled up the wrapper and set it on Ian's tray. "Isn't that my job?"

Ian waved a dismissive hand. "Whatever. You know you didn't want to do it anyway. That's why he offered."

The thing about the brothers was that they knew each other's strengths. Party planning definitely wasn't one of Myles's. In fact, he hadn't even thought about it until Ian had brought it up.

"You're right," Myles agreed. "What does he have in mind?"

"Vegas."

Myles thought about making that trip to Vegas. He'd only been a handful of times since they'd moved here. He didn't really care to go back, didn't like the vibe of the city. He'd much rather go to Brazil or Miami or Los Angeles. But he'd do whatever Ian wanted.

"Whatever you want, bruh. Just tell me the date and I'm there."

Ian held out his fist and Myles bumped it with his. "Word."

They spent the rest of their lunch catching up. Myles learned that Avery and El were having a boy, and that Drake and Love had decided to give Myles's adorable niece Zoe a little brother or sister. When Myles asked Ian if babies were in his future with Bailee, Ian told him to stand down.

Myles knew that their lives were branching off in different directions, but he hoped they would always find time for impromptu lunches, sip and paints, concerts in the park, and basketball games. And he wanted Aria to be there for it all.

Chapter 13

Aria stared at her newest work. It had taken her a week to find her groove with the painting, but it was shaping up quite nicely. She tilted her head, dipped her paint brush in the shade of green she'd just mixed and dabbed it on the canvas.

It seemed like June was just yesterday and now it was mid-August. In the last few weeks, she'd booked another exhibit at a small gallery in Novi, Michigan, and scheduled new shows in Manhattan and Chicago. As far as her own artwork, she was on fire and she couldn't be happier. Leaving New York had been just what she needed.

Her personal life had taken a turn for the better, too. When their schedules permitted, she and Myles spent as much time together as possible. Neither of them kept normal hours, but they'd made it work. Most nights, they'd slept together, either at her place or his. Aria had grown to love waking up in his arms. She'd grown to love him.

She blinked. *Love?* Where the hell did that come from?

Aria had no illusions. They'd spent weeks together, getting to know each other. They understood each other. She knew when he needed to spend time alone, and he let her immerse herself in her work without interruptions. It didn't matter that he still wore suits more often than not. It didn't matter that she had changed her hair color three times in the past month. He'd given her something she didn't realize she'd been missing from her life all along—acceptance.

Her father once told her that there would always be some reason to not get involved with someone. But if it works, then it's worth it. And Myles was worth it. What they had was worth it.

Aria hadn't told him how she felt with words, though. She'd been content to show him in different ways. Like driving all the way to West Bloomfield so Celeste could teach her how to make shrimp Alfredo. Like taking Ms. Pennie to her doctor appointments when Myles was stuck in the operating room. Like purchasing a keyboard to keep at her house for when he stayed over because she knew he hated being without his piano, even though he loved being with her. Smiling, she remembered the light in his eyes when she'd revealed her gift to him. Then, she recalled the way he'd thanked her—with his tongue, his teeth, his mouth, his… *Ooo-wee.* She shifted in her chair as memories of multiple orgasms followed by dessert ran through her mind.

"You're daydreaming." Brent walked into the studio and stood next to her.

Glancing up at him, she smiled. "Just thinking about the turn my life has taken."

"In other words, you're thinking about Myles."

She shoved him. "Be quiet." She turned to face him fully. "How are you? We need to schedule some time to just chill and catch up."

A few weeks ago, Brent had met up with a friend at the MGM Grand Casino, who just happened to know the star forward for the Detroit Pistons. The two struck up a conversation and the player hired Brent to create a tattoo for him. The tattoo went viral, and as a result InkTown had more business than her bestie could handle. He was so busy he was currently interviewing tattoo artists to join his team.

"I'm all right." He folded his arms over his chest. "I found someone to come in and rent a booth at the shop. I figured that was the easiest way to handle walk-ins. This way I can concentrate on my current clientele and their referrals."

"That's awesome. I always knew you would be a rock star in the tat world. I'm so freakin' proud of you."

He pulled a strand of her hair lightly. "I said the same about you. Did you make a decision on the building for the school yet?"

Aria sighed. The building she'd had her eye on recently went off the market. Now she was on the search again. "I lost the building. The seller had a better offer from someone else and accepted it without giving us the opportunity to counter."

"That sucks."

She shrugged. "It's life."

Aria had taken Myles to the building several times to talk about her dream for the space. He'd been supportive and even offered to invest. She'd thanked him for his encouragement later in the shower. On her knees.

"You'll find something," Brent said.

"I know. I'm not trippin'. I've been swamped with work here. The good news is the studio at my house is almost ready. So I won't have to spend so much time here in the evenings."

Cocktails and Canvas had seen an influx of customers over the summer, and she suspected that number would grow as the weather changed and people started looking for more indoor activities. She'd hired a manager and two artists to take over the classes, which had helped tremendously. But she still liked to drop in during the sessions to get a feel for how the customers enjoyed their experience.

"Oh, I'm glad you're here," Aria said. "Mel is leaving for New York a week early and wanted to have a get-together to celebrate and say goodbye to Michigan. She told me to invite you."

"Sounds like she wants a personal going-away present." He winked, then ducked when she threw a paintbrush in his direction. "You're so violent."

"Don't play, Brent. Stay away from Mel. The last thing I need is Myles trying to kill you. That would ruin everything."

He threw up his hands in surrender. "Okay. I'll bring a date so I won't be tempted to destroy your world."

She stood and gave him a hug. "Thank you."

"What's this we have here?"

Aria froze at the sound of her mother's voice and registered the low curse Brent spouted before he pulled away from her. Turning, she plastered on a smile. "Mother. You're here." *For the first time. Ever.*

"Imagine my surprise when your father told me you were dating Dr. Lawrence Jackson's son and that you invited him to dinner with you two. I suppose my invite was lost in the mail."

No greeting, no hug, no words of encouragement about her business. Aria shouldn't have been surprised by the lack of emotion or affection her mother showed her, but it still stung. As it always did. "Hi, to you, too."

"Why didn't you tell me you were dating such an accomplished man, Aria? I would have liked to join you for dinner."

The dinner in question had occurred a few days ago, when her father had to attend a conference in Ann Arbor and suggested they meet him for a meal. "Why am I not surprised you're upset about this?" Aria asked. "This isn't a competition. Why would I invite you for a random dinner with Dad when you've made it clear that you don't have anything to say to him?"

Brent glared at her mother. "Hi, Ms. Bell."

"Aria, we need to talk," Elizabeth said, ignoring Brent.

Anger simmered in her gut at the way her mother dismissed Brent. "Mother, Brent is talking to you."

Elizabeth rolled her eyes. "Hi, Brent. Can I have a minute with my daughter?"

Brent squeezed her arm, silently telling her he was good and to calm down. "I'm going to head out," he said. "Call me if you need me."

She nodded. "I will." Aria watched Brent leave the studio and whirled on her mother. "That is unacceptable, Mom. I won't have you disrespecting my friend."

Her mother scanned the room, her nose turned up and her lips a straight line. Disgusted. That was the word that came to mind when Aria wondered what she thought of the studio. "Oh, Aria. Calm down. Your *friend* is just fine. He seems like he's done a fine job living off you."

Aria's fists clenched together. "Mom, if you came here to start a fight, let me finish it. Get. Out."

Elizabeth reared back on her heels. "Excuse me?"

"You heard me. I have asked you to respect my friend time and time again. But you can't resist getting in your little digs. And I don't want to hear it."

Her mother sighed. "I'm sorry. Tell Brent I apologize."

The half-assed apology did nothing but piss her off even more. "What do you need?"

"Honestly, Aria, do you have to get so worked up about everything? I came here because I—"

The snicker that escaped Aria's mouth surprised her, but she wouldn't back down. "Please, I know why you're here. And it's not because you haven't seen me in a while and missed me. It's not even because you wanted to check out my business or even look at some of my art-work. In all the years I've been doing this, you've never supported me, never bought a painting, never attended a show. You seem to think that if you don't encourage me, all this work—which I suspect you see more as a hobby—will go away. So why would I think you were here for any other reason than to be nosy?"

"Who do you think you're talking to?"

"Elizabeth Bell," Aria said simply.

"Your mother. I'm still your mother."

This conversation felt surreal. Aria couldn't believe that her mother had the audacity to come to her busi-ness and want to know anything personal about her. As far as she was concerned, Elizabeth didn't deserve to have any piece of her life even if that piece was simple information.

"Okay, Mom." Aria let out a humorless chuckle. "I'm on my way out, so let's make this quick. You heard that I'm dating a Jackson and you wanted to confirm. Right?"

"Actually, I couldn't believe that you were dating anyone with that status. The Jackson family is extremely wealthy. Dr. Lawrence Jackson is a world-renowned plastic surgeon who's done work for several women at the club. I've even consulted with him about a little filler." She switched her handbag to the other arm. "If you are, I think it's great. But I hope that you know how to conduct yourself when you're around the family."

Aria tipped her head up toward the ceiling. "I can't believe this," she mumbled.

"I'm hoping that I can help you with your unfortunate fashion sense. If this relationship is to go anywhere, it might provide an impetus for better choices." Elizabeth gestured toward Aria's hair, which wasn't styled in any way her mother approved of. Her natural curls were wild and the green highlights she'd just applied the other day stood out like a beacon of light in a sea of dark waves. "I'm sure people of that ilk wouldn't appreciate that hair color."

"I've had enough!" Aria sliced a hand through the air. "You've never had anything good to say about me. All of my life, I've never felt like you loved me, and this is why. I've tried to have a relationship with you, but I can't do it anymore. Because you'll never be satisfied. There will always be something about me that you want to change. But guess what? I love who I am. It has taken years, but I've worked my ass off—with no support from you. One day, you're going to realize the error of your ways, but

I'm not waiting around for it. I'm successful, intelligent, and not too shabby to look at. I have my own money and I don't need a man to make me feel good about myself. You may not think so, but I'm a catch. Myles should be happy to have me."

Her mother gasped. "I did not teach you to be so conceited."

"You didn't teach me shit."

"Watch your tone," Elizabeth warned.

"No. Everything I learned about being a good human being I learned from my father and Celeste and Brent. The only thing you did for me was parade me in front of your peers like some made-up doll or try to pimp me out to the next wealthy bachelor."

"Aria!"

"I'll make this really easy for you. My relationship with Myles is my business. You have nothing to say to me that will make any difference."

"Just remember that when this all blows up in your face, I'm still going to be your mother and you'll wish you had behaved better toward me, that I could have helped you avoid disaster."

The thought of it all "blowing up in her face" sank like a brick in her stomach. She pressed her hand there to quell the ache that had set in. "Mom, I need to leave. Until you can come in here and accept me for who I am and support what I've accomplished, I don't want to see you anymore."

"You may not believe this, but I do love you. I want the best for you."

She had waited forever to hear her mother tell her she loved her. But the words didn't ring true, because it felt like they came with conditions. "I love you, too, Mom. But I don't love how you have always made me feel."

Aria brushed past her mother and headed toward the door. Opening, it, she turned and said, "I am closing up. I have to go."

Elizabeth lifted her chin in the air and approached Aria. She stopped next to her. "I hope…"

A moment of silence stretched between them as Aria waited for her mother to finish her sentence. Only Elizabeth didn't say another word. She simply left.

It didn't take long for Aria to get to Myles. She'd driven through the city in a haze, tormented by the realization that her mother had walked away without a fight. But Aria had vowed not to shed a single tear, because she shouldn't have to beg her mother to love her or accept her.

Using the key Myles had given her, she opened the door. She couldn't help but smile at her painting, the *Phoenix*, which was now sitting on the floor in the front room. They'd discussed the best place to hang it, but hadn't made a decision.

The house was silent. Frowning, she walked through the living room into the kitchen. His car was outside, so she knew he was home. *The music room.*

Aria poured herself a glass of water and slid her feet into his slippers. She'd grown used to wearing them while she was at his house. As she neared the music room, she heard faint melodies coming from within. He'd mentioned that he wanted to add another layer of insulation to make it completely soundproof.

After opening the door, she stepped in. Myles looked up from the piano and smiled at her. He didn't stop playing, though. And Aria was glad he didn't because the notes were soothing, comforting to her. She hugged him from behind, kissed his cheek and sat next to him on the bench.

She leaned her head against his shoulder as his fingers moved over the ivories, wringing emotion with every chord. When he finished, when his finger hit the last note, a lone tear fell from her eyes. She quickly wiped it away, hoping he didn't see it.

Of course, he did. He brushed her cheek where it had fallen. "What's wrong, baby?"

She moved away from his touch. "Nothing," she lied. "That's beautiful, what you were playing? What was it?"

"'Aria.'"

"What?" Aria focused on the keys, tapped one with her thumb. Anything to not look him in the eye.

"'Aria.' That's the name of the song."

Shocked, Aria stared up at him. "What?" she repeated.

"I wrote the song for you."

She blinked. "Are you serious?"

"Very. I couldn't get your voice out of my head. I memorized the inflections of it, the tone. And this just came to me. I recorded it for you, along with other original work. I've never let anyone hear it before."

Aria pressed her hand against her heart. "Oh," she breathed. Apparently, she couldn't find her words even though she knew he deserved to hear something other than *oh* from her.

Tears pricked her eyes. Aria was stunned because she was on the edge of an ugly cry, and it wasn't because she was thinking about the conversation she'd had with her mother. She wasn't sad. No, it was because she felt happy. It was because of him. *I'm probably crazy. Am*

I dreaming? Just to make sure, she pinched herself—a little too hard because she winced from the pain. *Ouch.*

Myles frowned. "Did you just pinch yourself?"

Damn. He had caught that. She felt her chin tremble. *Oh, no. Don't cry here, not in front of him.* A tear fell, followed by a dam bursting as she fought back a sob.

With a concerned stare, he used his sleeve to wipe her face. "Aria, talk to me. Are you okay?"

She stood abruptly. "Okay, so I just have to say this, and I want to caution you not to interrupt me or let it go to your head. Because that will ruin everything, which would be a shame." She backed away from him slowly.

"Okay."

"I really like you." She ignored the frown on his face and forged ahead. "Like really. A lot." He smiled, and it was like the sun came out of the clouds and bathed her in its heat. "I'm lying." His brows creased together again. "I'm pretty sure I'm falling for you. No, I'm already there." She swallowed. "I mean, there's no falling. It's more like…fell."

Myles laughed then.

Aria shifted on her feet, one side to the other, then back again. "You're laughing at me. Why are you laughing? This is not funny."

"It is." He stood and approached her. "I thought you were crying because something happened to you. I was worried."

"Something did happen," she admitted. When he opened his mouth to respond, she placed a hand over his mouth. "But it doesn't matter now."

His hand wrapped around her wrist, pressed against that pulse again. Closing his eyes, he whispered. "As long as you're okay."

"I am," she assured. "I did just say something pretty big, though."

Myles leaned his forehead against hers. "You did."

"Did you...? I mean, what do you think?"

"I think...good. Now, we're even."

She felt her lips turn up, and soon she couldn't stop the grin that spread over her face. *I'm not crazy.* And she didn't need to hear the words. Just the fact that they were "even" erased any fears she had about it. She dared to hope it was her reality.

Myles placed his fingers under her ear. "You once asked me why I always place my finger or lips against your pulse point?"

Aria nodded, her gaze locked on his.

"I love the feel of your heartbeat, the rhythm, the way it matches mine. It wasn't just your voice I memorized. I know every beat, every note of you. And..." Myles kissed her, then. Hard. "I love you, too, Aria." He smacked her butt. "Let's go get dinner."

Aria couldn't move. She couldn't even feel her legs. Because though she'd thought she didn't need the words, the sound of them seeped into her soul and bloomed. Dinner? She didn't want dinner. The only thing she wanted was him—his hands roaming over her, his body against hers, his tongue stroking hers and his teeth nipping at her skin.

"Myles?" She wrapped her arms around his waist and kissed his chin. "I don't want food."

With a raised brow, he rested his arms on her shoulders and buried his fingers in her hair. "What do you want?"

"You. Naked. Now."

* * *

Myles had an epiphany during his last surgery, one that changed everything. And he wanted—no, needed—to tell Aria.

He'd left the hospital early, abandoning a mound of patient files on his desk, and sped over to Aria's house. Because this was too big to wait until tomorrow.

Myles had been drowning in the details of his life for too long, turning his back on a huge piece of himself in the name of obligation. Now he could see clearly, and he knew what he wanted. It wasn't something he was willing to compromise for anything or anyone. Aria was right. He could do both. He could play and operate and love Aria. So, when Martel, the guitarist friend he'd taken Aria to hear, had texted him and asked him to join him onstage at Baker's Keyboard Lounge next week, he'd responded with one word. Yes.

Arriving at her house, he rushed to the door and used his key to unlock it. He found Aria engrossed in the painting she'd been working on all night.

Aria on a regular day was beautiful, but Aria in her zone, creating masterpieces, was stunning. Her eyes were narrowed, focused.

She glanced at him out of the corner of her eye and smiled. Then she returned her attention to her work. "You're here. I thought you were working late." She dipped her brush into an azure blue and swiped it over the canvas.

He registered the music playing through the surround sound speakers, then. His music. And he could barely contain himself.

"I'm almost done," she murmured. "Your song is so

beautiful, Myles. I can't stop listening to it." She babbled on about something, but he had no idea what she was saying because he couldn't concentrate. The sight of her working, listening to his music, made him want to strip her bare right there and make love to her. He didn't care if she was covered with paint.

He unbuttoned his shirt and pulled it off. He took his pants and his underwear off next. And Aria was still talking.

"Aria," he said. "Stop talking."

She glanced at him, and her eyes widened. "Myles, you're... You took your clothes off."

"I did." He nodded. "Now, take yours off." He stalked toward her, circling her like an animal would its prey. Reaching out, he turned her stool around, so she was facing him. "You're moving too slow."

He tugged her shirt off and tossed it behind her. Then he pulled her to her feet and pushed her yoga pants down.

"Myles, I can't. We can't do it right now. I have to take a shower."

He gripped the fabric of her underwear and yanked her to him, enjoying her sharp gasp as she crashed against his body. Soon her panties were a tattered mess at his feet. He cupped her breasts in his palm while his other hand brushed against her core.

"Oh, God," she groaned. Her head fell back, and he took the opportunity to kiss the delicate column. "The ladies... We're having Tacos and Tequila here tonight. I'm already running late."

He shushed her with a kiss, groaning at the feel of her tongue against his. "I want you," he whispered against her mouth.

"But—"

"Aria, quiet." He gripped her hips in his hands and

lifted her, backing her against the wall. He pressed his erection against her entrance. "Time to stop talking, baby."

A beat later, he was inside her. Myles closed his eyes, relished the feel of her around him. She was so perfect. They were perfect together, like they were meant to be. When she squeezed his hips with her long legs, he began to move.

"Go harder," she moaned.

Myles loved it when she told him what she wanted. Aria wasn't a timid lover. She met him thrust for thrust, taking as much as she gave. He picked up the pace as she whispered filthy words in his ear. He wasn't going to last. But he needed her to come with him. He slipped his hand between them, pressing his thumb against her clit.

Shit, please, yes, oh God, and I'm coming. He wasn't sure who'd said the words, but it didn't matter. The only thing that mattered was their intense connection, the love they made together.

Aria cried out, screaming his name as she came. Myles let go, kissing her deeply as his orgasm pulsed through him.

His legs nearly buckled from the pleasure, so he turned and slid down the wall with her still in his arms. For the next several moments, he tried to catch his breath.

Aria finally looked up at him with hooded eyes and a lazy smile on her swollen lips. "You're crazy." She kissed his jaw.

"Crazy, about you, baby."

"That's so cheesy!" She laughed.

"It's so true." He circled her nose with his. "I love you."

She wrapped her arms around him, hugging him to her. "I love you more."

Half an hour later, Aria emerged from the shower. "Do you have to go back to work?"

Already dressed, he wrapped a towel around her. "No. I'm headed out with my brothers." Since the ladies were getting together, Ian had suggested they hang out and watch the game. "We're headed to Buffalo Wild Wings."

"Fun. What made you stop by?"

Myles had been so distracted by her that he'd forgotten why he'd rushed over. "Oh, I have news."

"What is it?"

"Martel texted me earlier, asked me to sit in for his pianist."

Her eyes widened and she blessed him with one of her soul-snatching smiles. "Really? That's great. Did you say yes?"

"I did."

She jumped in his arms. "Oh, my God! I'm so happy. Finally."

"I figured it was time to stop hiding."

"I agree."

"I wanted to tell you first."

Aria fixed his collar and peered into his eyes. "I'm glad you did. Who knows? Maybe this experience will be a catalyst for you to do more."

"I want you to come."

"Are you crazy? I wouldn't miss it for the world. I will definitely be there. Cheering, you on. I'll wear good underwear, too, so you can destroy another pair later."

Myles chuckled. "Silly."

Her doorbell rang. "Oh, shoot. They're here. Go answer the door and leave. It's about the ladies tonight."

After a few more kisses and another "I love you" Myles said goodbye and left.

Chapter 14

Myles looked out at the packed Baker's Keyboard Lounge and sighed. Tonight he'd go out onstage and play with his friend. Over the past week, he'd thought of every reason in the world to cancel, but he didn't. Because it was time.

Although Martel had sent him the sheet music, he barely used it when practicing. He'd heard the music many times and thought he would be able to find his way. He eyed the piano off to the side of the stage. Martel had asked if he would rather play on the keyboard or the piano, and Myles had emphatically insisted on playing on the house Steinway. Having visited the establishment numerous times, he was excited to be able to use the same instrument that so many jazz legends had played on. He could barely wait to touch the keys.

On in fifteen.

In the audience, his family took up two of the larger

booths in the back and two tables right in front of the stage. All of his siblings had shown up, along with their spouses. Ms. Pennie had ridden with him and Aria. Brent had arrived a few minutes ago with a date.

"You good?" Martel stood next to him, his eyes on the crowd.

He glanced at his friend. The two had been friends for years, having met in college. Aside from Aria and his family, Martel was the only other person who knew he played as seriously as he did. He'd even let Martel use his in-home studio on several occasions to record.

"I'm okay," Myles said.

"I'm glad you said yes this time."

Myles let out a slow breath. "Me, too."

The announcer hopped up on stage. "Hello, everyone. We have a great act for you tonight. A crowd favorite, Martel Pierce, is in the house." A chorus of cheers, whistles and claps filled the air.

The announcer went on to give updates on the upcoming acts before he introduced the Pierce Band. Myles followed Martel out of the small hallway. He took a seat at the piano, ran his fingers lightly over the keys.

Martel didn't make any announcements, didn't pick up the microphone to wax poetic about the love of music or even to thank the audience for coming. That would come later, right after the first set. Instead, Martel just did the lead-in count and they started to play.

When Myles played his first chord, he knew he'd made the right decision. It felt amazing, his fingers on the keys, watching his fingers on the keys, playing for the audience. It felt like home. As his fingers pounded on the piano, found their groove within the rhythm, Myles got lost in the notes. The melodic wail of the saxophone, the distinctive sound of the trumpet, the beat of the drums, the boom of the bass and strum of Martel's guitar set the tone and the pace. Myles slipped into the fray like he'd been doing so for years.

The crowd shouted, some voices hollering out "yeah" or "go 'head." As the first song ended, they moved into a rendition of "People Make the World Go Round," originally recorded by the Stylistics. The transition was seamless, with no break between. Halfway through the song, Myles thought he could do this often. The rush, the feel of the dim lights on his skin, was addictive.

Martel raised a hand sometime during the third song, signaling them to drop the music to a lower octave. He picked up the microphone and thanked everyone for coming. "I want to thank you all for supporting me over the years. It's always good coming back to the Lounge, where the greats have played before me and the newcomers will play after me."

The crowd roared.

"I want to introduce you to my band."

Myles knew what came next. The solos. As Martel called each bandmate's name, that person would be able to do whatever on their instrument. He played along as his friend announced each of them.

"And I would like to introduce a special guest tonight," Martel said, after a sick solo from the bass player, Mike. "I'm down a pianist, and I called on a good friend." He pointed at Myles. "Dr. Myles Jackson. It's all on you."

Myles picked up the volume, tapping the keys with an intensity he reserved for home. The notes floated up in the air and spread out like he owned the place. Now, he really understood what Aria had told him all along.

He could play his music and perform life-changing surgery and be good at both.

When his solo was done, he registered the applause and the whistles that were no doubt coming from his brothers. Martel took over the stage, killing it with a guitar solo. Myles stared out into the audience, meeting the smiling gazes of his family members as they grooved to the music. There was one set of eyes he was searching for. Aria. He grinned when he saw her, one arm raised, eyes closed. The other hand was splayed over her heart as she swayed to the tempo. He couldn't look away from her. She moved like she was totally captivated by the music, and he was captivated by her. Finally she opened her eyes and caught his gaze. She smiled and blew a kiss his way.

The set was over far too soon, in his opinion. But the last song ended, and Martel announced they would be back in half an hour.

Once they were off the stage, Martel clasped his back. "That was sick, man. I'm telling you, I need you on the stage more often."

"I need to be on that stage."

They talked about the next set for a few minutes, before Martel excused himself. Myles walked over to his family. Big hugs, strong handshakes and a score of congratulations greeted him when he made it to them.

"Bruh." Ian gave him a man hug. "I have to say, I'm proud of you, man. You tore that stage up."

"Thanks, bruh. I had fun up there."

"I could tell. I think you caught the bug."

"You may be right," Myles agreed. "It was intense. I loved every minute of it."

"Good." Ian squeezed his shoulder. "I'm glad to be in the house for this."

Bailee hugged him. "Myles, I cried. You were so good."

"She cries at the moon nowadays," Ian said, flinching when Bailee socked him in the shoulder. "Just playin', baby."

"Anyway." Bailee rolled her eyes hard at Ian. "I'm going to tell everyone I know about this place. It's a gem. And that chicken was the bomb."

Myles laughed. Bailee was from Columbus, Ohio. She'd only lived in the area a little over a year. "My brother should have brought you here a long time ago."

"He sure should have," she agreed.

Mel wrapped an arm around Myles's shoulder and kissed his cheek. "My brother is a beast on that piano!"

Myles gave Ian a fist bump and waited for Ian and Bailee to take their seats again before he turned to embrace his little sister. "Thank you."

Mel leaned back, peered into his eyes. He saw the tears standing there. "I'm so excited for you, Myles. I can't wait to see your name on the Mylar."

"I think you're getting ahead of yourself, sis."

"I'm not. You just make sure you call me if that ever happens. I will be on the first plane back for that." Myles muzzled his sister's hair, laughing when she smacked his hand away. "Dude, stop messing up my hair. I have a date."

He looked over her head at the guy in question. He'd met him earlier and wasn't impressed. "Are you sure he's smarter than a fifth grader?"

Mel choked on the drink she'd just sipped. "Oh, my God. You're stupid!"

"I'm serious, Mel. He doesn't seem like he's on your level."

"Peter is an accomplished man," she argued. "He's a professor at University of Michigan."

"Sounds pretty boring."

"Says the serious twin?"

"Ha. You got jokes."

"Lots of them."

Mel would be leaving for New York in a few days. Myles thought this might be the last time they were all together in the same room for a while. He couldn't help but feel sad at that prospect, even though he was proud of his sister for stepping out on her own. He hugged her again. "Mel, I'm proud of you. I'm going to miss you."

She squeezed his neck tighter. "Stop making me cry in front of my date," she whispered. "I'm going to miss you, too, big brother."

Mel pulled away from him and went back to her man. Myles smiled at Ms. Pennie, who was tapping her foot to the recorded music playing over the speakers.

He leaned down. "I'm glad you made it."

When Ms. Pennie had told him she wanted to come, he was a little concerned about her being out so soon after a short stint in the hospital for pneumonia. But she'd insisted, telling him that if something should happen, at least she was around a bunch of doctors.

"Boy, you did it." Ms. Pennie kissed him on the cheek.

"I did. And it was because of you that I was able to get out there and do well."

She shot him a watery smile. "I didn't do anything. It was all you."

"What did you think of my solo?"

"Excellent." She gave him a high five. "Although, I wish you would have switched up the tone and gone softer in the middle before closing it out. And make sure you're sitting with your back straight."

Myles chuckled. "Always the teacher."

Ms. Pennie patted his cheek. "You did good, boy. I'm so proud of you. And Aria? That girl wouldn't stop smiling. She's in love with you."

"I love her, too."

"I knew it!" She barked out a loud laugh. "I want a front seat at that wedding."

"Ms. Pennie, slow down."

"Whatever, boy. You'll be married before next spring. Mark my words."

Myles talked to Ms. Pennie for a few more minutes before he stood, intent on making it to Aria before the next set started.

"Myles!" Avery shouted, blocking his path to Aria. "You are... Brother, you're amazing. I can't believe you haven't done more with your music."

"I know," he said.

"But that's all going to change. I have news."

He frowned. "What news?"

"I shared your CD with my production team, and they want to use one of your songs for the opening of my new show."

Myles blinked. "What?"

When had Avery heard his original work? The thought sobered his mood. While he'd made the huge step to play in public tonight, he had no intention of sharing his own music with anyone just yet.

"How did you hear my song?" he asked.

Aria.

"Myles, you're blessed with talent in so many areas," Avery said, ignoring his question. "I can't wait to work with you. We'll talk soon. I have to order some of that chicken."

Avery walked over to Love, and they broke out in a fit of laughter. Myles turned to Aria, who was talking to Brent. He wondered why she would let Avery hear something that was so private to him, something that he'd told her he hadn't let anyone hear.

Brent tapped Aria's shoulder and pointed at Myles. Aria turned and smiled before hurrying over to him. She hugged him.

"Baby, you were brilliant up there." She brushed her lips over his. "Oh, my God! You were in a zone. I'm so happy for you."

"Aria."

"See! I told you. You can pursue your music and still be a surgeon."

"Really?" A surge of anger shot through him. He'd chosen to go public with his music. It had been his choice. She knew how important that was, and she'd betrayed him if she'd given his music to someone else to use publicly. "Is that why you took matters into your own hands?"

She frowned and leaned back. "What? I don't know what you're talking about."

"I think you do know."

Needing to put some distance between them before he said something he regretted, he walked away.

Aria stared after Myles as he disappeared around the corner toward the bathrooms.

"Everything okay?" Brent asked.

"I don't know."

She replayed the conversation and couldn't figure out

what had happened. Onstage, Myles was perfect. He'd played with abandon, slipped into the music like he was born to play it. Even when the set ended, the smile on his face had still been there. She'd watched him talk to his brothers and Mel. She had seen him hug Ms. Pennie. Somewhere between them and her, things had changed. He was pissed. At her.

"Aria."

She turned, surprised to find Dr. Law standing there. *When did he get here?*

"Hello." She shook the older man's hand. Normally, she would give a hug, but she suspected it wouldn't be a welcome gesture. "I didn't know you were coming." She cleared her throat.

"I heard that my son was playing here tonight, and I wanted to see it for myself."

"Your son is excellent. He played wonderfully on that stage. You should be proud."

"Is this what you wanted all along?"

Aria folded her arms over her breasts. She wouldn't back down. Not tonight. Despite Myles's behavior toward her, she knew that he needed his father's support. "Excuse me?"

"I'm assuming you're the one that put this ludicrous idea of having a music career in his head. My son is a surgeon, with skilled hands meant to cut. Not play."

"Did you hear your son on that stage? I mean, really listen to him? His hands were made to touch those keys."

"So you can have a successful and wealthy musician as a beau?"

Aria shook her head. "I'm not sure who you think I am, but I don't need your son's money."

"I know who your father is, Aria Bell."

She shrugged. "Okay. And your point? What does *my* father have to do with *my* money? See, I don't need his money or Myles's money. I have my own, from years of making a name for myself in the art world, from my business bringing in money daily. This isn't about me. This should be about him."

"It is about him. And the fact that since he's been your *friend*, he's made decisions that have taken him off his path."

Aria tried not to flinch at Dr. Law's use of the word *friend*. He'd meant it like a slap to the face because that was exactly how it felt. "You mean *your* path for Myles."

"Whatever," Dr. Law said. "The point is, he was just fine working on something that will benefit his pockets for years. He doesn't have time to devote to flights of fancy." He turned his nose up at her, probably taking in the pink streaks in her hair.

"You know, I've been with Myles for a while. I've talked to him about his dreams and his goals. Music is a part of him, just like medicine. He can do both. That's all I've been trying to tell him from the beginning. I don't want him to give up one or the other. I've encouraged him to follow his heart. That's what a real *friend* does."

Dr. Law tilted his head and studied her, almost like he was seeing her for the first time.

"The fact is, I love your son," she continued. "I only want the best for him. I know that Myles would love to have your support on this. It would be nice if you could do that for him. Not because I'm asking, but because he's your son. And he's good. He's so amazing. At everything he does. He deserves to hear that from you." She wiped a tear that escaped from her eye. "Have a good night."

Aria walked around Dr. Law and took her seat next

to Brent, just in time for the next set to start. The band made their way back to the stage, and she watched as Myles took his seat at the piano. To a person that didn't know him, he probably looked normal, no different than he did before. But to Aria, he looked stiff and uncomfortable on the bench. His fingers moved over the piano keys with precision, but he didn't sound as free as he had during the first set. Still good, but she could tell his mind was on something else.

She thought about what he'd said to her. *Is that why you took matters into your own hands?* She turned his words over and over and couldn't figure out why he'd said that. What did he think she did? If he had something to accuse her of, he should have just come out with it. And it had better be true.

The crowd ate up the second and third song in the set, but Aria couldn't help obsessing over him. When Martel announced the final song a while later, she recognized it immediately. It was the same song he'd played for her at his house that first time. "In a Sentimental Mood." Memories of that night, the way he'd sounded, the way he'd smelled, the way he'd made love to her, filled her with hope and dread. Hope because she wanted to feel that again. Dread because she wasn't sure she would.

She stared at him, willed him to meet her gaze. But he wouldn't look at her. Once the last note was played, Myles stood with the rest of the band and waved at the crowd. Then he disappeared in the back while other band members joined their guests in the lounge area.

Sighing, Aria tapped Brent on the shoulder. "What are you doing tonight?"

"Taking her home." He gestured to his date, who was sitting with her arms clasped in her lap. "Why?"

"Do you mind taking me home?"

Brent frowned. "What about Myles? Didn't you ride with him?"

"Yes." She smiled. A little too wide for Brent not to know it was fake. "Look, don't ask any questions. Let's just go. I have a terrible headache."

"Okay. Are you ready now?"

Aria looked toward the hallway that led to the back room. She pulled out her phone and shot Myles a quick text. Bravo! Are you coming out?

Moments went by. No answer. She lifted her gaze to Brent. "Yeah. I'm ready."

Standing, Aria said quick goodbyes to everyone in attendance, ignoring the concerned looks on all of their faces.

"Bye, Ms. Pennie. I'm going to ride home with Brent."

Ms. Pennie frowned. "What? Are you okay, child?"

"I'm fine. I'll talk to you Tuesday. I'll come around noon to take you shopping."

"Okay," the older woman said. "How about I call you tomorrow?"

"Sounds good."

Aria waved one last time before she followed Brent and his date out of the place.

Chapter 15

Myles paced the small area in the back reserved for musicians. Martel had jumped back on the stage for a solo set, while the other band members were in the audience with their guests, so he had the room to himself.

He was torn between being upset at Aria for giving Avery his CD without asking and being upset with himself for reacting the way he did. Then, there was the unease in his gut, the feeling that he was missing something that didn't sit right.

When he'd talked to her, she didn't seem like she'd done anything wrong. *Maybe I'm wrong?* He knew Aria; he'd devoted himself to learning all of her quirks. He'd memorized the inflections in her voice and the lines in her face. He'd lost himself in the liquid pools of her eyes.

He'd given every bit of himself to her. And it felt better than anything he'd ever felt. She was the missing beat of his heart. The thought of her betraying his trust made his stomach roil in pain. She was an artist, which made it all the more painful. She understood how important it was for artists to control their own work, to decide when they wanted it released to the public. He'd respected that about her work, and he'd thought she'd do the same for him.

This wasn't how tonight was supposed to end, with him unsure about her. When he was up onstage during the first set he couldn't wait to get to her, to tell her how it felt to be there. He'd had plans for the night, after they left. He'd vowed to show her just how much she meant to him. The surprise he had in store for her was the ultimate grand gesture. Myles had looked forward to seeing her reaction, to celebrating with her all night. But now...

"Myles?"

He whirled around, blinking when he saw his father standing in the doorway. "Dad? What are you doing here?"

"I heard you were playing. Figured I'd come check you out."

Myles eyed him warily. It was unlike his father to do anything on a whim. "How long have you been here?"

"Since the beginning. I heard both sets."

"If you're here to argue with me about the business or tell me to stop playing, don't. I'm not in the mood."

Dr. Law walked into the room, scanning the small space. Pictures of jazz greats were spread over the walls. Ella Fitzgerald, Miles Davis, Nat King Cole, John Coltrane, Donald Byrd... All of them had played there. There was a wealth of music history within the walls of that place.

His father tapped the picture of Miles Davis on the

wall. "Davis. His recording of 'Seven Steps to Heaven' changed my life."

Myles's eyes widened. "What?"

A whisper of a smile stretched across his father's mouth. "I can hear it in my head today as clearly as I heard it the first time I listened to it. After I heard that song, I knew I wanted to play the trumpet."

This was all news to Myles. He'd never known his father to play any instrument. "You played?"

"I did." His father sat down on one of the stools in the room. "I played until my lips were swollen. I had to ice them every night because I couldn't stop."

Myles took the stool next to his father. "I didn't know that."

"You wouldn't. I never wanted you to."

"Why?"

"I made choices, son. Choices that took me far away from that dream of being a musician, of traveling around the world with my trumpet in hand."

Myles thought about his childhood, tried to remember some hint that his father understood why music meant something to him. He couldn't recall anything.

"The day I told my father that I was moving to California to become a famous musician with my girlfriend and my best friend was the day my father told me that I was dead to him."

His grandparents had died before Myles was born. El had told them all horror stories about them, but Dr. Law had never talked about them. At all. Now he knew why.

"Wow, that's…"

"Heartless," Dr. Law said. "But I didn't care. I left, with one suitcase, one hundred dollars and my horn."

"Was this before medical school?"

Dr. Law nodded. "Before kids, before your mother, before everything."

"What happened?"

"Not what I thought would happen. We drove to LA, rented a one-bedroom apartment and worked odd jobs around the city to make money. When we weren't working, we were practicing."

"Did you write your own music?"

"I did. I just knew someone would discover us. I met great people, though. Even met Miles Davis one day."

"Straight up?"

"Yes. He was playing at this little jazz club in town. I begged my boss to let me off work early so I could see him. I barely made it. The house was packed, people everywhere. Standing room only. Davis was on stage playing 'Blue in Green.' The sound from his horn could not be duplicated. It was the most beautiful thing I've ever heard.

"When he got offstage, I walked up to him and introduced myself. He didn't smile, he didn't shake my hand. He just told me to keep playing. And walked away."

Myles was blown away. He knew the song, 'Blue in Green.' He'd played it himself many times. The entire album, *Kind of Blue*, was one of his favorites. "Cool."

"That experience ranks up there with my most memorable. I rushed home to tell my girlfriend about it. When I walked in, I found her with my best friend, in my bed."

"Damn." Myles hadn't expected that plot twist. "Did you kill them?"

Dr. Law snickered. "No. I left."

"You came home."

"Yeah. I walked away. From my dream. Because of a woman. I scraped up my last money and hopped on the road. It took a week to get back. I slept in my car at night and drove during the day."

"What did your father do when you got back?"

"He told me I was a fool for leaving in the first place, but he let me come home. The next day, he paid for my tuition. I never looked back. Now, instead of a world-renowned musician, I'm a world-renowned surgeon."

"Do you regret it?"

"Every day. I'm sorry, son." Myles glanced at his father, noted the sincerity in his eyes. "When you were young, and you walked up to that piano and started playing, I didn't know what to do. All I knew was my own experience. I only knew how it felt to leave everything behind for all the right reasons, only to end up with a broken heart and nothing to show for it."

"So you made the decision for me? Took away my freedom and my options?"

"That's exactly what I did. I know now it was the wrong choice."

"Why now?"

"Because I listened to you. You have an amazing talent, one that I should have cultivated and not stamped down."

Speechless, Myles thought about all those years he'd had to play in secret. Even though it had hurt him, he couldn't regret it. Because if his father had encouraged him to play, he might have never met Ms. Pennie. If his father had been supportive, he might have quit playing because he didn't have to work as hard for it.

"I haven't been a good father to any of you," Dr. Law admitted. "I've done unspeakable things in the name of control. But I want you to know that you've been a great son. You've never given me any trouble. You've worked hard all of your life. And I'm proud of you."

Tears burned Myles's eyes, surprising him. He blinked several times.

Dr. Law patted him on his back. "I'm proud of the man you've become."

"Dad, thank you."

"Thank Aria. She made me see the error of my ways."

Myles stared at his father. "Aria talked to you?"

"She did." He chuckled. "She let me have it."

"I said some things to her tonight that probably ruined everything," Myles admitted.

"What was that?"

Myles told his father what happened with Avery and the CD and Aria. "I walked away from her without giving her the chance to explain. Still, she knew I didn't want that CD to be shared with anyone."

"Listen, there are two things I learned about Aria in my little interaction with her. She loves you. I don't believe she would do anything to hurt you. And she was right to encourage you to play. Because you're a phenomenal musician. Better than most. Even that Martel guy you played with."

Myles laughed. "Dad."

"Hey, what can I say? He's not as good as you." Dr. Law stood. "You better go see about Aria."

"I will." Myles hugged his father. "Thanks."

"About that meeting?" Dr. Law said. "Next week, we'll discuss the role you'll have with the business."

"The role of partner?" Myles asked.

"Whatever role you want."

Myles smiled. "Sounds good."

He hurried out of the room, through the crowd to his

family. He scanned the room, looking for Aria. She was nowhere in sight.

"She left," Mel said. "With Brent."

Myles pulled his phone out of his pocket and turned it on. He saw the text she'd sent earlier and cursed himself for not checking his device before now. As he started to respond to that one, another text came through. From Aria.

I decided to catch a ride with Brent. Since you walked away from me, I figured you would be okay with some time to deal with whatever is bugging you. Because I have no idea.

Shit. He dialed her number and cursed when it went straight to voice mail. "I have to go." He turned to Ian. "Will you drop Ms. Pennie off at home?"

"Of course," Ian said.

Without another word, Myles ran out and jumped in his car. He made it Ann Arbor in record time. Letting himself into her home, he called out her name, walked through every inch of the house. She wasn't there. *Where the hell is she?*

He stretched his neck to relieve tension that had set in. He dialed her again. Voice mail. He plopped down on her sofa. *What the hell did I just do?*

Aria opened her door the next morning and dropped her keys on the table near the door.

"Where have you been?" Myles walked into the living room from the kitchen, looking worse for the wear in black sweatpants and a hoodie.

"I stayed at Brent's last night. I didn't want to sleep here by myself." Because she was used to sleeping with him.

"We need to talk."

"I think you said enough." She brushed past him and headed for the refrigerator for a bottle of water. "Listen, I don't know what's wrong with you, but I didn't deserve to be treated the way you treated me."

"I'm sorry."

Myles never fought fair. He didn't hurl insults, throw tantrums or threaten to ruin her when they argued. He apologized if he was wrong. Every time.

Her chin trembled. "What are you sorry for?"

"Avery came to me and told me that she wanted one of my songs to be used for her show."

Aria couldn't help but smile. "That's great!" Then she remembered she was supposed to be angry, not excited for him. After that, she wondered how Avery knew about his songs. "Wait, how did Avery know about your music?"

Myles bowed his head and sighed. "Not from you, obviously?"

"Is that... You thought I told her?"

"I did," he admitted.

"Why would I do that? You told me not to share it. I'm an artist. I respect other artists' wishes."

"How else did she know about it?"

Aria thought about his question and it came to her. "Oh, no. She came over for Tacos and Tequila and it was still playing. I never turned it off."

"And she took the CD. She told me." Myles explained that after she didn't come home, he'd called Avery and asked her where she'd heard his music. Avery had told him that she'd swiped the CD at Aria's house and apologized for taking it. "When she heard it, she thought it would fit the vibe of the show. She said she meant to call and ask, but got so excited about it, she plowed ahead."

"Wow."

"I shouldn't have jumped to conclusions."

"Right. You should have known me better than that."

"I do." He stepped forward, but she retreated a step. "I reacted before I thought about it. But I know you. Even after I talked to you, I couldn't reconcile what Avery said with the Aria I know."

"If that's the case, why didn't you come back? Why did you play the way you did? Why didn't you look at me when you were onstage?" He'd hurt her. His action still stung in the light of day. "That's not what we're supposed to be about, Myles. You were supposed to talk to me, not shut me out."

"Aria, I'm sorry. I got wrapped up. My dad stopped in and... Aria, I never want to hurt you. I only want to love you."

"You're... You're an idiot."

"A big one," he conceded. "I need you to forgive me, though."

Aria did forgive him. Last night, she'd had a long talk with Brent. Her bestie had surprised her when he didn't jump on the pissed-at-Myles train. Of course, he'd listened to her intently, had even let her cry on his shoulder. But when she was done crying, he'd told her to give Myles a break, even going so far as to say she might have been too fast to leave without talking to Myles and hearing his side of the situation.

"I already do," she admitted. "You have Brent to thank for calming me down."

Myles smirked. "And my dad pointed out how much of an idiot I really am."

Aria frowned. "What?"

"My dad told me he talked to you."

She groaned. "Yes. It wasn't the most pleasant conversation."

"Well, it must have been okay because I think he likes you."

Laughing, Aria, shoved him. "Get out."

"I'm serious."

So, the formidable Dr. Lawrence Jackson does have a conscience. "I'm glad you two talked."

"I learned a lot about him last night. And I know that has everything to do with you." He tugged her to him. "I'm so sorry."

"Don't apologize. Just don't do it again."

He kissed her. "I promise to always talk to you first before flipping out."

Aria wrapped her arms around his neck. "Good."

Myles grinned. "Come on."

"Wait, I thought we were having makeup sex?"

He laughed. "Later. Take a ride with me?"

Aria took his hand and he led her to his car. Myles pulled out his phone and typed something quickly before he stuffed it back in his pocket. As they drove, she peppered him with questions, wanting to know where they were going, how long they were going to be there, and if their destination involved food because she was starving.

Twenty-five minutes later, Myles pulled up at the school Aria had wanted to purchase. She glanced at the building, then back at Myles. "Why are we here?"

"It's a surprise. Come on."

He hopped out of the car and jogged to her side, opening her door for her. With her hand in his they approached the door. She expected it to be locked, but he pushed it open. Her song played on a tiny speaker to her right and there was a table in the center of the long hallway.

"What's this?" She inched toward the table. It had a dome-covered silver tray on it. "Are we eating here?"

Myles shook his head. "No, woman." He gripped her shoulders in his hands, turning her to face him. "Aria, I love you so much. You're the perfect melody. You've touched my heart in a way even music hasn't. I feel so much better with you in my life. And I wanted to give you something to show you just how much I care."

He handed her an envelope and his handkerchief so she could wipe her teary eyes. Eyeing him, she ripped open the envelope, and read the top few lines. She glanced up at him. "You bought this building?"

"I did."

"You're the one who put in a bid on it?"

"No. Someone really did outbid you. I just outbid them."

Aria's mouth fell open. "You didn't."

"Oh, I did."

She jumped in his arms. "Oh, my God, Myles. You're..." *Enter the ugly cry.* Aria sobbed with joy. And Myles rubbed her back and let her. When she pulled back, she said, "I can't let you buy my building."

"Think of it as a partnership. I want to work with you to help this dream become a reality."

Aria licked her lips before she kissed him, long and hard. "I love you so much."

"Good."

Aria giggled, remembering the first time she'd told him how she felt. He'd said the same thing then. She twirled in the hallways, arms wide. "I can't believe this."

Once she stopped dancing, her eyes dropped down to the covered tray. "What is this?"

"Open it," he told her, a sneaky gleam in his eyes.

Slowly she lifted the lid off the tray. Sitting in the middle of it was a bowl of vanilla ice cream and a bag of chips. She squealed in delight. "Dessert for breakfast. You're a keeper." She dipped a finger in the ice cream and rubbed it on his lips. Leaning in, she licked the treat from his lips before she kissed him. "Ice cream melts. How did you pull this off?"

"I had one of my interns hook it up."

"Was that the text you sent when we got in the car?"

"Yes."

Aria sighed. "Well, can I just say that I'm glad it wasn't a ring? I'm not ready to get married yet."

Myles laughed. "I know. I'm saving that for October." With a raised brow, she met his gaze. She opened her mouth to speak, but he stuffed a chip inside. "Aria?"

"Hmm?" She bit down on the chip.

"Just stop talking. I love you."

"I love you more."

Epilogue

Aria and Myles strolled hand in hand up to the door. Today was the grand opening of the school they'd worked so hard to bring to life.

The past year had flown by like a whirlwind. Both Myles and Aria had put their homes on the market and purchased Ms. Pennie's house. In the end, it didn't make sense for each of them to have a place. And Ms. Pennie didn't want to sell to just anyone. They'd agreed to pur chase the house from her if she would agree to stay with them—in a separate mother-in-law suite, of course. The older woman had agreed.

Construction on two buildings at once had been a nightmare, but they'd made it work. Finally, they were settled into their home nicely.

Myles had agreed to let Avery use his song, which led
to more offers. He'd decided not to record a solo album
or anything, though. At least for now, as his first priority was the school and the private practice with his father. After he'd talked with Dr. Law, they'd agreed to
still go into business together. But only if Myles could
work the hours he wanted to work. The Jackson patri-
arch had agreed to Myles's terms, and the new practice
would open next spring.

Aria continued to paint every day and had even vended
at the Art Fair over the summer. She'd done a few shows
and was set to debut her latest collection in the Detroit
Institute of Arts next March.

"I can't believe this day is here," Aria said, as they
stepped onto the raised porch in front of the school.

Myles kissed the inside of her wrist, right over her
pulse point. "I know. Seems like yesterday that I presented you with the deed."

"What a day that was. The second-best day of my
life."

The first was their wedding day. True to his word,
Myles proposed right in the middle of a Halloween party.
All of his siblings and Brent were in attendance and,
apparently, in on the entire thing. Aria smiled, remembering when he'd dropped to one knee and told her he
wanted forever with her.

Aria had bawled like a baby—after she'd shouted yes.

They married in August, in a small chapel in Flor-
ence, Italy. The only people in attendance were Brent,
Ian and Bailee, and Ms. Pennie. The decision to elope
was an easy one. They wanted their day to be all about
them and no one else.

During the ceremony, they vowed to love each other,

to cherish one another, and to always do what was best for them. They kissed under the moon and retreated to a private villa for an extended honeymoon.

That was two months ago, and it had been nonstop working to get the school up and running since. Finally the day had come. The school had received many applications from eager students, ready to learn. Aria had been surprised by many things during the process. The funding process had been daunting, as she'd expected. But it was Dr. Law who had come through with the save. One day, he'd dropped by her and Myles's house with a sizable check in hand for the school. Aria had tried to give the check back, but he wouldn't have it. He'd told her then that he wanted to contribute. His only condition was that the school would offer art and music classes.

Now, as they stood in front of The Metamorphosis School of Fine Arts and Music, Aria couldn't be happier that they'd decided to make the change.

Their families were gathered. Her father, Brent and Celeste came out. And Myles's siblings, their spouses, and Dr. Law joined the celebration. Her mother had even shown up out of the blue. Aria wasn't fooled into thinking her appearance was a turning point in their relationship, though. Rumor had it that Dr. Law had mentioned it to her and strongly encouraged her to attend.

"Ready?" Myles asked, interrupting her thoughts.

Aria smiled. "I'm ready."

He handed her a pair of big scissors and Aria cut the huge red bow that had been hung in front of the door. The crowd cheered as she and Myles opened the doors, and encouraged their friends and family to explore the renovated space.

As people walked the halls, Aria hung back with

Myles. She bumped her hip into his. "I couldn't have done it without you." She looked at him. "And I wouldn't want to."

Myles kissed the corner of her mouth. "I love you, too."

"Good."

* * * * *

Soulful and sensual romance featuring multicultural characters.

Look for brand-new Kimani stories
in special 2-in-1 volumes.

Available October 15, 2019

His Christmas Gift & Decadent Holiday Pleasures
by Janice Sims and Pamela Yaye

Her Christmas Wish & Designed by Love
by Sherelle Green and Sheryl Lister

Christmas with the Billionaire & A Tiara for Christmas
by Niobia Bryant and Carolyn Hector

She took another step closer. "Mr. Millner—"

"I'm sure Annalise explained to you that I need an assistant for the weekends only. Your main priority would be typing my handwritten book, updating my social media accounts and running errands," he said, turning to stride across the room to stand next to the lit fireplace.

"You write by hand?" she asked, unable to hide her amazement and forgetting the reason for her visit.

"Yes," he said, his voice deep.

"And you've finished your new book in the Mayhem series?" she asked.

"So, you're familiar with my books?" he asked, his attention locked on the crackling fire.

Samira wished she could see his face. She felt almost like he was hiding it from her intentionally. "Yes," she finally answered. "My favorite is *Vengeance*."

He grunted.

She eyed him. There was something so powerful but still sad about his stance. The way he moved. The way his stare was downcast. She was surprised at how strongly she needed to know what gave him such a demeanor. It, plus the dark interior of the home and neglected exterior, was all so mysterious—maybe even more so than one of his novels.

The man was an enigma. How could someone so abrupt and insolent write with such emotion and rhythm that she was forever transformed by his words? The two did not match.

"I assume since you're here you made Annalise's round of cuts," he said.

Annalise? As in Annalise Ray?

"Absolutely," she lied, completing winging this unexpected interaction.

"I like that you don't talk much."

She pressed her lips together.

"Do you want the job?" he asked, crossing his strong arms over his chest.

She didn't miss the way the thin material stretched with the move. "Wait. What?" she asked, forcing her attention from his fit form framed by the light of the fire and on to his words.

A billionaire heiress working as an author's weekend assistant. The thought actually made her smile.

The smile widened.

And maybe a better chance to get to know him and just what his reservations are about selling the land.

She contemplated all the pluses and minuses of the ruse. Some work related.

Samira eyed the fine lines of his taut body and her body instantly responded to him.

Some not.

"Yes or no?" he asked, his tone brusque.

Is this crazy? Am I?

"Yes, Mr. Millner, and thank you," she said.

Will this work?

"Good. Ms.…"

She opened her mouth but closed it as she almost supplied him her real name. He might very well know the Ansah name. "Samantha Aston," she lied, pulling the name out of the air.

Ding-dong.

She briefly looked over her shoulder to the front door at the sound of the doorbell.

"Your first duty is sending away all the other applicants," he said, turning and leaving the room with long strides.

What the hell have I gotten myself into?

Don't miss Christmas with the Billionaire
*by Niobia Bryant, available November 2019
wherever Harlequin® Kimani Romance™
books and ebooks are sold.*